"It's just that I'm not going to be in Lucky Harbor much longer, so while I'm here, I'm aiming for ... fun," said Grace.

"Fun."

"Yeah. It's a new thing I'm trying."

"And you think I'm not," Josh said with a hint of disbelief, "fun."

"It's nothing personal."

"Hmm." He took a step toward her, and since there was already no place to go, she found herself once again sandwiched between the door and his deliciously hard body. His hands went to her hips, where they squeezed lightly and then slid up her sides, past her ribs, to her arms and her shoulders. By the time he got to her throat and cupped her face, her bones had gone AWOL.

"What are you doing?" she managed.

"Showing you how much fun I can be."

Oh, boy. Just his husky whisper sent a shiver down her spine, the sort of shiver a woman wasn't supposed to get for a man she didn't want to be attracted to. And then her body strained a little closer to him.

Bad body!

Josh's eyes met hers and held. He was purposely building the anticipation, along with the heat working her from the inside out.

"Still think I'm not fun?" he asked softly...

Praise for Jill Shalvis and Her Novels

Head Over Heels

"[A] winning roller-coaster ride...[a] touching, character-rich, laughter-laced, knockout sizzler."
—*Library Journal* (starred review)

"Healthy doses of humor, lust, and love work their magic as Shalvis tells Chloe's story...Wit, smoking-hot passion, and endearing tenderness...a big winner."
—*Publishers Weekly*

"The Lucky Harbor series has become one of my favorite contemporary series, and *Head Over Heels* didn't disappoint...such a fun, sexy book...I think this one can be read as a stand-alone book, but I encourage you to try the first two in the series, where you meet all the characters of this really fun town."
—*USAToday.com*

"The writing is, as always, very good. Shalvis makes her characters seem like reflections of ourselves, or at least our relatives. She also makes the scenarios real, not too sweet or too violent. Definitely a good choice for a rainy afternoon."
—*RT Book Reviews*

"A Perfect 10. A truly fun and engaging tale from beginning to end...readers will not be disappointed...Be sure to put this one on your book buying list and get ready to snuggle down for some hot reading."

—RomRevToday.com

"Chloe and Sawyer are my favorite couple of the series...These two set the pages on fire!...It's entertaining, sweet, steamy, and one of my favorite contemporary romances of the year!"

—GoodReads.com

"5 stars! A truly delightful read that had me chuckling while reading it...a nice blend of romance, humor, and drama. Definitely going on my keeper shelf. I highly recommend this one."

—SeducedByaBook.com

The Sweetest Thing

"A wonderful romance of reunited lovers in a small town. A lot of hot sex, some delightful humor, and plenty of heartwarming emotion make this a book readers will love."

—*RT Book Reviews*

"A Perfect 10! Once again Jill Shalvis provides readers with a sexy, funny, hot tale...The ending is as sweet as it is funny. Tara and Ford have some seriously hot chemistry going on and they make the most of it in *The Sweetest Thing*. Trust me: You'll need an ice-cold drink nearby."

—RomRevToday.com

"Witty, fun, and the characters are fabulous."

—FreshFiction.com

"It is fabulous revisiting Lucky Harbor! I have been on tenterhooks waiting for Tara and Ford's story and yet again, Jill Shalvis does not disappoint...A rollicking good time...If you have not read the first book yet, this one will certainly compel you to do so...*The Sweetest Thing* is shiny and wonderful book goodness."

—RomanceJunkiesReviews.com

"This is a fun and flirty story of past loves, secrets, and three sisters whose lives draw the reader in. For a good-time romance, check this one out."

—*Parkersburg News and Sentinel* (WV)

"A fun-filled, sexy, entertaining story...[satisfies] one's romantic sweet tooth."

—TheRomanceReader.com

Simply Irresistible

"Hot, sweet, fun, and romantic! Pure pleasure!"

—Robyn Carr, *New York Times* bestselling author

Forever and a Day

Also by Jill Shalvis

Simply Irresistible

The Sweetest Thing

Heating Up the Kitchen (cookbook)

Small Town Christmas (anthology)

Christmas in Lucky Harbor (omnibus)

Head Over Heels

Lucky in Love

At Last

Forever and a Day

Jill Shalvis

FOREVER

NEW YORK   BOSTON

This book is a work of fiction. Names, characters, places, and incidents are the product of the author's imagination or are used fictitiously. Any resemblance to actual events, locales, or persons, living or dead, is coincidental.

Forever

Hachette Book Group

237 Park Avenue

New York, NY 10017

www.HachetteBookGroup.com

Printed in the United States of America

First Edition: July 2012

10 9 8 7 6 5 4 3 2 1

Forever is an imprint of Grand Central Publishing.

The Forever name and logo are trademarks of Hachette Book Group, Inc.

The Hachette Speakers Bureau provides a wide range of authors for speaking events. To find out more, go to www.hachettespeakersbureau.com or call (866) 376-6591.

The publisher is not responsible for websites (or their content) that are not owned by the publisher.

It takes a village to write a book, and I'm grateful for mine.

To Christie and Carrie, for the invaluable advice on this book, not to mention the friendship, neither of which I could do without.

To Jolie and Debbi, for Mesquite 2011, where this book was plotted in its entirety while consuming far too much food and fun.

To Laurie and Melinda and Mary, for always being willing to read for me.

To Robyn and Kristan for having my back.

Love you all.

Forever and a Day

Chapter 1

Chocolate makes the world go around.

Tired, edgy, and scared that she was never going to get her life on the happy track, Grace Brooks dropped into the back booth of the diner and sagged against the red vinyl seat. "I could really use a drink."

Mallory, in wrinkled scrubs, just coming off an all-night shift at the ER, snorted as she crawled into the booth as well. "It's eight in the morning."

"Hey, it's happy hour somewhere." This from their third musketeer, Amy, who was wearing a black tee, a black denim skirt with lots of zippers, and kickass boots. The tough-girl ensemble was softened by the bright pink EAT ME apron she was forced to wear while waitressing. "Pick your poison."

"Actually, I was thinking hot chocolate," Grace said, fighting a yawn. She'd slept poorly, worrying about money. And paying bills. And keeping a roof over her head...

"Hot chocolate works too," Amy said. "Be right back."

Good as her word, she soon reappeared with a tray of steaming hot chocolate and big, fluffy chocolate pancakes. "Chocoholics unite."

Four months ago, Grace had come west from New York for a Seattle banking job, until she'd discovered that putting out for the boss was part of the deal. Leaving the offer on the table, she'd gotten into her car and driven as far as the tank of gas could take her, ending up in the little Washington State beach town of Lucky Harbor. That same night, she'd gotten stuck in this very diner during a freak snowstorm with two strangers.

Mallory and Amy.

With no electricity and a downed tree blocking their escape, the three of them had spent a few scary hours soothing their nerves by eating their way through a very large chocolate cake. Since then, meeting over chocolate cake had become habit—until they'd accidentally destroyed the inside of the diner in a certain candle incident that wasn't to be discussed. Jan, the owner of Eat Me, had refused to let them meet over cake anymore, so the Chocoholics had switched to brownies. Grace was thinking of making a motion for chocolate cupcakes next. It was important to have the right food for those meetings, as dissecting their lives—specifically their lack of love lives—was hard work. Except these days, Amy and Mallory actually *had* love lives.

Grace did not.

Amy disappeared again and came back with butter and syrup. She untied and tossed aside her apron and sat, pushing the syrup toward Grace.

"I love you," Grace said with great feeling as she took her first bite of delicious goodness.

Not one to waste her break, Amy toasted her with a pancake-loaded fork dripping with syrup and dug in.

Mallory was still carefully spreading butter on her pancakes. "You going to tell us what's wrong, Grace?"

Grace stilled for a beat, surprised that Mallory had been able to read her. "I didn't say anything was wrong."

"You're mainlining a stack of six pancakes as if your life depends on it."

"Because they're amazing." And nothing was wrong exactly. Except...everything.

All her life she'd worked her ass off, running on the hamster wheel, heading toward her elusive future. Being adopted at birth by a rocket scientist and a well-respected research biologist had set the standards, and she knew her role. Achieve, and achieve high. "I've applied at every bank, investment company, and accounting firm between Seattle and San Francisco. There's not much out there."

"No nibbles?" Mallory asked sympathetically, reaching for the syrup, her engagement ring catching the light.

Amy shielded her eyes. "Jeez, Mallory, stop waving that thing around—you're going to blind us. Couldn't Ty have found one smaller than a third world country? Or less sparkly?"

Mallory beamed at the rock on her finger but otherwise ignored Amy's comment, unwilling to be deterred. "Back to the nibbles," she said to Grace.

"Nothing to write home about. Just a couple of possible interviews for next week, one in Seattle, one in Portland." Neither job was exactly what Grace wanted, but available jobs at her level in banking had become nearly extinct. So here she was, two thousand miles from home, drowning beneath the debt load of her education and CPA because her parents had always been of the "build character and pave your own road" variety. She was still mad at herself for following that job offer to Seattle, but she'd wanted a good, solid position in the firm—just not one that she could find in the *Kama Sutra*.

Now late spring had turned to late summer, and she was *still* in Lucky Harbor, living off temp jobs. She was down to her last couple of hundred bucks, and her parents thought she'd taken that job in Seattle counting other people's money for a living. Grace had strived to live up to the standards of being a Brooks, but there was no doubt she fell short. In her heart, she knew she belonged, but her brain—the part of her that got that she was only a Brooks on *paper*—knew she'd never really pulled it off.

"I don't want you to leave Lucky Harbor," Mallory said. "But one of these interviews will work out for you. I know it."

Grace didn't necessarily want to leave Lucky Harbor either. She'd found the small, quirky town to be more welcoming than anywhere else she'd ever been, but staying wasn't really an option. She was never going to build her big career here. "I hope so." She stabbed another pancake from the tray and dropped it on her plate. "I hate fibbing to my parents so they won't worry. And I'm whittling away at my meager savings. Plus, being in limbo sucks."

"Yeah, none of those things are your real problem," Amy said.

"No?" Grace asked. "What's my real problem?"

"You're not getting any."

Grace sagged at the pathetic truthfulness of this statement, a situation made all the worse by the fact that both Amy and Mallory *were* getting some.

Lots.

"Remember the storm?" Mallory asked. "When we almost died in this very place?"

"Right," Amy said dryly, "from overdosing on chocolate cake, maybe."

Mallory ignored this and pointed her fork at Grace. "We made a pinky promise. I said I'd learn to be a little bad for a change. And Amy here was going to live her life instead of letting it live her. And you, Miss Grace, you were going to find more than a new job, remember? You were going to stop chasing your own tail and go after some happy and some fun. It's time, babe."

"I *am* having fun here." At least, more than she'd ever let herself have before. "And what it's time for right now is work." With a longing look at the last stack of pancakes, Grace stood up and brushed the crumbs off her sundress.

"What's today's job?" Amy asked.

When Grace had first realized she needed to get a temporary job or stop eating, she'd purposely gone for something new. Something that didn't require wearing stuffy pencil skirts or closed-toe heels or sitting in front of a computer for fifteen hours a day. Because if she had to be off-track and a little lost, then she *was* going to have fun while she was at it, dammit. "I'm delivering birthday flowers to Mrs. Burland for her eightieth birthday. Then modeling at Lucille's art gallery for a drawing class."

"Modeling for an art class?" Mallory asked. "Like... nude?"

"Today they're drawing hands." Nude was *tomorrow's*

class, and Grace was really hoping something happened before then, like maybe she'd win the lottery. Or get beamed to another planet.

"If I had your body," Amy said, "I'd totally model nude. And charge a lot for it."

"Sounds like you're talking about something different than modeling," Mallory said dryly.

Grace rolled her eyes at the both of them and stood. She dropped the last of her pocket money onto the table and left to make the floral deliveries. When she'd worked at the bank, she'd gotten up before the crack of dawn, rode a train for two hours, put in twelve more at her desk, then got home in time to crawl into bed.

Things were majorly different here.

For one thing, she saw daylight.

So maybe she could no longer afford Starbucks, but at least she wasn't still having the recurring nightmare where she was suffocating under a sea of pennies that she'd been trying to count one by one.

Two hours later, Grace was just finishing the last of the deliveries when her cell phone buzzed. She didn't recognize the incoming number, so she played mental roulette and answered. "Grace Brooks," she said in her most professional tone, as if she were still sitting on top of her world. Sure, she'd given up designer wear, but she hadn't lost her pride. Not yet anyway.

"I'm calling about your flyer," a man said. "I need a dog walker. Someone who's on time, responsible, and not a flake."

Her flyer? "A dog walker?" she repeated.

"Yes, and I'd need you to start today."

"Today . . . as in *today*?" she asked.

"Yes."

The man, whoever he was, had a hell of a voice, low and a little raspy, with a hint of impatience. Clearly he'd misdialed. And just as clearly, there was someone else in Lucky Harbor trying to drum up work for themselves.

Grace considered herself a good person. She sponsored a child in Africa, and she dropped her spare change into the charity jars at the supermarket. Someone in town had put up flyers looking to get work, and that someone deserved this phone call. But dog walking... Grace could totally do dog walking. Offering a silent apology for stealing the job, she said, "I could start today."

"Your flyer lists your qualifications, but not how long you've been doing this."

That was too bad because she'd sure like to know that herself. She'd never actually had a dog. Turns out, rocket scientists and renowned biologists don't have a lot of time in their lives for incidentals such as dogs.

Or kids...

In fact, come to think of it, Grace had never had so much as a goldfish, but really, how hard could it be? Put the thing on a leash and walk, right? "I'm a little new at the dog walking thing," she admitted.

"A little new?" he asked. "Or a lot new?"

"A lot."

There was a pause, as if he was considering hanging up. Grace rushed to fill the silence. "But I'm very diligent!" she said quickly. "I never leave a job unfinished." *Unless she was asked how she felt about giving blow jobs during lunch breaks...* "And I'm completely reliable."

"The dog is actually a puppy," he said. "And new to our household. Not yet fully trained."

"No problem," she said, and crossed her fingers, hoping that was true. She loved puppies. Or at least she loved the *idea* of puppies.

"I left for work early this morning and won't be home until late tonight. I'd need you to walk the dog by lunchtime."

Yeah, he really had a hell of a voice. Low and authoritative, it made her want to snap to attention and salute him, but it was also…sexy. Wondering if the rest of him matched his voice, she made arrangements to go to his house in a couple of hours, where there'd be someone waiting to let her inside. Her payment of forty bucks cash would be left on the dining room table.

Forty bucks cash for walking a puppy…

Score.

Grace didn't ask why the person opening the door for her couldn't walk the puppy. She didn't want to talk her new employer out of hiring her because, hello, *forty bucks*. She could eat all week off that if she was careful.

At the appropriate time, she pulled up to the address she'd been given and sucked in a big breath. She hadn't caught the man's name, but he lived in a very expensive area, on the northernmost part of town where the rocky beach stretched for endless miles like a gorgeous postcard for the Pacific Northwest. The dark green bluffs and rock formations were piled like gifts from heaven for as far as the eye could see. Well, as far as *her* eye could see, which wasn't all that far since she needed glasses.

She was waiting on a great job with benefits to come along first.

The house sat across the street from the beach. Built

in sprawling stone and glass, it was beautiful, though she found it odd that it was all one level, when the surrounding homes were two and three stories high. Even more curious, next to the front steps was a ramp. A wheelchair ramp. Grace knocked on the door, then caught sight of the Post-it note stuck on the glass panel.

> *Dear Dogsitter,*
> *I've left door unlocked for you. Please let yourself in. Oh, and if you could throw away this note and not let my brother know I left his house unlocked, that'd be great, thanks. Also, don't steal anything.*
> *Anna*

Grace stood there chewing her bottom lip in rare indecision. She hadn't given this enough thought. Hell, let's be honest. She'd given it *no* thought at all past Easy Job. She reminded herself that she was smart in a crisis and could get through anything.

But walking into a perfect stranger's home seemed problematic, if not downright dangerous. What if a curious neighbor saw her and called the cops? She looked herself over. Enjoying her current freedom from business wear, she was in a sundress with her cute Payless-special ankle boots and lace socks. Not looking much like a banking specialist, and hopefully not looking like a B&E expert either...

Regardless, what if this was a setup? What if a bad guy lived here, one who lured hungry, slightly desperate, act-now-think-later women inside to do heinous things to them?

Okay, so maybe she'd been watching too many late-night marathons of *Criminal Minds*, but it could totally happen.

Then, from inside the depths of the house came a happy, high-pitched bark. And then another, which seemed to say, "*Hurry up, lady. I have to pee!*"

Ah, hell. In for a penny...Grace opened the front door and peered inside.

The living room was as stunning as the outside of the house. Wide-open spaces, done in dark masculine wood and neutral colors. The furniture was oversized and sparse on the beautiful, scarred hardwood floors. An entire wall of windows faced the late summer sky and Pacific Ocean.

As Grace stepped inside, the barking increased in volume, intermingled now with hopeful whining. She followed the sounds to a huge, state-of-the-art kitchen that made her wish she knew how to cook beyond the basics of soup and grilled-cheese sandwiches. Just past the kitchen was a laundry room, the doorway blocked by a toddler gate.

On the other side of the gate was a baby pig.

A baby pig that barked.

Okay, not a pig at all, but one of those dogs whose faces looked smashed in. The tiny body was mostly tan, the face black with crazy bugged-out eyes and a tongue that lolled out the side of its mouth. It looked like an animated cartoon as it twirled in excited circles, dancing for her, trying to impress and charm its way out of lockup.

"Hi," she said to him. *Her?* Hard to tell since its parts were so low as to scrape the ground along with its belly.

The thing snorted and huffed in joyous delirium, rolling over and over like a hotdog, then jumping up and down like a Mexican jelly bean.

"Oh, there's no need for all that," Grace said, and opened the gate.

Mistake number one.

The dog/pig/alien streaked past her with astounding speed and promptly raced out of the kitchen and out of sight.

"Hey," she called. "Slow down."

But it didn't, and wow, those stumpy legs could really move. It snorted with sheer delight as it made its mad getaway, and Grace was forced to rethink the pig theory. Also, the sex mystery was solved. From behind, she'd caught a glimpse of dangly bits.

It—*he*—ran circles around the couch, barking with merry enthusiasm. She gave chase, wondering how it was that she had multiple advanced degrees, and yet she hadn't thought to ask the name of the damn dog. "Hey," she said. "Hey you. We're going outside to walk."

The puppy dashed past her like lightning.

Dammit. Breathless, she changed direction and followed him back into the kitchen where he was chasing some imaginary threat around the gorgeous dark wood kitchen table that indeed had two twenty-dollar bills lying on the smooth surface.

She was beginning to see why the job paid so much.

She retraced her steps to the laundry room and found a leash and collar hanging on the doorknob above the gate. Perfect. The collar was a manly blue and the tag said TANK.

Grace laughed out loud, then searched for Tank.

Turned out, Tank had worn off the excess energy and was up against the front door, panting.

"Good boy," Grace cooed, and came at him with his collar. "What a good boy."

He smiled at her.

Aw. See? she told herself. *Compared to account analysis and posing nude, this job is going to be a piece of cake.* She was still mentally patting herself on the back for accepting this job when right there on the foyer floor, Tank squatted, hunched, and—

"No!" she cried. "Oh no, not inside!" She fumbled with the front door, which scared Tank into stopping mid-poo. He ran a few feet away from the front door and hunched again. He was quicker this time. Grace was still standing there, mouth open in shock and horror as little Tank took a dainty step away from his *second* masterpiece, pawed his short back legs on the wood like a matador, and then, with his oversized head held up high, trotted right out the front door like royalty.

Grace staggered after him, eyes watering from the unholy smell. "Tank! Tank, wait!"

Tank didn't wait. Apparently feeling ten pounds lighter, he raced across the front yard and the street. He hit the beach, his little legs pumping with the speed of a gazelle as he practically flew across the sand, heading straight for the water.

"Oh, God," she cried. "No, Tank, *no!*"

But Tank dived into the first wave and vanished.

Grace dropped the purse off her shoulder and let it fall to the sand. "*Tank!*"

She dashed closer to the water. A wave hit her at hip level, knocking her back a step as she frantically searched for a bobbing head.

Nothing. The little guy had completely vanished, having committed suicide right before her eyes.

The next wave hit her at chest height. Again she staggered back, gasping at the shock of the water as she searched frantically for a little black head.

Wave number three washed right over the top of her. She came up sputtering, shook her head to clear it, then dived beneath the surface, desperate to find the puppy.

Nothing.

Finally, she was forced to crawl out of the water and admit defeat. She pulled her phone from her purse and swore because it'd turned itself off. Probably because she kept dropping it.

Or tossing it to the rocky beach to look for drowning puppies.

She powered the phone on, gnawed on her lower lip, then called the man who'd trusted her to "be on time, be responsible, and not be a flake." Heart pounding, throat tight, she waited until he picked up.

"Dr. Scott," came the low, deep male voice.

Dr. Scott. *Dr. Scott?*

"Hello?" he said. "Anyone there?"

Oh, God. This was bad. Very bad. Because she knew him.

Well, okay, not really. She'd seen him around because he was good friends with Mallory's and Amy's boyfriends. Dr. Joshua Scott was thirty-four—which she knew because Mallory had given him thirty-four chocolate cupcakes on his birthday last month, a joke because he was a health nut. He was a big guy, built for football more than the ER, but he'd chosen the latter. Even in his wrinkled scrubs after a long day at work,

his dark hair tousled and his darker eyes lined with exhaustion, he was drop-dead sexy. The few times that
their gazes had locked, the air had snapped, crackled,
and popped with a tension she hadn't felt with a man
in far too long.

And she'd just killed his puppy.

"Um, hi," she said. "This is Grace Brooks. Your...dog
walker." She choked down a horrified sob and forced herself to continue, to give him the rest. "I might have just
lost your puppy."

There was a single beat of stunned silence.

"I'm so sorry," she whispered.

More silence.

She dropped to her wobbly knees in the sand and
shoved her wet hair out of her face with shaking fingers.
"Dr. Scott? Did you hear me?"

"Yes."

She waited for the rest of his response, desperately
gripping the phone.

"You *might* have lost Tank," he repeated.

"Yes," she said softly, hating herself.

"You're sure."

Grace looked around the beach. The empty beach.
"Yes."

"Well, then, I owe you a big, fat kiss."

Grace pulled her phone from her ear and stared at it,
then brought it back. "No," she said, shaking her head as
if he could see her. "I don't think you understand. I *lost*
Tank. In the water."

He muttered something that she'd have sworn sounded
like "I should be so lucky."

"What?" she asked.

"Nothing. I'm two minutes away. I got a break in the ER and was coming home to make sure you showed."

"Well, of course I showed—"

But he'd disconnected.

"Why wouldn't I show?" she asked no one. She dropped her phone back into her purse and got up. Two minutes. She had two minutes to find Tank.

Chapter 2

Okay, so maybe chocolate doesn't make the world go around, but it sure makes the trip worthwhile.

Josh's day had started at five that morning in the gym. Matt and Ty, his workout partners, spent the hour sparring in the ring, beating the shit out of each other while Josh lifted weights. The three of them worked hard while retaining enough breath to sling ongoing insults and taunts. It was what friends were for.

By six-thirty, he was in the ER, patching up a guy who'd gotten in a bar fight in Seattle hours before but had been too drunk to realize he was bleeding profusely as he drove down the highway. From there, Josh had moved on to a heart attack victim and then to a two-year-old who'd swallowed a few pennies and was having understandable trouble passing them.

By noon, Josh wasn't even halfway through his day, and he'd already been overloaded and overworked and was quite possibly teetering on the edge of burnout. He could feel it creeping in on him in unguarded moments, like now when he was parking his car between his house and the beach to deal with Grace Brooks.

He knew who she was. He'd seen her around. Blue eyes, a quick smile, long, shiny blond hair, and a willowy yet curvy body that could drive a man right out of his mind if he gave it too much thought.

As he walked across the sand toward the water, doing his best not to give it *any* thought, he caught sight of her in the water. She was facing the waves, her hands on her head in a distraught pose. With a frown, he picked up the pace, just as something dashed toward him in his peripheral vision.

Something small.

Something evil.

Something named Tank. Josh scooped up the sand-covered puppy and held him away from him. The pug wriggled intently, running in the air, trying to get closer to Josh. Finally giving up, Tank refocused his attention on the woman in the ocean.

"Oh, I see her," Josh said. "And what the hell have you done now?"

Grace was panicked. It was one thing to lose a job. It was another thing entirely to lose *the* job. Damn. Her parents had always told her "keep your head down and work hard" and she'd done her best. She really had.

But she'd still screwed up. And it wasn't like she could call them for advice on this. Neither of them could possibly understand the thought process that had led her to a dog walking job, much less why she'd placed fun as her newest, highest priority. "Tank!" she yelled at the waves. "*Tank?*" Wading back in up to her waist, she turned in a full circle to rescan the beach, then went utterly still.

Standing on the sand was a man. His tall, broad stature implied strength and control, and he was rocking a pair of navy blue scrubs and dark wraparound Ray-Bans.

Holding her archnemesis.

Tank.

The puppy was panting happily away, and Grace could have sworn he was *smiling*. Forget the pig or alien theory—Tank was a rat. Relief at seeing the thing alive nearly brought her to her knees, but she'd have drowned, so she locked them—just as the next wave hit her from behind.

She was very busy fighting a full-facial, saltwater cavity wash when two big hands gripped her arms and hauled her upright.

Dr. Scott, of course.

She coughed and choked some more—very attractive, she was quite certain. Then she realized that she was up against her rescuer, held there firmly as the water swirled around their calves. "I'm okay," she gasped.

"Sure?"

"Yes," she said, but he didn't let her go. "Really," she promised. "I'm good."

He nodded and continued to hold her against him.

Except...he wasn't holding her at all. *She* was clinging to *him*, soaking up the warmth and strength of him radiating through his now-wet scrubs. Well, crap. Forcing herself to loosen her grip on him, she stepped back, working on searching for a different grip entirely—the one on her fast-failing dignity. Hiking her dress up to her thighs, she frog-marched out of the water as fast as she could so as to avoid being flattened by the next wave. By the time she hit dry sand, she was feeling a little bit like a drowned kitten. One glance down assured her that she didn't look like a drowned kitten. She looked like she was trying out for a wet T-shirt contest.

Yikes.

She decided not to look at herself again and made the mistake of looking instead at her rescuer. He was close, close enough to force her to tilt her head up to see his face, close enough to ascertain that he clearly hadn't shaved that morning.

The dark stubble on his jaw was incredibly disconcerting. And sexy.

"*Arf!*" Tank said from his perch, which was her purse, still lying on the sand. The little shit was standing on it like he owned it, wet, sandy paws and all. "*Arf, arf!*"

Nice. Grace gave herself a big mental thumbs-up for the "fun" that this job had been so far.

Josh nudged Tank off Grace's purse, then attempted to brush the wet sand from the leather. Tank gave a pretend ferocious growl and began a tug of war with the strap.

Heathen.

Josh gave him another nudge and rescued the purse. He was doing his damnedest to concentrate on the situation at hand, but that was proving difficult given the sight of Grace, her clothes plastered to her like a second skin. Half of her hair was in a topsy-turvy knot on top of her head, with the rest plastered to her face. The tip of her nose had gotten sunburned, and her mascara was smudged around her drown-in-me blue eyes.

And then there was her mouth.

She had a full lower lip, one that warmed him up considerably and made him think about sex. Actually, everything about her—the oh-shit expression on her face, the way she waved her hands like she was trying to explain herself without words, the delicate clinking of the myriad of thin silver bracelets she wore on her wrist—brought to mind sex.

Sex and chaos.

Pure, unadulterated, trouble-filled chaos. The thing was, he'd been there before, in another time and place, and was no longer interested in such things. No matter how hot the packaging was.

And the packaging was *very* hot. Grace was wearing one of those flimsy little summer dresses that had a way of messing with a guy's brain. The tiny straps had been designed with the sole purpose of making him want to tug them down—with his teeth.

Or maybe that was just him, and the fact that he hadn't had sex in so long he'd nearly forgotten how it felt.

Nearly.

The pulse at the base of Grace's slender neck was beating a little harder and faster than it should be. As a doctor, he knew these things. Plus, his own pulse was going too. Mostly because that hot little sundress was as sheer as tissue paper when wet, and she was most definitely wet.

And cold.

Her underwear was white lace. God bless white lace. And Jesus, he really needed five minutes of shut-eye. And possibly a lobotomy. Or maybe he just needed to get laid.

Like *that* was going to happen when he was working 24/7.

Blowing out a breath, Josh scooped up the puppy that

his sister had adopted with the sole purpose of sending Josh over the edge—which was working—and grabbed his shivering dog walker's hand. He led her to his car and directed her to the passenger seat and put Tank into the back.

"W-where are we g-going?"

"Nowhere." Josh cranked the engine and heater, then twisted around to extract his sweatshirt from the back-seat.

"N-no, that's okay," she said, shaking her head. "I'll g-get it all wet and sandy."

"Put it on before your teeth chatter out of your head."

Grace complied, then wrapped her arms around herself and huddled into the heater vents. "I'm sorry I lost Tank."

The puppy perked up at his name and took a flying leap into the front seat, landing in Josh's lap. Four paws hit the family jewels with precision. Sucking in a breath, Josh scooped Tank up and was promptly licked for his efforts.

"It's so great that you found him," Grace said.

"Yeah." Josh sighed in grim resignation, swiping the puppy drool off his chin. "*So* great."

Grace watched Josh set Tank onto the backseat. Again. Tank cried and leaped forward. Josh caught him in midair and dangled him in front of his face so that man and puppy were eye to eye. Tank panted happily, looking thrilled.

Not so the good doctor, though it was hard to tell what he was thinking behind his sunglasses. "You warmed up now?" he asked.

"Arf."

Grace smiled in relief. The puppy was okay. "I guess that means yes."

"I meant you," Josh said.

"Oh!" She laughed. "Yes, thank you."

He just looked at her, and she realized he was waiting for her to get out. Right. He had to get back to work. She opened the door, and he did the same, getting out with Tank tucked under his arm like a football.

"Want me to put him away for you?" she asked, thinking it was the least she could do.

"I've got him."

Grace watched him head toward his house. He was a big guy. Bull-in-a-china-shop big. But he had a way of moving with surprising grace. He was very fit, and *very* easy on the eyes. She wasn't often steered astray by bouts of lust, but she felt it stir within her now. No doubt he would be a very interesting item to add to her list of Fun Things to Do, but he was a doctor. Most would be attracted by that, but not Grace. She knew his world, knew the crazy hours, the life that wasn't really his own, knew what it was like to compete for even a smidgeon of attention. Fair or not, the initials MD after his name would keep him off her list. "You said you'd kiss me if I lost Tank."

The words popped out of her unbidden, and she covered her mouth. Too late. Turning back, Josh shoved the sunglasses to the top of his head and leveled her with a long, assessing look from dark brown eyes.

He looked exhausted. As if maybe he'd been working around the clock without sleep. "Ignore that," she said. "Sometimes I have Tourette's."

Some of the tension went out of his shoulders, and for a beat, his features softened into what might have been amusement. "You want me to kiss you?"

Oh boy. "You were happy I'd lost your puppy?"

He was looking like he was still thinking about smiling as he glanced down at Tank, tucked under his arm. "No. That would make me an asshole."

Right...

"And he's not *my* puppy," he said. "He belongs to my son, given to him by my evil sister, who I'm pretty sure bought him from the devil."

They both looked at Tank, who soaked up the attention as his due. He managed to roll in Josh's arms, over to his back, showing off his good parts with pride.

Such a guy. "If you don't want him, couldn't you just give him back?"

Josh laughed softly. "You don't have any kids, I take it."

Or dogs. "No."

"Trust me," Josh said. "I'm stuck with him."

"Arf," Tank said.

Josh shook his head, then started toward the house again, his wet scrubs clinging to those broad shoulders and very nice butt as his long legs churned up the distance with ease.

Apparently they were done here. "Uh, Dr. Scott?"

"Josh," he corrected.

"Josh, then." Since he hadn't slowed or looked back, she cupped her hands around her mouth. "Should I come by your house at around the same time tomorrow, then?"

His laugh was either amused or horrified. Hard to tell. "No," he said.

Grace paused, but really, there was no way to mistake the single-syllable word. No was ... well, *no*.

Which meant she was fired. Again. One would think she'd be good at that by now, but nope, she didn't feel good at it.

She felt like crap.

Chapter 3

♥

Happiness is sharing a candy bar. Even better is not having to share.

This is all your fault," Josh told the wriggling puppy as he walked toward his house.

Tank didn't give a shit. He'd caught sight of a butterfly and was growling ferociously, struggling maniacally to get free so he could attack.

Tank was the Antichrist.

"Look, we all know you think you're a badass, but that butterfly could kick your ass with one wing tied behind its back," Josh told him, tightening his grip as he used his other hand to reach into his pocket for his phone.

His *wet* phone, which—perfect—was fried. Seemed about right, given his day so far. "You could have kept running for the hills," he said. "Or at least stayed 'lost' long enough to get me that kiss."

Tank stretched his nonexistent neck and oversized pug head so he could lick Josh's chin again.

"Yeah, yeah." It didn't matter. Grace Brooks was a

beautiful woman, but he didn't have time to sleep, much less time to give to a woman.

Although, the way she'd hiked her dress up her bare, toned legs had definitely been worth the price of admission…He let himself into his house, trailing sea water and sand with him. No doubt he'd get a dire text from Nina, his pissy housekeeper, but his phone was dead.

Silver lining.

Toby had started kindergarten this week, so the house was void of the insanity of Zhu Zhu hamster pets and the *whoosh, vrrmm-whoosh* of Toby's ever-present Jedi saber. Anna should be in class—*should* being the operative word. His sister had yet to consider junior college any more seriously than her choice of fingernail polish.

Moving toward the kitchen to dump Tank, Josh stopped short in surprise.

Shit.

Literally.

Grinding his teeth into powder, Josh lifted his shoe, studied the bottom of it, then dangled Tank at eye level. "Have you ever heard of mince meat?"

Tank tried to lick his nose.

"*Not* cool, dog." Josh dealt with the mess. If he left it for Nina, she'd quit for sure since she'd already made it clear that nothing puppy related was on her plate. And that was *all* Josh needed, for yet another person to quit on him. It took a village to run his life, and his village was in mutiny.

He caught sight of the forty bucks still on the kitchen table. Hell. Grace hadn't taken the money. And she needed it, too, which he knew because this was Lucky Harbor. You could drop a pot of gold on the pier and a perfect stranger would hand it back to you, but you couldn't keep a secret to save your life.

Josh stripped out of his wet scrubs in the laundry room and slid Tank a long look. Unconcerned, Tank was snuffling around in his bed, turning his fat, little puppy body in three tight circles before plopping down with a snort and closing his eyes. Apparently he was satisfied with the destruction he'd left in his wake.

Definitely the Antichrist.

The house phone was ringing, probably because his cell was no longer working. Josh grabbed a set of fresh scrubs from the freshly delivered stack that he kept in the basket on the dryer and headed for the door. Later. He'd deal with it all later.

This is how he survived the daily insanity of his life, using his unique ability to prioritize and organize according to importance. Taking care of his family—important. Incoming phone call to inform him he was late—redundant, and therefore not critical.

Josh worked two shifts a week in the ER and four shifts at his dad's practice. His dad had been gone five years and Josh still didn't think of the practice as his own, but it was, complete with all the responsibilities of running it. When he could, Josh also donated a shift to the local Health Services Center. All the work made for a great stock portfolio, but it was hell on his home life.

Hell on Toby.

Something had to give, and soon. Probably Josh's own sanity, but for now, he headed back to the hospital only to be called into a board meeting.

He wasn't surprised by the topic at hand. The board wanted him to sell the practice, incorporating it into the hospital as many of the other local medical practitioners had done. The deal was they'd buy Josh out, pay him to stay on board, and also hire on another doctor to help him with the workload. Plus they'd guarantee the practice the hospital's internal referrals.

It was a dangling carrot.

Except Josh hated carrots.

This wasn't the first time the board had made the offer. They'd been after him all year to sell, each offer getting progressively more aggressive. But Josh didn't like being strong-armed, and he didn't like thinking about how his dad would feel if Josh let his hard-earned practice slip out of his control.

It was eight-thirty by the time he got home that night— half an hour past Toby's bedtime. Last night, the five-year-old had been in bed at this time, asleep on his belly, legs curled under him, butt in the air, his chubby baby face smashed into his pillow. He'd clearly gone to bed directly from the bath because his dark hair had been sticking up in tufts, the same way Josh's always did when he didn't comb it.

Toby's pj's had been—big surprise—Star Wars, and Josh had kneeled by the kid's bed to stroke back the perpetually unruly hair. Toby had stirred, and then...

Barked.

He'd been barking ever since Anna had brought Tank home. It was a passing phase.

Or so Josh desperately hoped.

Toby was the spitting image of Josh, but he had his mother's imagination and her temperament to boot. Josh could read that temperament in every line of his son's carefree body as he slept with wild abandonment. He wondered if Ally would be able to see it. But of course she wouldn't, because to see it, she'd have to actually see Toby, something she hadn't attempted in years.

Hoping the Bean was still up and using actual words tonight, Josh walked in the front door and stopped in his tracks.

Devon Weller, Anna's latest and hopefully soon-to-be-ex-boyfriend, was sitting on the half wall between the dining room and living room, eyeballing his cell phone.

Anna came into sight, arms whipping as she sped her wheelchair around the corner on two wheels. Hard to believe someone so tiny could move so fast, but Josh knew better than to underestimate his twenty-one-year-old sister.

She'd created a figure-eight racecourse between the two couches and the dining room table and was getting some serious speed. In her lap, squealing with sheer joy and possibly also terror, was Josh's mini-me—not asleep, nowhere close. With his eyes lit with excitement, cheeks ruddy from exertion, Toby was smiling from ear to ear.

Tank was right on their heels—or wheels in this case—barking with wild abandoned delight, following as fast as his short little legs would take him.

For a brief second, Josh stood there rooted to the spot by a deep, undefined ache in his chest, which vanished in an instant as Anna took a corner far too tight, wobbled, and tipped over, sending her and Toby flying.

"Damn," Devon said, and clicked something on his phone with his thumb.

The idiot had been timing the event.

Josh rushed past him to the crumpled heap of limbs. "Don't move," he ordered Anna, pulling Toby off her. He

turned Toby in his arms and took in the face that was so
like his own, except free of the exhaustion and cynicism
that dogged Josh's every breath.

Toby grinned and threw his arms around Josh's neck in
greeting. The kid's moods were pure and mercurial, but
he loved with a fierceness that always grabbed Josh by the
throat. He hugged Toby back hard, and Toby barked.

Letting out a breath, Josh set him aside to lean over
Anna, who hadn't moved. He didn't fool himself; he had
no delusions of being able to control his sister. She hadn't
stayed still simply because he'd ordered her to. "Anna."
Gently he pushed the damp hair from her sweaty brow.
"Talk to me."

She opened her eyes and laughed outright. "That was
sweet," she said.

Toby tipped his head back and barked at the ceiling,
his voice filled with glee.

Josh sat back on his heels and scrubbed a hand over his
face. "Toby should be in bed, Anna. And you could have
hurt yourself."

She started to crawl to her chair. "Been there, done
that, bought the T-shirt."

Josh scooped her up while Devon sauntered over.
Though how he could walk at all with his homeboy jeans
at half past his ass was a mystery. Devon righted Anna's
wheelchair, and Josh set her into it.

"Oh, relax," she muttered after Josh stood over her,
hands on hips. She tugged on Toby's ear. "Hey, handsome. Go get ready for bed, 'k?"

"Arf-arf," Toby said, and turned to the hallway.

Josh caught him by the back of his Star Wars sweatshirt. "You use soap and water today?"

Toby scrunched up his nose and scratched his head.

Josh took that as a no. "Use both now. And tooth-paste."

"Arf," Toby said slowly, all hurt puppy face.

But Josh had learned—never cave. "Go on. I'll be right there."

Toby went from sad to excited in a single heartbeat, because if Josh was coming, too, it meant a story. And for a moment, Toby looked young, so fucking painfully young, that Josh's chest hurt again.

Getting home in time to fall into bed exhausted was one thing. Getting home in time to crawl into bed with his son and spend a few minutes before they both crashed was even better. "Pick out a book," he said.

"*Arf!*"

Josh gave Devon a look, and the guy made himself scarce. Devon might be a complete loser but he was a smart loser.

Anna ignored Josh and pushed back her dark hair. She was tiny, always had been, but not frail. Never frail. She had the haunting beauty of Snow White.

And the temperament of Cruella de Vil.

Five years ago, a car accident had left her a highly functioning paraplegic. She was damn lucky to be alive, though it'd been hard to convince a sixteen year-old to see it that way. "If you can't get him to bed on time," Josh began, "just tell me. I'll come home and do it myself."

"Oh good," Anna said with an impressive eye roll. "You still have the stick up your ass." She headed into the foyer, grabbing her purse off the bench.

"You're still mad about me nixing your Europe trip," he guessed.

"Give the man an A-plus." She snatched her jacket off the low hooks against the foyer wall. "Always knew you were smart. Everyone says so. They say, '*Oh, that Dr. Scott's so brilliant, so sharp.*'" She turned away. "Shame it doesn't run in the family."

"No one says *that*," he said.

"They think it."

Josh's fingers curled helplessly as she struggled into her jacket, but if he offered to help, she'd bite his head off. He wasn't the only Scott family member who hated needing help. "So prove them wrong," he said.

She shrugged. "Too much work."

"Anna, you can't just traipse around Europe with Devon for the rest of the year."

"Why? Because my life is so busy? Because I've even got a life?"

"You've got a life," he said, frustrated. "You're taking classes at the junior college—"

"Yes, Cooking 101 and Creative Writing. Oh, and my creative writing teacher told me I should definitely *not* quit my day job."

He sighed. "You can do anything you want to do. Pick a major. You *are* smart. You're—"

"*Paralyzed*," she said flatly. "And bored. I want to go to Europe with Devon."

God knew what Anna saw in the guy who claimed to be going to a Seattle tech school at night while working on a roofing crew by day. Josh had never so much as seen Devon crack a book, and he sure as hell seemed to have a lot of days off. "How does Devon have the money for Europe?"

"He doesn't. My settlement money from the accident comes in two weeks."

Oh hell no. "*No.*"

"I'm going out," she said, both ignoring what he'd said and changing the subject since it didn't suit her.

"Where?" he asked.

"*Out.*"

Jesus. Like pulling teeth. "Fine. Be back by midnight."

"You're not Mom and Dad, Josh. And I'm not sixteen anymore. Don't wait up."

"Devon have gas this time?" Last week he'd run out of gas in his truck at two in the morning, with Anna riding shotgun up on Summit Creek.

In answer to the gas question, Anna shrugged. She didn't know and didn't care.

Great. "*Midnight*, Anna."

"Yeah, yeah."

"Wake me up when you're home."

She rolled her eyes again and yelled for Devon, who appeared from the kitchen eating a sandwich. He slid Josh a stoner-lazy smirk, then pushed Anna's chair out the front door and into the night.

Nice. Josh shut the door and ground his teeth. He was all too aware that he *wasn't* Mom and Dad. They'd been gone for five years, killed in the same accident that had nearly taken Anna as well. Josh had been twenty-eight, a brand-new father from his first and only one-night stand, and a single year out of residency when it'd happened. Overnight he'd lost his parents and had suddenly become responsible for a badly injured, headstrong, angry teenager along with his infant son. He'd held it together, barely, but it'd all been a hell of an adjustment, and there'd been more than a few times Josh hadn't been sure he was going to make it.

Sometimes he still wasn't sure.

He locked up, flipped off the kitchen and living room lights, and found Toby jumping on his bed with his Jedi saber, the iridescent green light slicing through the air.

Whoosh, vrrmm-whoosh.

Josh caught him in midleap and swung him upside down, to Toby's screams of delight. Then Josh tossed him onto the bed and crawled in after him.

Toby had a few books on his pillow. He was into superheroes, cars, trains... anything with noise, really. Being read to calmed him, and he snuggled up close and set his head on Josh's shoulder, pointing to the top book. The Berenstain Bears. The cover showed the entire family, but Toby stroked his finger over the mama bear.

He wanted *his* mama bear.

Like a knife to the heart. "Toby."

Toby tucked his face into Josh's armpit but Josh gently palmed the boy's head and pulled him back enough to see his face. "You remember what I told you, right? About your mom? That she had something really important to do, but that she'd be here with you if she could?"

Toby stared at him with those huge, melting chocolate-brown eyes and nodded.

And not for the first time in the past five years, Josh wanted to strangle Ally for walking out on them. For walking out and never so much as looking back. Leaning in, he pressed a kiss to Toby's forehead and then sighed. "You forgot the soap."

"Arf."

Josh woke somewhere near dawn, dreaming about being smothered. When he opened his eyes, he realized he'd fallen asleep in Toby's bed. The Bean had one half, Tank the other, both blissfully sleeping, limbs and paws akimbo.

Josh, bigger than both of them put together times four, had a tiny little corner of the bed. And he meant tiny. His feet were numb from hanging off, and the *Berenstain Bears* book was stuck to his face. Wincing at his sore bones, he shifted, and at the movement, Tank snuffled and stretched.

And farted.

The bedroom was instantly stink-bombed. "Jesus Christ, dog, you smell like a barn."

Tank just gave him a pug grin.

Josh shook his head and eased out of the bed, pulling the covers up over Toby, who was sleeping like he did everything in life—with 100 percent total abandonment.

Envying him that, Josh showered and went downstairs.

Nina was cleaning the kitchen and making Toby's lunch.

"I need you to walk Tank today," he said. "Twice. Once midmorning and once in the afternoon. He sure as hell better learn to hold it that long if he wants to live."

Nina carefully closed Toby's Star Wars lunch box. "No," she said.

"Okay, okay, I'm only kidding. I'm not going to actually kill him." *Probably.*

"No, I won't walk that dog." Nina was four and a half feet tall, Italian, complete with accent and snapping black eyes that could slay one alive. The housekeeper also possessed the baffling ability to organize Josh's place so that it looked like humans lived there instead of a pack of wild animals. She didn't cook, though. And she didn't mother.

The sole reason she made Toby's lunch was because Toby was the only one in the house she actually liked. "I do not care for *that* dog," she said. "He licks me."

"He's a puppy," Josh said. "That's what puppies do."

"He's a nightmare."

Well, she had him there.

Chapter 4

*The 12-Step Chocoholics Program: Never be more than
12 steps away from chocolate!*

Half an hour later, Josh had gotten Toby onto the school
bus, then driven to the office, still having no idea what
he was going to do about the damn dog. He would have
thumbed through his contact list, except he hadn't replaced his phone yet.

He could rehire Grace. She needed the money but hiring her again would involve being sucked into her sexy
vortex. Hell. He left his car, and instead of heading inside
the building, he crossed the small side street to the hospital, then walked around to the old west wing, which was
now the Health Services Center, run by Mallory Quinn.

She smiled when he entered. "Hey, Doc. Tell me
you're here to give me a shift."

"No. Don't you have Dr. Wells today?"

"He ended up with an emergency in Seattle and can't
show."

Shit. Josh eyed the filled waiting room. "Martin didn't get you a replacement?"

Mallory shook her head. They both knew Martin Wells thought he was too good to give his time to the HSC, that he felt the ER was lucky to get him once a week on contract from Seattle. "I don't know what I have waiting for me in the office," Josh said. "But I'll try to get back over here."

"Thanks," she said gratefully. "But if you're not here to work, what can I do for you?"

"I need to locate Grace."

Mallory arched a brow. "Grace?"

"I need her dog walking services again."

"But you fired her yesterday."

He grimaced. He'd been sort of hoping she wouldn't know that. Mallory was an amazing nurse, the fiancée of one of his closest friends, and she was as fierce as a mother about the people she cared about—Grace being one of those people. "Yeah, I might have been hasty on that," he said.

Mallory studied him. "She's something, isn't she?"

Yes. Yes, Grace was something all right. "So, do you have her number? My phone died in the ocean."

"Yes, I have her number."

He waited but she didn't give it to him. He looked at his watch. "Mallory."

"You have to promise to apologize for hurting her feelings yesterday."

"I didn't hurt her feelings."

Mallory just gave him a long look. Jesus, he didn't have time for this. Neither of them did. "Fine," he said. "I'll apologize for hurting her feelings. Just tell me where to find her."

"I'm sorry, I can't. It's against the code."

"The code?"

"Yeah, the code. Listen, if one of your friends had gotten hurt by a girl, and then that girl wanted his phone number from you, would you give it out?"

"Mal, you're sleeping with one of my friends every night. Why would I give some girl Ty's number?"

She sighed. "None of this matters right now anyway. Grace isn't going to answer her phone. She's working."

"Walking more dogs into the ocean?"

"Okay, that was your crazy puppy's fault, and no, it's Wednesday morning, so she's at Lucille's art class at the gallery."

"Thanks." Josh moved to the door, then turned back. "Can you call my office and tell them I'm running half an hour behind, and see if someone picked me up a replacement phone yet?"

"It'll cost you."

"Let me guess," Josh said. "Chocolate cake?"

She smiled sweetly. "From the B and B, please."

Tara, the chef at the local B&B, made the best chocolate cake on the planet. "Noted." Josh left HSC and drove through Lucky Harbor, past the pier to Lucille's art gallery. The place was an old Victorian, possessing 150 years of charm and character, sitting comfortably on its foundation in its old age. When he stepped inside, a bell above his head chimed, and Lucille poked her head out of a room down the hall.

She was somewhere near eighty. She favored pink polyester tracksuits and matching lipstick and was the heart and soul of Lucky Harbor—not to mention the Central Station for all things gossip. "Dr. Scott!" she said,

beaming in delight at the sight of him, patting her bun as
if to make sure it was still stacked on top of her head. "Are
you here to join our drawing class?"

"No, I need to speak to one of your students."

"Uh-oh. Do you think Mrs. Tyler's having another
heart attack?"

Christ, he hoped not. "Not Mrs. Tyler."

"Whew. Don't tell me Mrs. B's got hemorrhoids again.
I keep suggesting that she eat more prunes, but she
doesn't listen. You need to tell her."

Mrs. Burland was one of Josh's patients. In fact, she
refused to see any doctor other than Josh—but she didn't
listen to him any more than she did Lucille. "Not Mrs. B,"
he said. "I'm looking for Grace Brooks."

Lucille blinked in surprise. "Well, honey, why didn't
you say so? Sure, you can speak to her, but she's not one
of my students. She's our model."

"Your model?"

"Yes, today we're drawing the nude form."

Not much surprised Josh. Actually, nothing surprised
Josh. But this did. "Grace is the nude model?"

"Learning to sketch the nude human form is standard
practice for a beginning drawing class," she said. "We always hire a nude model. Last season I did it myself."

While he was adjusting to the horror of that, Lucille
went on. "The female form is the most beautiful form on
earth. Very natural." She pushed the studio door open, revealing Grace on a pedestal, a robe pooled at her feet, her
body twisted into some ballerina pose. Her blond hair was
loose, wavy to her shoulders, shining like silk, her limbs
bare and toned.

She wasn't nude. At least not completely. She was

wearing one of those long gimmick T-shirts so common in beach shops, with the form of a very curvaceous woman on it in a skimpy string bikini.

Lucille grinned at him. "She was feeling a little shy."

Holding her pose, Grace narrowed her eyes on Josh. "What are you doing here?"

"He came to see you," Lucille said.

Grace's eyes narrowed a little bit more. "You draw?"

"Not even a little bit," Josh said. She should have looked ridiculous. She had a knockout body, but it was completely covered up, from chin to shin, in that oversized shirt. Her feet were bare, her toenails painted a bright pink.

She didn't look ridiculous at all. She looked the opposite of ridiculous. In fact, she looked good enough to gobble up with a spoon. Without a spoon. He was thinking his tongue would work...

"Why are you here?" she asked.

"My dog needs a dog walker today."

Not saying a word or moving a single muscle, she managed to say no. It was all in the eyes.

She had amazing eyes.

"You're a dog walker?" Lucille asked Grace in surprise.

"No," she said.

This was news to Josh. "Your flyer said you were an 'experienced dog walker.'"

Grace winced at this, then bit her lower lip as she looked away.

"Hold still, dear," one of the budding artists said.

"Sorry." Grace cleared her expression and got back into her pose. "The flyer wasn't mine," she admitted to Josh. "You called the wrong number."

"I called the wrong number." He absorbed this a minute. "And yet you were willing to go work for a perfect stranger who needed his dog walked?"

"Hey, don't blame me. You were the one willing to hire a perfect stranger."

Unbelievable. "You had references on that flyer!"

"Did you actually call any of them?" she asked.

Suddenly, he needed Advil. "So you'd go work for anyone who called?" He hated that she needed work that badly. "Jesus, Grace, I could have been a psycho."

"Or *mean*," she pointed out.

"I wasn't mean."

Her expression said she thought otherwise. And then there was another thing. The T-shirt. It was hard to get past the huge cartoon breasts, stuffed into that cartoon itty-bitty bikini. And he couldn't help but wonder.

What was she wearing beneath the T-shirt?

"Honey, you're looking a little tense," Lucille said to Grace. "We haven't studied tense yet. Can you go back to serene?"

Grace did just that, and Josh dipped his head and studied his shoes for a long moment, until the desire to strangle Lucille had passed. "Fine," he said, looking up at Grace again. "I'm sorry I didn't keep you on as my dog walker."

"And yet you're not sorry for being mean."

It wasn't often that he didn't know what to do. But he honest to God had no idea what to do with her.

"Look," she said, still holding her pose. "I nearly lost your dog. You had to come into the ocean to save me, and I got you all wet. I was a mess and a terrible dog walker. I get it."

"You weren't *that* terrible."

"Are you just saying that so I'll come back?"

Well, yes. But even he knew that was a trick question. With a minefield all around it. "Please," he said.

Everyone in the room was following this conversation like they were at Wimbledon in the final match, but all eyes had landed on Grace now, waiting breathlessly for her answer.

"You weren't exactly friendly," she finally said, non-committal.

In unison, the heads swiveled back to Josh, eyes narrowed in censure.

He drew a breath, remembering what Mallory had told him, that he'd hurt Grace's feelings. He hadn't meant to, of course, but even he knew enough about women to understand that didn't mean shit. Once feelings were hurt, it took an act of congress to reinstate status quo. Since he wasn't used to apologizing for his actions, he kept it simple. "You're right. I wasn't friendly. I was overworked, stressed, and in a hurry. I'm sorry."

"Sorry, or desperate?"

Desperate? Hell no. *She* was the desperate one. But if he said so, he'd lose the tentative ground he'd just made. So he pulled out his ace in the hole. "I'll double the pay."

This got her attention enough to make her break the pose. Hell, it got *everyone's* attention.

Even Lucille set down her pencil. "What do you think, ladies?" she asked the room. "Should Grace give Dr. Scott another shot?"

They whispered among themselves like jurors debating his sentence. Josh slid Grace a look. She was looking at him right back, eyes lit with amusement, not looking particularly desperate for the job at all.

"Six to two," Lucille announced, "in favor of Grace giving Dr. Scott another shot."

Grace didn't react, and Josh had the feeling the vote was actually more like six to *three*. "*Triple* the pay," he said. No more messing around. He was already late, and he was sinking fast. The board didn't need another excuse to get on his ass about being unable to handle the workload.

Grace smiled, and it was a really great smile. So great that he felt something twinge inside him, something he'd thought dead. "What's so funny?" he asked.

"*Triple* the pay?" She was still smiling but there was something in her voice that warned him he was on thin ice, but hell if he knew what he'd done now.

"Yeah. Problem?"

Several of the women behind him snorted, the rest nodded in agreement, all of it adding up to him being an idiot.

"I'd have done it for that kiss you promised me," Grace said.

Well, *now* was a fine time to tell him that.

"*Aw.*" Lucille clapped her hands together in utter delight. "Break time, ladies! Let's give these two a moment." She slid a sly look in Josh's direction. "Go ahead, then," she whispered. "Pay her."

Josh shook his head. "My wallet's in the car—"

"Not money, Dr. Scott. The girl said she'd do it for a kiss."

Josh let out a laugh. "Lucille, she was just kidding."

Lucille studied Grace, then slowly shook her head. "No, I don't think she was kidding. Does anyone here think Grace was only kidding?"

Everyone in the room shook their heads in unison. A room full of damn geriatric bobblehead dolls.

Grace stepped down off the pedestal. "It's okay, Lucille," she said, still looking at Josh, her mouth curving slow and sensuous. "We're scaring him. Of course Dr. Scott doesn't have to kiss me to get me to walk his dog." She shrugged at him, like *Hey, this isn't my doing*.

Bullshit it wasn't her doing. But she had such pretty eyes, he thought insanely. Real pretty. And, hell, they were scaring him. Pride stinging just a little bit, feeling like he had something to prove—though he wasn't quite sure what—he stepped close to Grace and bent his head low, his gaze searching hers for a sign that she was being pushed into this.

Her smile broadened.

"You could put a stop to this," he said softly, and unbelievably, she made the sound of a chicken. He straightened and narrowed his eyes. "What does *that* mean?"

"You know what it means."

She was crazy, he decided. A crazy cutie. He had way too much on his plate for this. Too many people to take care of, and she had "take care of me" written all over her. And yet she thought that *he* was a chicken. Interesting.

Infuriating.

And a little bit of a turn-on. But fuck it, he was done thinking. The woman wanted a kiss, and hell if he'd try to talk her out of it. So he leaned in and brushed his mouth over hers. Peach. Her lip gloss was peach, and it was more delicious than anything he could remember.

So was the kiss, chaste as it was, which rocked his socks right off.

Chapter 5

*Chocolate is good for three things. Two of them can't be
mentioned in polite company.*

Grace closed her eyes to enjoy the feel of a man's
mouth on hers. Yep, just as heavenly as she remembered.
Maybe even more so. She definitely felt a spark.

Actually, she felt a full fireworks display.

When Josh pulled back, she opened her eyes to his
dark brown ones and caught his own flash of surprise before he masked it.

"We have a deal, then," he said. "For today."

He hadn't worded it as a question, of course, which
was just like a man. But he looked even more exhausted
today than he had yesterday, and that both intrigued and
worried her. She was extremely aware of his proximity,
that his big, bad self wasn't in wet, sandy ER scrubs today. He wore cargo pants and a fisherman's sweater, both
in black, both casual but expensive-looking, like he'd
walked right out of an ad.

But she was even more aware that the entire art class was watching them.

Avidly.

Her phone buzzed. The incoming text was from Lucille: *Honey, I don't mean to rush you but it's rumored that the good doc has got the best hands in all of Lucky Harbor. Go for it.*

Grace lifted her head and sent Lucille a look.

Lucille smiled innocently.

Grace rolled her eyes and nodded to Josh. "Fine. We have a deal."

He handed her a key to his house and left.

Grace watched him go, thinking that his hands weren't even his best part. "Excuse me a minute," she said to the class, before running to catch up with Josh in the hall.

He turned to face her, and she shook her head, her body still humming from his kiss. "What was that?" she finally managed. "Back there."

"You know what it was."

Yeah. Yeah, she did. Chemistry. Holy Toledo, some damn *hot* chemistry. "But it shouldn't be like this, not between us." They were night and day. Oil and water. He might not know it, but she did. "It was a fluke." That was all she could think, that it was a complete fluke. But his eyes darkened, and in response, her nipples got hard. "Okay, so maybe not," she muttered, and crossed her arms over herself and her fake triple Ds.

He stepped closer, his voice low. "I'd prove it to you, but I'm not into kissing by committee."

She looked over her shoulder and found Lucille and the entire art class leaning out the classroom door, unabashedly eavesdropping. She gave them the "shoo" signal, and they vanished.

"Impressive," he said. "Be sure to use that level of authority on Tank today and try to avoid another swim."

"I really thought he was in the water."

"He likes to play hide-and-seek."

"Good to know." And she still had to take that crazy puppy out for another walk...

"Interesting T-shirt," he said.

She looked down at herself, eternally grateful that she hadn't gone the full Monty route after all. "It's not as good as the real thing, but as it turns out, I'm pretty selective about who sees the real thing."

His smile softened. His eyes crinkled in the corners, and the laugh lines on either side of his mouth deepened, stealing her breath. "Good to know," he mirrored back at her.

It was a genuine smile from a man who didn't appear to do it too often, and it left her a little dazed. Or maybe it was the crazy amount of testosterone coming off him in waves.

"Let me know if you have any trouble today," he said.

"For what you're paying me, there'll be no trouble." And if there was, he'd be the *last* man she'd call, amazing kisser or not, because they had a connection, and she knew the power of it now.

Grace wasn't in Lucky Harbor to make a connection with a man she knew wasn't her type. She was looking for *fun*, that was it, and in spite of Josh being sex-on-a-stick, she wasn't sure he had a lot of fun in him. Steering clear was her smartest option here. And no matter how good he was with his hands, she was going to be smart, if it killed her.

* * *

A few hours later, Grace headed to Josh's house. As she
parked, she noticed she had an unread text from Mallory.

*Hey, head's up. The hottest doctor in town just came
by and coerced me into telling him where you were.
I folded like a cheap suitcase. Sorry, but he's hard
to say no to. Don't be mad. I owe you a cupcake.*

Yeah, an entire batch. Grace shook her head and let
herself into Josh's house without incident. This time, she
carefully leashed Tank *before* she opened his baby gate,
and then as a double precaution, she just as carefully
picked him up and carried him outside.

She might not be a blood-born Brooks genius, but she
was quick on the learning curve.

She avoided the beach entirely, instead setting Tank
down to walk alongside the quiet street. Tank sniffed every single rock, every last tree, and then finally chose a
spot to hunch and do his business.

"Hey!" A man stuck his head out of a window of the
house. "Don't think I don't see that you're not carrying a
doodie bag! You come back with a doodie bag and clean
that up!"

A doodie bag? Grace had seen a stack of plastic bag-
gies by Tank's leash. Guess she knew what they were for
now. She scooped Tank back up. "I hope you're done."

Tank snorted and licked her chin.

"I mean it!" the man yelled at her. "Make sure you take
care of that mess or I'll call the cops on you."

Grace took Tank back to the house, securing him in
the laundry room. Then she reluctantly grabbed a bag to

go do her "doodie" duty. As she turned to the door, she nearly tripped over a young woman in a wheelchair. She was twentyish, petite, dark-haired, her eyes as dark and alluring as the man she had to be related to.

"Anna," she said, introducing herself. "The crazy sister. And you must be the nude girl he kissed."

Grace choked. "*What?*"

"Yeah, you haven't seen?" Anna pulled her phone from a pocket and thumbed a few buttons, then turned the screen for Grace.

It was Lucky Harbor's Facebook page, and a picture of Grace in the bikini T-shirt that was going to haunt her for the rest of her damn life. And her lips were indeed connected to Josh's. The kiss had lasted only a heartbeat, but one would never know it by the picture, which had been captured at just the right nanosecond, showing Grace leaning into Josh with her entire body, both hands on his chest.

She hadn't realized she'd touched him so intimately, but now she could remember the heat radiating through his shirt, the easy strength of him beneath. And he'd smelled delicious.

But God, had she really looked at him so adoringly?

Josh hadn't been so innocent either. He had one big hand cupping her jaw, his thumb clearly stroking her skin in a way that seemed both tender and yet somehow outrageously sexy.

"Cozy," Anna said dryly.

"It's not what it looks like," Grace said, giving her back the phone.

"No?" Anna asked, looking down at the screen again. "Because it looks like you're kissing. You're not kissing?"

"Okay, so we're kissing, but that's only because the day before he'd said he'd kiss me if I lost the dog and then..." Grace trailed off, unable to remember exactly how it was that she'd ended up with Josh's mouth on hers.

On the Internet.

Anna arched a brow.

Grace sighed. "Well, this is embarrassing. We're not...I mean, he and I aren't—"

"Oh, no worries," Anna said. "I know you're not his girl toy. He wouldn't have hired you if you were."

"Girl toy?"

"Yeah, Josh doesn't bring his women home."

Well ouch. "Okay, good." *Great.* Because, hey, she'd already decided that the two of them weren't going to do this. This being anything. So yeah, this was really great.

"Hang on," Anna said. "I just want to share the link with everyone I know..." She hit a few keys, then smiled. "There. God, how I love it when he does something stupid. It's so rare, you know? And then when he finally does it, he really does it right." She unlocked the baby gate, freeing Tank just as a young boy came tearing into the kitchen. He was waving a lightsaber and making some sort of war cry as he ran circles around the kitchen table.

Tank took off right on his heels, barking so hard his back legs kept coming off the floor. Quite the feat, given that his belly swung so low.

The kid was wearing a Star Wars T-shirt. His jeans were streaked with dirt and low enough on his narrow little hips to reveal his underwear waistband, which was also Star Wars. His battered athletic shoes lit up with each step he made, and the right one was untied. He was maybe five, with dark hair that definitely hadn't seen a brush that morning, and his melting, dark chocolate eyes matched Dr. Josh Scott's. He stopped short at the sight of Grace, and Tank plowed into the back of his feet, then fell to his butt and gave out a little startled yelp.

"Toby," Anna said. "You're going to stay here with Grace. I'll be back in an hour."

"Wait...what?" Grace shook her head. "No, I'm just the dog babysitter."

"Yeah?" Anna asked. "Are you babysitting the dog right now?"

"Well, yeah, but—" She broke off at Anna's amused look and whirled around to find the puppy chewing on the kitchen table leg. *Crap.* "Hey," she said. "No chewing on that."

Tank kept chewing. Grace went over there and pried him loose but she was too late. He'd left deep gouges in the beautiful wood.

Anna tugged affectionately on a lock of Toby's hair. "The dogsitter will make you an after-school snack. Don't do anything I wouldn't do, Slugger."

Grace was still shaking her head. A dog was one thing. But a kid? There was no counting the number of ways she could screw this one up. "Wait a minute."

But Anna wasn't waiting. She was actually at the door. "No worries, he's easy. The regular nanny, Katy, ditched Toby today, so we picked him up from school, but I've got things to do, so..."

"We?"

A horn sounded from out front. Grace looked out the window and saw a rusty pickup truck.

"Gotta go," Anna said, and wheeled out.

"But..." But nothing. Anna was gone, gone, gone.

And Grace had just been promoted to a job for which she had absolutely no qualifications. She looked at Toby.

Toby looked at her right back, solemn-faced, his dark eyes giving nothing away.

"Hi," Grace said.

"Arf," he said.

"Arf," Tank said, dragging a running shoe that was bigger than himself. He'd already chewed a hole in the toe. Eyes bulging, tongue lolling out the side of his smashed-in face, Tank sat and panted proudly at the prize he offered her.

It was going to be a long hour. She liberated the shoe and searched her brain for some way to relate to a five-year-old kid holding a toy lightsaber. Who barked. "So are you a Jedi warrior?"

Toby swung the lightsaber wide. It lit up and went *whoosh, vrrmm-whoosh.*

Tank promptly went nuts, so naturally Toby swung again.

Whoosh, vrrmm-whoosh.

Toby hit a home run with a cup of juice that had been on the kitchen table, sending it flying through the air. Luckily the cup was plastic. Not so luckily, the juice was grape, and purple sticky liquid splattered like rain on the table, the floor, the counters, Grace, and both Tank and Toby. Even the ceiling took a hit.

Toby dropped the lightsaber as if it were a hot potato.

Tank scooped it up by the handle in his sharp puppy teeth and began running circles around the table again, both belly and lightsaber dragging on the ground, still lighting up, still making *whooshing* noises.

"It's okay," Grace said to a stricken-looking Toby,

grabbing a roll of paper towels from the counter, swiping at the kid first. But the sticky clothes didn't appear to bother him any because he stepped free and headed toward the fridge.

Tank dropped the lightsaber, redirecting his reign of terror to licking the floor.

"Toby?" Grace asked. "Where's the trash?"

The boy made a vague gesture over his shoulder toward the back door and stuck his head into the fridge.

Grace went to wipe down the table and instead stared at the stack of twenties, underneath a grape-splotched sticky note that had *Grace* scrawled across it in bold print. She picked up the money and started counting. Twenty, forty, sixty, eighty... *One hundred and sixty bucks.* It took her a minute to figure it out—forty for yesterday, triple that for today.

It was ridiculous, of course, and yet... the things she could do with a hundred and sixty bucks. Staring at it longingly, she thought of her overloaded credit card, her student loans, and the weekly rent she had coming due at the B&B where she'd been living.

Not to mention the cleaning bill for getting grape juice out of today's sundress. Shaking her head, she pocketed forty. Nothing for yesterday since she'd screwed up, and forty for today. Because she wouldn't screw today up. Leaving the rest, she stepped out the back door with the sticky paper towels, which she dumped into the trash can. Now that she had a moment of privacy, she pulled out her cell phone and hit Josh's number to fill him in.

He picked up, sounding harried. "Dr. Scott."

Her brain stuttered at the sound of his low voice, the same low voice that had prompted her into a moment of insanity earlier. That kiss... "One hundred and sixty bucks?" she said in disbelief. "What exactly are you expecting for this hundred and sixty bucks?"

There was a beat of silence. She figured he was probably wondering who the crazy lady was, so she decided to clarify. "It's Grace," she said, trying for calm efficiency. She was used to calm efficiency, after all. Used to order. Used to things balancing.

Or she *had* been used to those things, back when she'd been gainfully employed, making something of herself, something very big and very important. Back way before she'd come to Lucky Harbor and taken on the first job she'd ever had that was completely over her head.

"You needed the money," Josh said. "Right?"

"Well, yes," she admitted reluctantly. "But a hundred and sixty dollars?"

"It's what we agreed on, triple yesterday's pay."

"I didn't mean to accept that. The kiss was my payment." The crazy, wild kiss. The crazy, wild, *wonderful* kiss. She turned back to the door, which had shut behind her.

It was locked. *Uh-oh.*

"What?" he asked.

Had she said that out loud? "Nothing." She peered into the window, thankful that the shades on it were open, but didn't see Toby in the kitchen. "Well, nothing except your sister brought Toby home, and I'm watching him for her for an hour or so."

There was another beat of silence while Josh processed this. Though he was a guy, and therefore a master at hiding his emotions, his thoughts weren't all that hard to decode. Surprise and shock that somehow the same person who'd lost his dog yesterday was now in charge of his kid, and irritation at his sister. "Anna left you in charge of Toby?"

"I guess your nanny got sick, and Anna's boyfriend picked Toby up from school."

Nothing about that sentence seemed to bring him comfort. And it wasn't even the worst bit of news she had to tell him. That honor belonged to the Facebook photo, which she decided he didn't need to know about right now. Or ever. "It's only for an hour," she said, trying to make the best of the situation. "How much can happen in an hour?" She tried the door again. Still locked. She knocked.

Tank came tearing back into the kitchen, running more circles around the table with the lightsaber. But still no sign of Toby. She knocked again.

Tank stopped running in circles and panted at her. Then he turned his attention to the cabinet under the sink, where he started nosing around with what appeared to be a small trash container.

The container wobbled but didn't tip.

Tank then sank his teeth into the plastic liner and tugged until the thing fell over, spilling trash across the kitchen floor. *Crap.* Grace looked around her. She was in the side yard, with two gates at either end—both locked. "I have to go," she said.

"Don't even think about it. What's wrong?"

Oh, so many, *many* things. Tank was going to town on the trash, inhaling whatever he could get at. Toby was still nowhere in sight. That couldn't be good. She knocked again, harder this time.

The puppy looked up from his mission of destroying the world and growled at her.

Grace whirled around, searching for a doormat. Everyone hid a key beneath a doormat. But there was no mat. Most likely because it was safer for Anna in her chair that way. So where would they hide a key?

"*Grace.*"

She gave up. "Okay, where is it?" she asked him. "Where do you hide the key for the stupid people who get locked out?"

"You got locked out?"

"No, I'm just asking for the stupid people."

"Where's Toby?"

She took another peek in the window, and oh thank God, there he was, standing on the other side of the door, staring up at her with those big eyes. She pointed to the door.

Toby just looked at her.

Grace sighed. "He's in the kitchen."

"Go to the second planter from the porch," Josh instructed. "Reach into the sprinkler valve box."

Holding the phone in the crook of her neck, Grace smiled at Toby in what she hoped was a reassuring manner and again pointed to the door handle, gesturing for him to let her in.

Instead, he turned and walked out of the kitchen for parts unknown, his shoelace trailing on the floor, his little Star Wars undies sticking out of his jeans in a way that he'd probably spend the next fifteen years purposely trying to mimic.

"Toby!" she called. "Toby, don't leave the kitchen. *Toby?*"

"Hurry, Grace," Josh said in her ear.

She rushed to the second planter and at the sight there,

she dropped her phone. There was a very large spiderweb guarding the valve box. Heart pounding, she scrambled to pick up her phone. "Sorry. You there?"

Nothing. She smacked her phone on her thigh and tried again. "Josh?"

"Yeah. Do you see the key? It's in the metal hide-a-key."

Yeah, she saw the metal hide-a-key. She also saw the spiderweb. The *massive* spiderweb. She toed it and a big, fat, hairy brown spider crawled with badass authority into her line of sight, giving her the evil eye. He was ready to rumble. *Gulp.* Not much truly terrified Grace. Well, aside from clowns and glass elevators. But spiders? Spiders topped her list, and the hairs on the back of her neck stood up.

"Grace?"

"Yeah?" she whispered. Was it her imagination or was the spider giving her a "bring it" gesture with two of its spindly legs?

"There's a pool out back," Josh said. "You can't get to it from the side yard where you are. Toby can swim, but..."

Oh, God. The image of Toby running outside and into the pool on his own was too awful to bear. She closed her eyes, plunged her hand into the sprinkler box while silently chanting "pleasedon'tbitemepleasedon'tbiteme," and pulled out the hide-a-key.

Without getting bitten.

She ran to the back door and let herself in, racing through the kitchen, skidding to a halt in the living room, where Toby was standing on the couch, lightsaber once again in hand, whipping it around.

Whoosh, vrrmm-whoosh.

Grace nearly collapsed with relief. She'd handled millions of dollars of other people's money without breaking a sweat, and yet at this, just one little boy and a puppy, she needed a nap. "Well, that was a fun fire drill."

"Toby?" Josh asked in her ear.

"All in one piece." She sank to the couch and put her head between her knees. "Your house is a little crazy, Dr. Scott."

"You must feel right at home, then."

She heard herself let out a weak laugh. "Hey, *you're* the crazy one." She fingered the money in her pocket. "You can't go around paying people so much money for menial work. They'll take advantage of you."

"I'm not easy to take advantage of."

Okay, so that was undoubtedly true, she thought. "But—"

"Did you lose Tank?"

Only for a minute . . . "No."

"Did he shit in the house?"

"No."

"Then you're worth every penny," Josh assured her. "Listen, I'm sorry about Anna. I'll get there as soon as I can."

"But—"

But nothing. He was gone. She lifted her head and found Toby standing there, a lock of dark hair falling across his forehead, lightsaber still in one hand, a squirming Tank in the other.

He really was pretty damn cute, she thought. This would be okay. She could totally do this for an hour. It'd be like the time she had to babysit the guys in payroll.

Toby wrinkled his nose like something was stinky, then hastily set Tank down.

The puppy was panting, and his stomach looked uncomfortably full. *Uh-oh.* "Tank," she said, trying to get him outside.

Too late. Tank hunched over and horked up all the trash he'd eaten.

On her feet.

"Arf," Tank said, looking like he felt all better.

"Arf," Toby said.

Chapter 6

There are four basic food groups: plain chocolate, milk chocolate, dark chocolate, and white chocolate.

One painfully long hour later, Grace was exhausted. This was *nothing* like babysitting the guys in payroll. First of all, Tank never stopped moving.

Or barking.

He'd found a forgotten stethoscope from somewhere and had dragged it around and around the living room. Around the couch, up and over the coffee table, until he'd inadvertently trapped the end on a chair leg and been caught up short. A sound like air leaking out of a balloon had come from his throat, and he'd fallen over, legs straight up in the air.

Grace had thought he'd killed himself and had gone running toward him, but before she'd gotten to him, he'd rebounded.

Good as new, he'd been chewing on her sandals five minutes later.

And five minutes after that, the wooden kitchen chairs.

And the wooden banister poles.

And someone's forgotten hat... ·

She was considering giving him an electrical cord to chew on next when she heard the front door open. Josh stepped inside wearing a white doctor's coat over his sexy office clothes, a stethoscope around his neck like a tie. He picked up Toby and flung him over his shoulder in a fireman's hold, making the kid squeal with abandon.

Josh gave a tired smile at the sound and turned to Grace, Toby still hanging upside down behind him. "Anna?"

"Present," Anna said, rolling in the front door. The driver of the pickup was with her. Twentysomething, with an insolent smile, he slouched against the doorjamb.

Josh nudged the guy back a step until Slacker Dude stood on the other side of the jamb. Josh then shut the door in his face.

"Josh!" Anna was horrified and pissed. "You can't do that to Devon!"

"Just did."

"You—"

"*Later*," he said curtly.

Anna whirled in her chair and sped off down the hallway. Two seconds later, her bedroom door slammed hard enough to shake the windows.

Josh ignored this. "Thanks," he said to Grace, who felt as rattled as the windows. Five-year-old boys, as it turned out, were aliens. They owned battery-operated hamster pets called Zhu Zhus that chirped and whistled and skittered randomly, terrifying pug puppies and temp babysitters alike.

Josh reached into his pocket and pulled out some cash.

"Oh no," she said, backing away. "You don't have to…"

"We didn't negotiate for babysitting fees."

"It's okay."

He gave her a speculative gaze. "Is this one of those 'I would have done it for a kiss' deals?"

She laughed, even as her tummy quivered. "I just meant that this one's on me."

"No," he said softly. "I owe you."

The air between them did that snap-crackle-pop thing again, like static electricity on steroids, and Grace's breath caught. "Okay," she said, just as softly. "You owe me."

Two days later, Grace entered the diner, still thinking about kisses, deals, and sexy doctors named Josh.

And oddly enough, her résumé. She supposed she could add dog walker to it. She'd done it four days in a row now with no mishaps, at least no major ones. She didn't count Tank biting the mailman's pant leg yesterday, because Tank didn't actually break skin. Nor did she count Toby dumping his bottle of bubbles into the pool because, hey, she'd always wanted to see what would happen too. And the pool guy had come right out and fixed everything, so all was okay.

In fact, she could probably now add babysitter to her new and constantly changing résumé as well, since it went nicely with dogsitter, model, and floral delivery person.

Not that any of that went with being a banking investment specialist.

She did finally get calls for interviews. She had a

Seattle appointment tomorrow morning. The Portland interview was the following day, early, and would be conducted by Skype. This worked out in her favor because this way she wouldn't miss modeling for Lucille's class. The budding artists were drawing feet this week, so Grace had no wardrobe worries, at least from her feet up.

She tried to imagine her mother or father modeling their bare feet, but couldn't. Because they took life much more seriously than that. They were the real deal.

And Grace was a poser.

It wasn't that she didn't love Lucky Harbor. She did. It was just that what she could find here in the way of a career wasn't...big enough. Important enough. She plopped into the back booth next to a waiting Mallory. Amy showed up two minutes later and dropped a shoe box onto the table. She untied her pink apron, tossed it aside, and sank into the booth, propping her feet up by Grace's hip. "Off duty, thank God."

"What's with the shoe box?" Grace asked, nudging it curiously. "New boots or something?"

"Or something," Amy said. "Somehow, I'm selling like crazy." She was a sketch artist, and she'd found a niche for herself creating color pencil renditions of the local landscape. Lucille's gallery was selling out of everything Amy created nearly as fast as she brought it in. "I can't keep up."

"Keep up?" Grace asked.

"Yeah. At first, I just took people's cash or checks and shoved the receipts into my purse or pockets or wherever."

She was talking about her accounting, Grace realized with horror. She might not be a bean counter anymore, but she still had a healthy respect for the process. "You said at first. What are you doing now?"

"Well, I decided I was being irresponsible," Amy said, "so I started a file."

"That's not a file," Grace said. "That's a box."

"Yeah, whatever. A box worked better." Amy pushed it toward her. "For you."

Grace opened the box. It was full of...everything. There were napkins with numbers and dates scrawled on them, little pieces of paper with more numbers and dates, bigger pieces of paper, receipts, some folded, some crumpled, some not. Grace lifted a round cotton pad with a number scratched onto it in what looked like eyeliner and stared at Amy in disbelief.

Amy shrugged. "So bookkeeping isn't my thing. It's yours, right?"

"Well, yeah, I suppose."

"And?" Amy looked at her expectantly.

"And...?"

"You going to help me or what?"

"How?" Grace asked in disbelief. "By getting you a bigger box?"

"No, by keeping track of my shit." Amy waved her hand. "You know, create a system so I don't look like just another idiot with a box come tax time."

Grace looked at Mallory, who laughed. "Better do it," she told Grace. "Before the IRS takes her away."

Grace pulled the box near her and sighed. "Fine. I'll do the damn books. But it's going to cost you."

"Big bucks?"

"Chocolate cupcakes. *Tara's* cupcakes." Tara was Grace's landlord at the B&B, and there was little that compared to the exquisiteness of Tara's baking. Not that Grace could afford her.

"Done," Amy said. "But I'm going to pay you as well, so be sure to bill me."

"On what, a napkin?"

"Funny."

Over chocolate cupcakes—not Tara's, unfortunately—they discussed the latest and newest. Amy was moving in with her sexy forest ranger, Matt Bowers. Mallory was planning to elope with Ty, a local flight paramedic, to a beach somewhere in the South Pacific—though she wanted a big reception here in Lucky Harbor when they got back. And Grace told them about dog walking for Josh, laughing a little because dog walking hardly compared to relationships. "I didn't realize it would be an ongoing thing," she said. "But the good doctor has this odd ability to get his way."

"Yeah, you know who else is like that?" Amy asked. "*All* men. Is his pug's name really Tank?"

"His sister brought the puppy home for the kid," Mallory said, knowing much more about Josh than any of them since she and Josh worked together at the hospital. "Without asking, I should add. It's Anna's life mission to drive Josh insane."

"Why?" Grace asked.

"I don't know. I think she's trying to make him pay for her being in a wheelchair, which of course isn't his fault. Between her, Toby, and the hospital board all up Josh's ass about selling them the controlling percentage of his practice, he's got to be close to losing it completely."

Actually, every time Grace had seen Josh, he seemed perfectly calm, perfectly in control, and perfectly . . . yum.

If not entirely too exhausted. "Why would he sell the controlling percentage of his practice?" Grace asked.

"People don't realize how much work a sole practice is," Mallory said. "If something happens to a patient, it's his fault. If a billing error's made and a procedure's wrongly claimed, that's fraud—also his fault. The list is endless, and he's responsible for all of it. That doesn't even count the med school loans, the license requirements, insurance bills, office costs, support systems..." She shrugged. "People think doctors have it easy, but they don't. Josh inherited the practice from his late father, but his first love is the ER. If he sold, he could spend more time there. Or with Toby."

"Then he *should* sell," Grace said.

"Not that easy," Mallory said. "His father was very popular around here, and he built that practice out of love. People come from all over to go see Dr. Weston Scott's son, out of loyalty and affection. It's a huge obligation on Josh's shoulders."

Grace nodded. Oh boy, did she understand family obligation. Hers was to become *Someone Important*. Instead she was walking dogs and delivering flowers and kissing sexy doctors named Josh... She realized conversation had lagged and that Amy and Mallory were staring at her. "What?"

"You tell us what," Mallory said. "Miss Staring-Dreamily-Off-into-Space."

"I wasn't," Grace said. "It's nothing."

"It's something," Amy said.

"Oh, it's something all right," Lucille said helpfully, getting out of the booth to their right. "She left out the kiss." She pulled out her cell phone. "Here."

Oh boy, Grace thought. *Déjà vu.*

And indeed, Lucille produced the infamous Facebook pic.

Mallory's and Amy's eyes cut straight to Grace, and she grimaced. "Okay, so I maybe left a teensy little part out," she admitted.

Amy took Lucille's phone and cocked her head sideways. "What are you wearing? That's one hell of a tiny frigging bikini. I had no idea pink polka dots were your thing."

"Oh, for God's sake." Grace snatched the phone and handed it back to Lucille. "It was you. *You* posted this thing."

"Well of course I did. It's been a slow week. Nothing exciting—until you kissed the town's favorite bachelor." Lucille winked, snagged a cupcake, and went on her way.

Intending to do the same, Grace slid her purse on her shoulder and picked up Amy's box of receipts. "It's getting late." She made a move to slide out of the booth but Amy blocked her exit with one very wicked-looking kickass boot.

"*Fine.*" Grace sagged back. "We kissed, okay? No big deal. And I didn't tell you guys because I didn't want you to make a bigger deal out of it than it is."

"You kissed the hottest doctor in town," Mallory said in disbelief. "Maybe the hottest doctor *ever*, and you don't think it's a big deal?"

"He kissed *me*," Grace corrected, grabbing another cupcake since her exit was blocked. "And are you sure he's the hottest doctor ever? I mean, you've seen *Grey's Anatomy*, right?"

"*Ever*," Mallory maintained, and shrugged helplessly

when both Amy and Grace stared at her. "So sue me, I have a thing for late-bloomer nerds."

Grace choked on her cupcake and it almost came out her nose. "Late-bloomer nerd? Are you kidding me?" Josh was six foot four and solidly built. He had melted dark chocolate eyes and a smile that did more for her than the cupcake she was eating, and a way of moving his big, gorgeous self that always made her clothes want to fall right off. "Nothing about him says nerd." *Nothing.*

"Well, I went to school with him," Mallory said, carefully peeling her cupcake out of its baking paper. "He hit high school at like five-five and was the scrawniest thing you've ever seen. He wore glasses and *still* couldn't see worth shit. Oh, and he was head of the science club and got beat up by the football players unless he did their homework."

"Damn," Amy said, sounding impressed. "He sure turned things around for himself. I bet he enjoys his reunions, being a big-shot doctor and everything. Not to mention he looks like he could kick some serious ass if he wanted."

"He kicks serious ass every single day," Mallory said. "By saving lives. He raised his sister. He's raising his son."

"Speaking of which," Grace said, "what happened to Toby's mom?"

Mallory did a palms-up. "She wasn't from around here and she didn't stick. That's all anyone really knows. Josh doesn't talk about it." She'd finished her cupcake and licked some chocolate off her thumb before concentrating on Grace. "I know you planned to just blow through Lucky Harbor and ended up staying longer than you meant to. And we're glad about that, so very glad." She said this with fierce affection, reaching for Grace's hand. "Because the three of us, we give each other something."

"A hard time?" Grace asked.

"*Hope*," Mallory said. "And courage. You wanted the courage to add some badly needed fun to your life. The kiss with Josh sounds like a good start to me. That's all I'm saying. So don't sweep it under the rug as a fluke or try to forget about it. Enjoy it."

Grace blew out a breath. "Well, sure, cloud the issue with logic."

Mallory smiled. "We made a pact to change our lives, and that's what we're doing. All of us. No man left behind."

Grace was incredibly touched by the "we." She'd never had siblings. Her parents had given her everything they had but they weren't warm and fuzzy by nature. She'd had girlfriends, but they were always schoolmates or coworkers. Her relationships had always been born of circumstance.

Like her.

This wasn't the case with Amy and Mallory. They were the real deal, and better than any sisters she might have spent her childhood wishing for.

Mallory pointed at her. "I mean it!"

Grace ignored her suddenly thick throat. "It's hard to take you seriously when you have a chocolate mustache."

Mallory swiped it off with her forearm. "And it's not like I saw this life of mine coming down the pike, you know. Opening up a Health Services Center, falling in love...I mean, I am so not sitting in a European sidewalk café right now, rearranging my desperately alluring miniskirt and thinking about whether it's too early to ring up U2 or go shopping." She grinned. "That was my secret high school fantasy. But I wouldn't trade this for the world." She looked at Amy. "And you changed your life too. Tell her."

"She knows."

"*Tell* her," Mallory insisted.

"I changed my life," Amy intoned.

Mallory rolled her eyes and gave Amy a shove.

"Fine," Amy said. "I changed things up, opened myself to new experiences. Like...*camping*."

Mallory sighed. "Killing me."

"And love." Amy gave Mallory a little shove back. "See, I can say it. I found someone to love me. *Me*," she repeated, clearly still boggled by that fact.

Grace understood the sentiment. She'd had boyfriends— some had lasted a night; some that had lasted much longer. She'd even fallen in love and gotten her heart broken. She'd learned a lot—such as how to keep her heart out of the equation.

"The truth is," Amy said, "I came to Lucky Harbor searching for myself. Even though deep down, I was afraid that whatever I found wouldn't be enough. But actually, my real self kicks ass."

"Yeah, it does," Mallory said softly, smiling at her.

Grace stared at the two of them. "You're a pair of saps."

"Look, forget us," Mallory said. "We're not the point. The point is that you're not living up to what you said you'd do. You're not having fun."

"I don't know," Amy said slowly, studying Grace.

"Posing in the nude, walking McSexy's dog...Sounds like fun to me."

"I didn't pose nude," Grace said. "*Sheesh!*"

"Well maybe you should," Mallory told her. "And maybe you should have fun with the sexy doctor while you're at it. He's just about perfect."

Grace understood the logic, convoluted as it was. But there was a flaw, a fatal one. Having grown up trying to live up to being damn near perfect, she refused to date it.

The diner door opened, and a man strode in wearing paramedic gear with FLIGHT CARE in white across his chest.

Ty Garrison.

Mallory took one look at the man she was going to marry and grinned dopily. She brushed her hands off and headed straight for him, meeting him in the middle of the nearly empty diner. In her scrubs and sneakers, she seemed tiny compared to the tall, leanly muscled flight medic as she leaned into him. Tiny and cute.

Ty must have thought so, too, because he bent and kissed her with lots of heat, easily boosting her into his arms, the muscles in his shoulders and back rippling as Mallory wrapped herself around him like a pretzel.

"Aw," Grace said in spite of herself.

"Get a room," Amy said.

Behind Ty's back, Mallory flipped Amy the bird and kept kissing her fiancé. They were holding on to each other, and even from the length of the diner, Grace could see how much Ty loved Mallory. It was in every touch, every look. She sighed and pulled out her phone, which was ringing. "Crap," she said, looking at the caller ID.

"Bill collector?" Amy asked.

"Worse. It's my mother."

"The rocket scientist?"

The one and only. Grace sucked in a breath and looked down at what she was wearing before she got a hold of herself and remembered that her mother couldn't actually *see* her. "Mom," she said into the phone. "Hi, what's wrong?"

"What, a mother can't call her only daughter?"

Grace smiled at the imperious tone and could picture her mother in her lab, working in Dior and a white doctor's coat to protect the elegance and sophistication that she couldn't quite hide behind all the degrees and doctorates.

Grace didn't have elegance and sophistication emanating from her every pore because of one simple truth—she hadn't been born into it. She'd done her damnedest to absorb what she could and fake what she couldn't. "It's not the first weekend of the month," Grace said.

"True, but I just finished up that three-week seminar on the design for NASA's new deep-space exploration system, and I realized I missed our monthly check-in. How are you doing, darling?"

This wasn't a "tell me about the weather" sort of question. This was a request for a full, detailed report, and guilt flooded Grace. She quickly scanned through her options. She could tell her mom what she'd been up to—which was that she'd been using her fancy college education not at all—or continue to slightly mislead in order to keep her happy.

Mallory disconnected her lips from Ty and led him back to the Chocoholics' table. He took a cupcake, kissed Mallory, and left.

"And how's Seattle?" Grace's mom asked. "How's your new banking job? You the CEO yet?"

Grace grimaced. "Actually, I've sort of moved on to something else."

"Oh?"

Grace looked down at Amy's shoe box full of receipts. "Something more accounting based." Vague, and hopefully impressive. But there was no denying it truly was a total and complete lie, which meant she was going to hell, doubly so for telling the lie to her own mother.

"A lateral move, at least?"

A beep sounded in Grace's ear, her call-waiting. *Saved by the beep.* "Hold on, Mom." She clicked over. "Hello?"

Nothing. Damn phone. She'd dropped it one too many times. She slapped the phone against her thigh and clicked again. "*Hello?*"

"Grace. You available for tomorrow?"

Josh and his deep voice, the one that continuously did something quite pornographic to every womanly part in Grace's entire body. *Was she available?* Unfortunately, yes. "Hang on a sec." She clicked back to her mom and decided that since she was going to hell, she might as well make her well-meaning mom happy before she did. "I've made a lateral move from my usual banking specialist schtick. Nothing quite as exciting as being a rocket scientist or a biologist, but I am working for a doctor."

"Sounds fascinating," Josh said wryly. "Do I know this doctor?"

Grace froze. *Crap.* "Just a minute," she managed. She smacked herself in the forehead with her phone; then, ignoring both Amy and Mallory gaping at her, she clicked over again. "Mom?"

"Yes, of course, dear. Who else?"

Who else indeed. Grace swiped her damp forehead.

Mallory and Amy, both clearly fascinated by the Grace Show, were hanging on her every word.

Grace twisted in the booth, turning her back on them.

"So tell me about your job," her mom said.

"I'm...working for a doctor," she said again.

"Using your CPA to handle his finances? Or research on that dissertation you never finished?"

She was saved from having to answer when her phone beeped again. "Hold on." She clicked over. "Josh, I can't talk right now."

Nothing.

Good Lord. She really needed a new phone. She smacked it again for good measure and clicked back to her mom. "Sorry, Mom. Yes, I'm going to be putting my CPA to use." She looked at Amy's box. "Sort of. I'm trying some new things out. And some...research. But listen, I've really got to—"

"Trying new things," Josh said. "I like the sound of that."

"Oh for God's sake— *I have to go.*" She clicked again and drew in a deep breath. "Mom?"

"Yes. Darling, you sound quite frazzled. You're working hard?"

"*Very*," Grace managed, rubbing the spot between her eyes.

"What? Hello? Grace, I can't hear you—"

Silence.

Grace swore and hit the phone again. "Mom? Sorry,

bad reception. But yes, I'm working hard, very hard. Hey, I'm a Brooks, right? That's what we do."

"This conversation just gets more and more interesting," Josh said.

"Oh my God! I thought I told you I had to go!" Grace disconnected him and fanned herself. "Damn, is it hot in here?"

Mallory and Amy were wide-eyed. Mallory opened her mouth to speak, but Grace pointed at her, then grimaced as she spoke into the phone. "Mother?"

"Yes. Grace, what are—"

"Going into a tunnel, Mom. We're going to lose reception—" Grace disconnected, closed her eyes, and took her medicine like a big girl. "I suppose you're still there," she said into the phone.

"Yep," Josh said. "So the dog walking. Overqualified much?"

"I don't want to talk about it."

"I bet."

"I'm going into a tunnel," she said desperately.

"There are no tunnels in Lucky Harbor, Grace."

"Then I'm throwing myself under a bus."

"You can run," he said, clearly vastly amused, "but you can't hide."

And that's where he was wrong. She'd been hiding all her life, right in plain sight. Pretending to be a Brooks, when the truth was, she wasn't pedigreed. She was mutt. She disconnected, tossed her phone to the booth seat, and thunked her head onto the table.

"Wow," Amy said approvingly. "When you embarrass yourself, you go all the way, don't you?"

"I'm going to go to hell for that."

"Nah," Amy said, pushing the tray of cupcakes closer to Grace. "I don't think people go to hell for making an unbelievable ass of themselves. My grandma used to say you go to hell for abusing yourself."

Grace thought about how she'd abused herself in the shower just that very morning and sighed.

Chapter 7

If not for chocolate, there would be no need for control-top hose. An entire garment industry would be devastated.

Thanks to a crazy ER shift, Josh didn't get home until 3:00 a.m. He crawled into bed and immediately crashed, dreaming about a certain beautiful, willowy banking-specialist-slash-model-slash-dog-walker in a wet sundress that clung to her curves and made his heart pound.

And thanks to his own stupidity, he could also dream about kissing said beautiful, willowy blonde.

He got one glorious hour of sleep before he was woken by a puking Anna. Not the flu, but a hangover. Good times.

When he finally got to his office, he found he'd been double booked, but that was nothing new either. First up was Mrs. Dawson, who was experiencing hot flashes and other signs of perimenopause. She'd been coming in once a week or so for months, bringing him casseroles along with her list of gripes and symptoms. At the end of each appointment, she asked him out. Each time, he politely turned her down, saying he never mixed business with pleasure. Today when he gave her the standard line, she pulled out her phone and showed him the Facebook pic of him and Grace kissing.

"Looks like a pretty definite mixing of church and state," she said.

Josh stared at the picture, a little surprised to find that his and Grace's crazy chemistry had absolutely translated to the screen for the world to see. "She's not my patient."

"She's an employee. You pay her to walk your dog."

There was no use in getting annoyed that she knew Grace was his dog walker. Everyone knew it. This was Lucky Harbor, after all. He rose, pulled off his gloves, and tossed them into the trash bin. "See you next week, Mrs. Dawson."

"Humph," Mrs. Dawson said.

Josh walked to the next patient room and pulled the chart from the door holder. Mr. Saunders was dealing with kidney stones. Josh entered the room and pulled on yet another set of gloves. He'd once wondered how many hours a year he spent pulling on and tearing off gloves and figured he didn't really want to know. "How are you doing today, Mr. Saunders?"

"Dying."

"Actually, you're not," Josh said. "It's kidney stones. Once you pass them, you'll feel better."

"You sure?" Mr. Saunders asked.

"Yes."

"Sure sure?" Mr. Saunders asked. "Because it doesn't feel like kidney stones. Last night, I felt like I was having the most painful orgasm of my life. I guess I was probably just passing one of the stones, huh?"

Josh had to keep his head buried in the file as he nodded because how the hell do you confuse passing a kidney stone and an orgasm?

And so his day went, leaving him to wonder if everyone was crazy or if it was just him. By noon, his head was going to blow right off his shoulders, and he knew he couldn't go on like this. He either had to start turning patients away or give up the ER shifts.

"It's a no-brainer," Matt said. He'd brought five-inch-thick deli club sandwiches for lunch. They were spread out in Josh's office as the men watched ESPN highlights on the computer. "Sell the practice to the hospital. Let them bring in another doc, and all your problems go away. You work the hours you want. Simple."

Nothing was ever that simple, but the appeal was growing, and Josh had been thinking about little else for months. It meant giving up his dad's dream, which he hated, but the truth was that Josh couldn't do the dream justice. He'd tried.

When Matt had gone back to work, Josh brought up the contract offer, which he'd read a hundred times. A thousand. He'd had his attorney go over it with a fine-tooth comb. All he had to do was accept the offer with an electronic signature and hit SEND.

His finger hovered over the ENTER key, but then he set his head down on his desk to think about it for a minute. The next thing he knew, Dee, his nurse-practitioner, was calling his name.

"Hey," she grumbled from the doorway, "if you get to nap, so do I." She was in her fifties and resembled Lucy from the Peanuts comic strip. She was that perfect mix of no-nonsense and sweet empathy with his patients, though she rarely felt the need to impart any of that sweet empathy on him.

"Need you to get your cute ass out here," she said. "You've got Nancy Kessler in room one with a bladder infection that she wants cleared up before she goes to Vegas this weekend with her new boyfriend. Randy Lyons is in room two. He nail-gunned his thumb to the roof again. And Mrs. Munson's in three, saying the high pollen count is going to kill her dead."

"You take the allergies," he said. "I'll get the other two."

"Three. You've got thirteen-year-old Ben Seaver in four. He stuck his ding-dong into the Jacuzzi vent."

"Christ," Josh muttered. "*Again?*"

"Here." Dee handed him her coffee. "You probably need it more than I do."

"Thanks." It had far too much sugar and milk in it, but she was right. He needed it bad.

"Your father was never this busy," Dee said.

"Because we've doubled his practice."

"*You* doubled his practice," she said, and gave him a rare pat on the arm. "He'd be proud, but he wouldn't want this for you. Just sign the damn contract, Doctor. Before you burn out."

"I'm not going to burn out."

"Okay, then sign the damn contract before *I* burn out." With that, Dee nabbed back her coffee and left.

Josh's other office staff members consisted of two front office clerks, Michelle and Stacy, and an LPN named Cece. An hour later, Michelle poked her head into the exam room. "Mrs. Porter on line two. Needs to see you today. Says she's dying."

Mrs. Porter wasn't dying; she was lonely. Her kids lived on the East Coast, so she came in at least once a week for attention. Last week she'd had an eye twitch and had self-diagnosed a brain cancer. "Tell her we can get her in tomorrow," he said to Michelle.

"She says she'll be dead tomorrow."

"All right, fine. Squeeze her in today, then."

An hour later, the waiting room was still full. Dee gave Josh the stink eye when he slipped into his office to take an incoming call. It was Toby's school.

Toby hadn't been picked up by Katy, his nanny.

Josh immediately headed for the door, giving a pissed-off Dee an apologetic wave. He got into his car while dialing Katy. She was the sister of one of the nurses at the hospital and had come highly recommended. Problem was, she was only a temporary fix because, soon as her husband's transfer came through, they were moving to Atlanta.

Before Katy, they'd had Trina, who'd quit because of complications. Those complications being Anna. And Suzie, the nanny before Trina, had also left unexpectedly.

Josh was sensing a pattern, and he didn't have time for it.

Katy picked up and immediately said, "Don't hate me but I'm getting on a plane."

Josh let out a breath. "No notice?"

"I couldn't get a hold of you yesterday. I talked to Anna."

Josh considered thunking his head against his steering wheel. "A *day's* notice, then?"

"I'm sorry, Josh," she said with real regret. "But I think

my replacement should be *two* nannies. And maybe an enforcer."

Josh called Anna next. She didn't pick up. Shock. He pictured Toby waiting at school with no one there and his stomach cramped. He sped up while mentally thumbing through the contacts on his phone, slowing at Grace's name.

Stopping.

Moving on.

Backing up.

Don't do it, man. She was smart as hell but she was also a really, *really* bad dog walker. No way should he burden her with his kid too. Except she'd already handled Toby yesterday for an hour, and everyone had lived to tell the tale.

She'd come through for him, twice now. Which really begged the question—*exactly who was helping whom here?*

The truth was, she'd already proven more reliable than half the people in his life. And damn if there wasn't something in her eyes that pulled him in like the tide, something extremely unforgettable. He knew she was a little lost, searching for something. He had no idea what but he wanted to help. Which was a very bad idea. He needed another person on his plate like he needed a hole in his head, but he couldn't turn back now. He was drawn to her.

She answered on the third and a half ring with a question in her "hello," as if maybe she'd been playing chicken with her voice mail.

"So," he said. "Daughter of a rocket scientist?"

"I don't want to talk about it."

He laughed. "You busy?"

"Not anymore. Just got back from an interview in Seattle."

This drained his amusement real quick, and his gut tightened—both in relief for her and regret for how he'd feel when she left Lucky Harbor. "How did it go?"

"Good. I think. I just got back and already walked Tank for you. And there were no accidents and no near drownings. No incidents at all, actually. Oh, and whatever your neighbor says about me isn't true. Mostly."

"Mostly?"

"Well…Tank sort of defiled Mrs. Perry's petunias. Twice."

Mrs. Perry was dead serious about her petunias. A few months back, when Josh had been teaching Toby to ride his bike, Toby had ridden through the flower bed.

Mrs. Perry had called the police, claiming vandalism.

Sheriff Sawyer Thompson had shown up on Josh's doorstep doing his damnedest to hide his smile, suggesting that Josh might want to think about teaching Toby to ride in a deserted parking lot instead of making potpourri out of Mrs. Perry's petunias.

The following week, Anna had brought the Antichrist home, and Toby had given up riding his bike, preferring instead to run with the puppy.

And bark.

"Forget Mrs. Perry," Josh said. "I've another job for you."

"Doing?"

He hesitated, not wanting her to say no. "It's a one-time temp position."

"My specialty," she said. "Do I get a hint?"

"I need a babysitter for Toby. Just for an hour or two."

She fell quiet, and Josh didn't want to rush her, but he

had patients waiting, a sister to strangle later, and Toby, who was hopefully not waiting alone at the curb at the school that Josh was still five blocks from.

"Was I your last choice?" she finally asked.

"You were my *only* choice."

"Aw," she said. "We're both such accomplished liars."

He laughed softly, and there was another beat of that crazy chemistry, right through the phone.

"I'll do it," she said. "I'll watch Toby for you."

He let out a breath of relief. "Meet us at the house. And, Grace?" He paused. "Thanks."

"Yeah, you probably shouldn't thank me yet."

Josh disconnected and pulled up to the school. Toby stood on the curb, one hand in his teacher aide's, the other clutching a Kung Zhu Ninja warrior to his chest.

Josh got out of the car and crouched in front of him. "Hey, Little Man. Sorry Katy wasn't here to get you. She's moving a little sooner than expected."

Toby nodded and studied the tops of his battered Star Wars sneakers. He had newer pairs but he refused to wear them.

Josh met the teacher aide's eyes. She sent him a censuring look that said, *Epic Fail, Dad.*

Message received, thank you annoying, condescending teacher aide. "Appreciate you waiting with him."

"It's my job," she said. "And you should know, Toby pulled another vanishing act on us today."

"I didn't get a call."

"Because we found him," she said. "Thirty feet up the big oak tree in the playground."

Little black dots floated in Josh's visual field. As an ER doctor, he'd seen exactly what a thirty-foot fall could do to a body. He'd seen everything. "What were you doing up there?" he asked Toby.

Toby had another silent consult with his athletic shoes, so the aide answered for him. "He had a tree frog clenched in one fist."

"Toby doesn't have a frog."

"No," she agreed. "But we do. It was liberated from its terrarium in the kindergarten classroom."

Ah. Now it made sense. Josh looked at Toby. "You saved the frog, huh?"

Toby nodded.

"Oh, and he spoke today," the aide added.

"Yeah?" This was great news. "What did you say?" he asked Toby. "Wait. Let me guess. You solved world hunger. Or...created peace on earth. No, I know, you asked a girl out."

Toby wrinkled his nose like, *Ewwww, a girl?*

Josh grinned at him, and Toby giggled, the sound music to Josh's ears.

"He wanted to know if I'd be his new mommy," the aide said.

Uh-oh. That one had Anna written all over it. Josh sucked in a breath and slid another glance at Toby. "Your aunt teach you that?"

Toby shrugged.

Oh, yeah. *Anna.*

"He also asked the lunch aide and vice principal. And the janitor."

Josh kept his expression calm as he rose and took Toby's hand. Toby used his other to pull up his sagging jeans, and because his Star Wars T-shirt was only half tucked in, there was a strip of pale skin revealed.

His son was going commando.

Josh had no idea why, and hell if he'd ask in front of Judgmental Teacher Aide, so he filed the question away for later. "Ready to go home, Little Man?"

Finally a spark of life. "*Arf.*"

Chapter 8

♥

If chocolate is the answer, the question is irrelevant.

Grace had been at the grocery store when Josh had called and was checking out when she got stopped by Jeanine Terrance, who owned a pottery shop.

"I hear you're an accountant," Jeanine said. "*And* that you're fixing Amy up with a bookkeeping system. I could *really* use a better bookkeeping system."

"Oh," Grace said. "Well, I'm not—"

"Amy swears by you," Jeanine said. "I'd do it myself but the left side of my brain is resistant to numbers. I'd pay you, of course, and not just in pottery either. I'm doing really well this quarter. Or so I think. I'll know better when you fix up my books."

"Yes, but I didn't really plan to start bookkeeping..." Grace broke off at Jeanine's hopeful expression. Hell. One small pottery shop. How much work could it really be? "I guess I could come take a look at what you've got."

"Oh, that's so wonderful!" Jeanine hugged her, then

spared a guilty smile. "Um, you should probably know that I'm not quite as organized as Amy."

Since Amy's entire financial portfolio had been shoved into a shoe box, this was cause for some alarm, but Grace had already said yes. She promised to go by later, and drove to Josh's.

Certain parts of her—her naughty parts—were doing the happy dance at getting to see him again. Her other parts—her *smarter* parts—were more reserved. After the humiliating Phone Call Incident where he'd heard way too much about her through her conversation with her mom, she'd sort of hoped to keep some healthy distance between her and Josh for a while.

Like forever.

But he'd dangled this job, and she couldn't really afford to turn it down. She'd told him the truth about the Seattle interview going well, but she didn't have an offer yet. Next up was the Portland interview. And then all she had to do was wait.

She hated waiting.

When she knocked on the front door, wild barking came from inside. Josh answered, looking pretty damn fine in black pants and an azure blue button-down, the ever-present stethoscope around his neck. Grace's morning had been spent in a meeting with several men just as well dressed, just as handsome, but not a single one of them had affected her breathing.

Why did he affect her breathing?

His gaze tracked right to her lips, and a shot of hot, wet desire went straight through her, heading south.

Oh no. No, no, no, she told herself sternly. No matter how good-looking he was, or how he made her knees wobble with just one glance, he wasn't for her. Not even close. He was the kind of man she'd spent her entire life trying to live up to, driven, focused, workaholic...Ain't happening. Not here, not now, not ever. She repeated that to herself a few times, but her body didn't buy into the hype. Her body wanted him.

The barking seemed to have increased in decibels. "Don't tell me it multiplied," she said.

"Okay, I won't tell you."

Hmm. He was also extremely cool and calm under pressure. Something she'd never managed on her best day. And sexy as that was—so damn sexy—she'd discovered that men who had the cool, calm thing down were cool and calm *everywhere*, including their relationships.

She didn't want cool and calm in a relationship. She wanted passion. The big bang.

Fun.

"Arf, arf!" Toby yelled, coming running around the corner.

Josh swung him up and around so that he carried the boy piggyback style. Now there were two faces looking at Grace, both so similar as to be eerie, though Toby's was minus the fine stress lines outside the eyes and the world of knowledge in them.

"Toby's going to try real hard to be good," Josh said.

Toby nodded. Tank was at their feet, running in circles, chasing his own tail. With Toby still on board, Josh bent and scooped up the puppy too. "I can't promise the same for Tank."

Tank panted proudly. "Arf!"

Grace gave the pug a steely-eyed look that said, *Eat*

my shoes today and die, which didn't cow him at all. But
she had a genuine smile for Toby. "Hey there."

"Arf!"

"Are you and Tank brothers?" she asked him.

Toby smiled and started to speak, but Josh adjusted his
hold on Tank and reached back, covering Toby's mouth.

"Wait," Grace said. "I think he was going to actually
use words."

"Yeah, but trust me, you don't want to hear them."

Toby pulled Josh's hand away. "Are you my new
mommy?"

Grace's mouth fell open in shock, and Toby giggled at
the sight.

"Okay, Tiger," Josh said. "You know I love the sound
of your laugh, probably more than any sound in the
world, but I will squash you like a grape if you say that to
one more woman today."

Toby pointed to Anna, who rolled into the living room
behind them.

"Yeah, I know," Josh said mildly, sending his sister a
glance. "I'm going to squash Anna like a grape too."

Grace was horrified he'd say such a thing to a sweet
little boy, much less to his handicapped sister, but Toby
just grinned.

Anna did, too, and without a word, continued rolling
through the house, ignoring all of them.

Josh set Toby down. "How about you go find something to do that won't get you in trouble," he said.

When the kid was gone, Josh looked at Grace. "I called
Mallory."

"You did? For what?"

"I realize that this is a favor, *my* favor," he said. "But

I had to make sure you're everything you seem, even with the multiple degrees and what sounds like an...interesting family. And just out of curiosity, what kind of research are you doing for me, by the way?"

She groaned and covered her face. "I told you, I don't want to talk about it."

He laughed softly. "So we're okay?"

"Maybe. What did Mallory say?"

"That I'd be lucky to have you as Toby's nanny. And that she'd hurt me if I hurt you."

"What would you have done if she'd said something bad about me?"

"I'd have brought Toby with me to work. I've done that before."

She couldn't be sure, but it seemed like the big, bad, tough doctor shuddered at the memory. "You won't have to do that this week," she said.

He gave her a smile that conveyed gratitude, and also a good amount of something else, something that wobbled her knees as he gestured her inside. Every other time she'd been here, the place had been very neat, but not today. Today it looked like a bomb had gone off, especially the kitchen. There were dishes in the sink and ingredients and utensils all over the counters.

"It's my housekeeper's day off," Josh said, and scooped Toby up, eliciting a squeal of delight. This got even louder when Josh hung Toby upside down before finally setting the kid into a chair in front of a loaded plate.

"After-school snack was Toby's choice today," Josh explained. "Luckily this coincided with a lunch break for me, and I made what we like to call 'guilt pancakes.'"

From the ingredients and stuff scattered on the counter,

Grace could tell they were wheat pancakes with blue-
berries, accompanied by turkey bacon. Her own father
wouldn't know a spatula, much less how to turn on the
stovetop, so this was impressive.

Josh poured a little dollop of syrup onto Toby's plate,
then ruffled the boy's hair, his expression soft with something Grace had never seen from him before.

Affection.

"Be right back, Short Stack," Josh said. "Eat up."

Toby held up his lightsaber with one hand, which was,
of course, driving Tank nuts. The little pug was doing
his circle-the-table thing, growling ferociously at every
whoosh, vrrmm-whoosh, posturing like he was a Jedi as
well.

"Napoleon complex," Josh said to Grace. "He thinks
he's bigger than he is."

Toby grabbed a pancake in his free hand. Flattening
it on the table, he rolled it up before dipping it into the
syrup and then into his mouth.

"Utensils," Josh said.

Toby sighed and dropped his lightsaber to reach for a
fork.

Tank's growl came to an abrupt stop when the lightsaber hit the floor, and with a startled snort, he ran off
with his tail between his legs.

Toby, holding a fork in one hand, used his other to stuff
a huge bite into his mouth.

Josh tapped the unused fork in Toby's hand, then
turned to Grace, gesturing that he wanted a word in private. He led her out the back door, shutting it behind
them.

She turned to look inside to see if Toby was using the

fork or his fingers, but today the blinds on the window were closed.

"Okay, so here's the deal," Josh said. "I lied about it being for an hour or two."

That had Grace turning back to face Josh. "So I'm not the only one going to hell?"

Josh shoved his fingers through his hair, making it stand up on end. He was so broad that he blocked the sun, and with his arms up and bent, he was really testing the seams of his dress shirt in a way that worked for her, big-time.

Suddenly he dropped his arms back to his sides as if they weighed far too much. "Look," he said. "The truth is that I'm late. I'm overbooked. My sister's going to give me a heart attack. I need someone to watch the Bean for me today, and you need money. Plus, he's a good kid, really good, even if he refuses to use utensils or speak English. He will, however, bark at will, and he's excellent at catching spiders."

This stopped her cold. "You have more spiders?"

"No," he said without missing a beat. "No spiders."

"You said spiders," she said. "And I saw a big one in the side yard, in the sprinkler well."

"That spider went south for the winter."

"It's summer."

"He wanted to be the first to get out of town."

"Look at you, with all the lies." But she had to admit, "the Bean" *was* pretty damn cute. And the Bean's father was even cuter—though she was sure he'd object to such an innocuous word as *cute*.

Josh had spoken in a calm, quiet manner, but everything about him said exhausted tension. Not to mention how much he appeared to hate having to ask something of her.

She understood pride. God, how she understood pride. But seriously? Was she really thinking of doing this simply because he was in a bind?

No, a little voice inside her head said. *It's because he's hot...* "How long?"

Josh didn't move, didn't give away any sign of relief, but his eyes warmed. "Eight o'clock, at the latest."

Five hours from now. Grace had no idea what to do with a kid for five hours.

"Offer to kiss her again."

They both whirled around to find the back door cracked and an eyeball peering at them through that crack—at hip height.

Anna, in her wheelchair.

"Sorry," Grace told her. "That ship sailed."

Anna snorted.

Josh pushed the door shut and held it closed with one hand, the other resting on the wood next to her head. "Sorry about that." He leaned into her, forcing her into a door-and-Josh sandwich.

Not a bad place to be when it came right down to it. "So," she said, annoyingly breathless, "eight o'clock, then?"

"Yes, and there's a but."

If it was *his* butt, she was in.

"It's not just for today," he said.

This was the proverbial bucket of ice water. "What?"

"I need help for the rest of the week," he said. "From two until eight...ish."

"Oh my God, Josh." *All week...* "I don't know."

"I'm hiring a replacement nanny. I've already got feelers out. You and Toby can do the preinterviews and save some time if you want. I'd ask Anna to watch him, but she does the early mornings and late nights already. Plus, she's not been all that reliable, and Toby's been through enough."

"Josh…"

"A thousand bucks," he said.

"*Oh my God.*"

"Yes or no, Grace."

He was all hard, unforgiving lines of tough sinew, wrapped in a double dose of testosterone, but it was hard to concentrate on his yummy goodness at the moment, as unbelievable as that was. "A thousand dollars?" she said, dazed. "For half a week? You can't be serious."

"It also comes with free room and board. There's a guesthouse behind my pool. That's where a couple of our nannies have stayed, though not our last one; she was married. It's only seven hundred and fifty square feet, but it's furnished."

Grace shook her head, but the truth was, he'd had her at *free*. She'd been staying at the local B&B, and loving it. The three sisters who ran the place, Tara, Maddie, and Chloe, had been lovely, but the B&B wasn't exactly bank-account friendly. "I'll have more job interviews this week." *Hopefully.*

"We can work that out," he said.

She nodded, but she was thinking that he smelled amazing, even better than chocolate. So much so that she wanted to bite him.

And was he suddenly closer? She leaned her head back on the door to look up at him, into those warm, mocha eyes. Yeah, he was closer. She *could* actually bite him if

she wanted. But she was going to be good. "There's no
family to help you?" She knew his dad had passed away,
but that was all she knew. "What about your mom, or
maybe other siblings? Or...Toby's mom?"

"Both my parents are gone," he said. "And I have no
other siblings. As for Toby's mom, she's not available."

His face was an impassive mask. Impossible to read.
Not too hard to guess his thoughts, though—the guy was
in a rough spot with no support system in place. Maybe
she was nothing but a sucker, but there was something so
appealing about a guy supporting his kid, his sister, and
an entire medical practice all on his own, doing everything he could to make it all work. "Okay," she said softly.
"I'm in. I'm not sure about the guesthouse; I'll let you
know. But I'll take care of Toby for the week." She expected him to back up and let her go, but he didn't. Her
entire visage was the sheer expanse of his chest.

"There's one last thing," he said.

She wondered if he looked as good without his clothes.
"What?"

"*That ship sailed?*" he asked, repeating her earlier
words to Anna.

Again she tilted her head up. "I just meant we've been
there, done that. We already kissed, remember?"

His gaze heated. Yeah, he remembered.

"And it was...fine."

He'd probably shaved that morning but he had a
shadow coming in. And his eyes. Fathomless dark pools,
as always, giving nothing away of himself or his secrets.
"The kiss was...*fine*," he repeated, eyes narrowed.

"Well, yeah." *Fine plus amazing times infinity.*

He just looked at her.

"Okay," she admitted, sagging back against the door. "So it was a little better than fine. But I'm not looking for this. For a guy like you."

"Like me," he said slowly, as if the words didn't quite compute any more easily than "fine" had.

And probably they didn't. Look at him. He could have chemistry with a brick wall. "It's just that I'm not going to be in Lucky Harbor much longer, so while I'm here, I'm aiming for...fun."

"Fun."

"Yeah. It's a new thing I'm trying."

"And you think I'm not," he said with a hint of disbelief, "fun."

"It's nothing personal."

"Hmm." He took a step toward her, and since there was already no place to go, she found herself once again sandwiched between the door and his deliciously hard body. His hands went to her hips, where they squeezed lightly and then slid up her sides, past her ribs, to her arms and her shoulders. By the time he got to her throat and cupped her face, her bones had gone AWOL.

"What are you doing?" she managed.

"Showing you how much fun I can be."

Oh boy. Just his husky whisper sent a shiver down her spine, the sort of shiver a woman wasn't supposed to get for a man she didn't want to be attracted to. And then her body strained a little closer to him.

Bad body!

Josh's eyes met hers and held. He was purposely building the anticipation, along with the heat working her from the inside out.

"Still think I'm not fun?" he asked softly.

"You're not." She swallowed hard. "You're..."

He quirked a brow.

Hot and sexy, and damn. *Fun.* Which meant that she was in big trouble here, going-down-for-the-count kind of trouble. Time to wave the white flag, she decided. And she would. In just a minute...

"Say it, Grace."

"Okay, so maybe you're a *little* fun," she admitted. "But—"

He nibbled her lower lip, soothing it with his tongue, then stroked and teased her with his mouth until she let out a helpless murmur of arousal and fisted her hands in his shirt.

His eyes were heavy-lidded and sexy when he pulled back. "Bullshit, a *little* fun." His mouth curved as he looked down.

Following his gaze, she realized she was still gripping his shirt. She forced herself to smooth her fingers over the wrinkles she'd left. "Fine. You're a barrel of fun. Happy now?"

"Getting there." His eyes were dark with lust and focused on hers, his hands on her back, fingers stroking her through the thin material of her dress. When he lowered his head, he did it slowly, giving her plenty of time to turn away.

She didn't.

Their eyes held until his lips touched hers, and then her lashes swept down involuntarily. She couldn't help it; his lips were warm, firm, and oh how just right...

With a deep, masculine groan, he threaded his hands through her hair and tilted her head to better suit him, parting her lips with his, kissing her lightly at first, then not so lightly. And then everything felt insistent and urgent, and all her bones melted.

By the time he broke the kiss, Grace was unsteady on her feet, and her breathing was more in line with a marathon run. "I'm not sure what that proved exactly," she managed. Except he was the best kisser on the planet...

His eyes were heavy-lidded. His shirt was half untucked—her doing. He stood there looking dangerously alluring and hotter than sin.

He slowly shook his head. Obviously he didn't know what that proved any more than she did. "I'm not looking for a relationship with you either," he said quietly. "I'm not looking for a relationship period. You've seen my life, Grace. Hell, you're living it. You know I'd be crazy to bring a woman into this mess."

"So we're on the same page," she said with relief. Except not really. She *should* feel relief, but didn't, which made no sense. Neither of them wanted this. Where was her relief?

His gaze dropped to her mouth. "Thanks for agreeing to watch Toby for me this week."

"Any time," she whispered, then went up on tiptoes so that when she repeated the two words softly, her mouth brushed his with each syllable.

He groaned, and the sound of it was so innately male, so sensually dominating, that she tingled all over. She leaned into him, and when he groaned again, it rumbled from his chest to hers. "Grace."

"I know." She lifted her hands from him and backed away, right into the door, of course.

His hand, low on her back, slid up until he cupped her head in his palm. "Careful."

They stared at each other some more. Then her hands made their way up his chest, around his neck, her fingers gliding into his hair.

He made another sound low in his throat and pulled her back to him. She wasn't sure which of them made the next move after that, but then they were kissing again, and damn, she'd been right. The man could kiss, *really* kiss—

The knock on the other side of the door caused her to nearly jump out of her skin.

Josh didn't jump or let go of her. He pressed a kiss to the soft spot just beneath her ear. "You're lethal," he whispered before pulling her clear so he could open the door to Anna.

Toby was in her lap eating a Popsicle, his mouth rimmed in purple.

Anna was smirking. "Whatcha doing?" she asked.

Josh just sent her a long look, one that would have had Grace quivering in her boots if it'd been directed at her.

But Anna wasn't cowed in the slightest. "Oh, I know," she said. "You were checking each other's tonsils."

"Anna," Josh said, his tone mild but laced with a clear warning.

She just smiled. "Toby wanted to remind you that you have open house night at school later. And you're supposed to bring cupcakes for something or another tomorrow."

Still sucking on the Popsicle, Toby nodded his agreement on this.

"Neither of those things are on the schedule," Josh said.

"Oops," Anna said. "They must have gotten erased. Like my Europe trip."

A muscle twitched in Josh's jaw, but he softened his expression for a solemn Toby, ruffling the boy's hair in reassurance.

Tank was at their feet, squealing and snuffling, trying to coax someone into picking him up. "Arf," he said.

"Arf," Toby said.

Grace's uterus contracted, which she couldn't have explained to save her life. "I can handle the cupcakes," she heard herself say.

Josh looked at her with the expression of someone who was drowning but hadn't expected a rope tossed to him. "Yeah?"

"Yeah." She smiled at Toby. "I'm something of a cupcake expert. Especially *chocolate* cupcakes."

Josh's phone buzzed from the depths of his pocket. He pulled it out and looked at the screen, mouth grim. "Gotta go." He kissed the top of Toby's head. "Be good." He sent Anna a long warning look, then went on the move, towing Grace along with him, his hand on her wrist, forcing her to practically run to keep up with him. They strode through the house and out the front. Josh shut the door firmly, then pressed her back against it, dipping down a little to look into her face.

"We have got to stop meeting like this," she said.

He didn't smile. "We still on the same page?"

"The no-relationship page in spite of the fact that we tend to burn up all the oxygen in a room when we're in it together?" she asked. "Hell yes, we're on the same page. Who needs all that crazy chemistry." She forced a laugh. "Not me . . ."

"Grace." He wasn't smiling. "If this is too much—"

"No, of course not. We have a deal. I'll watch Toby.

Another reason to minimize the whole kissing thing, right? Because I don't kiss my bosses. In fact, my last job didn't work out because I wouldn't..." She grimaced. Damn big mouth of hers. "You know."

Josh's expression was suddenly even *more* serious. "No," he said quietly. "I don't know. Tell me."

Well hell. How did they get here? She rolled her shoulders and looked at the ocean across the street, uncomfortable with the subject *and* the memory she didn't want to tell him about. "It's no big deal. He wanted...things. I didn't want to give him things. The end."

Josh studied her for a moment. "But first you sued the pants off him, or at least smacked him around a little, kicked him where it hurts, right?"

She let out a low laugh. "No." Nothing nearly so satisfactory. She'd simply left Seattle, not willing to fight for the job that she'd realized she'd never be comfortable in. Unnerved about what had happened, scared about her future, she'd gotten in her car and headed out. She'd been thinking only about putting some distance between her and what would have been a bad decision, and then she'd ended up here in Lucky Harbor.

A complete accident that had turned out to be the best accident of her life. A glorious break from the fast track of her life.

"Grace," he said, and waited for her to look at him. "I'm not that guy."

"I know." And she did. "Which is how"—she waved her hand between them and let out a low laugh—"it got a little out of hand just now. My fault, I know, but I just don't want you to think—"

"I don't," he said. "I wouldn't. And you weren't

alone in letting it get out of hand." He shook his head. "Not even close. I acted inappropriately. I'm sorry, Grace."

In her world, blame was assigned and cast upon the closest target. In her world, people did not take responsibility for their own mistakes. She met his gaze and gave him the utter, terrifying truth. "It didn't feel inappropriate," she admitted. "It felt..."

"Fun?" His tone was lighter now. Teasing. And she knew they were truly going to be okay. He didn't want this; he didn't have time for this. That made two of them. She'd be leaving soon, going back to her "real life." Soon as she found it. "Anything critical I need to know to ensure Toby's well-being?"

"He's shy and won't tell you if he's hungry or thirsty. He eats dinner at five-thirty, and there's stuff in the freezer with directions included. Be careful not to deviate—he has food allergies. There's a card on the counter listing all the no-nos. And don't let him feed Tank any of his Zhu Zhus. Tank is the Antichrist himself, but even the Antichrist can't digest metal and plastic. That painful lesson cost me six hundred bucks last week."

"Ouch," she said, grateful not to have a pug puppy. Or a Zhu Zhu. "So feed and water the kid, and keep Tank away from the Zhu Zhus. Got it."

"And Anna..."

"I'm thinking she can tell me when she's hungry and thirsty. And she probably knows not to try to inhale any Zhu Zhus, right?"

Josh let out a breath. "Yeah. But she's not your responsibility. Don't let her drive you off."

"She won't need any help?"

"No. Trust me on this, no. And I should probably apologize ahead of time for her."

"We'll be fine, Dr. Scott."

He let out a half laugh. "Back to that, are we?"

"Don't you like it when people call you doctor?"

"Only if they're sitting on my exam table."

She looked into his eyes for a sign that he was being falsely modest, but he wasn't. There was nothing but a mild impatience in his gaze.

And a lingering heat that stoked hers back into flames. "You gotta go."

"Yeah." He leaned in and brushed his mouth over hers, then kissed her with some serious intent before pulling back. "Shit."

She wobbled unsteadily and had to laugh at the both of them, shaken by a kiss. "It's still there."

"Yeah. It's still there."

Chapter 9

♥

*There's no Chocolate's Anonymous because no one
wants to quit.*

Josh went back to the office, and as he worked through
his patients, all he had to do was look at a door and he'd
think about the full-body press he'd given Grace.

Twice.

He wanted her, which was just about as crazy as it got,
since she was a woman with nothing more than fun on her
mind. But he'd been there, done that, and had had his life
changed forever. It was how he'd gotten Toby, which he
wouldn't change for the world.

But he wasn't about to do it again.

So it made no sense to him, his crazy attraction to
Grace. She wasn't his type. Okay, so he didn't have a
type. His requirements were warm and sweet—except in
bed, where he preferred decidedly not warm and sweet.

But Grace wasn't going to end up in his bed. They'd

both said so. They'd agreed to be on the same page in this matter—the no-relationship page. Very grown up.

Christ, he hated being grown up.

"Room one," Dee said as they passed each other in the hallway.

Mrs. Carson was waiting on him. She'd accidentally mixed up her blood pressure meds with her husband's Viagra. Unfortunate that she was also hard of hearing. "Mrs. Carson, you need to get the pill dispenser that we talked about to prevent this from happening."

"What is that, dear?" she yelled, an arthritic hand curled around her ear. "I'm going to grow taller and harder?" She grinned at her own joke, slapping her knee, completely unconcerned that everyone in the building could also hear her. "Not that I wouldn't mind being able to take care of myself in that manner, mind you," she went on. "Paul's a good man, but he's not built for much downstairs, if you know what I'm saying."

Josh did. He just wished he didn't.

"Aw. Your father would have laughed. You're not much fun."

Gee, where had he heard that before?

Josh's next patient was Kenny Liotta, a truck driver who came in every six weeks without fail with a new STD. "You ever think about getting smart?" Josh asked.

Kenny grinned. "Your dad used to ask me the same thing. Problem is, my dick's in charge. And my dick's not the one with the IQ."

Josh shook his head and wrote a script. "Your dick needs to read *Dicks for Dummies*, or it's going to fall off before your next birthday."

Kenny laughed. "But what a way to go, right?"

"No," Josh said. "It's not a good way to go. Go with a hot tub full of blondes in some seedy hotel, from a heart attack of pleasure. Not from an STD."

Kenny nodded. "Yeah, I see your point. You're a good man, Doc. You're not going to sell the practice, are you? Like all the others around here have?"

It was common knowledge that the hospital had been slowly but surely procuring other county medical facilities, from labs to pediatricians to specialists of all kinds. By absorbing them all under one umbrella, it gave the medical center a huge boost in popularity and reputation. This translated to big bucks, of course. Just about every doctor Josh worked with in the area was a part of the hospital in some way.

He was one of the lone holdouts. "I'm thinking about it."

"It's like some socialist takeover. What did they threaten you with, broken kneecaps?"

This made Josh laugh. "You're watching too much TV. If I sell, the world will go on spinning the same way. The level of care here will remain the same as well."

"You sure about that?"

"Yes," Josh said firmly. But if he truly believed it, why hadn't he signed already?

The board didn't understand either. Neither did Matt when he called to see if Josh was ever going to go rock climbing with him again.

"I can't get away," Josh said.

"Jesus. Sign already."

"I'm still thinking."

"Are you still going to be thinking when you're too old to hang off a cliff without worrying that you'll drop your dentures?"

Josh sighed. "Call Ty. He'll rock climb."

"He'll rock climb never. The guy who jumps out of helicopters to rescue people for a living doesn't like heights."

This was true. "Take Amy."

"No go," Matt said. "She told me if I tried to wake her up before dawn again, she'd kill me with my own gun."

This was undoubtedly also true. Amy Michaels was beautiful, sharp, and tough as hell.

"You need some more hours in your day," Matt said. "You're not any fun. Anyone ever tell you that?"

Okay, now this was starting to piss him off. "I'm plenty of fun," Josh said.

"Yeah? When?"

When his tongue had been in Grace's mouth. That had been pretty fucking fun.

"*Sell*," Matt said, and disconnected.

"I'm fun," Josh repeated to no one. He slid his phone away and thought about Grace some more. That was fun all in itself, actually. Too much fun. She was a complete time sink, not to mention a threat to his peace of mind. She made him want things. She made him want to step outside of the box of his life, something he absolutely couldn't do.

No matter how tempting.

He got home at eight-thirty, half an hour late. Toby was bathed and ready for bed, a Zhu Zhu warrior hamster in one fist, his Jedi lightsaber in the other, Tank compliant at his feet. Two perfect angels.

When Grace had arrived at his house earlier, she'd looked soft and willowy in a sundress, cropped sweater, and sandals, her wavy blond hair falling silkily to her shoulders, facial expression dialed to easy, curious intelligence. During their moment against his back door, her hair had gotten mussed—his doing—and her expression hadn't been nearly so calm. Her eyes had been dilated, her mouth wet from his, her nipples hard.

He'd liked that look, a lot.

Now her hair had been put up in some sort of knot, held there by a LEGO piece, with long silky strands escaping wildly, making her look a little bit like a mad scientist. Her sweater was gone, she had something streaked and stained down the front of her sundress, and her expression wasn't serene or aroused.

She was laughing. She and Toby were in the kitchen, counting the cupcakes on the tray at the table, cracking up. Just looking at them had the tension draining from his shoulders. "Sorry I'm late," he said.

"You have an emergency?" she asked, turning a concerned face his way.

"A sixteen-year-old girl pierced her own tongue, and it abscessed. She didn't tell her parents for three days, not until it swelled, blocking her breathing passage."

"Oh my God."

"She's okay. Grounded for life, but okay."

She just stared at him. "Wow. That makes my day seem like a piece of cake. Or as it turns out, a cupcake." She gestured to the tray. "We had to make two batches. We don't want to talk about batch number one."

Toby giggled and shook his head.

"You *made* them?" Josh asked, impressed.

"Yeah. At the expense of your kitchen."

The kitchen was a complete disaster, like a bomb had gone off. Dishes piled high in the sink, chocolate everywhere. "Hey, at least everyone's still alive," he said.

"Well, if that's your only requirement."

He smiled. "You smell like a chocolate cupcake."

Anna wheeled into the kitchen, her attention riveted to the open book in her lap. "Found it, Josh's freshman pic," she said. "He's the one with the thick glasses, braces, and black eye. The black eye happened when he let himself get stuffed into his own locker. He was a lot smaller back then. He was a total loser."

Josh eyed the book. "Is that my yearbook?"

"Relax," Anna said. "It's not like I showed her a pic of your tattoo."

Josh rubbed his forehead. "Has she been dishing out my dirty little secrets all day?" he asked Grace.

"Like candy."

Perfect.

"And tattoo?" Grace asked, her gaze running over his body. "Where?"

"His ass," Anna said helpfully.

Josh covered Toby's ears. "*Hey.*"

"Sorry," Anna said. "His butt."

Grace raised a brow at Josh, clearly trying not to laugh, though whether it was in horror or genuine amusement, he had no idea.

"What is it?" Grace asked.

"I lost a bet," Josh said in his own defense. "And I'm not telling."

Now she *did* laugh. "I thought you were a late-bloomer nerd, not a reformed bad boy."

Anna snorted. "Yes to the nerd. No to the bad boy."

"*I lost a bet,*" he repeated in his defense. *Jesus.* "It's all Matt's fault."

"You could get it removed," Grace said, "if you're embarrassed."

"I'm not embarrassed." Much. "And besides, nobody ever sees it because nobody's ever behind me when I'm..." He tightened his grip on Toby's ears. "Bare-assed."

At this, Grace burst out laughing, and the sound made him smile in spite of himself. She moved to the sink and began washing dishes. Anna, apparently allergic to cleaning up anything, ever, suddenly remembered she had to get online for something. Toby climbed onto a chair to help Grace. Josh shook his head. "You know the rule about standing on chairs, Tobes." Which had been put into place six months ago after an incident involving three stitches above Toby's eyebrow.

"Oh, he's okay," Grace said. "The back of the chair's turned out to keep him from stepping off."

Which is exactly how it'd happened the first time. "It's also that drying sharp knives is a bad idea."

Grace turned to Toby, who was drying a wooden spoon. She arched a brow at Josh. *Overprotective much?*

Josh shook his head, rolled up his sleeves, and joined them. When they were finished, Grace helped Toby down and squatted in front him, her eyes soft and warm. "Sleep tight," she said, hugging him. "Don't let the bed bugs bite."

Toby hugged her back. "Night."

Josh's jaw dropped. A *word*, not a bark.

Grace smiled. Toby smiled back, and the sight of it grabbed Josh by the throat so that he couldn't breathe for a second.

Grace rose and grabbed her purse, and Josh walked her

out. At her car, she tried to open the driver's door but it
stuck.

"Dammit," she muttered.

"Here, let me—"

"No," she said. "It always sticks. I've got it." She
yanked hard, and it opened so fast she nearly fell to her
ass but he caught her.

He turned her to face him. "You got him to use words."

"I told him that I didn't understand puppy talk." She
smiled. "You've got a great kid, Josh."

"I know. And thanks," he said. "For today. For everything. Have you thought about the guesthouse?"

The moonlight slanted over her features. "Some."

He didn't push, not in all that much of a hurry himself
to have her sleeping so close. "Tell me how it went today."

She looked at him for a long moment. "He needs more
of you."

He drew in a slow, deep breath. "I know."

"And you're right on Tank being the Antichrist, by
the way. Although he's possibly the cutest Antichrist I've
ever seen."

"And?" Because he was pretty sure there was one.

"And your sister. She…" Grace shook her head, at a
loss for words.

"Yeah," he said on a low laugh. "She has that effect on
people."

"I think it'd help if you loosened the reins on her a little."

He shook his head. "That's the opposite of what she
needs."

"What she needs is to be challenged," she said. "She's
bored. And *any* bored twenty-one-year-old is trouble.

Plus, I don't know how to tell you this, but she's not nearly as handicapped as she likes people to believe."

Josh was impressed. "It usually takes people weeks to get her number."

"Hmm." She tilted her face up to his. "Would you still be amused if I told you she said that while you're a great doctor, you're also a control freak, only a so-so dad, a totally crappy brother, and an even more totally crappy significant other?"

"No, since it's all mostly true."

She studied him a long moment. "You want to expand on any of that?"

"You've seen my life, Grace. It's ... busy." His mouth quirked when she snorted at this newsflash. "My schedule's insane, and I *have* to be somewhat of a control freak to keep it all managed."

"Which is what makes you a great doctor."

"And only a so-so dad," he said, and Christ how he hated *that* admission. "I'd argue the crappy brother part, but she's pretty much dead on about the rest."

"The significant other?" she asked.

"I don't have one, but if I did, yeah, I'd be crappy at that too."

Something crossed her face. Disappointment? That couldn't be. She'd been the first one to say that they weren't going there.

"Toby's got a project at school," she said carefully.

Josh felt a fishing expedition coming.

"A family tree," she said.

Yeah, definitely a fishing expedition.

"He said he couldn't fill in the mom because he didn't have any pictures."

"Toby has a picture of his mom," Josh said. "It's just an older one." He paused. "We split when he was a few months old. He doesn't remember her."

"You have full custody."

"Yes."

She waited, clearly hoping for more. But he didn't have more, and he was too tired to even try.

"He hasn't seen his mom since he was a few months old?" she asked.

"She isn't from this area."

"Aw. That's rough." She softened, clearly feeling sorry for him.

He hated that, both for Toby and himself. They'd done just fine on their own. Well, mostly. He rubbed at the beginning of a headache right between his eyes.

"You're tired," she said softly. "Try to get some sleep." And then she patted him on the arm like he was a pathetic loser.

He stared down at her, torn between showing her just how *not* tired he was and wanting her to leave before he did exactly that.

She patted him again, and he caught her hand.

She stared at his fingers on hers, sighed, then dropped her forehead to his chest. "Do you have to smell good?" she asked, voice muffled. "Like, *always*?"

"I—"

"No, don't answer that." She lifted her head and kissed him on the cheek. Her breath was warm, and she still had that cupcake scent going, and damn if her lips didn't linger. Not one to need an engraved invite, he turned his head and look at that, his mouth lined right up with hers.

Oh yeah. *This* was what he'd needed. All damn day

long. His tongue teased the corner of her lip. When she opened for him, hunger took over, setting him on fire. Hauling her up against him, he took control of the kiss, deepening it. She rewarded him with a soft moan that said she was right there with him, and he felt a whole hell of a lot better.

Finally, Grace stepped back, smacking up against her car. Laughing at herself, and him, too, he suspected, she got into her car.

Josh watched her drive away, turning only when he heard Anna's wheels hit the porch behind him.

"Where are you going?" he asked her.

A truck pulled up to the curb and honked, answering his question.

"He should come to the door for you," Josh said.

"God, you're old," she said. "And *he* has a name."

They all had names. Josh had discovered it was easier to just think of each of them as the Boy. Still, Devon had staying power. Not surprising, since Anna was coming into her settlement. He snagged a quickly escaping Anna by the back of her chair. "First, tell me about today."

"There were no casualties, and your girlfriend managed to stay the whole day without quitting on you."

Josh knew better than to let her engage him in a semantics war, so he let the "girlfriend" comment slide. "You were on your best behavior, then."

Anna smiled.

Hmmm...

"Like I said, she stuck it out," Anna said.

"Maybe tomorrow you can resist doing your best to make me look like an ass," he said.

"Maybe tomorrow you could not be one."

"Anna—"

Devon honked again.

Josh slid Anna a look and she shrugged. "He'd come in, but you scare him."

"Bullshit."

"Okay, you don't," she agreed. "But he's got authority issues. Anyway, he did some research and came up with a European itinerary. I e-mailed it to you."

"What about school?"

"School's dumb," she said.

"No. Dumb is quitting school."

"You don't understand."

The family therapist had told Josh not to pretend to understand. That he was never going to know what it was like to be a hormonal teenage girl who'd lost her parents at a critical age, not to mention the use of her legs.

What he *did* understand was that, as usual, *he* was the bad guy.

Anna pushed off toward the truck, and when she was gone, Josh went inside. "Just you and me," he said to Toby. "Ready for bed?"

"*Arf.*"

Chapter 10

Einstein was eating chocolate when he came upon the theory of relativity. Coincidence? I think not.

Grace went back to her room at the B&B that night and sat on the bed watching TV while she eyeballed the balance of her checking account on her laptop. Five hundred dollars cash. That's all she had left to her name, unless she broke into her saved-for-a-rainy-day investments. But it wasn't raining, not quite yet. She'd gotten a call for a second interview on the Seattle banking position, and tomorrow morning was the Skype interview with Portland. An offer from either of them would change everything.

Until then, she could stay here in the B&B and watch her balance dwindle further away or she could go to Josh's guesthouse.

It was no contest, really. Besides, by this time next week, she'd probably, hopefully, have one of the jobs.

And a direction.

There was a knock at the door, and she opened it to one of the B&B owners. Chloe was wearing little hip-hugging army cargoes, a snug, bright red henley, and matching high-tops. Her glossy dark red hair cascaded down her back in an artful disarray that Grace might have hated her for if it hadn't been for Chloe's friendly smile and the plate of chocolate chip cookies in her hands.

"Tara had extra," Chloe said. "I tried to steal 'em but Tara said I had to give them to our guest."

Grace tried to take the plate and laughed when Chloe didn't let go of it. "Want to come in and share?"

"Hell, yeah." Chloe stepped inside. "For a minute there, I was afraid you weren't going to ask me."

They ate cookies and watched a dog training class on TV. The instructor was saying that there were no bad dogs, just bad dog owners.

"Huh," Grace said, thinking of Tank.

And Tank's big, bad, gorgeous hunk of an owner.

"You think an alpha guy can be trained as easily as a dog?" Chloe asked.

Chloe was engaged to Sheriff Sawyer Thompson, definitely an alpha guy, and Grace laughed. "Good luck."

After Chloe left, Grace spent a couple of hours on Amy's shoe box, enjoying the task more than she thought she would. She knew accounting was dry to most, but somehow the numbers soothed her. By the time she went to bed, she had Amy shockingly organized.

The next morning, Grace showered, dressed, and paid up for her stay at the B&B. She'd be sorry to leave the very lovely inn, even more so since they gave her an extra plate of chocolate chip cookies as a going-away gift.

She drove to Josh's place. It was early but she had that

interview, and she wanted to make sure she was set up somewhere with Internet.

The front door opened before she knocked. Josh was dressed in a T-shirt and basketball shorts, a messenger bag slung over one shoulder and a duffel bag over the other. To the gym and then to work, she figured. He was also carrying the cupcakes on a tray and had Toby, with his Star Wars backpack, by the hand.

Both man and boy looked at her from twin chocolate gazes, and her heart did a little somersault in her chest. She smiled at Toby. "Enjoy the cupcakes."

Josh eyed her own big duffel bag. "You're going to stay in the guesthouse."

"If that's still okay."

"Very. Give me a minute." He walked with Toby to the end of the block just as a yellow school bus pulled up. They both disappeared onto the bus, and then after a few minutes, Josh reappeared without the cupcake tray.

"The bus driver's a friend," he said to Grace when he'd walked back to the house. "She'll make sure Toby gets into school without getting mobbed on the bus for the cupcakes." He took in Grace's interview suit. "You have an interview today."

"Yes, in an hour."

"I e-mailed you the file of nanny applicants so far."

She nodded. "I'll get on that today and hopefully help you find someone perfect for Toby."

"Thanks." He dropped his bags and took hers. "I'll show you the guesthouse. Whatever you do, don't let me come in with you."

"Why not?"

His gaze ran over her body, tingling and heating every

inch it touched, and it touched a lot. "It would be a bad idea," he said in a voice that scraped over her erogenous zones. "For both of us."

She checked her clothes to make sure they hadn't gone up in flames. He was right. It would be a very bad idea.

But at the moment, *very bad* was sounding *really great*. Because once again, he smelled amazing. His T-shirt strained over his biceps and pecs but was loose over his flat, hard abs. When he turned to lead her through the house, the material stretched tight over his athletic-looking back. And then there was his butt in those basketball shorts. Edible. That's how it looked, and she wanted to sink her teeth into—

He turned to say something and caught her staring. She quickly pretended to be watching her own feet. Look at that, her heels were looking a little worn. "Pretty hardwood floors," she said.

"You weren't looking at the floor. You were looking at my ass."

Giving up, she sighed. "Okay, yes," she said as primly as she could. "But it's impolite of you to point it out."

He laughed.

She walked past him so that *she* was in the lead, thinking at least now he couldn't see her face.

"Grace?" he said from behind her.

"Yeah?"

"Your ass is ogle-worthy too."

She bit her lower lip to try to keep her smile in and kept walking. "We're being inappropriate again."

"You started it."

Going out the back door, he led her around the pool to the small guesthouse. There he pushed open the door, dropped her bags inside, and very purposely remained in the entryway.

He was right—the place was tiny. But cute. The living room, kitchen, and bedroom were all open to each other, done in soft blues and neutral colors.

"The bed's behind that screen," Josh said, pointing. "The kitchen's minimally supplied. You've got wireless, but the electrical is crap. Can't run the toaster and the heater at the same time. I'll work on that this weekend."

Grace turned to him in surprise. In her experience, men were either cerebral or good with their hands. And never the two shall meet. She'd pegged this "late-bloomer nerd" as the cerebral type. Not too much of a stretch, given that he was an MD. "You do electrical?"

He gestured to himself. "Not just a pretty face."

This made her laugh. "I just meant because you're a doctor. Doctors usually can't do anything other than... well, doctor."

"Hey, don't judge us all by our pedigree."

She met his gaze, knowing she'd just done exactly that. And she of all people knew better. "Are you really not coming in?"

His eyes darkened, and her body reacted with feminine predictability. "If I come in, you're going to miss your interview."

Her heart skipped a beat. "Oh."

His mouth curved very slightly. "Not in our best interests," he said softly, giving her another of those searing looks that made her knees wobble. "Lock the door behind me, Grace."

When he was gone, she let out a shaky breath and locked the door. She looked over her new place and felt… right at home. She'd had a lovely childhood home back East but she hadn't lived there in years. She'd gone to college, then on to her own places, none of which she'd stayed in too long. She'd attributed that to restlessness, the need to climb the ladder of success. But it'd never mattered what size her place had been or how much it cost; she'd never really found home.

Obviously, this wasn't it either, but the fact that she wanted to unpack and nest reminded her that it had been a damn long time since she'd felt at home like this.

Too long.

"A week," she said out loud to remind herself what she'd told Josh. "This is only for a week."

She did her Skype interview and scored a request to come to the Portland offices for an in-person interview in a few days. Then she texted her parents with the news. She wasn't a complete loser! After that, she left for her modeling job, dropping Anna in town at the girl's request.

To Grace's surprise, Anna was waiting by her car when she came back out of the gallery an hour later. "Aw," she said to the frowning Anna, "you missed me. How sweet."

Anna snorted and got into Grace's car, then sat there like a queen while Grace wrestled with getting the wheelchair folded and into the trunk. "You know," Grace finally said, swiping her brow with her arm, "if you learned how to do that yourself, you could have your own vehicle. One of those adapted vehicles that you could drive yourself."

"Oh, actually I do usually handle it by myself."

Grace gave her a long look, and Anna lifted her hands. "Sorry! But people like to help me, you know? Makes them feel better about being with me." She smiled sweetly.

Grace shook her head. "Don't give me that crap. You were totally amusing yourself by watching me fumble ineptly with your chair."

"Or that." Anna grinned. "You and Josh are the only ones to call me on this stuff, you know that?"

"What else does Josh call you on?"

Anna shrugged. "He says I'm not good at toeing the line. And that he'd get me a special van to drive but that I'm too angry to be on the road."

"So get unangry. Learn to toe the line. I could teach you. Once upon a time, I was most excellent at toeing the line. At least the pretense of it."

"He treats me like a child."

"Then stop acting like one," Grace said. "And while we're on the subject, he cares about you very much. You know that, right?"

Anna shrugged.

"I figured you didn't know, seeing as you treat him the way you do."

"And how do I treat him?" Anna asked.

"How do you think?"

Another shrug.

"I bet if you treated him nicer, he'd loosen up a bit with the reins," Grace said.

"He's not the boss of me."

"So you can do whatever you want."

"Exactly," Anna said.

"And what is it that you want?"

Anna didn't answer for so long that Grace figured she wasn't going to get one. But then Anna finally spoke. "I want my mom and dad back."

Grace kept her eyes on the road but her throat went

tight as she nodded. "I can only imagine. But it makes me doubly glad you have other family. Toby, for instance."

"Yeah, the rug rat's pretty cute."

"And Josh," Grace said.

Anna turned away and looked out the window. "Anyone ever tell you that you drive like a girl?"

"I am a girl. Don't you have class today?"

"Missed the bus."

"I'll drive you."

"Missed class already."

Grace looked at her. "Call me crazy, but I'm getting the feeling you don't like your cooking and writing classes."

"Gee, ya think?"

"So why don't you go for something more challenging?"

"Like?"

"Like a degree," Grace said.

"In what? I'm in a wheelchair."

"Are your eyes and brain paralyzed?"

Anna rolled her unparalyzed eyes.

"What interests you?" Grace asked.

"Getting home to see if Devon's there."

"Is he a good guy? Good to you?"

A shrug. "Yeah."

"What do you like about him?"

"He's hot."

"Boys are like drugs," Grace said. "You're supposed to just say no."

This earned her another eye roll. "He doesn't care that I'm..." Anna waved at her legs. "He thinks I'm pretty. And...sexy."

There was something about the way Anna said it that

made Grace take another look at her. "You are pretty. You're *beautiful*. But a guy that age thinks *everyone's* sexy."

There it was again, the odd look flickering in Anna's eyes. Uncertainty. "Anna. He's not pushing you for anything you're not ready for, is he?"

"I'm ready for anything."

"Sex. Is he pushing you for sex?"

"I'm paralyzed, not stupid. I'm not a pushover, for anyone."

"Good," Grace said, not feeling better, because Anna's posture didn't match her words.

"Yeah. Good," Anna said.

Grace sighed and took her home. In the driveway, Anna didn't make a move to get out, just faced the side window as she spoke. "So how old were you when you first..."

Grace did the math. Anna had been paralyzed and lost her mom at age sixteen, most likely before she'd had her first anything, leaving her without an influential female in her life. And Grace sincerely doubted Anna would go to Josh about these things. "Forty-five."

Anna snorted.

"Look," Grace said. "There's no right age. Just as long as the guy is right. Are you telling me that Devon is right?"

"He's into me."

"That's not enough. You have to be into him. And not just because he's hot either. You're so smart, Anna. You need a guy to be into you *and* be just as smart."

Another shrug.

"Just promise me you won't let him rush you."

Anna went noncommittal on that, rolling inside the house.

Grace went to the guesthouse and opened her laptop, where she began to weed through the interested applicants for the nanny position. First up was a patient of Josh's, and all she wanted to know was if Josh was still single. Delete. The next applicant was sixty-five and had asked if there was a retirement plan.

Also deleted.

Feeling somewhat discouraged and desperate, Grace finally found two semi-promising applicants and set up interviews for Josh. Then she got Toby from the bus.

"Arf," he said in greeting.

"Arf," she said back. "But I was sort of hoping we could speak in English today too. 'Cause we're going to make pizza for dinner, and dogs don't eat pizza."

"I like pizza!"

She smiled, took his hand, and walked him the half block home. They worked on his handwriting and made pizza, and after that, worked on their Jedi lightsaber skills, dueling in the living room.

"Gotta be the bestest Jedi warrior in all the universe," Toby told her, swinging his lightsaber.

"Awesome," Grace said. "Why?"

"'Cause if I'm the bestest, then my mom'll come."

Grace hunkered before him and stroked a lock of hair from his face. "Actually, I think you already *are* the bestest Jedi in the universe."

He beamed at her for the compliment but went back to practicing. *Swoosh, vrrmm-swoosh.*

Josh got home at eight, looking hot as hell in wrinkled dark blue scrubs and athletic shoes, his hair rumpled, his eyes tired and unguarded. Toby and Tank jumped him on the spot, and the three of them wrestled on the floor like a pack of wolves until suddenly Toby sat straight up, looking green.

"Uh-oh," he said, and threw up on Josh's shoes.

Josh grimaced but handled the situation with calm efficiency, scooping up a distraught Toby, cleaning the mess, and corralling the crazy pug that was running worried circles around a sniffling Toby. Finally, Josh sat the now-shirtless Toby on the kitchen counter and handed him a glass of water. "What did you have for dinner?"

"Pizza," Grace said.

Josh slid Grace a look.

"No pepperoni," she said quickly. "It was on his list of no-nos. Just sausage."

"He's allergic to pork."

Oh, shit. *Double shit.* "It didn't say that on the list. It just said salami and pepperoni."

"Because he doesn't like sausage."

Grace looked at Toby, who was clutching his lightsaber and staring at his bare feet. And she got it. He'd wanted to please her.

Triple shit. She was such an idiot. "I'm so sorry. Do we need to do anything?"

"I think his body took care of it," Josh said dryly. "And where was Anna? She should have known better."

"She went out with friends."

"She was supposed to stay home tonight."

"She said she'd be back before she turned into a pumpkin," Grace told him. "An exact quote."

Josh's mouth was grim but he kept his thoughts on the matter to himself. Grace busied herself picking up the disaster that the house had somehow become over the past few hours. In the living room, in the middle of the chaos, Tank lay on the couch. He was on his back, feet straight up in the air like he was dead, snoring away.

"You don't have to clean up," Josh said, coming into the room behind her, stopping her from picking up by taking her hand in his and pulling her around to face him.

She stared up at him as time stuttered to a stop for a second. Yearning. Aching…

He looked into her eyes, then broke the spell with clear reluctance, stepping back from her as he noticed the puppy, looking like road kill. "How the hell did he learn how to get up on the couch?"

Toby had spent the better part of an hour teaching the pug how to jump that high. Grace nudged the sleepy Tank down, earning a reproachful look and a soft snort. "Sorry about Anna," she said to Josh. "But maybe if you let up on her just a little—"

"You're Toby's babysitter. Not mine."

Right. Gee, she'd almost forgotten there for a moment. Well, clearly she'd done enough here for the night. She grabbed her purse and headed for the door.

"Grace—"

"It's late," she said. She'd had a lifetime to learn how to read the people around her, down to the slightest nuances. Her parents' moods had been quiet, subtle. So she knew exactly when she'd overstayed her welcome. And that was now. "'Night, Josh."

Chapter 11

In heaven, chocolate has no calories and is served as the main course.

The next night when Josh got home, Toby was just getting out of the tub. Grace made a quiet escape to the pool house, which Josh knew was to give him some alone time with his son.

Or she wasn't all that interested to be in his company.

His fault, of course. He'd been an ass the night before. "Tobes," he said, "get into your pj's. I'll be right back." He paused, watching Toby pull on his pj bottoms, sans underwear. "What's with the commando thing?"

Toby shrugged. "Feels best."

Hard to argue with that. "Pick out a book. Give me five minutes." He jogged through the house and caught up with Grace at the back door. "Hey."

"Hey yourself." She smiled, and it was sweet, if not quite meeting her eyes.

Also his fault. He searched for a way to make it right

and came up with nothing. Which really, he figured, was for the best.

"Well," she said, a little too brightly, "see you tomorrow—"

Suddenly unable to let her go until he'd at least *tried* to fix this, he caught her hand in his.

She went still, even dug her heels in a little as he turned her to face him.

"I was an ass last night," Josh said.

Grace met his gaze and felt his struggle. She told herself not to care, but she couldn't help herself. "You were tired."

"Okay, so I was a tired ass. I'm still sorry."

This time when she smiled at him, it was a real one. She had no idea what it was about a guy who could say he was sorry...

"Everything go okay today?" he asked.

"You have two interviews for babysitters on Friday."

He nodded. "Good. Thanks. You want to sit in?"

"I'll be in Portland on an interview myself."

Something came and went in his eyes—regret?—but he nodded. "Your Skype interview went well, then."

"Very." She'd gotten the call today that they'd liked her and wanted another interview.

"That's great," he said.

"Yeah." She was trying to work up some enthusiasm. It was, after all, her future, and she wanted a good one. But she also wanted to stop thinking about it. It wasn't hard to distract herself with the view.

She could tell by Josh's dress clothes that he'd worked in his office today. He wore dark trousers that fit his butt perfectly—which she knew because she'd checked it out when he'd bent to pick up Toby earlier. His button-down was dark chocolate brown and shoved up to the elbows. No stethoscope or tie today, but his five o'clock shadow had a five o'clock shadow, and his eyes...His eyes gave her a lot, telling her how much he'd seen, done, been through. When he looked like this, a little rumpled, a lot tired, it softened his features, allowing her to see more of him than he'd probably like. He didn't feel quite so impenetrable to her tonight. He felt...human. Just a regular man, a man who'd most likely saved someone today, probably more than one someone. He did more every day than she could possibly imagine, and she admired him for it, greatly.

She also wanted to hug him. Instead, she reached up to push a lock of hair off his forehead, then caught herself. But before she could pull back, he wrapped his fingers around her wrist and slowly reeled her in.

"Thanks for today," he said quietly, his other hand going to her waist.

She stared at his chest, trying not to notice how her pulse had leaped. "You don't have to keep thanking me. You're paying me."

"I'll do both. And speaking of paying you..."

"Uh-oh," she said, tilting her head up to his.

"I think I need another week to find the right nanny," he said. "You up for that?"

Was she up for a second week of being overpaid and having another excuse to put off her life? "Sure."

"Arf, arf, arf!" came Tank's bark.

"Arf, arf, arf!" came another bark.

Toby's.

Josh dropped his forehead to Grace's shoulder and sighed.

"He spoke English all day," she said. "Until you came home."

He lifted his head and looked at her. "So it's me. He's barking because of me."

Grace hesitated, knowing she had to tell him but hating to add to his full plate of things to worry about. "You know he wants to be a Jedi warrior, right?"

"*Everyone* in Lucky Harbor knows he wants to be a Jedi warrior."

"Yes, but did you know he wants to be the best Jedi warrior ever so that his mom will come home?"

Josh stared at her for a blink, then closed his eyes. "Shit."

The barking increased in intensity, and he pulled free. "I have to go."

"I know." And she did know. A guy like Josh would always have to go: to work, to his family . . . to everyone but the woman in his life he didn't have time for, or want.

She knew this. She'd been okay with this. So when exactly had that begun to change?

The next morning, Grace woke up early to work on Jeanine's books for her pottery shop. It was icy cold, so she cranked on the heat and then went to the kitchen, where she'd stowed the few groceries she'd bought yesterday. Trying to decide between yogurt and a bagel, she thumbed through her texts, stopping at one from her father.

Hi Pumpkin, your mother tells me how well you're doing. Expect to hear great things from you! Keep it up. Love, Dad

Still staring at the text, she popped a bagel into the toaster. Something sizzled, and then the lights went out. And then Josh's words came back to her, a little too late.

Can't use the heater and the toaster at the same time.

"*Crap.*" There wasn't much to see by, just the predawn light filtering in through the windows. No flames. That was good. But what if she'd started an electrical fire in the walls? Worried, she threw on a robe and ran for the big house. The back slider was locked, but she could see through the living room to the kitchen table. Toby was sitting on it, Indian-style, with Tank in his lap. The two of them were eating cereal out of a huge plastic container. The *same* huge plastic container.

Not a surprise. Tank loved anything edible. Especially if Toby was eating it.

Grace waved. Tank leaped off the table and came barreling at her. Losing traction, he slid on the tile floor and crashed face-first into the slider door. Bouncing back on his butt, he sat there a moment, dazed, before shaking his oversized head, barking at her.

Grace, who'd been working with him on commands since she'd seen that doggie training show, pointed at him. "Tank, *quiet.*"

Tank sat.

He did not, however, stop barking. Grace sighed and caught Toby's eye, gesturing to the locked door.

This went no better than it had the last time she'd been locked out. Apparently thinking she was waving, Toby waved back, then arced his lightsaber through the air. "Toby. Come open the door."

He finished *whooshing* first, then having apparently satisfied himself that he'd thoroughly impressed her, opened the door.

Tank was still barking.

"Tank, *quiet*! Toby, where's your dad?"

Toby pointed in the vague direction of the hall. Grace headed that way. The first door—Toby's—was open, revealing a bedroom that looked like a disaster zone of epic proportions.

Anna's door was shut.

Josh's bedroom was at the end, partially open, allowing Grace to peek in. And oh, goodness, there he was, sprawled out flat on his back in the middle of the bed. He was shirtless, and the sheets rode low enough on his hips to reveal a mouth-watering chest, abs to die for, and a happy trail that vanished beneath the sheet and made her want to do the same.

Probably he was naked, and just the thought gave her a hot flash. "Josh?"

He didn't move, so she stepped into the room. She set a hand on his shoulder, but before she could say his name again, he'd grabbed her and tugged hard, rolling her beneath him.

Yep, he was naked.

Very, very naked.

"Mmm," he rumbled. "Like the robe. It's soft." Dipping his head, he nipped at her throat. "I'm over the no-kissing thing, Grace. I want a new deal."

She let out a breathless laugh, her hands wandering over his shoulders and back because, hello, she was only human. He was warm and solid and felt so good nuzzling her neck. Not at all sure he wasn't still in dreamland, she nudged him. "You awake?"

"Shit." He sighed. "Yeah. And Toby's probably up."

Josh was "up," too, and the thought gave her a shiver of arousal. "Toby *is* up. He's eating an entire box of cereal out of the same bowl as Tank."

"Perfect." Josh rolled off her and then stood—still very naked, impressively so. And utterly unconcerned about it in the way that only a man could possibly be.

"Um," she said, losing her train of thought, riveted to the part of him that was the *most* awake, telling herself to close her eyes and preserve his modesty.

But she didn't close her eyes.

He grabbed a pair of jeans off a chair and pulled them on, adjusting himself and giving her another hot flash.

Think, Grace. You came here for a reason. "I've got a problem."

"What now? Anna?"

"No."

He finished buttoning his fly. He stood there, hair tousled, no shirt, no socks, nothing but those loose, low-riding jeans, and it was damn hard to think. "I turned on the heater and—"

He lifted his head. "Not the toaster."

"And the toaster," she admitted.

"Shit, Grace." He headed out the door.

"Sorry!" Feeling like an idiot, she flopped back onto his bed, staring at the ceiling. *Such an idiot.* And since she was, she rolled over and pressed her face into Josh's still-warm pillow, inhaling him in.

"What are you doing?"

She squeaked in horrified surprise at Josh's voice and leaped off the bed to find him in the doorway.

"Were you going back to sleep in my bed?" he asked, looking amused.

And since that was far less embarrassing than the truth, she lifted a shoulder. Noncommittal.

Not fooled, he shook his head and tugged her up to go with him to check on the guesthouse. Toby tagged along as well, wanting to see the "big fire!"

Luckily there was no big fire. There was no fire at all. She'd only tripped an electrical breaker, but she'd learned her lesson. And that lesson was, don't go to Josh's bedroom or she'd see things that she wanted but couldn't have.

"I wanted to put out the big flames with my lightsaber," Toby said, disappointed. "That'd make me the bestest warrior ever." He paused. "After you, Daddy. 'Cause you're the first bestest."

Grace's heart cracked in two, and she looked at Josh. He crouched before Toby, hands on his skinny little hips. Toby stared down at his battered Star Wars athletic shoes.

Josh put a finger beneath Toby's chin and gently tilted up his face. "You're already the best warrior there is, Little Man. The very best."

"I'm too small to be the bestest. I want to be as big as you."

"It's not about size."

"It's 'cause I don't have a mommy. Sam and Tommy and Aiden and Kyle, they all have mommies. Kyle's mommy told Tommy's mommy that I don't have one because you wouldn't share me."

Josh didn't say anything for a moment. When he

spoke, his voice was a little hoarse, but it was filled with conviction. "This might be hard for you to understand, but once in a very great while, sharing isn't the best thing to do."

"But *everyone* has a mommy," Toby said. "How can I be the bestest Jedi without one?"

"I don't have a mom," Josh told him. "Does that make me less of a Jedi?"

Toby shook his head adamantly. "No, you're still the bestest, Daddy."

"Then how about we be tied?"

Toby thought about that, then nodded solemnly. When Josh opened his arms, Toby walked right into them, curling tightly into Josh's chest.

Grace didn't drop to her knees and crawl into Josh's arms too.

But she wanted to.

Josh watched his son run back to the big house ahead of him and Grace, not surprised when Grace stopped him with a question in her eyes.

"Tommy's mom knew Toby's mom," he said quietly. "But she has only one side of the story."

"What's the other side?"

That Josh had grown up the nerd, the bookworm, the kid who got frisked for his lunch money and stuffed into the lockers. By the time he'd gone to college, he'd finally grown and learned how to fight back. But even as recently as five years ago, a gorgeous woman blowing through town for a wedding and picking him for one hot night together had been more than a little shocking.

And flattering.

He'd fallen for the charming words and amazing body, hook, line, and sinker. And then gotten his heart broken, just the same as Toby. "The other side of the story isn't relevant," he finally said.

"I hear ya," Grace said softly, making him wonder what kind of a story *she* had.

But it was none of his business, even if she was staring up at him with those gorgeous, heart-baring eyes. Open. Sweet.

Welcoming.

He could drown in her if he let himself. The trick was not to let himself.

On Friday, Josh got up at 4:00 a.m. to squeeze in a rock climb with Matt. It'd been weeks since he'd gone, and he needed the icy predawn air, the Olympic Mountains...Plus Matt had said he'd kick Josh's ass if he didn't show.

Not too worried about that ridiculous threat, Josh got ready. He'd seen Ty yesterday when their paths had crossed in the hospital, and Ty had claimed that Matt had been seen muttering something about diamond rings.

Josh had to hear this for himself. He checked on a sleeping Toby, then made sure Anna was in her room. He left her a note reminding her that she'd promised to get Toby dressed, fed, and to the bus stop on time.

As he quietly exited the house, he was surprised to see Grace heading toward her car as well. "What's up?" he asked.

"Heading to Portland," she said. "It's an early interview, and it's a long drive."

Three hours. She was wearing another suit that was all

business, softened by high-heeled sandals that had a bow on her ankles. Her hair was in a sophisticated twist, made cute by a few loose strands brushing her temples. It was quite a different appearance than the bathrobe look she'd rocked a few days before, which he'd loved. But he loved this too. She looked like a million bucks, which wasn't why he ached at the sight of her. He didn't care what she wore. There was just something about her that made him feel like a kid on Christmas morning. Like he couldn't wait to see beyond the packaging, couldn't wait to touch. And not just physically, which was what really disconcerted him.

He wanted to touch her from the inside out, which made no fucking sense at all. "Good luck today," he said. "I hope you get what you want."

"It's not what I want. It's what I *require*," she said, and when he arched a brow, she sighed. "Never mind. It's just one of those things my parents always say. Requirements need to be met before needs."

He gave her a longer look, beyond the pretty packaging now, and realized she was taut with tension. "You don't talk much about yourself or your past," he said.

"Nothing really to talk about."

"Everyone has something in their past to talk about."

She lifted a shoulder. "I had a boring childhood."

She was even better than he was at protecting herself. Interesting. "Doesn't sound boring, what with the rocket scientist and all..."

Another shrug. And though he hated when people pushed him for answers he didn't want to give, he couldn't help but push her. "What about *after* your childhood?"

Her gaze slid to his. "You mean like college? Jobs? Boyfriends? Which?"

"Yes."

She let out a short laugh. "I went to college in New York. Interned at a big financial institution and got my CPA. Then got a banking job complete with a nice place to live, a few boyfriends, yada yada. My parents were proud. The end. That answer all your questions?"

Not even close. She was suddenly as defensive as hell, and he was good at reading the symptoms and coming up with conclusions. She hadn't been as happy as she'd wanted to be. "Parental expectations suck."

This forced another laugh out of her. "A little bit, yeah. But they just want the best for me. They always have."

Josh knew the value of silence, and he was rewarded when she sighed. "I'm adopted," she said. "So this whole being an overachieving genius isn't exactly natural for me."

He absorbed what she said, and all she didn't—that she clearly didn't feel she was equipped with the right genes to be on the same level as her adoptive family. Just the thought of her feeling that way gave him a physical ache in his chest. "I hope that they took into account what your hopes and dreams for yourself were, not just theirs."

"What they took into account was that my IQ was high enough to do well for myself."

"They had your IQ tested?" he asked.

"When I was in middle school, to help determine my career path."

"When you were in middle school," he repeated. In middle school, Josh's dad had played football with him, not had his brain tested.

"There's no time to waste when you have high achieving to do," she said.

"In *middle* school?"

"Hey, they love me," she said. "In their own way."

"By making you try to be like them?"

"Not *exactly* like them," she said. "I never did quite get the hang of science, which was a huge disappointment. And anyway, I *wanted* to be like them."

No doubt this was a big part of why she worked so hard at finding the right job now. To please them. To show she deserved the Brooks name.

He didn't give a shit how smart her family was; he wanted to wrap his hands around their necks and rattle the teeth out of their heads for seeing that the baby they'd adopted had grown into an amazing woman.

"What about you?" she asked. "Did your parents expect a lot from you?"

"They expected me to be happy."

"Aw." Her mouth curved into a soft smile. "That's just about the loveliest thing I've ever heard. So are you? Happy?"

Well if that wasn't the million-dollar question and far too complicated to answer at this hour. Instead, he took the computer case from her and set it on her backseat before opening her driver's door. The door didn't stick for him, and she rolled her eyes. "I shouldn't be surprised that you're good with your hands," she said.

His smile heated, and she put her hands to her hot cheeks. "I didn't mean that the way it sounded."

"It's okay. It's true. I'm very good with my hands."

She gave him a laughing shove. "It doesn't matter how good you are," she said. "Since we're not going there."

Yeah. Damn.

Grace looked away, then back into his eyes. "I'll be back in time to get Toby from the bus stop."

"Thanks. I got a bunch more calls on the nanny position."

"Want me to weed out the crazies?" she asked.

"More than I want my next breath."

She laughed again, and the sound of it made him want to smile. "Let me know if you need anything," he said.

"What about if *you* need something?" she asked.

"What?"

"What if *you* need anything, Dr. Scott? You're always the one doing all the caregiving—in your job, here at your house, everywhere. I realize I'm not exactly the best nanny/dog walker, but I'd be happy to help. If you need anything..."

Something actually fluttered in his chest. "You are the perfect nanny/dog walker," he said. "But I'm not all that great with accepting help."

Her mouth quirked. "Tell me something I don't know." She patted him on the chest, got into her car, and in her sexy suit and heels, drove off.

Chapter 12

And on the Eighth day, God created chocolate.

On Monday morning, Grace got up early for a few hours of floral deliveries, and then an hour with Anderson, the local hardware store owner. His bookkeeping system had crashed, and he needed her help. When she asked why he'd called her, he'd said, "because everyone knows you're the go-to accountant in town."

She wasn't sure how she felt about that.

She'd just gotten back to Josh's place and was slipping out of her wedge sandals when she heard the knock at the door. She looked out the glass into the dawn's purple glow and felt her heart leap.

It was Josh, dressed for his office in dark pants, a dark slate button-down, and a dark edgy expression.

She opened the door, and because they were chronic idiots, they stared at each other before she stepped back to let him in.

He shook his head.

Right. He wasn't coming in. Because it was a *bad idea*.

Disappointed, she bent to pick up her computer bag, and when she straightened, she collided with Josh.

Who'd apparently changed his mind about coming in. Her hands went to his chest to keep her balance, and the warm strength of him radiated through his shirt. Maybe her hands slid over him, just a little.

Or a lot.

She couldn't help herself. He had a great chest. Great abs too. He had a six-pack— No, she corrected, her fingers wandering...An *eight*-pack. And then there were those side muscles, the obliques, the ones that made even smart women stupid.

"Grace." His voice sounded husky and just a little tight as he grabbed her hands, making her realize they'd been headed south.

"I'm sorry." She tried to snatch them free, but he held on. "I guess I'm feeling a little conflicted about what I want here," she murmured.

"So the mixed signals," he said. "You're doing that on purpose?"

"No." She paused. "Maybe." She grimaced. "*I don't know.*"

"It's okay, take your time." He backed her up against the doorjamb. "You just let me know when you decide."

At the connection of his body to hers from chest to thighs and everything in between, she heard herself whimper in pleasure, the sound shocking in its need and hunger. "Maybe I was hasty about the not-going-there thing," she whispered. "Maybe the not-going-there thing needs to be temporarily revisited."

His eyes were still dark. Still edgy. "You have my undivided attention."

Actually, she didn't. His hands were gliding down her legs and back up again, beneath the hem of her skirt now.

"Josh?"

"Still here."

No kidding. His fingers. Lord, his fingers. "Kiss me," she managed. "That'll help me figure this out—"

She hadn't even finished the sentence before he'd lowered his head and covered her mouth with his. Gentle. Then not so gentle, and when she kissed him back, she felt the growl reverberate deep inside his chest, a soulful, hungry sound that made her go damp.

"Decide anything yet?" he asked, his voice thrillingly rough when he pulled back.

"Another minute." She tugged him back to her.

Apparently that worked for him because he kissed her, his mouth open on hers, igniting flames along her every nerve ending. Her purse clunked to the floor, and her arms wound up around his neck, her hands gliding into his soft, silky hair.

His hands were just as possessive, going straight to her bottom, squeezing, then lifting her up.

The only barrier between them being his pants and her sundress, which was hiked high enough now that it was really only her panties. "Toby? Where's Toby?"

"Already on the bus." His mouth was busy at her ear, his movements masculine and carnal, arousing her almost beyond bearing.

"Anna—" she gasped.

"In her cave, probably still sleeping. Or stirring her cauldron." He slapped his hand to the lock on the door.

The click of it sliding home hung in the air along with their heavy breathing as they stared at each other.

"So we're doing this?" she asked. "We're—" She broke off on a startled gasp when the halter top of her dress gave.

He'd untied her.

"Okay," she breathed on a shaky laugh. "So we are. We're doing this." She let the material slip away from her, baring her breasts.

With a rough groan, he dipped his head and kissed her collarbone. Then lower. When he licked a nipple as if she were a decadent dessert, she heard herself sigh in sheer pleasure.

He pulled back just enough to blow lightly on her wet skin, eliciting a bone-deep shiver. "You're going to be late for work," she murmured, unbuttoning his shirt. In her impatience, she tore off two buttons.

His mouth was on her, gliding from one nipple to the other, then gently nibbling, and he didn't respond.

Quivering from head to toe, she arched back against the wall, giving him more access. "*Josh.*"

"You're right," he said silkily, giving her a teasing nip as he moved between her thighs, rocking against her. "I'm going to be late."

She let out an unintelligible sound, and Josh lifted his head. "Tell me you want this, Grace. Because I do. At this moment, I'm right where I want to be." He kissed his way to the outer shell of her ear, his breath hot, chasing a shiver down her spine.

At the moment . . .

She understood the words, understood the meaning behind them. "I want this," she said, pressing against him. "I want you." She tugged off his shirt, running her fingers over his abs, which quivered at her touch. Her dress was pretty much a belt around her waist by now. No deterrent for Josh, who dipped his head, taking in her bright red thong with a U.S. flag front and center.

"God bless America," he said.

She laughed. He had one hand on her ass, the other on her breast, which was still wet from his mouth. She was halfway to orgasm, and she was laughing.

So was he.

Then their eyes met. The laughter faded, replaced by a driving need to do this. Turning, he gently pushed her to the couch. He followed her down, covering her body with his own as he kissed her, his warm hands shoving her dress up a little more, his fingers sliding to the edge of her panties.

And then beneath.

"I love your sundresses," he said against her mouth. "You always look so cool and calm, except for your eyes. Your eyes show it all."

"My panic?"

"Your passion," he breathed. "For everything."

"I—" She gasped when he slid a finger into her. Then again when it left her, but before she could make a protest, he was back with two fingers, his thumb stroking right over the center of her gravity. "Oh my God."

"Good?"

She bit his shoulder rather than cry out with exactly how good it was.

"So wet," he said hoarsely, his fingers working magic, stroking her just right so that the pressure built shockingly fast.

"Josh—"

He kissed her deep, his tongue mimicking his fingers,

moving in the same unhurried motion as she writhed beneath him, lost, completely gone. When she came, it shocked her into crying out his name as she rode the wave.

He stayed with her to the end, patient enough to let her come down at her own speed. When she blinked him into view, she didn't know whether to be embarrassed or thank him. "Has it really been a whole year for you since you did this?" she managed.

"And two months."

"You don't seem out of practice."

"Like getting back on a bike…" He slid down her body. Before, he'd simply scraped her panties aside for quick access, but now he hooked his fingers in the material low on her hips and slowly pulled them down her legs.

"I—" she started, with no idea where she was going with that sentence because he put a big palm on each leg and spread them for his viewing pleasure. Leaning in, he kissed first one inner thigh, then the other.

And then in between.

"Um—" Again, she broke off, unable to remember what the hell she'd wanted to say. She couldn't even remember her own name. She was rocking up into his mouth, biting her lip to keep herself quiet. This wasn't quite effective; she was still making noises, horrifyingly needy noises and little hurry-up whispers and pants as she burst again.

Two orgasms.

Always she'd had to strain for even one, and he'd just given her *two* with shockingly little effort. "Oh my God."

He crawled up her body and kissed her. "Oh my God good?"

"*Amazing.*"

"Amazing works. Grace…"

She met his gaze and saw the seriousness in it. "What?"

"I don't have any condoms."

She stared at him. "*What?*"

His laugh was low and a little wry. "You heard the part about a year and two months, right?"

She let out a very disappointed breath, body still humming, mind whirling. "I'm just off my period. It's been a long time for me, too, and I'm clean. We could—"

"No," he said softly but with utter steel laced beneath. "I'm clean, too, but no. No taking chances."

She figured this had something to do with how he'd gotten Toby, so she nodded and blew out another breath. It didn't help. She wanted him, bad.

"It's okay." His smile was tight as he shifted, making her extremely aware that he was still wound up tight, and hard. *Very* hard. Sitting up, she pushed him back and straddled him.

"Grace—"

"Shhh," she said, kissing her way down his incredible chest, paying special homage to every muscle she came across, and there were many. "Since you're already late…" When she scraped her teeth over one of his flat nipples, he sucked in a breath. His head thunked back to the couch as he let out a heartfelt groan, his hands going straight to her ass.

Clearly, it was his favorite part of her anatomy.

As for *his* anatomy, she couldn't possibly pick one favorite part. His entire body was an erotic playground. She spent a moment on his abs, licking him like a lollipop, then slid farther to her knees on the hardwood floor. He was straining the front of his pants, a situation easily remedied. She unbuttoned, unzipped, and slid her hands inside, wrapping them around a most impressive erection. This elicited another rough sound from Josh. Leaning over him, she began to kiss her way up his length, prompting him to slide his hands in her hair and—

His phone went off.

"Ignore it," he said hoarsely.

She nodded and readjusted her grip, starting again at the base with her tongue. His fingers tightened in her hair, more a show of need than domination, as he didn't try to direct her. He groaned, and then...his phone buzzed again.

"Fuck." He let go of her to fish through his pocket, pulling out his phone, glaring at it. "*Fuck.*" He sagged back and stared up at the ceiling.

She rose up on her knees and looked at him. "Problem?"

"I have to go." But he didn't move.

"Josh?"

"Yeah." He let out a slow breath and straightened, pulling her off the floor and into his lap. He held her close for a minute, kissed her shoulder, then her neck while he straightened out her dress for her. When he was done with that, he kissed her mouth. He sighed again, then set her on the couch next to him and got to his feet. He stuffed himself back into his pants, which appeared to be *very* uncomfortable. Shaking his head, he made an adjustment, then grabbed his shirt from the floor. He put it on inside out, swore, yanked it off, then righted it and tried again.

"You going to work like that?" she asked.

He looked down at his hard-on. "That bad?"

"Boy Scouts could camp in there."

He snorted, and Grace found herself laughing again. She was trying to remember that they weren't well suited, that he was the opposite of everything she'd ever wanted, but it wasn't working.

Not even close.

She wanted to tug down his pants and finish what she started.

"Christ, Grace," Josh said on a groan. "Don't look at me like that." He closed his eyes. "I'm standing here trying to mentally recite chemical elements to calm down, and you're looking at me like you want to eat me for breakfast."

She slapped a hand over her eyes. "Oh my God. I was not."

"Yeah, you were."

Okay, she had been doing exactly that. "Sorry!" She paused, lowering her hands. "And you can recite the chemical elements?"

His hands gripped her arms and hauled her up against him. He kissed her and said, very quietly, very seriously, "We okay?"

"Well." She gave him an embarrassed smile. "*I* am..."

Letting out a laugh, Josh let her go and turned for the door. His cell phone was vibrating from the depth of his pocket again. He was already on it before the door shut behind him.

Grace took a moment to fix herself, even though the truth was she needed a lot more than a moment. Her hair was a complete wreck, her body still quivering, but she couldn't seem to get rid of the grin that came from two pretty great orgasms. She did the best she could to look presentable and entered the big house, nearly tripping over Anna. "Sorry!"

Anna studied her for a beat. "You just missed Josh."

Grace worked on looking innocent as they went into the kitchen. "Oh?"

Anna shook her head. "Amateur."

Grace sagged, giving up the pretense. Tank was jumping up and down in hopeful entreaty behind his baby gate, snuffling and snorting. Grace released him from his doggie prison. The puppy immediately caught sight of the lightsaber lying on one of the chairs and began posturing, growling fiercely at it.

"You drive him crazy," Anna said. "You know that, right?"

"It's the lightsaber."

Anna rolled her eyes. "My brother. You drive my brother crazy."

"Actually, I'm pretty sure that's you." Grace gave Tank the signal to sit.

He didn't. Instead, he barked.

Grace took a doggie cookie out of a container on the counter. "*Sit.*"

Tank rolled over. Twice.

"Tank, *sit.*"

Tank offered her a paw to shake, and Grace gave up.

"So," Anna said, "are you going to fall for Josh like the other nannies? Because I don't recommend it. Falling for him is the fastest route to getting fired. Or dumped."

"What are you talking about?"

Tank whirled in circles, then rolled again, clearly going through his entire repertoire of tricks for another cookie.

"Didn't you interview your employer before you took the job?" Anna asked Grace.

"Well, I..." Not this time, she hadn't. "This job sort of happened in a hurry."

Plus she hadn't wanted to probe. Which was entirely different from not wanting to know. Because she did want to know.

Bad.

"You never wondered why none of your predecessors are still around?" Anna asked. "Or why such a great guy with such a great family"—she stopped here to flash a grin so similar to Josh's that Grace blinked—"can't keep a nanny? Or a girlfriend? It's because they all fall hard for him. And he doesn't have a heart, so he doesn't fall back."

"Wow," Grace said.

"I know. You really need to get it together."

"No, I mean you're pretty mean. Anyone ever tell you that?"

Anna didn't seem to take this personally at all. "Mean as a snake," she agreed. "I'm majoring in it at college."

"No, you're not. You're majoring in not-going-to-class."

Anna sighed. "Is this going to turn into another lecture?"

"You're taking cooking and a creative writing class," Grace said. "A *saint* would be bored. I'm telling you, try something more challenging."

Anna shrugged.

"But why not?" Grace asked. "I don't get it. If you're

smart enough to be as mean as a snake, then you're smart enough to do something with yourself."

"Like?"

"Like whatever you want," Grace said. "It's wide open. Hell, you could play softball if you wanted."

"Hello, I'm in a wheelchair."

"No, I saw it on the Washington University website," Grace said. "They've got a whole handicapped athletic program, including softball and soccer and self-defense classes."

Anna blinked twice.

"Run out of excuses?" Grace asked her.

Anna snorted. "Didn't anyone ever tell you that you're supposed to be nice to the poor handicapped girl?"

"You have to earn nice."

Anna narrowed her eyes, and Grace shrugged. "It's true. You don't get an ass-pass just because you're handicapped, no matter what you think. And to be honest, you don't seem all that handicapped."

Anna sputtered at this. "Are you blind?"

"No. Are you?"

Anna just stared at her. "I'm *paralyzed*."

"I know. You keep telling me."

"I'm paralyzed from a car accident that killed my parents," Anna said with great emphasis. Clearly she had this routine down, and just as clearly, it usually worked for her. "You're supposed to feel sorry for me. Everyone feels sorry for me. It's what they do."

"Listen," Grace said softly. "I *hate* that you went through that. It must have been hell. *No one* should ever have that happen to them." In fact, just thinking about it brought a punch of emotion that blocked Grace's windpipe, for Anna, for Josh. She physically ached for him and what he'd faced, and she had no idea how he'd managed to keep it all together. "But you lived," she reminded Anna softly.

"So? I still can't play soccer."

"Could you before?"

"Yes! I was *great* before."

"Then you're still great," Grace said. "Play wheelchair soccer."

"That's stupid. And pathetic."

"No, stupid and pathetic is not doing anything at all but bitching about not going to Europe, when really, if you wanted to go, you'd just go. I mean, as you keep saying, you're a grown-up."

Anna let out a low, disbelieving laugh. "I take it back. I don't like you better than the last few babysitters at all."

Grace smiled sympathetically. "They babied you, huh?"

This got some spark. "I don't need babying."

"No kidding!"

That got a very small smile out of Anna, but a genuine one. Then her attention turned to the guy coming down the hall from her bedroom in nothing but boxers, yawning.

"He's gone, right?" Devon asked, his voice sleepy and thick. "Your brother?"

"Yep," Anna said.

"You fell asleep on me last night," Devon said.

Anna let out a laugh that was so completely fake that Grace's eyes flew to her, and then to Devon. But Devon either missed that fact entirely or didn't care. He scratched his head, then his chest. If he scratched his ass next, Grace was going to throw up in her mouth a little bit.

"What do you want to do today?" Anna asked him, so clearly wanting him to get dressed and out of the house that Grace nearly shoved him out the door herself. She wanted to tell Anna to grow a set and kick his ass. But when Grace had been Anna's age, she'd have highly resented anyone telling her what to do. In fact, it would have made her do the opposite, so she bit her tongue, hard.

"Thought we'd go to Seattle and hit some stores," Devon said. "The new snowboards are in."

"Don't you have physical therapy?" Grace asked Anna, trying to toss her a life preserver.

But Anna didn't want one. "Seattle sounds great," she said.

"Cool," Devon said. "But I don't have my wallet."

Anna shrugged. "No problem."

Okay, that was it. "You," Grace said, pointing at Devon. "Out."

"What?"

Grace opened the front door and gestured with a jerk of her chin.

"Dude," he said. "I'm not dressed."

"*Dude*, I don't care. Come back when you can pay your own way."

Devon stalked stiffly out, and Grace shut the door on him. Actually, she slammed it.

Anna's eyes narrowed. "Is this your idea of helping me toe the line? Because it sucks."

"There's the line, and there's common sense. You figure out the difference, and we'll talk."

Anna glared at her for a minute, then shrugged. "I'll need a ride to PT in an hour."

"I'll be here." Grace watched Anna vanish down the hallway, then turned to the little pug demon puppy. "So how do you feel about chocolate pancakes?"

"Arf!"

Chapter 13

♥

Beware of chocolate squares; they make you round.

For several days, Josh was up to his eyeballs in patients with the flu and strep throat. Throat cultures and breathing treatments became his favorite words. By the end of the third day, he was practically swaying on his feet in exhaustion. "We done?" he asked Dec, knowing he still had to face the mountain of paperwork on his desk. "Anyone left to see?"

"No." She knocked on wood. "Don't jinx it or someone'll come knocking. Run while you can."

"What about Mrs. Porter? Didn't I see her on the schedule earlier?"

"She was here, but she got tired of waiting. Said you were cute, but not *that* cute, and she'd see you another day."

"What brought her in?" he asked.

"Headache. She said it was probably because she'd lost her glasses and would just get another pair from Walmart later instead of bothering you."

Josh spent twenty minutes at his desk facing the torturous pile of files before he was paged into the ER. One of the on-contract doctors couldn't show up for the first half of their nightshift, and they needed Josh. He called Anna, who informed him she couldn't babysit the rug rat because she had a date. So Josh called Grace. "I hate to ask," he said, "but—"

"I've got him right here. I heard your call with Anna. We're just getting back."

"Back?"

"I took Anna and Toby to see a soccer game."

This surprised him. Anna had been a big soccer player before the accident. Ever since, it was as if she'd erased soccer from her vocabulary. "Really?"

"Wheelchair soccer."

It wasn't often he was rendered speechless. "She went willingly, or did you have to kidnap her at gunpoint?"

"She went willingly," Grace said, sounding amused. "And said she could have done better than half the girls on the field."

An odd emotion blossomed in Josh's chest. "I owe you," he said softly.

"Actually, at the moment, I owe *you*."

Surrounded by hell, his life completely not his own, he found himself smiling for the first time in days. "I'm open to a deal."

"Sounds promising, Dr. Scott. Talk to you later."

Josh was still smiling when he headed into the ER. The shift was a little crazy, but that was the nature of the beast in any hospital. There was a purpose to all of it, to every orchestrated movement, and unlike everywhere else, here he thrived on chaos.

You thrive on the chaos that is Grace Brooks as well...

Grace might think she was winging life at the moment, but everything she did, everyone she helped along the way, everything she said or felt, came from the bottom of her heart.

He loved that.

It was 1:00 a.m. before he left the ER. He had a few hours to get home and sleep before the madness started again.

He was halfway to his car when he got the call.

Mrs. Porter had just come in, DOA.

Josh ran back into the hospital, but of course, there was no rush. Not for the dead. He grabbed the chart. There'd be no official cause of death until the autopsy, but all signs pointed to an aneurysm.

Josh stared down at Mrs. Porter's body in disbelief. The possibility of an aneurysm had never been on his radar. It was a silent killer. So of course he hadn't seen any signs of any impending illness, and it certainly hadn't been in her patient history, which he knew by heart. Over the years, he'd probably spent a total of *months* talking to her. He knew she liked her margaritas frozen, her music soft and jazzy, and was a secret office supply ho. She didn't have much family or any pets, she'd always said she was allergic to both, and she'd never missed a single episode of *Amazing Race*. She'd planned on someday being the oldest winner.

Soon as she could get over her fear of flying.

And now she was dead.

It wasn't his fault. Logically, he knew this, but he felt guilty as hell, and sick. *Sick* that he hadn't moved his patients along faster earlier in the day so that she'd have waited for him. Because if he'd seen her, maybe there'd have been signs, maybe he'd have somehow known that today was different, that she'd really needed medical care and not just a little TLC.

"I'm sorry," he said, touching her hand, tucking it under the blanket alongside her body. "So damned sorry."

Only utter silence greeted him. Devastated him. Still in his scrubs, he drove home in a fog and found Grace asleep on his living room couch. She sat up, sleepy, rumpled, an apologetic smile on her face. "Didn't mean to fall asleep," she said.

He helped her to her feet, then pulled his hands back from her warm body and shoved them into his pockets, not trusting himself to touch her right now. He felt her curiosity but managed to walk her to the guesthouse without a word.

"Josh?" Standing at her door, bathed in the moonlight, she touched his face. "Bad night?"

Her eyes were fathomless, and as always, he knew that if he looked into them for too long, he'd drown.

But he was already drowning.

She shifted closer and brushed her willowy body against his. Soft. Warm. He could bury himself in her right now and find some desperately needed oblivion.

But taking his grief out on her would be an asshole thing to do. "I'm fine." Still numb, he waited until she went inside to go back to the house.

Not to bed, though. No, that wasn't the kind of oblivion he planned to settle for. He went to the cabinet above the fridge for the Scotch, and then to the couch where Grace had fallen asleep waiting for him. It was still warm beneath the blanket from her body heat. And it smelled like her.

He inhaled deep and poured himself a few fingers.

He'd lost track of the number of shots he'd drunk by the time someone knocked softly on the glass slider. When he didn't move, Grace let herself in.

Josh wasn't drunk but he was close as he eyed her approach. She was wearing a camisole and cropped leggings. No shoes. Her hair was down. No makeup. He wanted to tear off her clothes, toss her down to the couch, and bury himself so deep that he couldn't think.

Couldn't feel.

He watched her cross the room, and some of his thoughts must have been obvious because she stopped just short of his reach and gave him a long, assessing look.

"Saw that the lights were on," she said. "You can't sleep."

He shrugged and tossed back another shot.

"I'm sorry about Mrs. Porter."

He went still, swiveling only his gaze in her direction.

"Since you were doing your impression of the typical tall, dark, and annoyingly silent male," she said, "I went to the source. Facebook." She paused. "Mrs. Porter was very sweet. And I know she adored you. You're a good man, Josh. A good doctor. Don't blame yourself for her death."

Too late.

"It wasn't your fault."

Maybe not. But plenty of other shit *was* his fault. Anna, still floundering in her new life. Toby thinking he had to be a Jedi warrior to warrant his mother's return. His dad's practice getting too big for its britches and losing the personal attention each patient deserved...

And Grace—the last lethal shot to his mental stability that had come out of nowhere.

She stood there, his own personal, gorgeous goddess, running his world in her own way along with her huge heart. She looked so soft and beautiful in the ambient light. So...his. His heart revved at just the sight of her, so he closed his eyes and let his head fall back to the couch. "You need to go."

"Can't."

He didn't ask why not, but she told him anyway. "I think maybe that's the problem," she said softly, and he could feel her leg brush his now.

She was getting braver.

"People go away in your life, don't they, Josh?" she asked. "You get left, abandoned, whether by choice or through no fault of anyone."

He heard more movement; then she tugged off one of his shoes. She was kneeling at his side, a position that brought dark erotic thoughts to mind. "I don't want to talk about it," he said.

"I know." Having gotten his shoes off, she rose up on her knees. "But you aren't okay. And I'm not leaving you."

He stared at her, ashamed to feel his throat tighten. "Grace. Just go."

"No." She lay her head down on his thigh and stroked his other with a gentle hand. "Tell me what to do to help you."

She could start by moving her mouth about two inches to the right.

She didn't. What she *did* do was take the shot glass dangling from his fingers and set it on the coffee table.

Then she stood and pulled him up with her, hugging him.

His throat tightened beyond use as he buried his face in her hair and held on to her hard.

"You're going to be okay," she whispered.

No. No, he wasn't. But rather than admit that, he took a deep breath. He didn't want her concern.

She pulled back, and keeping a hold of his hand, led him down the hall to his bedroom.

Bad idea.

The worst sort of bad idea.

Stop her...

He had her by a good foot and at least seventy pounds. It wouldn't be difficult to free himself, but instead he followed along after her like a lost little puppy.

She turned off the lights, and darkness settled over them. Over him. *In* him. He was just about as on edge as it got.

And he wanted her.

Needed her.

But he'd never been very good at asking. Not that she was making him ask...

She pulled him into his bedroom, nudging the door shut with her foot. "Come here."

"You're shaking," he said, wrapping his arms around her trembling body.

Her hands glided up his chest to cup his face. "Not me," she said very gently, eyes shadowed. "You. *You're* shaking."

Well, hell. He tried to pull back, but she gripped him tight and refused to budge. "Josh—"

"I need to go—"

"Honey, this is *your* place." Her fingers slid into his

hair, gentle and soothing. Tender. So were her eyes when she tilted his face down to hers to see it in the dim light. "No one's going anywhere," she said. "You're already right where you need to be." Then she locked the door and gave him a push that had him falling onto his bed.

Shit, he was pretty fucking far gone if she could catch him off guard like that. He came up on his elbows, and there she stood in that shimmery top and leggings, looking like everything sweet and warm and caring. *Too* caring. He didn't want that. He wanted her naked and sweaty and screaming his name. "I want to be alone," he said.

"You don't need to be alone tonight."

"You don't know what I need."

She stared down at the hard-on he was sporting, the one straining the front of his scrubs. "I think I have a pretty good idea." She let the straps of her camisole slip to her elbows, and the whole thing fell to her waist. She urged it past her hips with a little wriggle, and it hit the floor. "You sure you don't want to talk about it?"

Sitting up, he settled his hands on her rib cage, fingers spread wide.

"It might help if you did," she said.

He took in her pretty pink bra. It was one of those half-cup things that gave him tantalizing peek-a-boo hints of nipples, which were already hard. They puckered up even tighter, and his mouth watered.

"Josh?"

"Sorry. I haven't heard a word since you took off your top." He closed his eyes. "You shouldn't be here."

"Give me one good reason why not."

He didn't have any logic skills in that moment. None. He searched for words. "I'm temporarily unavailable."

"Incapacitated, maybe." With a hand to the center of his chest, she pushed.

He fell flat to the bed and stared up at the ceiling, which was twirling. And there was something else. He badly wanted to roll her beneath him and take her. Take her hard and fast and dirty. "You need to go, Grace."

"Yeah? And why's that?" she asked. "You might actually let your control slip? Or worse yet, an emotion?" She shook her head, a small smile curving her lips. "You've seen *me* reveal lots of emotions. Fear, sadness, anger... You've seen me totally out of my element and freaked out. You've seen me *everything*. So I think I can handle whatever you've got, big guy."

He blinked. "Big guy?"

She crawled onto the bed and then over him, letting her stomach brush over his erection. "Feels big to me."

Through his haze, Josh felt her hands stroke his thighs. And then higher as her fingers deftly untied and tugged enough to free him. "I'm not feeling gentle," he warned.

"I don't need gentle." She smiled at him. "Remind me sometime to show you my sexual fantasy list. It's quite comprehensive. In fact, you in your scrubs are on it. Being *not* gentle."

He groaned.

"We play doctor. And in a variation, *I* get to be the doctor."

Jesus. "Grace—"

"Shhh," she murmured, her warm breath brushing over him as she wriggled some more, right out of her leggings. At the feel of her bare legs entangled with his, he groaned again.

"I have your attention?" she asked.

"You *always* have my attention."

"Good to know." As light and teasing as her words were, she made a little movement that rubbed her thighs together, and it occurred to him that she was as turned on as he was. He felt himself twitch at the thought. "Grace—"

"No." She covered his mouth with a finger. "You just sit there and look pretty."

His low laugh turned into a husky groan when she grasped him with her hands and let her lips slowly descend over him.

"Oh, Christ." He had to close his eyes after that, his hands fisted tightly in the bedding instead of in her hair, because she was right—he wasn't at all sure he could control himself. Two minutes in, he was drowning in pleasure and hot, desperate need. "Grace—" he gasped, trying to warn her.

She merely let out a hungry little murmur and tightened her grip, humming her approval, and blowing his mind right along with his favorite body part.

He came fast and hard, and he figured he should be mortified—tomorrow. For now, all he could muster was a blissed-out exhaustion...

When he woke several hours later to the alarm, he was all alone, leaving him to wonder—real or Memorex?

The next day came too early, and Grace cursed her alarm. It'd been two when she'd left Josh sprawled out spread-eagle on his bed, eyes rolled back in his head. She'd been pretty sure he'd still been breathing.

He must have been, because his car was already gone.

She drove into Seattle for an interview at a second firm

that had called late yesterday, and it went well. On her way back to Lucky Harbor, she got a phone call from Anna.

"Toby's school called. He fell into a mud puddle, and he needs a change of clothes."

"Okay," Grace said. "I'll be there in twenty." When she got to the house, she went through Toby's dresser and pulled out a pair of pants.

"Don't forget socks," Anna said from the doorway.

"Socks." She grabbed those too.

"And shoes. And a shirt. And a coat..."

Grace looked at Anna.

"Apparently, he's quite the mess."

Grace drove the change of clothes to the elementary school, and Anna had been right. Toby was a mess, but a happy one.

"I didn't need new clothes," he said, not quite so happy now that he had to change. Apparently little boys like to wear their mud like badges of honor.

Grace handed him the clothes and gave his hair a tousle. Or tried. Her fingers caught on the mud in his hair. "What, did you bathe in the stuff?"

He grinned, and she shook her head. "See you at the bus stop in a little while, handsome."

She left the school and met Amy and Mallory for a late lunch at Eat Me. Lunch was chocolate cupcakes, of course.

"So sad about Mrs. Porter," Mallory said. "We're all taking it hard at the hospital. Especially Josh." Her eyes cut to Grace. "You hear from him?"

Not since she'd left him boneless and panting on his bed. She shook her head and peeled her cupcake from its wrapper.

"He might need some TLC," Mallory said.

"Whatever you do, don't call it TLC," Amy said. "That'll scare an alpha into next week. Just do him. That's all the TLC he'll need."

Grace, who'd just taken an unfortunate bite of her cupcake, inhaled it up her nose. By the time she'd stopped coughing and swiped at her streaming eyes, both Mallory and Amy were waiting, brows up.

"Stop," Grace managed. "You guys read far too much into everything. Must be all that *TLC* you're both having. It's making you think everyone else is having it too."

"So you're saying that there's nothing going on with you and the doc?" Amy asked.

Well, hell. She couldn't exactly say that. "I'm saying that this was supposed to be just fun. Not anything real. I'm interviewing for jobs that I'm actually trained to do, and—"

"That your *family* wants you to do," Mallory reminded her. "Because if you ask me, life here in Lucky Harbor suits you pretty nicely."

"My parents mean well," Grace said. "They want me to succeed."

"Well of course," Mallory said. "They love you. But I'm thinking success and happiness don't get along. Sometimes you have to sacrifice one for the other."

Grace had strived hard for success all her life, wanting to live up to being a Brooks. It meant a lot to her, but it'd also cost her. Until now she'd not managed to have any real relationships in her life, at least not long-lasting ones. They'd not been important. But now she couldn't imagine her life without Mallory and Amy in it.

"Happiness should always win," Mallory said quietly.

Grace sighed. They ate in companionable silence for a few minutes.

"So on a scale of one to Taylor Lautner," Amy said to Grace, "how good is he?"

Grace thought about hers and Josh's two extremely memorable...moments. "It's not what you think." She paused. "But Josh is ten-point-five Taylor Lautners. No, make that eleven."

This caused a moment of silent appreciation.

"He makes you happy," Mallory said softly.

Grace looked into her friend's warm eyes. Mallory wanted the best for her. She also wanted the best for Josh. It was natural that her romantic heart would want the best for *them*, together. "I've always been a little short on the happy," Grace admitted. "So it's hard to say. But it's what I said I wanted. Fun."

Mallory's gaze never left Grace's as she squeezed her hand, and Grace knew what she was thinking. What they were all thinking. Yes, Grace had said she wanted only fun. But somehow, when she hadn't been looking, she'd begun to yearn for more.

Far more.

That she'd already set the parameters with Josh was her own fault, so fun it would be. And no more.

"You could do this the easy way and just tell him," Mallory said.

"Tell him what?" Amy wanted to know.

"That she's falling for him," Mallory said.

Grace shook her head. She wasn't falling. She couldn't be falling. Because Josh had a very full life, and there wasn't room for her in it. And she was quite over trying to squeeze herself in where there wasn't room. She'd done that with her parents all her life. And every failed relationship.

No more. Her heart wasn't strong enough to take it.

Amy looked at Mallory. "She's going down the same path I did, poor baby. The path of most resistance."

"I'm not taking *any* path," Grace said, feeling grumpy now as she reached for another cupcake. Her grumpiness hit a new level when both Amy and Mallory merely laughed at her.

"Is watching Toby as hard as you thought it would be?" Mallory asked when she'd controlled herself.

Trick question. Grace had honestly believed that taking care of Toby would be easier than watching after Tank. It hadn't been at all, but she couldn't remember ever enjoying a job more. Not sure what *that* meant. She lifted a shoulder. "Little boys aren't all that different from big boys."

Amy grinned. "Now *there's* a lesson that should be taught to every female in kindergarten to save years of frustration and heartache."

"You really don't think you're falling for him?" Mallory asked Grace.

She shook her head. Her life had always been about the bottom line, about numbers, about getting to the top. It'd never been about emotions, about heart and soul. About falling in love...She knew better than that. "Josh isn't looking for that."

Mallory looked amused. "I meant Toby."

Oh. Right.

"But good to know where you're at," Mallory said.

Yeah. Good to know. Grace's phone rang. A number she didn't recognize.

"Grace Brooks?" came an unfamiliar voice in her ear.

"Yes."

"This is Serena, the nurse at Lucky Harbor Elementary. Toby's not sick or hurt or anything."

"Okay..."

"But he fell in a mud puddle again..."

Since there was only a half hour left of school, Grace just took Toby home with her. She buckled him into his booster seat and slid him a look in the rearview mirror. "Do I want to know?"

"Camel flaunting," he said very solemnly. "Me and Tommy needed to camel flaunt."

This baffled her for a beat; then she had to laugh. "Camouflage?"

"Yes," he said.

"For a battle."

"Yes!"

Grace had never really pictured herself with kids. She didn't know why, exactly. Maybe because she'd never been around them, or because she figured she'd be married to her career as her parents were. But in that moment, sharing a grin in the mirror with Toby, something deep inside her squeezed hard in yearning.

They'd just walked in the front door and let Tank loose when Grace got a call from Anna.

"Need a ride," was all Anna said.

Grace could hear something in the girl's voice. *Tears?* Whatever it was, Grace's stomach dropped. She knew that Anna was supposed to be at physical therapy, but she also knew that Devon was a weasel, and once Anna was in his car, she was pretty much at his mercy.

Grace had tried talking to Anna about it twice since the other day, but Anna was good about avoiding talking.

A definite Scott thing.

Still, Grace couldn't get past the gut feeling that Devon was pushing for things Anna didn't want to give him. "Where are you?" she asked.

Anna rattled off an address that was just outside of Lucky Harbor. It was an area that Grace knew from delivering flowers, and it was not an especially good neighborhood. She looked at Toby, who was swooshing his Jedi lightsaber and making Tank nuts. "On my way." She disconnected. "We're going for a ride, Tobes."

"Tank and I are in the middle of a battle."

"You can finish when we get back."

"A good Jedi never stops in the middle of a battle."

She hunkered down and looked him in the eye. "We have another battle to fight."

He looked excited. "Yeah?"

"Yeah. Picking up your aunt."

His face fell. "Aw, that's no fun. And you promised we'd go to the park."

"Yes, but sometimes things happen."

"Not to Jedis. Bad things like not going to the park never happen to Jedis." Still holding his saber, he took off, his little feet pounding down the hallway. The next noise was the slam of his door.

Okay, so *someone* needed a nap. Though technically, that could apply to Grace as well. She followed him to his room and opened the door. She saw a little boy tush and a little pug tush, both adorable, sticking out from behind Toby's large beanbag chair. The classic "if I can't see you, you can't see me" pose. "Toby? Tank?"

"Don't answer," came a little boy whisper, and then a muffled snort.

A *pug* snort.

"Gee," she said. "Wherever could the Jedi warriors have gone?"

Another pug snort.

And then a giggle. "What a shame I'm all alone," she said. "'Cause I'm really in need of a couple of Jedi warriors, the very best of the best. There's an epic battle ahead. We have to save Aunt Anna."

The two tushes wriggled free, complete with warrior yells and lots of barking. Grace was just leading Toby outside when Josh pulled up.

He got out of his car looking like the day had already been too long. "Need my laptop," he said, eyes shadowed, face drawn. He made time to stop and crouch down to hug Toby before straightening and meeting Grace's eyes.

She wanted to ask him if he was okay. She wanted to give him a hug like he'd given Toby. She wanted to give him a chocolate cupcake and warm milk. She wanted to have him beneath her again, shuddering, her name on his lips as he came.

But mostly she wanted to ask him if there was any chance that he was feeling like this thing might be getting uncomfortably close to being a lot more than just fun. "Hey," she said, and then rolled her eyes at how breathless she sounded.

He'd been pretty far gone last night, both in alcohol and exhaustion, and she suddenly realized he might not even *remember* what had happened.

His dark gaze searched hers for a long beat, but he

gave nothing away. Something else he was extremely good at. "Where are you guys going?" he asked.

"Anna needs me to pick her up."

"Devon flake on her again?"

"I don't know. This is where she is." She showed him the address she'd scrawled onto a piece of paper.

He frowned. "That's nowhere close to her PT." He looked at his watch. "My car. Let's go."

They drove in silence. Well, except for the noises Toby and his Zhu Zhu warriors were making in the backseat. Josh turned onto a run-down street, and they all eyeballed the apartment building. Weeds in the asphalt cracks, dead lawn, peeling paint, and bars on the windows of the lower floors. Nice.

Anna was in her chair waiting on the front walk. At the sight of Josh's car, she scowled, and then again when he got out to help her.

"I called Grace," she said unhappily. "Not you."

"Hello to you too." He crouched in front of her, gaze narrowed. "You okay?" He reached out to touch her cheek where her mascara had run as if she'd been crying.

She slapped his hand away. "I'm fine. Just get me out of here."

The drive home was tense, with Josh keeping an eye on a silent Anna, who was huddled in the backseat. Back at home, she rolled into her room, slammed the door, and all went quiet.

Toby picked up his lightsaber. "Can we go to the park?"

"Not right now," Josh said.

"Swimming?"

"Not right now."

Toby tossed up his hands. "You don't let me do anything." And then he walked down the hall and slammed his bedroom door.

In a perfect imitation of Anna.

Josh looked like maybe he wanted to tear out his hair. He moved down the hall and knocked on Anna's door.

"Go away!" she yelled.

Josh strode back into the living room, looking as if he needed a long vacay.

"You okay?" Grace asked him.

"I don't know." He lifted his head and pinned her with his gaze. "Tell me about last night."

"What about it?" she asked carefully, not wanting to fess up to anything he couldn't remember.

He looked at her for another long moment, during which she did her best to look innocent.

"You could start by showing me the rest of that sexual fantasy list," he said.

Okay, she thought with a blush, so he *did* remember.

Gaze dark, he stepped toward her, but his phone went off. Josh swore, grabbed his laptop, then strode to the door.

Grace let out a breath, then sucked it in again when he turned back and lifted her up so that they were nose to nose.

"Now *I* owe *you*," he said softly, then set her down, brushed a kiss over her mouth, and vanished.

Chapter 14

I would give up chocolate, but I'm not a quitter.

It was a long day. At the office, every patient Josh saw wanted to talk about Mrs. Porter. They were devastated. His staff was devastated. By the time he got home, he was more done in than he'd been last night, and that was saying something.

He'd called ahead. Toby was asleep. Anna was heading out as soon as he got home. He could have done whatever he wanted with the evening.

But there was only one thing he wanted to do.

Grace.

The lights in the guesthouse were blazing. Through the windows, he could see Grace sitting on the couch, but she wasn't alone. She was with Mallory and Amy, talking and laughing. In front of them on the coffee table was an opened file box, and papers were scattered across the entire table, bookended by an open laptop and an adding machine.

It was a visceral reminder that Grace had a whole other life outside of his.

She'd taken on two more clients, which he'd heard from Dee, who'd heard it from Lucille, who'd heard it from Anderson at the hardwood store, since he was one of those clients. The other new client was the ice-cream shop on the pier and the two brothers who ran it. Lance and Tucker probably had no bookkeeping system at all, so Grace had her work cut out for her—not that it would be a problem. She seemed to have a way of getting to it all, making everything all work out. He admired that. She was just a sweet, smart, hard-working woman doing her best to find herself. No complaining, no feeling sorry for herself, doing what she had to do to get by.

She had her hair pulled up in a ponytail, but a few pale silk strands had escaped, framing her face, brushing her throat and shoulders.

Just looking at her had his body humming. And though she couldn't possibly see him standing in the dark night, she went still, then turned her head, and peered outside.

Unerringly looking right at him.

She said something to Mallory and Amy, then rose in one fluid motion and stepped outside, shutting the door behind her.

They met in the shadows near the shallow end of the pool.

"Hey," she said, looking like a vision in a loose white top that fell off one shoulder and white shorts showing a mile or two of sexy leg.

"Hey yourself," he said. "How did your day go?"

"Well, I didn't kill Tank, Toby continues to master

the English language, and Anna didn't run off today. Progress."

"Great, but I meant you. How are *you*?" She looked surprised, which he didn't like. "You think I don't want to hear about you too?" he asked.

She nibbled on her lower lip.

"Grace?"

"This thing between us . . . it's still just fun, right?"

He studied her a moment. "How does that translate into me not caring about you?"

She blew out a breath and looked away. "I'm sorry. I guess I'm not very good at this. I don't mix well with a guy like you."

"A guy like me," he said, trying to figure out what that meant.

"Look, it's all me, okay? I knew going into this thing that it couldn't possibly work, but I just kept . . ." She broke off and looked away. "I'm sorry."

"A guy like me," he repeated again. "Grace, I'm trying like hell to follow you but . . ."

She looked at him and blinked, as if she didn't understand how he wasn't catching the obvious. "We're so different," she said. "You've got your life in gear, all planned out. I don't know what I'm doing. I'm trying to know but . . ." She trailed off and looked at him again, as if expecting him to nod in agreement.

But he was still clueless. "If you think my life is working on some *plan* that I've set out," he said, "you haven't been paying attention. *Nothing* is how I planned it. And as for mixing well, I think we mix pretty fucking well."

"Yes, but isn't that just sex?"

"Not yet," he said with grim amusement. "But not for

lack of chemistry. And there's no 'just sex' about it."

She stared up at him, apparently speechless. There weren't crickets out tonight, but if there had been, they'd be chirping Beethoven about now. That's when it came to him like a smack upside the back of the head. "Who was the guy?" he asked.

"Guy?"

"The one who screwed you over, the one with some big, grand plan, I'm guessing. A plan that didn't work out in your favor. Was he a doctor?"

Grace drew an audible breath to speak and then shook her head. "That obvious?"

"No," he said. "Or I'd have caught on a lot sooner. And you'd think I would have since I was once burned by a big, grand plan too."

She sighed. "Bryce Howard the third."

"Sounds like a dick already."

She choked out a laugh that spoke more of remembered misery than humor. "He's a friend of the family. His parents are well-known and respected biomedical engineers, on the pioneer front of cardiovascular research."

"Never heard of them."

"We always knew we'd end up together," she said. "It was sort of expected, actually."

"Expected? Didn't anyone realize it's the twenty-first century?"

"It wasn't like that," she said quietly. "I liked Bryce."

And then Josh *really* got it. Christ, he was slow on the uptake. "You loved him."

"Yes." She let out a shaky breath. "I did. I loved him until the day after our engagement, when he came home and told me to pack because we were moving to England for his job, which was a six-year study grant. It was a great opportunity, but..."

"You didn't like being told what your life would look like for the next six years," he guessed.

She shook her head. "And you know what the really sad thing was? If he'd so much as asked, or even gave a thought to me and my job, I'd have junked it all to go with him."

"So what happened?"

"He left the next day," she said. "And shortly after, my job vanished when the economy dived."

"You could have looked him up," he said. "Gone to him then."

"Thought about it," she admitted. "But by then I was seeing someone else."

"Another PhD?"

"Yes, but a bank guy this time," she said. "Stone Cameron. He lost his job the same day I lost mine, only he'd invested in property instead of stocks. He had a house in Australia. He went there to go surf out the economy problems."

"He ask you to go with?"

"Nope." She shook her head. "This time, I wasn't in the plans at all."

Josh was starting to get the whole picture now, and he didn't like it much. "So your parents had big life plans for you. Bryce had big life plans for you. Stone just had big plans. And no one ever asked you *your* plans."

"No," she said softly. "And I realize I didn't actually have my own plans, but I'd have liked to be asked."

He nodded. He could understand that.

"So I'm just saying, you don't have to feel a responsibility to me just because we ... sort of had sex." She let out a low laugh that was far more natural now. "Twice. I'm still okay with this being ..."

"Fun."

Her gaze met his, clear and utterly unfathomable. "Yes."

"You think I'd feel a responsibility to you because of good sex," he said slowly.

"Well, it was better than good," she said. "But yes. I think you're exactly the type to feel a responsibility for those who cross your path. You're a rescuer."

Okay, so now on top of assuming he only wanted her out of some sense of responsibility, she'd also lumped him into the same category with all the other mistakes she felt she'd made. And hell if that didn't piss him off. She didn't want him to care. He got that, loud and clear. He didn't want to care either.

But he did. "Look, Grace, no matter what you call this thing between us—fun, a pain in the ass, nothing at all—it doesn't matter. Just don't judge me by the assholes in your past. I deserve more than that, but more importantly, *you* deserve more than that."

She stared up at him, then slowly nodded. "You're right. I'm sorry." She turned back to the guesthouse, and he grimaced.

"Grace—"

"Toby lost a tooth tonight," she said quietly over her shoulder. "He was excited and tried to wait up for the Tooth Fairy, but he didn't make it. She arrived the minute after he'd conked out."

He slid his hand into his pocket. "Thanks. How much—"

"You're paying me a thousand bucks a week." She faced him again. "I think I can cover it. I can cover a lot of stuff, actually. Except at the end of the day, I'm still just the babysitter. And he's still just an adorable, motherless five-year-old. Who also deserves better." With that last zinger, she let herself into the guesthouse and shut the door quietly.

He stood there for a moment, then nodded. Point for each, which meant it was a draw. Which didn't explain why he felt she'd lanced him alive.

Inside he found Toby deeply asleep, wrapped around both Tank and the lightsaber. The Berenstain Bears book was there, too, with the mama bear front and prominent.

Josh ignored the pain in his chest, the one that said he was *still* failing the people in his life, and gently pulled the lightsaber from Toby's slack grip. Next, he eyed the dog.

Tank opened one eye and gave a look that said, *Don't even try, pal.*

Josh gave up and covered them both.

Tank licked his hand.

Josh bent over Toby and kissed his temple. His son smelled like peanut butter and soap, which he took as a good sign. So was the way the kid smiled in his sleep. A smile with a gaping hole in the front.

"Love you," Josh whispered, the words a heavy weight on his chest.

Toby rolled away, pulling Tank under one arm and the Berenstain Bears book under the other, sighing softly in his sleep. "Arf," he whispered.

The next morning, Grace climbed back onto the modeling pedestal in Lucille's gallery. Today she was artfully draped in a sheet, supposedly like a Grecian goddess, though she suspected she looked more like she was going to a toga party.

"I wouldn't mind being twenty years younger, like you, Grace," Mrs. Gregory said conversationally. "Back to when my boobs were as good as yours."

"You mean *fifty* years," Lucille murmured.

"It's just that I'm tired of hoisting my boobs into a bra every morning." Mrs. Gregory pointed to Grace's breasts. "You don't have to hoist anything. Those babies are standing up on their own."

"That's because it's cold in here," Grace said in her own defense. She was counting down the last twenty minutes of class as she held her pose. After this, she was picking up Anna from PT, and then she had a few more calls to return to applying nannies. She was determined to find the best possible person for Toby. And Tank. And Anna, even though the twenty one-year-old would deny needing anything from anyone.

And Josh...

Grace could admit that she also wanted the best possible person to take care of Josh. Which was silly. Very silly. Obviously, the man was more than capable of taking care of himself, not to mention everyone around him. He'd proven that managing more than the average human should ever have to between his practice, the ER, Toby, Anna...the loss of his parents.

Sure, he was very used to taking care of people, and it was an extremely appealing part of the man. But maybe he just needed to know it was okay to be on the other side of the fence occasionally.

"Time," Lucille called out to her students, and Grace

relaxed. She jumped down off the pedestal and dropped the sheet, revealing the short, strapless sundress she wore beneath. Grabbing her cardigan and purse, she headed to the door. "Gotta go."

"Hold on, dear," Lucille said, and handed her a check and a bottle of wine.

"Oh," Grace said. "Thank you, but I'm not much of a drinker—"

"Check out the label."

It was a color pencil sketch of the Lucky Harbor pier at night, lit up with strings of white lights that glowed out over the water beneath a full moon. Grace had seen the original. The Chocoholics had celebrated Amy's sale of the drawing to the winery a month ago. When she recognized it, pride filled her. "It's beautiful," she said.

"Keep it," Lucille told her. "Maybe you'll have use for it on a date over a nice romantic dinner with the doctor."

"We're not dating—" She broke off at Lucille's smile and shook her head. "Listen, I know you're like the gossip guru in town, but there's no gossip here."

Lucille smiled. "Are you sure?"

"Very," Grace said firmly, ignoring the little ping inside her. Maybe if she'd stop giving Josh reasons *not* to fall for her... "I'm just watching Toby and Tank. Helping Josh out, is all."

"*Josh*, is it now?"

"Yes, that's his name."

"Actually, honey," Lucille said, "we all call him Dr. Scott. Well, unless he's not within hearing distance, and then we call him Dr. McHottie. And none of *us* get to live with him."

"I'm just the babysitter," Grace said. "I stay there because of the crazy hours he keeps. It makes things easier on him. And I'm in the *guesthouse*, not the main house, and only until we find him a replacement. There's no dating going on."

Everyone's ears perked up at this.

"I could take on one more kid," Jenna Burnett said. "For Dr. McHottie, I'd take on quadruplets."

Jenna was a single mom in her midforties, running a day care out of her home. Her three children were teenagers and helped when they got home from school. Jenna was sweet and kind, and probably a viable option for Toby.

"Ask him," Jenna said, seeing that Grace was actually thinking about it. "Tell him I'll give him a great deal!" She smiled warmly, but damn, there was definitely something just a little bit hungry behind it.

"Hey, I want to throw my name into the hat too." This from Sierra Hennessy. Sierra owned an upscale clothing shop in Seattle that she paid someone else to manage. The designs were Sierra's own, and because she had four ex-husbands, each more wealthy than the last, she didn't care that she sold only a few dresses a season. She also didn't care that she was considered a man shark. "What's Dr. Scott's stance on marriage?"

Grace managed a smile. "I'll let him know about both your offers. We'll be in touch about interviews." Then she hightailed it out of there. She got to Anna's PT office just in time to see the girl roar off in Devon's truck, flashing a peace sign at Grace.

Grace gritted her teeth and drove to the house, where she waited for the bus. When Toby hopped off it, he was bouncing up and down with excitement. It was Back-to-School night, and later Josh would get to see Toby receive the Student of the Week award. Afterward, Josh had promised him an ice-cream sundae, and then Toby was having his first sleepover at a friend's.

He was so excited he could hardly contain himself. He and Grace walked the half block home, where from hard-earned knowledge, Grace let Tank and Toby run wild laps around the yard until they expelled enough energy in tandem that Toby could sit and do his homework. While he did that, Grace worked on Tank's so-called obedience. This was more an exercise in patience for Grace than anything else, but she was determined.

They had mac and cheese and turkey hot dogs for an early dinner—no deviating from the planned menu—and then waited for Josh to show up to take Toby to Back to School night.

Except he didn't show.

Grace called Josh but got no answer. She called Anna. No answer there either. Finally, she drove Toby to his elementary school herself, pretty much steamed at everyone with the last name of Scott except for Toby.

Toby's teacher was thrilled to see him. "Sadie had her kittens, Toby. Want to go look?"

When Toby whooped and raced off, Grace looked at the teacher. "How much time before the awards?"

"At least half an hour."

"Can I leave him here while I go get his father?" Grace asked.

"Dr. Scott?"

"Yes. I'm sure he just got hung up at the office…"

One of the moms sidled close. A tall, perfectly-put-together, gorgeous brunette. "I'm sorry, but I couldn't help overhearing. Angela Barrison," she said, introducing herself. "I'll be happy to keep an eye on Toby while you go get Dr. Scott." She smiled a sort of tiger smile. "And if you could let him know that *I'm* the one watching Toby for you, that'd be great. I'd like to apply for the position."

"The nanny position?" Grace asked.

"*Any* position."

Grace shook her head all the way to her car.

Josh's office was in the building directly adjacent to the hospital. She tore into the lot, stomped up to his suite, and yanked open the door. Righteous anger was blooming within her, propelling her forward, ready to tear him a new one for missing something so important to Toby.

And something else was blooming too.

Worry.

This was unlike him, very much so. He never blew off anything that anyone needed, but especially Toby. His son came first with him. Family always came first. So this bothered her.

She hadn't expected to feel worry for the man who appeared to have it all. Hell, she hadn't meant to feel anything for him at all, but she did.

Far too much.

The waiting room was empty, the front office lit but also empty. And her worry amped up a notch. "Josh?" she called, walking down the hallway.

She came to a large office decorated in masculine dark wood, the huge mahogany desk loaded with paperwork and files. The lamp was lit. There was a mug of something on the corner and an open laptop in the middle.

Behind the desk was a large executive chair. In it was one Dr. Josh Scott, leaning back, feet up.

Fast asleep.

Chapter 15

Forget roses, send chocolate.

Josh hated falling asleep in his office chair. It never failed to give him a kink in his neck and make him grumpy as hell. So when he leaned back and let his eyes drift shut, he told himself he was merely resting his eyelids.

"Josh?"

Her voice, Grace's voice, came to him on a breath of air, and he relaxed into the leather chair.

"I have a case for you, Dr. Scott." Grace stood in his office doorway in a nurse's uniform, but not any uniform that Dee might wear. Nope, this one had come right out of the Victoria Secret catalog, complete with stilettos.

Looking holy-shit-hot, she sauntered into his office and slid between his legs, leaning over him in the chair, blocking him in with her body. His hands went to her hips to pull her in even closer, needing her so badly he was shaking but he refused to rush. If this was all they were going to have, this erotic dream, then he wanted it to last. He kissed her neck, then traced his tongue over the spot, elic-

iting the sweetest, most sensuous sigh he'd ever heard.
This fueled a bone-deep desire to mark her as his, and he
sucked the patch of skin into his mouth.

"Josh…"

No. No talking, or he'd wake up. He kissed the spot,
slipping his hands beneath the short hem of her uniform,
and groaned. No panties. God, he was a goner…

"Josh."

He grabbed her wrist and tugged so that she fell into
his lap with a gasp that had him opening his eyes.

No nurse's uniform. Damn. It really was just a
dream…

"Sorry," Grace said, wriggling, trying to free herself.
"I didn't mean to startle you awake. You were really out."

Med school and residency had taught Josh how to
sleep light and come awake fast, but apparently he'd forgotten the art of both. Then again, certain parts of him
were *very* awake, getting more so by the second thanks to
the squirming Grace was doing.

She wore another of her sundresses, this one sky blue,
the color of her eyes. It'd risen high on her thighs, and he
decided to help it along, sliding a hand up her leg, pushing the material as he went.

"What are you doing?" she asked, nice and breathless.

"Seeing if I should salute the flag on your panties," he
said. "I'm patriotic, Grace."

"These don't have a flag on them."

Aw, now see, that was just a challenge, and he'd never
been able to resist a challenge. His fingers tangled with
hers, trying to work the hem while she rocked around
some more.

That had enough of a noticeable effect on him that

her eyes widened at the feel of him hard beneath him. "Um…"

He met her gaze.

"You're…"

"Yeah," he said thickly. "I've been like this all week."

Okay, so not really. It was hard to maintain a boner while treating the flu or putting in stitches, but he'd given it the old college try.

And it *had* been a hell of a week. "I was dreaming about you. You were modeling for me."

"In the bikini T-shirt?" she asked.

"Try again."

She met his gaze and blushed gorgeously at whatever she saw on his face. "I…"

"Go ahead, guess," he said. "It's from your sexual fantasy list."

The air crackled around them.

"And not that I'm *not* completely enjoying this lap dance of yours," he said, "but what are you doing here and where's Toby?"

She looked at him as if maybe he wasn't as awake as he'd thought. "You're late for Back to School night. You weren't answering your cell. I came to check on you."

"Ah, shit." He stood up and let her slide down his body, but not before he caught a quick flash of peach silk. He *loved* peach silk.

But Toby was waiting, and Josh had indeed known about tonight. Damn, he couldn't believe he'd fallen asleep like that. Or maybe after eighty hours at the job this week so far, he could believe it. He shut his laptop, grabbed his keys and his phone, and keeping his fingers wrapped around Grace's wrist, began to tug her to the door. But then he stopped and looked down into her concerned face. She'd come to get him because she cared about Toby.

And because she cared about him too?

He thought maybe she was getting there. More than she planned to, and that did something to him.

People had cared about him before, of course. Toby loved him, unconditionally. His patients liked him. Ty, Matt...his staff. Hell, even his sister, though he wouldn't bet against the house on that one. But how often could he say that any of those people had put him first?

"Josh?" Grace murmured. "You okay?"

"I will be." Letting go of her, he moved back to his desk, opening his laptop again. He didn't have to bring up the hospital's contract offer; it'd been up for weeks. Months. His dad no longer needed him, but Toby did. Anna did. And Josh needed to do what was right for him too. He'd loved his dad, loved the memory of his dad right here in this office, helping people.

But it was no longer as relevant as making his own life work. Josh scrolled to the end, electronically signed on the bottom line, and hit SEND.

Done. Carrot bitten. Hell, carrot *swallowed*.

Just like that—though there were no trumpets, no fat ladies singing—Josh's life was irrevocably changed. He moved back to Grace at the door.

She was staring at him very solemnly. "What did I just miss?" she asked.

Josh didn't really have words. He felt a little off his center of gravity, like he was standing at the edge of a cliff with one foot in the air already. It was a new feeling for him. "Nothing yet," he said, and because she was standing so close, looking so cute and yet utterly, effort-lessly sexy, he backed her to the door.

"Josh," she said. Just that, just his name as her hands went to his chest.

Not to push him away, he noticed with some satisfac-tion. Though she wasn't exactly sold on this, on them, not yet. Not even close. But the way her pulse beat at the base of her throat told him the move had excited her.

"You feel warm," she said, and gave him a worried frown.

He pressed into her a little. Yeah, he *was* feeling warm. He was starting to feel a bunch of things. "Don't worry, it's not contagious."

Her brow creased more tightly in that adorable expres-sion of concern. "You're sick?"

"Probably." He slid a hand down her back to her very nice ass and rocked her into him. "Definitely."

She blinked, then caught onto his light, teasing tone. She relaxed, letting out a little sigh that went straight through him. "You poor man. All work and no play."

Yeah. But that was going to change.

Or so he hoped.

Too bad that by the time it did, she'd probably be long gone, having taken a job and a life that suited her far more than *his*. Leaning in, he kissed her, soft and light, then pulled back. "Let's go get Toby."

They made it to the school in time to see Toby get his Student of the Week award. Grace watched Toby beam with happiness at his father's presence and felt her heart clutch. Josh's expression was much more subdued but no less genuine, and Grace's heart kicked again.

After, she left to give them some alone time, heading to the diner to meet Amy and Mallory. Jan, the diner's owner, stopped her at the door. Jan was short and round and appeared to cut her dark hair by putting a bowl over her head to use as a guideline. She wasn't big on customer service, rarely speaking to her customers unless it was to yell at them to pipe down because *American Idol* was on the TV. "Got something for you," she said.

This took Grace by surprise. In all the time she'd known Jan, the woman had never spoken directly to her.

Jan held out a memory stick.

"What's this?" Grace asked.

"My laptop died. This is my backup bookkeeping. I need you to get on it ASAP. I'm a little behind."

"Okay…"

Jan was looking impatient to be back in front of her TV. "You're a number cruncher, yes?"

"Well, actually," Grace said, "I'm in banking—"

"You're doing Amy's books," Jan said.

"Yes, because she's my friend."

"And Lance's and Tucker's. And Anderson's. And Jeanine's."

Yeah, okay, so she'd gotten shystered into doing a lot of bookkeeping. She was good at it. And as it turned out, she also liked it. She liked the way numbers balanced at the end of the day, how she didn't have to take her work home with her to stress about at night. "These are all one-time things," she said to Jan. "Really. I'm just sort of setting them up."

"I'll pay you," Jan said. "And also give you free food. As much as you can eat."

Grace had her mouth open to refuse but she closed it,

inexcusably drawn in by this. "As much as I want?"

"As much as your skinny ass can take," Jan said, waving the memory stick enticingly.

Grace sighed and took it. Skinny? Not even close. "How long ago did your laptop die?"

"A month."

Great...

She made her way to the back booth. "Sucker," a waiting Mallory said.

Amy came out from the kitchen, making a big deal about setting the tray of cupcakes down just right, twisting the tray and nearly blinding Grace and Mallory with...

"*Oh my God*," Mallory said, and screamed.

Grace put her fingers in her ears but grinned wide.

Amy was wearing a rock on her ring finger.

Mallory jumped up and down and screamed some more, and then wore herself out and sank into the booth for a cupcake.

"I actually don't even need chocolate," Amy said, staring at her ring in dazed marvel. "Never thought I'd say that."

Mallory laughed and took a second cupcake. "I'll eat it for you."

"I'm getting married," Amy said softly. She looked up at the two of them, her eyes shiny. "Can you believe it?"

Grace knew that Amy hadn't had much luck in love before coming to Lucky Harbor. But Matt Bowers, a very sexy forest ranger and all-around great guy, had changed that for her.

Mallory's life was changing too.

Everyone's life was changing.

Except for Grace's.

Mallory squeezed her hand, making her realize she'd gone quiet. "You okay?"

"Oh, I'm good, and *very* happy for both of you." And she meant that, from the bottom of her heart. "I love how you've both figured out what was missing in your lives and went out and got it for yourselves."

"You know that what was missing wasn't a man, right?" Amy asked. "Because I didn't need a man to make me whole. I just needed to open myself up to new experiences. The man part sort of fell in my lap."

Mallory grinned. "Ditto."

"Well, thankfully, I don't need a man to make me whole," Grace said. "Because there's a definite man shortage in my life."

"Liar," Amy said.

"Hey," Grace said. "I'm just his dog walker and part-time nanny. It's temporary. Very temporary."

Amy turned to Mallory. "Time for the big guns."

Mallory pulled out her phone, thumbed to Lucky Harbor's Facebook page, and showed it to Grace. The latest entry read:

> *Ladies, our favorite doc, Josh Scott, is actively seeking a new nanny. Many have applied, and all have been turned down by his interim nanny, Grace Brooks.*
> *Is she just being extraordinarily careful?*
> *Or is she saving the position for herself?*
> *A picture is worth a thousand words...*

Accompanying this was indeed a picture, taken from inside the elementary school's kindergarten classroom.

Toby was up on the makeshift stage, accepting his award.

The class was full of proud, smiling parents.

And in the back of the room stood Grace, beaming at the stage, a flush on her cheeks.

That wasn't the most damning part. Nope, that honor went to Josh, standing just behind her, his arms around her, his shoulders much broader than hers, his jaw pressed to her temple as he also looked toward the stage. There was something about the stance, the body language, the way the air practically shimmered between them. Not that there was any air between them. He was so tight to her that a sheet of paper wouldn't have fit.

"Well that's just…" Grace trailed off. Sexy.

Hot.

In fact, she was getting a hot flash right now.

"Standing a little close, aren't you, for nanny and the professor?" Amy asked dryly.

"Doctor," Grace said absently. "He's a doctor."

"So is that why he's close enough to take your body temperature without a thermometer?"

Grace shook her head. "This picture couldn't have been taken even an hour ago." And that wasn't all. She looked happy in that picture.

"The good stuff travels fast in Lucky Harbor," Amy said. "You know that."

"And that's not the only fast thing," Mallory said. "You guys have moved pretty fast."

"Says the woman who slept with her fiancé on the first night she met him," Amy said dryly.

"*Second* night," Mallory said primly.

"This picture was taken out of context," Grace complained. "*Completely.*"

"Of course," Mallory agreed, nodding. Then she shook her head. "Um, so how do you take a picture out of context?"

Amy snorted.

"The classroom was packed," Grace said. "Standing room only. We were forced to be so squished."

"Interesting how his arms look quite comfortable around her," Mallory noted to Amy.

"And notice the postcoital look about her," Amy offered back.

Grace bit her lower lip and stared at the picture. She did seem to have a certain orgasmic glow. Jeez, how long did such a thing last anyway?

Josh didn't have the glow. Even though technically he'd been the last one to, um, *have* an orgasm, he was looking a little edgy, a little rough and tumble. Like maybe he needed another reason to glow. Grace bit her lip harder at the thought. "We haven't been together. Not exactly."

"*Not exactly?*" Amy asked, brows up. "Is that what you kids call it these days?"

Mallory cracked up at this, and Grace sighed. "It's more like coitus interruptus. Twice. Once because he was called into work and another because he fell asleep."

Amy grinned. "Anyone ever tell you you're supposed to keep them awake for the good stuff?"

Mallory was smiling but her question was serious. "So are you two going to be a real thing, then, not just a fun thing?"

Something clenched deep inside Grace at the thought, but she couldn't decide if it was a good clench or a bad one. *Liar, liar...* "I've run the numbers," she said. "It wouldn't work. First of all, he's a doctor. He gets a lot of points taken off for that."

"People usually add points for doctors," Mallory said.

"Not me," Grace said. "I was raised by a few of them, remember? Trust me, they don't make good relationship material."

Mallory squeezed her hand. "Honey, Josh isn't like your family. He's warm and loving."

"Not to mention hot as hell," Amy added.

Grace shook her head. "Sorry, the points are already deducted. And taking into account his schedule, and then the standard deviation from the *average* man's schedule, I figure ninety percent of his time would go elsewhere. I'd never get uninterrupted coitus."

"Penis math," Amy said. "Impressive." She looked at Mallory. "See, this is why a guy shouldn't date an accountant."

"I'm not an accountant," Grace corrected. "I'm a floral-delivery-girl-slash-model-slash-babysitter."

"Slash doctor's sort-of girlfriend?" Amy asked.

Both she and Mallory cracked up.

Grace grabbed a cupcake, stood, and headed to the door.

"Aw," Amy called after her. "At least grab a second one for Josh. Chocolate is the next best thing to sex..."

Chapter 16

*If at first you don't succeed,
have chocolate and try again.*

*M*uch later that night, Grace was lying in the bed of
the guesthouse. The sheets were soft, and she could tell
they'd been washed in the same detergent as Josh's because her nipples got hard at the scent. When she found
herself pressing her face to them instead of sleeping, she
got out of bed and strode to the windows.

The night was hot. Muggy. The lights in the big house
had been off when she'd gotten back from the diner. She
knew Toby had gone to a friend's house to sleep for the
night. She had no idea where Josh was; either he was out
or he was sleeping.

Anna could be anywhere.

Just in front of her, the pool gleamed, the water looking dark and inviting. Grace stripped out of her camisole
and panties and pulled on a bathing suit. She'd just go
cool off, and maybe then she could sleep. To help with
that, she grabbed the bottle of wine Lucille had given her

the other day. She found a corkscrew in the kitchen but couldn't locate a wineglass. No problem. She simply took the entire bottle with her and headed outside, where she sat on the edge of the pool and let her feet dangle in the water.

Heaven.

She watched the moon and stars and sipped wine for a while, wondering if this counted as fun. It felt decadent and different. But fun?

Maybe if she wasn't alone.

Maybe if Josh was with her...

That was a disconcerting thought, so she took another sip of the wine, set the bottle at her hip, and slipped into the pool with hardly a ripple.

It felt so good that she dived deep. The deliciously cool water rushed over her body, instantly bringing down her body temp. She swam a few laps, then lazily floated to the far side of the pool. She leaned on the edge, kicking gently, looking out at the rising moon, sipping more wine. Eventually she realized that some time had gone by and that there was now a light on in the big house. Her dreamy haze was interrupted by a disturbance in the water at the other end of the pool, and suddenly Josh was there, emerging at her side.

Her heart stopped, then started again when he leaned close, the heat of his body instantly enveloping her even as the chlorine-scented water rushed off his face and shoulders. He could stand up here where she couldn't, the water hitting him midchest.

Their eyes met. His lashes were wet and spiky, his eyes dark and deep and intense. He didn't speak, and neither did she. Reaching out, he stroked the wet hair at her temple, drawing his finger slowly down her cheek to the corner of her mouth, his gaze following the movement.

Suddenly the cool water felt as heated as the air around them, and she shivered. "Josh—"

He put a finger over her lips, then paused for a beat before lowering his face to hers. Replacing his finger with his mouth, his tongue traced the line of her lower lip.

She heard a moan. Hers, of course, low and throaty as Josh's hands slid up her back. Using the water's momentum to curl her into his chest, she fell into him willingly. He nuzzled her neck, his lips warm against her now-chilled skin, and she sucked in a breath.

Lifting his head, he met her gaze. His fingers cradled her head so he could run his lips along her jawline to the soft skin of her neck. Oh, God. His tongue there, right there on the vulnerable spot beneath her ear, and just like that, he had her.

Whatever he wanted…anything. Because she wanted it too.

He kissed her, slow and hungry and powerful, and the night, the moon, the stars, everything spun all around her. He deepened the kiss, turning it into a second one and then a third, and then so many more she lost count, his warm hands brushing her breasts and then her bare nipples.

He'd untied and removed her bikini top.

He raised his head, and she arched in the moonlight, wanting him to touch her some more, wanting his mouth on her.

But he just looked at her, and she couldn't tell what he was thinking. Needing some more liquid courage, she reached for the wine bottle, but he took it gently from her fingers. Watching her intently, he took a sip from the bottle, and then another, drinking more deeply. Catching up.

She couldn't take her eyes off him.

He set the bottle down and kissed her. His mouth was chilled from the wine, but fiery desire flamed through her, through him, too, if the groan that rumbled up from his chest meant anything. He offered her another sip from the bottle, then drank again himself. Lifting her up, he put his lips to her nipple, his fingers dancing down her spine, making her shiver. Everything he did felt so sensual, so slow and dreamlike.

Erotic.

She nearly went over the edge right then and there. With one more touch she might have, but his eyes met hers. They were dark, showing nothing but a reflection of the moon.

Nothing of the man.

She slid her hands up his delicious abs and up to his chest, humming in pleasure at the feel of all the firm muscle at her disposal. It wasn't enough. She needed more. "Josh—"

He kissed her throat, her collarbone, her shoulders as his fingers trailed down her belly, caressing her through the fabric of her bikini bottom. It didn't deter him. He merely slid the material aside and then his fingers touched her, knowingly caressing, then dipping inside her as he kissed her deeply, his tongue mirroring his hand's motion.

Grace pressed tight to him, loving the feel of his hard, wet body against hers, and he *was* hard. Everywhere. She palmed him gently, using her thumb to tease him, and his hips jerked into her touch. Fisting a hand in her hair, he kissed her harder, his mouth searing and very serious. "Out of the pool," he finally said, his voice low and commanding. And then he lent his hands to the cause, vaulting himself out in one easy economical movement that had all his muscles bunching. Reaching back for her, he pulled her out with no effort at all. "Come on."

She had no idea where to, and she didn't care. She willingly followed.

Josh pulled her wet bod in close. Her skin was deliciously chilled against his and her breath warm against his throat. They ground against each other, and he wasn't sure what she was thinking, but he was sure of one thing.

They were finally doing this.

He kissed her again, swift and rough, and she moaned and clutched at him eagerly.

"Now, Josh," she whispered. "Please now."

Hell yeah. He pulled back and eyed their surroundings. There was the patio table, but one of the legs was faulty. He had two plush lounge chairs only a few feet away, just beneath the terrace, protected by the bushes he'd yet to prune back for the year.

Perfect.

He pulled Grace over to one, nudged her onto it, and followed her down. Her mouth caught his attention first, and he kissed it long and hard, leaving it swollen and wet as he shifted down toward her breasts. He laved at one gorgeously pebbled nipple, loving how that made her gasp. She was making little panting whimpering sounds that were fueling his lust and need to the point of no return. He should stop this and get them inside, but he didn't want to move. The cool air, her hot body squirming beneath his, her hands running over him ev-erywhere she could reach, it all felt so good. He slid a hand to the small of her back, then to her ass, tilting her so that her sweet spot caught his thigh as she rocked her hips. They were still learning about each other, but he was starting to know her body now, and what she needed. Mouth on hers, he set a rhythm, and her legs tightened on him like a vise.

"*Josh.*"

"I know."

Her nails dug into his biceps as she squirmed some more, her breathing gone heavy. Close, he thought, so close, and then she tore her mouth from his. "Oh, God. I'm going to—"

"Come. Do it."

She burst into wild shudders in his arms. Absorbing her cry, Josh held her to him and watched as she rode out the waves of pleasure.

She was the sexiest thing he'd ever seen.

When she finally sagged back onto the lounge, she tugged him down over the top of her. "Tell me you have a condom. You'd better have a condom!"

"In my pocket."

This caused some trouble since his shorts were still drenched from the pool, but she managed to get her fin-gers on the packet when he sat up a little. Slapping his hands away, she insisted on doing the honors herself, which meant that by the time she'd painstakingly rolled the condom down his length, he was quivering, vibrating with need.

"Now," she said, and guided him home.

Nothing had ever felt so good. Then she arched her hips

and he saw fireworks. "Grace," he whispered hoarsely, nipping at her jaw. "We've got to slow down."

"Later."

She was completely out of control, he thought. And she wasn't alone. Already breathing crazily, he set his forehead to hers with a little groan as she continued to rock up against him as he moved within her, trying to get him to speed up.

"Please," she whispered sweetly, her fingers in his hair, her body straining and moving with his in a way that took him straight to the edge. He could feel everything tightening within him as he barreled like a freight train to the end of the line. "Grace, Christ. Don't move."

But of course she kept moving. His fingers dug into her hips, but there was no hope of reining her in. He didn't even know why he'd tried. She drew him deeper into her body, and, he suspected, into her heart and soul.

There was no holding back, not then, and not when she cupped his face and looked up at him, letting him see everything as she burst again. Her eyes went opaque, his name torn from her lips as her muscles contracted, clenching him so tightly it was his undoing. He came right along with her, thrusting hard into her body before finally falling over her in a boneless heap. He tried to pull back but she wouldn't let him, keeping her arms and legs wrapped tight around him. Finally she allowed him to shift his hands from her ass to the lounge, to support his own weight again.

They remained like that for a few long moments, his head resting beside hers on the cushion, breathing the same air, their damp limbs entangled.

It was the most perfect moment he could remember,

and he planned to rewind and repeat the entire experience. Just as soon as he could move.

Grace lay there wrapped up in a big, warm, sated Josh, thinking she'd never felt so amazing when she heard the slider open.

"Hey, Josh?"

Anna.

Grace's head shot up and bashed Josh in the chin hard enough to cause stars to dance in her vision.

"Josh," Anna yelled. "I've been calling you for ten damn minutes!" Oblivious, she rolled outside, staring down at the cell phone in her hand, grabbing up Josh's cell as she passed the patio table where it lay discarded.

"Oh my God," Grace whispered, staring up at Josh in horror, shoving at him, trying to get the big lug off of her.

Josh, of course, didn't budge. There was no budging him unless he wanted to be budged. With his still sleepy, heavy-lidded gaze locked on hers, he spoke over his shoulder to his sister. "Give us a minute."

Anna finally looked up. She had no way of seeing much. The night was dark, only a sliver of a moon. They were in the shadows, and Josh still had his shorts on, preserving most of his modesty. He was completely covering Grace, not that *that* helped any.

Anna narrowed her eyes as if trying to see through the dark, then slapped a hand over her eyes. "*Eww!* Are you *kidding* me?"

"A minute," Josh repeated in his no-nonsense, calm but steely voice.

"Fine. But call your son, who's been demon-dialing you for half an hour." With that, Anna whirled, then wheeled back to the house, dropping Josh's phone onto the table without further word.

Josh dived into the pool's depths to find Grace's bikini top. Once he'd retrieved it, he tied the straps at her back and neck while she adjusted her bottoms. He helped her make sure everything was back in place because she was pretty much a bowl of jelly. Then he strode directly to his phone and called Toby.

"Well?" Grace asked worriedly when he'd hung up.

"He's fine. He just wants to come home." His gaze met hers. "Grace—"

"If you're going to say you're sorry, please don't. Or if you regret it, or if it was just plain awful and—"

He shut her up with a kiss. A really great kiss, with lots of heat and tongue. When they ran out of air, he pressed his forehead to hers. "I was going to thank you. I needed you tonight. You were there for me."

It took her a moment to understand he didn't mean the sex on the lounge, but when she'd come to his office. What didn't take a moment was the realization that he'd said he needed her. Not someone. Or anyone.

Her.

That this big, strong, proud man who never needed anyone had said such a thing moved her far more than she'd expected. Reaching up, she cupped his jaw. "You were having a bad day?"

"A bad year." He hesitated, then covered her hand with his. "I sold my practice to the hospital tonight."

She controlled her instinctive gasp. "You did?"

"Yeah."

She was blown away. "Are you okay?"

He brought her hand to his mouth and kissed her palm.

"At the moment, I don't have much blood in my brain to be anything but very okay."

She smiled.

He smiled back, then kissed her. "'Night, Grace."

"'Night."

Chapter 17

Chocolate is nature's way of making up for Mondays.

Josh went through several straight days of craziness at work. He never second-guessed his decision to sell, but there was no immediate magic opening of his schedule. After the smoke cleared, there were a hell of a lot of people who wanted to talk to him. His staff was safe; that had been a nonnegotiable condition of the contract. Everyone still had jobs, status quo.

But even though he'd discussed it ahead of time with everyone in his office, now that it had been done, they all needed reassurance. Josh understood that, but it didn't help with the insanity, which also included more hospital board meetings. The board had been ecstatic about his decision, and as planned, they brought in another doctor to lighten the load.

Dr. Tessa McGinley. Josh knew her. They'd gone through residency together. Though they were the same age, Tessa had a warm, almost grandmotherly appeal to her that made her seem twice his age. She wasn't made for ER work, but that was a benefit as far as Josh was concerned, since he coveted the ER. The bottom line was that Tessa had been tailor-made for a practice like his, where patient care was the number-one priority.

Best yet, starting tomorrow, she'd be splitting Josh's days at the office, giving him room to add more ER shifts. More time for Toby.

A life.

He thought about that as he dealt with four flu sufferers, three routine physicals, two cases of strep, and a partridge in a pear tree. He thought about a lot of things, such as Grace. He hadn't seen her since the night they'd christened his lounge chair. He had no idea what her plans were, but his were leaning toward Operation: Get Her Alone in the Pool Again.

But he was gritty-eyed with exhaustion. He thought maybe he could lie down on his bed and sleep for the rest of his life.

Going to get better now, Josh told himself. Starting tomorrow. Tomorrow he wouldn't be too tired to give something more to the people in his life.

For now, he left work and headed to the pier. It was the night of the Summer Festival, an annual event featuring music, food, and booths from the local merchants. He'd promised Mallory that he'd put in an hour at the Health Services Center booth, making nice and taking blood pressure readings for the passersby.

In exchange, and since Grace had gone for another interview in Portland—something he didn't want to think about too much—Mallory had arranged for a babysitter for Toby. Thanks to the teen center that she ran as a part of the HSC, she had lots of money-hungry teenagers at her disposal, and tonight she'd lined him up with Riley. Riley wasn't a local girl but a teen Amy had rescued from the streets not too long ago.

Toby loved her.

So with Toby taken care of, Josh arrived at the pier. The hot, muggy day had turned into a hot, sultry night, and he rolled up his sleeves as he walked through the salty ocean air. He spent an hour in the booth, taking the blood pressure of every senior citizen in Lucky Harbor. When it was Lucille's turn, she merely winked at him when he suggested her blood pressure was a little too high and that she needed to slow down some.

"I'll slow down when I'm dead," she said, and waved in her entire blue-haired posse for their turn. Mrs. Tyler asked how Josh felt about cougars, and he really hoped she meant the kind in the wild.

Mrs. Munson grabbed his ass.

Mrs. Dawson asked him for a breast exam.

Josh was thinking about moving to the South Pacific and living on a deserted island beach when Dr. Tessa McGinley showed up to relieve him.

"Careful," he warned her. "They bite."

She was just over five feet, adorably round, and had one of those contagious smiles. "Want me to defend your honor?" she asked, laughing at him.

"You think I'm joking. I'm telling you, stay on your toes."

She didn't look perturbed in the slightest. "I think I can handle anything that comes up."

Josh was thinking *good luck* when Matt and Ty rescued him. The sun was sinking on the water, and the festival was kicking into high gear as the three of them sat on the pier near the dance floor.

"Hey," Ty said, toasting Josh with his beer. "Heard you got lucky."

Josh scowled. "How the fuck did you hear that?"

Ty went still for a beat and then laughed. "I meant regarding getting Dr. McGinley as a partner. But let's talk about what you thought I meant."

Josh slouched in his chair. "Let's not."

Ty and Matt were grinning at him, the assholes. "Shut up," he said without any real heat, and watched the dancers. Amy and Grace were dancing together in the center of the rambunctious crowd.

Matt was watching Amy. "Amy's worried that Grace'll take the first decent job to come along simply because it's what she's been told she should do," he said. "Rather than follow what makes her happy."

Josh had worried about the same thing. But it wasn't his deal to decide for Grace what made her happy. "And?"

"And so, if something or someone is making her happier than a fancy job but is being a pussy about saying so, he should step up."

Josh shook his head. "You don't know what you're talking about."

Matt laughed. "I'm currently 'getting lucky' every single day because I stepped up. I think I know what I'm talking about."

"I'm not you," Josh said. "And Grace isn't looking for that kind of relationship. Being here is a diversion for her, nothing more."

"Bullshit," Matt said. "Women don't work that way."

"Okay," Josh said. "So maybe I'm not looking for that kind of relationship either."

"More bullshit," Matt said, shaking his head at Ty like, *Can you believe this idiot?*

Ty pointed his beer at Josh. "Want to know what I think?"

"No," Josh said.

"I think you have a case of being a little girl. Maybe you should prescribe yourself a heavy dose of man-the-fuck-up."

Josh rolled his eyes as the two of them laughed their asses off over how clever they were. He turned to the dance floor again, watching Grace move with an easy rhythm.

Last night, she'd arranged for two babysitter interviews for him, vanishing instead of taking part in the interview process. He hadn't understood until he'd talked with Jenna Burnett and Sierra Hennessy. Jenna had wanted to know how much downtime they would get to spend together without "the kid," and Sierra had wanted to discuss his stance on prenups.

Not a big surprise that neither were going to work out.

He had two more interviews for tomorrow, and he wasn't sure he had any faith that either of them would be any more right for them than Jenna or Sierra had been. He knew he needed to step up and get more involved in the interview process because the clock was ticking down. Any day now, Grace was going to find a job, and she'd stop playing Mary Poppins.

He'd deal with it. He'd pick up the pieces and go on. But for now, watching her move so gorgeously and easily to the music, he wished time would stop. She wore a

lacy camisole top, one of those sheer numbers, with another camisole beneath it, showing off lean, toned arms.
Her skirt was short and made of a lightweight gauzy material that flirted with her thighs and blew his brain cells
right and left. Her strappy sandals had heels, making her
bare legs look long and sleek. The need to start at her toes
and lick his way up those legs to the promised land was
strong.

"You might be too much of a pussy to claim *your*
woman," Matt said, rising to his feet, "but I'm not." He
headed for Amy, moving in close to her, reaching out to
tuck a stray strand of hair behind her ear.

Josh watched Grace smile at the couple as she moved
aside, leaving room for Matt to wrap his arms hard
around Amy.

Josh pushed to his feet and met Grace on the edge of
the dance floor.

She smiled. "You dance?"

He gave her a boogie move that had gotten him laid
once or twice in college and made her laugh. "I didn't
know," she said.

"There's a lot you don't know about me."

"Like the time you and the sheriff got drunk and went
streaking on the pier?" she asked sweetly.

He sighed. "Why do you listen to Anna?"

She was grinning wide. "Did you really?"

"Yeah." He grimaced, making her laugh again.

"Honesty," she said. "I like that. Is lying against the
doctor's oath or something?"

"Hell, no. I lie all the time. Just tonight, on the walk
from my car to the pier, I told Mrs. Lyons that she was
looking good."

"Is she the one wearing the chartreuse green spandex shorts?"

"Yes," he said. "And for the record, we were stupid punk-ass seventeen-year-olds who thought we had something to show off to the world."

"Oh, you *do* have something to show off, Dr. Scott."

Shaking his head, he reached for her, pulling her into him as the music slowed. She fit against his body like the last pieces of a puzzle, and he felt himself relax for the first time in days.

"So what are some of your other lies?" she asked.

"Hmm…" He thought about it. He'd just lied to Ty and Matt about this being nothing more than a diversion. Not that he planned on saying *that*. Which probably counted as yet another lie. "This morning I told Toby that Santa Claus was alive and well and making toys as we speak."

"Aw. That's sweet, Josh."

His jaw was pressed to hers. He could feel her thighs and breasts pressing against him. She had one arm wound up around his neck, her fingers playing in his hair, making him want to purr like a big cat. "Sweet," he repeated.

"Yeah." She nudged closer. "*Sweet*."

"I'm not feeling sweet, Grace."

She very purposely rocked against the zipper of his pants. A zipper that was slightly strained. "Mmm. I suppose not," she murmured. "Just as well, really. Sweet's overrated."

Then she rocked again, laughing softly when he tightened his grip on her. He had a hand low on her back, itching to go lower, to run up her bare leg and beneath her skirt. He'd been thinking about doing that, or some version of it, all damn day. For two damn days really, ever since the pool, when he'd had her bare, wet body in his hands.

Scratch that. He'd been thinking about getting his hands on her since he'd accidentally hired her to walk Tank and gotten the call that she'd lost the dog. He could still see her, standing on the beach, her sundress plastered to her like a second skin, completely see-through.

She'd looked like a sun-kissed goddess.

Another couple bumped into them. Lucille and Mr. Wykowski. Mr. Wykowski was eighty, but he had all his own teeth and still had a driver's license, so every female senior citizen in Lucky Harbor was constantly chasing him. He winked at Josh. "It's a night for getting lucky, eh, boy?"

Josh met Grace's gaze as the other couple had danced off. "It's a night for something," he said.

The music was shifting again, gearing up for a faster-paced song. Night was upon them, the sun a mere memory on the horizon. All around them people danced, laughed, talked, drank. No one was paying them any attention, so Josh took Grace's hand and led her off the dance floor.

The bar was run by an old friend, Ford Walker.

"How's it going?" Ford asked. "Hear the little guy is doing great."

"Student of the week," Josh said proudly. He looked at Grace. "A drink?"

"A beer, please."

Ford served them up two longnecks. "So now that you're going to have all this free time, I can finally get you on our basketball team, right? Three on three. It's been just me and Jax ever since Sawyer pussied out. Pulled his Achilles. We need your height."

"Count me in," Josh said, and took Grace down the pier, lit by strings of white holiday lights that twinkled in the dark. Instead of walking to the end, where they'd be highlighted as if they were in a fishbowl, he directed her to the wood stairs that led down to the beach.

The sand was damp and giving, the water pounding the shore hard enough to drown out most of the sounds of the festival as they walked and sipped their beers. It'd been a long week, a big week. A week of irrevocable change. Josh had made a lot of mistakes in his life, and he'd tried to learn from all of them. He definitely tried to not repeat them.

Hiring Grace had been his favorite mistake so far. That he'd gotten to this place where he'd sold the practice and was going to live his life in a way far more suited to him was because of her. Even knowing she was going to leave, he still felt that way. "Have you heard back from any of the jobs you've interviewed for?" he asked, trying to sound neutral.

"I think Seattle and Portland are both going to offer. They're both good, strong opportunities in my field."

He wasn't the only one who sounded carefully neutral. She had her face averted. He tilted her head up and searched her eyes. "Is that what you want?" he asked.

"I'm working on figuring that out." Her gaze was unguarded, letting him see her hopes and dreams and doubts and fears. It was the last that got him.

She was at the proverbial fork in the road, and he'd been there, right there, wanting to do the best thing, the *right* thing. "I gave up my dad's expectations for me when I sold the practice," he said quietly. "I let it all go, knowing, or at least hoping, he'd understand." He paused.

"Maybe you need to give up your parents' expectations and do what's right for you."

She drew in a deep breath and nodded. "I know. But I've been living for their expectations so long, it's taking me some time to figure out what mine are."

Around them, the ocean continued to batter the shore. The silence was comfortable as he took in the fact that oddly enough, their problems weren't all that different from one another.

·"How about you?" she asked after a few minutes. "What do you want for yourself?"

What did he want? For things to be different. For this to be what *she* wanted. "I want to have time to breathe."

"You think that will happen now?"

"Christ, I hope so," he said. "I haven't seen enough of Toby."

"I helped him with his homework earlier," she said. "It was that family tree thing." She paused. "You and his mom weren't married?"

"No. Technically, we weren't even dating."

"A one-night stand?" she asked.

"Sort of."

She gave him an expectant look, and he blew out a breath. Was he really going to do this? He *never* did this. "You don't know this about me," he said. "But I wasn't exactly the cool kid on the block growing up."

"I do know. You were the late-bloomer nerd."

He sighed, and she smiled. "People like to talk about you," she said.

Yeah, and how he loved that. "Well, nothing much changed for me between being that kid who'd get stripped and tied to the flagpole and graduating high school."

"What?" She straightened, eyes flashing fury for the kid he'd been. "Who did that to you?"

"Easy, Tiger. I'm just saying, you grow up getting picked on, you aren't exactly prepared when the summer before college you suddenly grow a foot and women start paying attention to you. Then add a few years and the initials M. and D. after your name, and it gets even worse."

She blinked. "So women started throwing themselves at you? That must have eased your pain quite a bit."

Yeah. A lot, actually. But it didn't mean he'd instantly known what he was doing. "I met Toby's mom at a friend's wedding. She was from Dallas, and just in town for the weekend." It'd been the day from hell. He'd lost his first patient that day, a teenager who'd coded out on the table from an overdose before Josh could help him. Josh had gone to the wedding in a fucked-up frame of mind. Aided by a few beers, a beautiful stranger, and apparently one faulty as-hell condom, he'd done his best to forget the day.

Which had turned out to be impossible. "Ally had been working as a waitress to earn enough money to go to Nashville and have a singing career," he said. Wildly enthusiastic about everything, she'd sucked him in like a crazy breath of fresh air from the only life he'd been living at the time—the hospital. She'd done everything big—live, laugh, love. And God, that had been his undoing, her abundant passion. He'd fallen for her, hook, line, and sinker. "When she found out she was pregnant, things changed."

"Did she stay in Lucky Harbor to be with you?"

"For a little while." Josh had thought Ally would come to love him, too, but love hadn't been the draw for her.

She'd liked the idea of being a doctor's wife and had figured it'd pay off better than being a singer. "She was going to have a perfect life," he said, "but she figured out pretty quickly that I was about as far from perfect as one could get. Not to mention already married—to my job."

Grace's eyes flashed with fire again, but when she finally spoke, her voice was gentle. "So what happened?"

"Toby was born. I caught him, actually, held him in my hands and cut the cord." His heart still caught at the memory, every single time. One minute he'd been living the selfish life that came with his job, the life he'd always wanted. And the next, he'd been holding this gloppy, squirming, pissed-off little rug rat. He'd held Toby in his hands, stared down into his own dark eyes, and had felt something open wide deep inside him.

Then Toby had yawned and gone to sleep on him. "He changed my entire life." Ally's too, but in a different way. She hated the 24/7 care the baby demanded. She hated the changes in her body. She hated that Josh was gone so much working. "One day I came home after a brutal double shift, and Ally handed me Toby. Said he was changed and fed. Then she grabbed her keys and her purse and walked out the door."

She hadn't looked back, not once in the past five years.

Grace looked horrified. "So she left you alone with Toby? She just walked away from you?"

"I really was a pretty crappy partner," he said. "I was at work all the time. And she wasn't cut out for the domesticated sort of home life a baby required."

"But to just leave you and Toby. That must have been awful for you."

"I didn't have much time to dwell. A month later, a

drunk driver hit my dad's car head-on and killed both him
and my mom. And then Anna came to live with me too."

"Oh my God, Josh."

He shrugged. Yeah, those first two years with Toby and
Anna and his work had been a deep, dark hell. He didn't
like to remember the terror of having a baby, of dealing
with Anna's injuries, not to mention her mental state—
which hadn't been anything close to the downright sunny
nature she displayed now in comparison.

Grace was quiet a moment. "Did you know I've never
even so much as had a dog?"

He smiled, rubbing his jaw against her hair, loving that
she wasn't going to shower him with sympathy that he
didn't want. "That fact wasn't on your dog flyer."

She let out a low laugh. "My parents were too busy
trying to save the world to have pets. I'm surprised they
made time to adopt me. I have this recurring nightmare
where I've turned into a rocket scientist and my ass has
gone flat."

He laughed, and the hand he had low on her spine slid
down a little, giving her a quick squeeze. "It's perfect."

She smiled up at him.

"What?"

"I like your laugh," she said.

"Maybe it's the hand on your ass that you like."

"Why, Dr. Scott, are you flirting with me?"

"Desperately," he said. "Is it working?"

She laughed. "Depends on the end goal. And also, if it
matches my end goal."

"Maybe you should spell yours out for me. Slowly and
in great detail."

She smiled, a demure little smile that belied the heat

in her eyes, and hell if the woman didn't turn him completely upside down and sideways.

And turn him on...

Then she went up on her very tiptoes and leaned in, her lips brushing his earlobe as she did what he'd suggested, telling him in detail *exactly* what her end goal was.

He nodded solemnly, memorizing everything, every last little detail, before taking her hand and heading up the stairs.

Chapter 18

Chocolate is better than sex. It can't make you pregnant, and it's always good.

Grace had to take three steps for every one of Josh's much longer strides, but she was laughing as she did. "Gee, Dr. Scott, in a hurry?"

He didn't bother to answer her, just continued to steer them across the sand with the single-minded purpose of a man on a mission. She laughed again, and he tossed a look over his shoulder at her that had her swallowing the amusement and shivering in anticipation.

All her life she'd done what was expected, taken the "right" path. But Lucky Harbor, and her time in it, was supposed to be different.

She'd made it different. She'd made it hers. She'd never forget it.

Or him. "Where are we going?" she asked.

"Somewhere more secluded than this."

"And the hurry?" she asked.

"I want to get you alone before you forget any of your end game or we're interrupted again."

"No worries," she said. "I was very serious about my end game."

Their eyes caught. "Thought you don't do serious," he said. "You do fun."

"Is that what you're looking for tonight?"

His gaze was fathomless. "It's a start."

She quivered. "I need to tell Mallory and Amy I'm leaving. Give me a minute?"

"I'll get the car."

Grace found Amy and Matt sitting at a booth sharing a pitcher of beer and trying to swallow each other's tongues. Since Mallory and Ty were still on the dance floor doing the same thing, Grace texted them both without disturbing them. This had the additional benefit of not having to explain that she intended to go do the same thing that they were doing.

Heading toward the lot, she walked past a bunch of tables, all filled with people enjoying the night. Something niggled at her, and she turned back, realizing that one of the people was Devon.

With a girl who wasn't Anna.

Grace stared at him in shock. "What are you doing?"

Devon turned away, pulling the girl with him into the shadows, and in another heartbeat they were gone, vanishing into the night.

Grace wondered if Anna was here as well, but she hadn't seen her all night. It'd probably be impossible to maneuver around the crowded pier and the beach in her chair. Not only was the girl missing out on the festival, but also her boyfriend was a rat-fink bastard. Grace turned to walk away and plowed into a brick wall.

A brick wall that was Josh's chest.

"Hey," he said, catching her. "I got held up." He took a second look at her. "What's wrong?"

She couldn't tell him, not here. He and Anna rarely saw eye to eye on anything, *especially* Devon, which was mostly due to his fiercely protective instincts, not to mention the fact that Devon was a complete ass. If Grace gave Josh proof of that right now, she wasn't sure exactly what he'd do, but he'd do *something*.

And then there was how Anna would feel to not be the first to hear about Devon's indiscretions, "Nothing's wrong," she said.

Josh didn't buy it, but he didn't push either. He obviously had other things on his mind at the moment. Such as getting her alone.

On the way to the car, they were stopped multiple times by people wanting to tell Josh their ailments. Everyone wanted to talk to him, to let him know that their throat hurt, or that they were feeling better, or that they planned on calling his office for an appointment next week.

"How do you do it?" she marveled. "How do you keep track of everyone's various ailments and quirks and needs?"

"I don't know. I guess I've always had a good memory. My brain retains everything, even really stupid, useless stuff."

"Yeah?" she asked. "Everything?"

"Just about."

"What was I wearing that day you hired me?"

"White lace panties."

She laughed. "What?"

"You were all wet from the water. Your dress was sheer."

"That's not your brain's memory," she said. "That's your *penis's*."

He grinned and leaned in to nip at her bottom lip. "I love it when you say *penis* in that prim schoolteacher tone, like you're saying a forbidden word in public."

She felt herself blush. "What would you rather I call it?"

His eyes darkened. "We'll go over our body parts, and what they like to be called, in great detail tonight. But we have to get out of here first. The key is lack of eye contact. Don't look at anyone. I don't care if it's God himself, just keep moving, got it?"

"Yes, sir."

"I like that. More of that," he said.

"Um, excuse me, Grace?" It was Mindy, who owned the florist shop that Grace delivered for. She sent both Josh and Grace a shy smile. "I hope I'm not interrupting…"

The look on Josh's face was resigned, but to his credit he did make respectful eye contact. "It's okay," he said.

Mindy relaxed slightly. "It's just that I haven't been sleeping."

Josh let out a breath. "I have office hours tomorrow," he said. "From eight to—"

"Actually"—she turned to Grace—"it's you I need to talk to. I need some bookkeeping help. I heard you're the one in town to go to for this sort of thing. You helped Lucille, Anderson, and Amy, right?"

"Yes, but—"

"I'll pay," Mindy said. "Whatever they're paying."

Since Amy was paying in cupcakes, and Grace needed more cupcakes like she needed another sexually frustrated alpha male standing impatiently at her side, she started to shake her head, but Mindy grabbed her hands.

"It would mean so much to me," she said urgently, "to have someone trustworthy handling my books. My ex, he"—she drew in a shaky breath—"he screwed things up for me financially. Like I said, I really need your help."

Grace felt her stomach clench in sympathy and understanding and nodded. "Okay."

"Oh, thank you. Thank you so much! Now?"

"No," Josh said. "Not now." He took Grace's hand in a firm, inexorable grip. "Tomorrow. She'll help you tomorrow." And he pulled her away, through the crowd, across the lot, once again moving so that she was practically running to keep up with his long legs and relentless stride.

"That was rude," she said breathlessly.

He didn't bother to respond.

"People are going to think we're in a hurry to…"

He slid her a look that said, *We* are *in a hurry to …*

There were people milling around in the lot. One or two called out to Josh, but the man was on a mission and didn't veer from his path.

"Josh," Grace said on a breathless laugh. "Slow down."

He didn't, not even a little. And when several ladies from the drawing class she'd modeled for tried to wave her over, he tightened his grip on her. "No eye contact," he reminded her, and beeped his car unlocked, practically shoving her into the passenger seat. She might have objected to the way he was manhandling her except his big, warm hands were sliding over her body, making themselves at home, and she couldn't quite catch her breath.

He shut the door and was in the driver's seat before she could so much as blink.

"What if those ladies needed to talk to me?" she asked.

"*I* need to talk to you."

She laughed. "You want to talk? Really? Because you're looking a little bit like the big bad wolf over there. But if you want to talk, hey, I'm game." She leaned back in the guise of settling in comfortably. "How was your day?"

Josh reached across the console and pulled her into his lap.

"So it was a good day, then?" she teased.

"Fantastic. Tell me it's about to get even better."

She rocked a little, feeling his arousal beneath her, hard and quite insistent. "Mmm. Maybe..."

"Don't tease me. I'm beyond that."

"Aw. Poor baby."

"I mean it," he said in a low, very serious voice. "If we're interrupted again..."

She laughed. "At least we made it to the end last time."

"That wasn't the end. That was just the beginning." His dark eyes met hers. "A year, Grace. I went without sex for a whole year. I have some moves stored up."

"Yeah?" she asked, breathless at the thought. "Show me."

He covered her mouth with his, sliding a hand into her hair to angle her head the way he wanted it. She was getting to know him, and she knew that he was a man who rarely acted without thinking. His moves were always rational, calm.

Controlled.

But there was nothing controlled about him now as his hands wandered madly from her face to her waist to her hips, ending up back in her hair while he kissed her hard, his tongue tangling with hers.

And suddenly a Josh-induced orgasm right here, right now, seemed like the best idea she'd had all night.

Needing to touch him, Grace wrapped her arms around him and pushed her hands beneath his shirt, encountering sleek, smooth sinew.

His groan rumbled in her ear, and she pressed even closer. He was breathing unevenly, a fact she liked, very much. His hands were busy, the heat of them seeming to scald her skin as they dug into her hips. He was huge and hard and pressed up against her core, which worked for her. He'd completely forgotten their surroundings, which she liked even more. Then his hands slid beneath the hem of her dress, and she forgot their surroundings, too, beginning to pant before he'd even touched anything vital. He moved his lips to her neck, kissing and tracing his magic tongue down her throat as his wandering fingers stroked the wet silk of her panties.

The knock on the window startled them.

It was Lucille, one hand covering her eyes. "Sorry!" she yelled through the glass.

"I know I took an oath to save lives," Josh muttered, "but I'm going to kill her."

Grace scooted back into the passenger seat, desperately righting her clothing as she did. Josh checked her progress, then rolled the window down an inch.

"I'm sorry!" Lucille told him again, eyes still covered. "But a couple of the guys were messing around on the pier, and Anderson fell in. He hasn't surfaced. They're looking for him but—"

Josh was already out of the car. "Call nine-one-one,"

he called back to Grace, and took off running toward the pier.

Grace called 911, then took Josh's keys and locked up his car, moving quickly with Lucille to the water, anxious to know if Anderson had been found. An almost hushed crowd was gathered down on the beach, and they headed that way, taking the stairs as fast as Lucille could move.

There was a huddle in the water, three people making their way toward shore, a figure being carefully supported between them. One of the men was bent over the still one. It was too dark to see what he was doing or even who he was—but Grace knew.

Josh.

He and the others staggered ashore. Josh dropped to his knees, situating the overly still man between them, careful with his neck and spine.

"Oh thank God, they found him," Lucille breathed, and put her hands to her mouth. "I just hope they were in time."

The other men crouched on the opposite side of Anderson, water streaming off all of them. Grace recognized one of them as Sheriff Sawyer Thompson. The other was Ty, Mallory's fiancé. Sawyer borrowed a phone from someone on the beach and was on it, probably to dispatch, while Josh checked for a pulse. He must have gotten one because he nodded to Ty before beginning compressions, his movements quick and efficient.

"Oh no," Lucille whispered, and clutched at Grace. "He's not breathing."

"Josh'll fix it." Grace gripped Lucille's icy fingers and prayed that was true. In her heart, she knew that if Anderson could be saved, Josh was the man to do it.

But Anderson was awfully still, and there was blood on his face and head. He could have broken bones too; she couldn't tell from here but knew Josh was worried about the same thing given the extremely cautious way he'd handled Anderson's body. Just as he stopped to once again check for a heartbeat and pulse, sirens whooped, and red-and-blue flashing lights lit up the night as the ambulance pulled into the lot above.

And then, an even more welcome sound—Anderson choking up seawater, convulsing with the violence of it, his muscles spasming.

Sawyer and Ty let out audible breaths of relief. Sawyer stood up and pushed the crowd back. Ty accepted several jackets from people standing near, using them to cover Anderson.

Josh had deftly turned Anderson on his side to more effectively cough up what looked like gallons of water. As the EMS team ran down the pier stairs and hit the beach, Anderson tried to push himself up but Josh held him down, talking to him quietly.

"Damnit," Lucille said, her eyes glistening, tears of relief on her cheeks. "I can't hear what they're saying."

Grace didn't need to hear to know that Josh was working to keep Anderson calm and still. She was riveted to the sight. All of the men were drenched, but none of them appeared to even notice, worried only about Anderson.

Josh gave out orders to the EMS, and working together they got Anderson on the gurney, covered him in blankets, and then loaded him into the ambulance. Josh hopped into the back alongside his patient, and the doors closed. A minute later, the ambulance pulled out of the lot, lights going, sirens silent.

"Everyone in town is here," Lucille said to Grace. "They won't have any traffic on the road."

Grace nodded a little numbly, struck by the sudden feeling of fragility. Life was fragile.

Short.

Too short. Fingering Josh's keys, she left the pier and drove home. Well, not home exactly, she reminded herself.

Josh's home. Which he'd managed to make for himself and his family in spite of believing that he'd not given them much. It was a good home, too, warm and safe. But for now, tonight, it was silent and dark. Lifeless without Josh in it.

She found Anna by the pool, staring into the moonlit water. "Hey." Grace plopped down on a lounge chair near her. "You missed the action tonight."

"I can't maneuver the pier by myself."

"I'd have helped you."

This had Anna looking at her. "Why?"

"Why? Well, why not?"

"Because I've been a bitch to you."

"Yeah," Grace said. "But you're a bitch to everyone, so I never take it personally."

Anna laughed. It sounded a little rusty. And unhappy. Grace knew that what she had to tell her wasn't going to help. "I think I saw Devon there," she said carefully.

Anna shook her head. "He's in Seattle. At a family thing."

Grace grimaced. "Okay, let me rephrase. I *definitely* saw him at the festival. With a girl."

Anna went still. "Just when I thought I could learn not to hate you."

"If I were you, I'd want to know," Grace said, not hurt by Anna's words. She understood. She might not know firsthand the tragedy of losing her parents and becoming paralyzed, but she knew boy pain.

"You don't know anything about our relationship," Anna said.

"I know you like him." Grace wished Anna would open up to her so she could try to help—although she knew how everyone in the Scott family felt about accepting help. Stubborn to the end, the entire lot of them. "And I know that the way you feel about him means that you don't want him feeling it for someone else."

Anna shook her head but didn't speak as she turned away so Grace couldn't see her face.

Grace's heart squeezed tight. She knew damn well that Devon had been pushing Anna for sex. It didn't take a rocket scientist to figure out that if Anna wasn't ready, then Devon had gone after it somewhere else. "I'm proud of you for not caving to the pressure."

"You don't know what you're talking about," Anna shot back.

"So explain it to me."

"I *want* to cave to the pressure. I want to..."

"Have sex?"

Anna didn't answer, and Grace sighed. "Honey, if you can't even say the word, you're so not ready."

"I am," Anna said unconvincingly, and began wheeling toward the house.

Grace sighed. "If you need anything—"

"I won't."

"If your brother needs anything—"

Anna let out another rusty-sounding laugh, this one

with a hint of tears in it, but she stopped at the door, her back still to Grace. "He won't."

"He had a rough evening," Grace said quietly.

"Yeah, because he called me earlier to check in and told me I needed to stop seeing Devon. I read him the riot act."

"Actually, I didn't know that," Grace said. "I meant that Anderson nearly drowned tonight at the festival, and Josh had to perform CPR to save him."

Anna turned to her, eyes hooded. "That's what Josh does. He saves people."

Grace paused, wondering at the bitterness in Anna's voice. "You say that like it's a bad thing."

Anna was quiet a moment. "Do you think everyone should be saved?" she finally asked.

Okay, they were definitely not talking about Anderson. Grace moved closer. "Anna—"

"I'm fine. We're Scotts. We're always fine. Haven't you learned that yet?"

When Anna had rolled into the house, Grace pulled out her cell phone and called the hospital, inquiring after Anderson. She was told that no information could be given out about a patient, so she went to the next best source.

Facebook.

Luckily, Lucille was already on the case:

Thanks to the swift, heroic measures of Dr. Josh Scott, one of our very own was saved tonight.

Anderson, manager of Anderson Hardware Store, fell off the pier, hitting the water and his head. He'd have drowned if not for the three men who dived into the dark ocean after him: Sheriff

Sawyer Thompson, flight care paramedic Ty Garrison, and Dr. Josh Scott.

And, oh my, can I just say how incredibly handsome these three hunks looked all wet and sweaty from their efforts?

Anderson's at General, suffering a mild concussion, broken ankle, and probably a few sore ribs.

Thanks, Dr. Scott. You are one Hunkalicious Doctor.

Anderson, get well. And stay off the pier!

Grace logged off, crawled into bed, and hoped that wherever he was, Josh had at least gotten some dry clothes.

She had no idea how long she'd been out when she awoke suddenly, heart pounding in the dark. She peered at her cell phone on the nightstand.

Midnight.

She sat up just as a soft knock sounded on her door. Padding barefoot across the room, she peered out the peephole.

Dark, disheveled hair. Dark and shadowed eyes. Scrubs. Grace's heart kicked hard as she opened the door to one clearly exhausted Dr. Josh Scott.

Chapter 19

A chocolate in the mouth is worth two on the plate.

Josh had told himself he was going straight to bed. He needed the sleep. But his body got its wires crossed, and he ended up at the guesthouse instead.

Grace answered his knock with a sleep-flushed face and crazy hair, wearing a little tank top and boxers—emphasis on *little*.

Cute.

Hot.

"Anderson?" she asked, brow furrowed, eyes concerned.

He didn't want to talk about Anderson. He wanted Grace naked and screaming his name. But if there was a way to say that without sounding like a complete asshole, he didn't have the brain capacity to find the words. "He's got a hell of a headache and sore ribs, but he's going to be okay."

"That's what Facebook said too," she said. "Are you okay? You must be dead on your feet. Come on, come in and take a load off. My bed's warm."

He raised his head and looked into her sweet baby blues. "Anyone here?"

"No."

"Anyone *due* to be here?"

"No."

"Are you planning on starting a fire with the heater and toaster? Is anyone going to call you and need you to count their money?"

"No." She bit her lower lip to hold back a smile, the sexy witch. "Why? Do you have nefarious intentions?" she asked with a soft hopefulness that had lust and amusement warring for space within him.

He took a step and bumped into her, crowding into her space. "Yes. I have nefarious intentions. Lots of them. You should be running for the hills, Grace."

She held her ground, sliding a hand up his chest, hooking it around his neck, not speaking.

Josh didn't remember moving, but then he had her up against the wall, his arms tight around her, her legs around his waist. "The whole fucking place can come down," he said against her mouth. "We're not stopping."

"Show me," she said.

Grace hadn't meant the words as a dare but Josh appeared to take them that way. He lifted his head and held her gaze, one hand on her ass, the other reaching out to hit the lock on the door. "Phone?"

"On the counter."

Still holding her, he walked over to her phone and shoved it inside the fridge.

"Yours?" she asked.

"DOA from the ocean. Again."

"What if someone needs you?"

"Fuck the rest of the world," he said, his voice thrillingly rough.

She cupped his face and offered him a slow smile. "How about just me?"

His eyes darkened as he backed her to the bed and nudged her onto the mattress. "Tell me you still have condoms."

She rolled to her hands and knees and crawled to the nightstand. He groaned, making her realize the sight she'd just presented. Deciding to own it, she wriggled her hips and was rewarded with another rough sound from him, inherently male, as she yanked open the drawer to reveal a full box of condoms.

"That's a good start," he said, setting a knee on the bed. He moved so fast she didn't have time to react before his warm hand wrapped around her ankle and tugged.

She fell flat, facedown on the bed, laughing when he yanked her toward him, giving her a world-class wedgie. Then he flipped her over to face him. Her cami had risen up a little, and his gaze swept over her body, heating every inch it touched. His deep, rumbling groan was low and possessive, and everything within her quivered.

"Your shirt," she said. She needed it gone, yesterday.

He impatiently tore it off and tossed it behind him.

Oh, that was better, she thought, taking in his broad, sculpted chest, feeling herself go damp at the sight of all those muscles bunching as he moved. *Much* better.

As if reading her mind, his lips curved, sending more heat through her because she knew exactly what those lips could do to her, the places he could take her. He had a way of making her feel sexy, beautiful. Like she was special. He had a way of sending all her doubts scattering, of reinstating her confidence.

Her parents had educated her and made sure that her horizons were broad. But Josh had given her something new.

He made her *feel*.

The soft material of her cami gave him no resistance when he lifted it over her head and sent it sailing somewhere in the direction of his discarded shirt. "Mmm," he said, bending to kiss a breast as he hooked his fingers into the silk boxers low on her hips. They hit the floor next. "Christ, you're beautiful," he said as he stroked a hand up her leg, settling it low on her belly. "And wet." His thumb glided over her, spreading her a little on each pass, making her moan and shift impatiently. But he simply continued to tease and torment, that knowing finger nearly driving her right over the edge. "Please..." she finally gasped.

"After you come."

"But—"

"Shhh." Then he dropped to his knees beside the bed, pulled her to the edge, and put his mouth on her. The first stroke of his tongue shot her heart rate to the moon. "Did you just...*shush* me?" she barely managed to ask.

He pulled back just enough to blow a breath over her, making her shiver and moan and pant. "There's a code," he said. "A guy code."

Her only response was a throaty moan because his tongue was back. And good Lord, she could no more ignore that tongue than she could have stopped breathing.

"The guy code says you get yours first," he said.

She opened her mouth to say something to that, she

had no idea what, but all that came out was a low, desperate cry as he very gently nibbled at her.

And then not so gently.

And in less time than it would take to make toast and screw up the electricity, she nearly burst out of her skin. "*How* do you always do that?" she gasped.

"I know your body." He climbed onto the bed, caressing his way up her thighs, wrapping her legs around his hips. "I love your body."

And she loved his. "I hope the guy code says it's time."

He smiled as he cupped her butt in one hand. Leaning over her, his other hand slid up her back and into her hair as he whispered, "Yeah, it's time." He pressed a kiss at her damp temple, her cheek, her mouth, while she lay still trembling in little aftershocks from the orgasm. Lacing their fingers together, he slid their hands up over her head, and then executed a slow grind against her that had her eyes closing from the pleasure of the friction.

"Grace," he said softly, nipping at her lower lip until she looked at him. When she did, he kissed her deeper, harder. She could feel the burn low in her belly as she began to rise to peak again. Wrapping her arms around him, she had the sudden, irrational wish that she'd never have to let go. Not exactly in keeping with this being just fun. But then he slid into her in one thrust, and she could no longer think at all. She whimpered for more, and he gave it, slow and steady, until she adjusted to him, then hard and fast as they climbed together. She clutched at him, panting his name, giving herself over to him fully, wondering if he could possibly feel what she was feeling. Which was entirely too much.

His head was thrown back, his big body taut as a bow.

Pressing her harder into the bed, he tightened his grip on her and plunged deep. Moving together in just the right rhythm, her toes curled, and he shuddered against her as they rode each other to a mind-blowing completion.

When he finally sank down over her, muscles quivering, hands still possessively gripping her butt as he fought to catch his breath, she smiled. "Feel better?"

He rolled to his back so that she was straddling him. "Getting there."

A long time later, they were a tangle of damp sheets and exhausted limbs in the warm night. Grace couldn't have moved to save her life.

Josh pulled her in close, wrapped his arms around her, and let out a long, slow breath. Relaxed to the bone, she thought. It gave her a surge of feminine satisfaction that she'd gotten him there and it put a big grin on her face.

"Hmm," he said in a voice so low on the register she could barely hear it. "I'd swipe that smile off your face, but my body isn't working."

"Later," she promised him, hearing the exhaustion in his voice, snuggling in closer, stroking a hand down his back. "Josh?"

"Yeah?"

"Watching you tonight, working so hard to save Anderson..." She shook her head, moved again at the memory. "It was amazing." She snuggled in close and kissed one corner of his mouth, then the other. "I was so proud of you," she whispered.

The words seemed to rejuvenate him. He tugged the sheet from her, an urgent energy behind his movements that resonated within her as well. In a blink of an eye, he was pressing her back into the mattress, the sure and solid weight of his body as comforting as it was arousing.

It felt more right than anything she'd ever felt. *He* felt right.

He came up on his forearms, his eyes locked on hers as he slowly pushed inside her. Unable to keep still, she arched up with a soft gasp, wrapping her legs around his waist.

"So good," he murmured, then lowered himself again, his hands sliding up her back, pulling her in close. "Always so fucking good with you." He brushed his lips over hers, his eyes never leaving her face as he began to move inside her, slowly at first. She met him thrust for thrust, trying to urge him on by biting his lower lip. He hissed in a breath and gripped her hard, holding her still, forcing her to take the slow, tortuous climb, making her feel every single inch of him.

And she did feel him, she felt everything, and when the pure emotion overtook her, she felt her throat tighten, her eyes sting. She sobbed when she burst, feeling his release hit him too. Afterward, he pulled her in tight and held her close. Lulled by the feel of his warm strength, the comforting scent of him surrounding her, she drifted off, with him still buried deep.

Josh knew he needed to get up, but lying here with Grace wrapped around him like he was her own personal body pillow was really doing it for him.

He'd shown up here tonight and pretty much taken what he'd needed from her without a thought to the after. This wasn't supposed to keep happening, and yet it did. And each time, feelings got deeper.

At least for him.

He had no idea what that meant for them now and wasn't all that eager to find out if things had changed between them. Of course they'd changed, because in his experience, right about now was when things tended to go to shit.

"Hey," Grace murmured, her head on his chest, fingers gliding back and forth from pec to pec. "You okay?"

"That was going to be my question to you."

She lifted her head and looked into his eyes. "Nice deflection, Dr. Scott."

He blew out a breath and lay back, staring up at the ceiling. He felt unsure, and that was an extremely new and uncomfortable sensation.

"Are you ... feeling claustrophobic?" she asked. "Maybe contemplating a trip to Australia to go surfing?"

He shook his head at her polite tone. "Not all men are dicks like your exes, Grace."

"Touché. And right back at you."

He tilted his head down and met her gaze. "I haven't dated anyone with a dick."

"You know what I mean."

"Actually, I don't."

"It means," she said, coming up on an elbow to lean over him, eyes flashing, "that I might have called this 'just fun' but that doesn't mean I'd walk away if the going got tough."

God, she was gorgeous when riled up. "So that wasn't some sort of pity fuck?"

She pulled back to stare at him, then laughed, dropping her head to his chest.

"Just what a man loves. Being laughed at in bed."

"I don't do pity fucks," she said, still grinning, pissing

him off a little. "And I especially don't do pity fucks with doctors. Doctors don't need pity fucks."

Some of his annoyance drained away. "What *do* doctors need?"

She climbed on top of him, effectively taking care of the rest of his annoyance. "I'll show you," she said.

It was 3:00 a.m. before Josh could move again, and his blanket—a warm, sated, boneless Grace—murmured in soft protest. He stroked a soothing hand down her back.

She let out a sexy little purr and fell back into a deep sleep. He managed to untangle himself and rolled out of the bed without her stirring.

As he moved around the room searching out the scrubs he'd carelessly discarded earlier, his gaze kept wandering back to the bed. To the woman in it.

Dead to the world.

When he was dressed, he bent over her and brushed a kiss over her mouth. "'Night," he whispered.

She let out a barely there snore that made him smile as he left the guesthouse, carefully locking the door behind him. He entered his house and moved down the hall. Toby's door was open but he wasn't there; he was still at his friend Conner's. Anna's door was also open, and he found his sister sitting in her chair at her bedroom window, staring out into the dark night.

"Hey," he said, startled to see her. She did her best to avoid him these days. Something else he was going to have to fix in all his new spare time that he didn't yet have. "No adventure tonight?" he asked carefully. Something was obviously wrong. Not that she'd tell him.

"Hard to have an adventure on wheels."

His chest ached, and he drew a slow, painful breath. "What adventure would you like to have?"

She sighed, then wheeled to face him. "Don't you ever get tired of trying to make my life work for me?"

"No."

She stared at him and then shook her head. "Well I do. I hate being a pathetic burden."

"Anna, you are smart, attitude-ridden, and scary as hell. You're a lot of other things, too, but you are not, nor have you ever been, a pathetic burden."

She shrugged.

"What if it was me?" he asked her quietly. "Me hurt in the accident. Me in a chair. Would you think of me as a burden?"

"Would I have to wipe your drool?"

He sighed. Her teen years had been hell on wheels. Literally. Once in a while he thought he saw glimpses of the gentler, kinder version of Anna that she'd been as a young girl, but right now wasn't one of those times.

"Fine," she said, caving. "I'd kick your ass every day until you no longer felt sorry for yourself."

"So consider your ass kicked," he said.

"I'm still going to Europe."

He'd done a lot of thinking about this, and the idea of Anna alone in Europe gave him the cold sweats. But she was twenty-one, and the truth was, he couldn't stop her. And he did understand her need to go, to prove her independence. He really did. He just was terrified for her. "You can get adventure closer to home and closer to your support system."

"My support system works twenty-four-seven and doesn't have time for his own life, much less mine."

Guilt sliced him. "That's going to change. You know I sold the practice."

"I'm still doing this."

Since there was nothing to say to that, he turned to go.

"Josh?"

He looked back, wondering what she was going to fling at him now. "Yeah?"

"Thanks."

He was so surprised she could have knocked him over with one little push. "For?" he asked warily.

"For not seeing me as pathetic."

Chapter 20

*Coffee makes it possible to get out of bed but chocolate
makes it worthwhile.*

Josh walked into his office the next day and found his
office staff and Tessa huddled over the scheduling computer. They looked up in unison, paused, and then—still
in unison—grinned.

"Nice," Dee said to him.

"What?" He looked behind him; he was the only one
there.

"You got some," Dee said.

Michelle and Tessa smiled and nodded.

Josh worked at not reacting. He had a good staff, but
they were a pack of vultures. If they sensed a weakness,
they'd attack.

"'Bout time, if you ask me," Michelle said. "So it's a
good day to ask for a raise?"

"I'm thinking you don't have enough work to do," Josh
said in his boss voice.

They all scattered, except for Tessa. "I'm beginning to

see why you signed on the dotted line," she said. "Having a life looks good on you."

The morning went so smoothly that Josh got an actual lunch break. He met Ty and Matt at the Love Shack, Lucky Harbor's bar and grill. They'd beaten him there and were seated at a table hunched over *Cosmo* magazine.

"It was on the table when I got here," Matt said in his defense.

Josh eyed the open magazine. "You don't already know how to satisfy your boyfriends in bed?"

Matt ignored this. "Did either of you know there's ninety-nine ways to give a blow job? That's *ninety-nine* nights of blow jobs."

"Look at you with the math skills," Josh said.

Matt flipped him off while Ty flipped the page. " '*How to Give Your Hoo-Ha a Spa Day*.' Huh," he said. "I didn't know a woman's hoo-ha needed a spa day."

Ford came out from behind the bar to take their order. "Saw you on FB," he said to Josh.

"Ty was a part of the rescue too."

"I meant with the pretty babysitter at your son's Back-to-School night." Ford laughed. "Caught by Lucille, huh? Gotta be stealth, man. Geriatric stealth."

Josh didn't bother to sigh. "Like you didn't get on Facebook all last year when you started seeing Tara."

At this, Ford let out an unabashed grin, because they all knew it was true. While dating Tara, he'd found himself in the middle of an all-out whose-dick-is-bigger contest with her ex, which had been splashed across the entire town like it'd been first-line news. Ford was a world-class sailing pro and had a gold medal and buckets of money, but to this day, he was most famous for that abs contest, which had been legendary. As had the fallout, which had involved Ford breaking his leg climbing an apple tree to impress the girl.

"At least I didn't end up in my ER getting my leg set in a cast," Josh said.

Ford laughed good-naturedly and took their order. When he was gone, Matt looked at Josh. "So how's it going with your Grace anyway? Still having fun playing house?"

He'd been working at not replaying every detail of last night in his head over and over again. Working, and failing. Last night had been... incredible. "Says the guy who just put a rock on his girlfriend's finger."

Matt shrugged. "Turns out I like commitment. Who knew?"

"Yeah? And what's your excuse?" Josh asked Ty.

Ty's lips curved. "I took a page from your book."

"Mine?"

"I like the idea of the whole family thing, like you have with Toby and Anna. I want that. I want that with Mallory."

Their food came, and while Josh ate his chicken sandwich, he thought of his "whole family thing." He had his sister, who missed their mom and dad like she missed her own legs and was dating a first-class asshole. His son, who had spent far too many nights going to bed without any parent at all. The family unit everyone thought he had wasn't what it was supposed to be, and that killed him.

He'd made the first step—selling the practice. He only hoped he'd done it in time to repair his relationships. It wasn't something he could write a prescription for.

He couldn't order a scan and diagnose a solution. "I've fucked it up."

"Yeah?" Ty asked. "With the hot nanny?"

"No." *Yes*. "Never mind."

"That's the first sign of losing it," Ty said. "Disagreeing with yourself. And trust me, I should know."

Josh managed a brief smile at the memory of Ty coming apart at the seams not so long ago but Matt kept his eyes on Josh. Concerned.

"Stop," Josh said to him. "I'm not losing it."

"Maybe you should."

"Huh?"

"You're wrapped pretty tight," Matt said. "You should get in the ring with one of us. Release some tension."

"I've seen you two in the ring," Josh said. "It's like Extreme Cagefighting. On steroids. I like being able to walk out of the gym after a workout."

"One time," Ty said. "I only needed help one time. And it's because he sucker punched me."

Matt smiled smugly. "That's what happens when you stop to take a call from your fiancée when you're still in the ring."

"I'm not getting in the ring," Josh said, and stood. He dropped cash on the table. "I've got to get back."

His waiting room was calm and quiet. The front desk was calm and quiet. Everything was calm and quiet.

"There's no one waiting for me?" he asked Michelle.

"Tessa's got it moving along pretty good."

He eyed the schedule. "What about Mrs. B?"

"Oh, she's already been seen. She had some arthritic flare-up."

Josh was stunned. Mrs. B. had never been willing to

see anyone else before. "And Lisa Boyles? She was bringing in her three kids for sports physicals."

"Tessa finished early and offered to see them, and Lisa took her up on it. That's who she's with right now."

"Okay..." He felt a little off center. "I'll go get some charting done."

"Sure."

But when he got to his office and sat down, the charting didn't appeal. Where was a fast-paced ER emergency when he needed one? Anderson couldn't fall off the pier now?

He saw patients that afternoon but it remained quiet and sedate. Not at all what he was used to.

But what you wanted...

Except suddenly he wasn't keeping the world going around. It was going around without him, all on its own.

And he didn't know if he liked it.

That night for the first time in months, Josh got home in time for dinner. He walked into his house and blinked. His living room had been turned into a fort. Blankets and sheets had been stretched across the couches, tucked into the entertainment center, into shelves, anywhere and everywhere. He crouched down, and yep, it was filled with what appeared to be every single toy Toby owned.

He entered the kitchen to find Toby and Grace sitting on the counter, eating chocolate cupcakes. Josh met Grace's gaze, and the air did that unique crackle thing while her slow smile brought back memories of the night before.

Slow hands. Deep, wet, unending kisses. Bodies hot and damp and meshed together. Heady, erotic pleasures...

"Daddy, *cupcakes*!" Toby said.

"I'm sorry." Josh pretended to scrub out his ear. "Was that *English*?"

Toby grinned.

Josh pulled him up for a hug and came away a little sticky. "You're supposed to eat the dessert, not bathe in it."

This earned him another grin. "Try it!" Toby demanded, holding out his cupcake.

Josh took a bite, and he had to admit that the soft, spongy chocolate cupcake was pretty damn amazing. He took another bite, pretending to go for Toby's fingers, earning him a belly laugh.

Best sound ever. He started laughing as well when he turned and found Grace watching them with a smile. "Hope you don't mind," she said. "It's a backward dinner."

"We *love* backward dinners!" Toby said.

They'd never had a backward dinner.

Tank was sitting on the floor at Toby's feet. He let out a loud "arf!" followed by a pathetically sad whine.

"He's sad 'cause Grace said he can't have chocolate," Toby said. "Chocolate's bad for dogs. They go like this…" He mimed choking on his own tongue, complete with bugging-out eyes and the sound effects to go with it, before dramatically falling off the stool to the floor. There he kicked once, twice, and then "died."

"Nice," Josh said.

Toby smiled proudly and sat back up as Tank climbed into his lap, licking his face.

"We don't feel sorry for Tank," Grace told Josh. "He got his dessert."

"He ate a bag of powdered sugar," Toby said.

Josh looked at the tiny Tank. "When you say bag of powdered sugar…"

"The *entire* bag, including the paper." Grace shook her head. "He has an eating disorder."

They all looked at Tank, who snorted, then burped, emitting a little puff of white.

"You gonna eat with us, Daddy?" Toby asked. "We're having mac and cheese!"

"My favorite," Josh said dryly.

Toby grinned. "No, it's *my* favorite."

Josh thought about the nutritional content of the un-opened box of mac and cheese on the counter, which probably was about as healthy as eating the actual box, and grimaced. "Where's Nina?"

"On a date!" Toby said.

Now that Toby had regained his mastery of the English language, apparently he felt the need to speak in exclamation points.

"You should join us," Grace said, her voice sounding a little husky now, reminding him of how she sounded the night before, when he'd been buried deep. *Oh, please, Josh*, she'd said in that same voice. Pretty sure he *had* pleased, he cleared his throat and looked at the box again.

"Afraid?" she asked

"Yes. For my arteries."

She pointed to the counter and the half-empty bag of baby carrots there. "We're combating it with veggies."

"Toby doesn't eat carrots."

"I do so!" Toby claimed, and shocked Josh to the core by picking up a carrot. Of course he dipped it in a bowl of what looked like salad dressing until there was no carrot to be seen before jamming it into his mouth, dripping dressing everywhere.

Josh let out a breath.

Grace was looking at him, amused. "It's nonfat vanilla yogurt."

Josh shuddered at that combination but had to admit he couldn't object. "Where's Anna?"

Grace's smile faded some. "Out. Not sure where. How was work?"

In the past, the answer to this question would have been "*crazy*." But that didn't apply today. "Manageable."

"You sound surprised. Dr. McGinley not doing a good job?"

"She's doing a great job." So great that Josh still felt discombobulated at how easily his world had gone on without him. He looked at the box of mac and cheese and decided he just couldn't do it. He went to the freezer and pulled out a couple of steaks. While he defrosted them in the microwave, he headed out the back door and started the barbeque. The thing was brand spanking new and huge. He'd bought it two years ago and had never used it, not once, but it started right up with a big, satisfactory *whoomph*, not so unlike Toby's lightsaber.

Grace was standing in the open door watching him. "Feeling manly?"

He took in her pretty little sundress as she stepped outside. It had spaghetti straps and tiny buttons down the front and came to midthigh. "I'm feeling something."

She smiled. "What is it with men and big toys that turns them into Neanderthals?"

"It's not the toys. It's the 'big.' We like everything big."

"Well you have no worries there."

He wasn't touching that one with a ten-foot pole. Or a nine-inch one... "Are we playing?"

She looked him over from head to toe and back again. It wasn't the first time Josh had been undressed by a woman's eyes, but it was the first time it'd given him a hard-on. And he knew she liked what she saw because the pulse at the base of her throat kicked into gear.

Liking that, he took a step toward her, planning on showing her more of his "Neanderthal" side.

"Arf, arf!" Tank came barreling out the back door, chased by Toby with his lightsaber, both heading right for Grace full speed ahead.

Josh stepped in front of her to bear the brunt of the inevitable impact, bending low to grab for Tank just as Toby swung the lightsaber—

And accidentally collided with Josh's head. Josh staggered back and tripped over Tank. The puppy yelped, and Josh shifted his weight, but the damn dog wound his way between Josh's legs. To avoid killing him, Josh shifted again, and this time lost his balance. He fell, hitting with teeth-jarring impact, smacking his head on the concrete. Stars burst behind his eyeballs, and then...

Nothing.

Chapter 21

♥

*Always have chocolate on the To Do list to make sure
you get at least one thing done.*

Josh?"

He heard the voice coming at him from far away. It sounded urgent, and old habit had him responding to that urgency. He blinked his eyes open, then immediately wished he hadn't as pain sliced through his head, making him want to toss his cookies.

Or in this case, cupcakes.

"Josh, oh my God. Can you hear me?"

"Shhh." He closed his eyes again. Shit, that chocolate had been a very bad idea. "Toby—"

Grace was on her knees at his side. "He's fine. The dog's fine. I'm fine, thanks to you. We're all fine. Now please open your eyes again and talk to me."

Hell, no. If he did that, he'd *definitely* toss his cupcakes.

"Arf! Arf, arf, arf!"

Oh, Jesus, the Antichrist's barking was going to split open his head.

"Quiet, Tank," Grace said. "Toby, baby, grab him and put him in the laundry room, please. Anna, good, you're back. Get a phone in case we need to call nine-one-one."

"Got it," Anna said, sounding so unusually shaken that Josh did open his eyes. Look at that, Antichrist number two was worried about him. Nice change. "No nine-one-one."

"You need a doctor," Grace told him.

"I *am* a doctor. What the hell did I hit, a Mack truck?"

She held him down when he tried to sit up, and did so with surprising strength. "Stay," she said, like he was Tank.

"I'm fine." Except her fingers looked like...long French fries.

And she had two heads. And as strong and sure of herself as she sounded, all four of her eyes were filled with concern.

So sweet. He was used to doing the worrying. Hell, he was good at it. The best...

But it was nice to have someone else doing it for a change. He concentrated on that for a moment, then let his gaze wander. Four breasts too. Mmm. That was even nicer than having her worry about him. Four perfect handfuls— Wait. He'd need four hands for this. He lifted his hands to his face. One, two, three, four...ah, perfect. "It'd work," he said, and closed his eyes again.

Grace's heart was in her throat as she ran her fingers through Josh's hair, looking for the bump. She found it at the back of his head, a nice goose egg that had panic sliding down her spine. "Time to call nine-one-one," she said to Anna.

"On it," Anna said.

"No." Again Josh stirred, and it was like trying to hold back a stubborn mule. A two-hundred-pound, six-foot-plus stubborn *ass*, she thought grimly, sitting back on her heels. "Josh—"

"Ice," he said, snatching the phone from Anna's hand with surprising reflexes, especially given that a second before he'd been out cold. "I just need a bag of ice."

Anna rolled her eyes at the command but went wheels up to the kitchen.

Josh managed to get to his feet, looking like he felt the world spin on its axis before staggering two steps to sink rather heavily to the porch swing.

"Josh, you need to take it easy for a change."

He was green and getting greener and was covered in a fine sheen of sweat. He looked over at Toby standing there silent, somber, clutching his lightsaber in two little fists. "I'm fine, Squirt, no worries."

"Do you have blood?" Toby asked in a small, wavering voice. "Because when a Jedi warrior bleeds, he dies."

Josh ran his fingers through his hair, then showed his blood-free fingers to Toby, who didn't look convinced.

"I'm okay," Josh promised. "I'm going to live to fight another battle."

At that, Toby smiled a little, revealing the gap in the front where he'd lost his tooth. Adorable, but Grace was over the macho bullshit. "You need to go be checked out, Josh."

"I'm fine."

Did he really think he could fool her the way he fooled Toby? "If you're fine, how many fingers am I holding up?"

He focused in on her with what appeared to be great effort. "Two."

Lucky guess and they both knew it. Unfortunately, he was a man through and through, and therefore had a penis, which meant that there'd be no reasoning with him.

Anna came back with a bag of ice.

Josh placed it on the back of his thick noggin and settled more carefully on the swing, leaning his head against the wall behind him. Eyes closed. "Hey, Little Man," he said to Toby, "didn't you want to watch *Transformers*?"

"You said no 'cause I already watched too much TV this week."

"I counted wrong," Josh said. "Go ahead. Have Anna put it on for you."

Toby swung his lightsaber, *whoosh, vrrmm-whoosh* and ran back into the house, followed by a much slower moving, more reluctant Anna. "If you die," she said, pointing at Josh, "I'll kill you."

When she was gone, Grace moved in. "Nicely done. Now tell me what to do for you."

"How long was I out?"

"A minute."

"A minute, or a few seconds?"

"Seconds," she admitted. "But—"

"I'm good, Grace. I just need to sit here for a bit."

"Josh—"

"Tea," he said. "Can you make tea?"

"Sure." She jumped up and went in the kitchen. There she found Anna, with Devon.

"What are you doing here?" Grace asked him.

"Visiting." He hooked an arm around Anna's neck and

pulled her in, making her chair squeak as it slid sideways. He gave her a kiss on the temple.

Tender. Sweet. And full of shit. Grace tried to word-lessly convey to Anna that she was better than this. That she deserved more.

But Anna wasn't having the silent conversation. Or any conversation. "I came home to get a sweatshirt. We're heading back out," she said, only her eyes revealing the concern at leaving Josh right now—which of course she was far too stubborn to actually voice out loud.

Devon took the handles of her chair and turned her, wheeling her out of the kitchen. Just before they got to the door, he looked back over his shoulder at Grace and sent her a fuck-you smile.

Dammit!

Okay, one problem at a time, she thought. Josh first. She made the tea as quickly as she could, checked on Toby—blissfully watching *Transformers* with Tank on the couch—and rushed back out to Josh.

Who hadn't moved, not a single inch as far as she could tell. His big, long body was stretched out in the chair, his head back, cushioned on the ice against the wall.

Far too still.

Heart in her throat, she set the tea down and crouched at his side, laying a hand on his thigh.

He jerked, swore beneath his breath, then sent her a dark look.

"Sorry," she said on a relieved breath. "You were just so still. I thought…" She shook her head. "I brought your tea."

"I don't drink tea."

"Then why did you have me make it?"

"So you'd stop hovering."

She grated her teeth, then sat beside him and—what the hell—drank the tea. "Luckily for you," she said, "I can't hurt someone who's already hurt. Now tell me how you really feel."

"Could use a few aspirin. Or ten."

"Is aspirin okay with a head injury?"

"Grace."

Right. He was a doctor. He knew such things. She stood up, then narrowed her eyes. "Wait a minute. Is this another one of those things where I go running to get you the aspirin and then you don't want it?"

"Actually, it's one of those I'm-going-to throw-up things, and I want you to be far, far away."

Grace wasn't thrilled that Josh had gone to bed instead of joining them for dinner. She'd cooked the steaks, checking up on him every five minutes until the stubborn lug told her to go away and not come back. She was pretty sure he meant just for a little while, and not for the rest of his life.

She put Toby to bed and sat at the kitchen table working for her bookkeeping clients, still surprised that she'd somewhat accidentally started a business, albeit a small one. Nothing nearly so impressive as working at a big-time investment firm or bank in Seattle, but she was enjoying it anyway. She had no idea what she'd do if she got one of the jobs she'd tried for, and since she'd gotten a call today from Seattle for a final interview tomorrow, that seemed likely.

She was still working when Anna came home a few hours later. Grace stood up to make another drive-by check on Josh.

"Why do you get to act all crazy over a guy and I don't?" Anna asked.

"You have to earn the crazy," Grace said. "You're not old enough yet."

"He doesn't like it when people hover," Anna warned.

"How about when they care?"

"Nope," Anna said. "He's not overly fond of that either."

"Are you sure it's not just him being a stupid guy and not knowing how to deal with someone caring about him?"

This stopped Anna. "I don't know," she finally said after giving that some thought. "He's just always been the one to do the taking care of." She hesitated. "Now that you mention it, I don't know if that's because he's had to, or if he'd actually welcome help."

"Maybe you should find out sometime," Grace suggested. She moved down the hall to Josh's bedroom.

The room was dark, but she'd left the bathroom light on. His bedroom furniture was dark wood, masculine. The bed was huge and dominated the room. Josh lay sprawled on his stomach, face turned away.

She moved into the room and sat on the edge of the bed, gliding her fingers over his forehead, brushing his hair back.

He sighed. "It's been two minutes."

"Twenty. Do you feel nauseous?"

"Grace, I'm fine. Go away."

"What's your name?"

He let out a long breath. "Ticked off and looking for a new nanny."

"Funny. Follow my finger."

He smacked her finger away.

"You are such a big baby," she told him. "If one of your patients acted like this, you'd—"

"Assume they were good to go."

She could see that he'd showered, which freaked her out. He could have fallen, and she had no idea what she'd have done with a two-hundred-pound, wet, unconscious male. She knew what to do with a two-hundred-pound, wet *conscious* one, but that was entirely different.

He'd pulled on a pair of sweatpants, barely. They were so low on his hips as to be indecent, giving her a good look at his broad back that led down to a very sexy pair of twin dimples, and a hint of a tattoo.

Grace grinned wide, unable to help herself as she ran her fingers over the sweats, nudging them down enough to expose... a lightning bolt. She laughed softly, and he muttered a very bad word.

"Why are you still here?"

"You have a concussion," she reminded him. "I'm not leaving you alone."

"*Mild* concussion. Jesus. Stop hovering."

"Okay, I'd like to talk to Dr. Scott, not Asshole Josh."

He snorted, then let out a long-suffering breath. It hadn't escaped her that he hadn't moved. And he was looking extremely tense, his muscles rock hard with strain, which was confirmed when she stroked her hand along his back and felt the stress there.

Aw, the poor baby. Leaning over him, using two hands, she began to work the tension from his shoulders and back. She thought about massaging his ass as well, but she didn't want to take advantage of the man when he was down. "Tell me what I can do for you," she said softly as she worked.

He let out a muffled groan into his pillow. "That. Don't stop. Ever."

"I won't." Especially since touching him was pure pleasure. His skin was warm, smooth, and smelled so good she wanted to eat him up with a spoon. "What else do you need? Anything."

He groaned again. "I'm going to hope that promise doesn't have an expiration date."

She went still, then laughed softly. "You can think of sex *now*?"

"I can think of sex always. It's a special, God-given talent. Wake me up later."

"But—"

"*Much* later."

Hmm. "Tell me what to look for, Josh."

She couldn't see his eyes since they were closed, but she sensed them rolling around in his head in annoyance. "Brain damage," he said. "Bleeding, swelling, loss of muscle control. Death."

She gasped. "*What?*"

"But if I'm still in pain, death is fine," he said. "Just leave me dead. DNR."

Do not resuscitate. Doctor humor. "That's not funny, Josh."

"Look, it's not a big thing, okay? As long as my elevator goes to the top floor, let me be."

"But how will I know?"

"Grace." His voice held annoyance, frustration, and—his saving grace—affection. "You'll know."

"Okay, but you need to get better soon," she said, just as annoyed, frustrated, and affectionate. "So I can smack you."

Chapter 22

Life without chocolate is like a beach without water.

"Josh?"

He had no idea how much later it was when he heard her whisper his name. He thought how odd it was that only the day before the sound of his name on her lips would have made him hard. Now he wanted to strangle her. "*No*," he said.

"I haven't asked you anything yet."

He pried open one eye, noted the clock on his nightstand said midnight, and closed it again. Maybe she'd think he'd died.

"*Josh.*"

He sighed and rolled to his back. She wasn't going to give up. Ever. He knew that now. "I'm still breathing."

She sank to the bed at his hip and put her hand on his bare chest. Her fingers stroked him lightly, from one pec to another, her pinkie dragging over his left nipple.

His annoyance abruptly faded, and the age-old question of whether or not an injured man could get aroused was answered.

Yes, he could.

"Are you nauseous?" she asked.

"No. And I know my name, and I'm not hot or cold. I'm just right."

"Can you follow my finger?"

"Grace, I have a finger for you."

She sighed. "Fine. I'll see you in a few hours."

"Eight," he said. "*Eight* hours."

"Uh-huh..."

He knew she was totally humoring him, but her hand was *still* gliding over him, and her touch felt so good that he didn't give a shit. In fact, he fell asleep just like that, sprawled out like a dog begging for his parts to be stroked...

And woke up a few hours later, overheated. It *was* a fever, he thought dazedly. He'd joked about dying, he'd mocked death, and now he really was going to kick the bucket.

Then his blanket moved. And moaned softly.

Not a blanket. It was Grace.

It was two in the morning, dark except for the bathroom light, which slanted over his bed.

Grace was still in her cute, gauzy little sundress. No shoes. He was under the covers, and she was on them, so she must have fallen asleep during one of her million checks. He was flat on his back, and she was curled up into his side, her head on his shoulder, hair in his face, breathing steadily, deeply, doing that almost-but-not-quite snoring thing, which made him smile.

The smile made his head hurt and reminded him why

she was here in the first place. But he hurt a lot less than he had several hours ago. So much so that he rolled, tucking her beneath him.

She came instantly awake with a confused, befuddled, "What?"

He stroked the hair from her face. She'd stayed with him. She'd worried about him. She'd not left his side. He tried to remember the last time someone had been there for him instead of the other way around—and couldn't. "You nauseous?" he asked.

She blinked. "Uh..."

"What's your name?"

She blinked again and narrowed her eyes. "You're making fun of me. I've been worried, you know, and—"

"Are you feverish?" He pressed his lips to her temple. "Nope." He stroked a hand down her throat to her chest, spreading his fingers wide as she'd done to him, stroking sideways. He loved her breasts. They were full and soft.

Except the nipples.

Her nipples were always hard for him.

"What are you doing?" she asked.

"Seeing if you're getting a chill."

"By copping a feel?"

"Are you cold, Grace?"

"No."

He smiled and lowered his head, lightly clamping his teeth on her nipple over her thin sundress.

She gasped.

"If you're not cold," he said, "then you're turned on."

"There are other options!"

"Name one." He switched to her other nipple, and she

moaned, arching up into his mouth, her fingers gliding into his hair and over his injury.

Which made him hiss in pain.

"Oh God, I'm sorry."

Keeping a hold of her, he rolled to his back so that she straddled him. Then he urged the spaghetti straps to her elbows and tugged her dress to her waist. "Always."

She frowned. "Always what?"

"You always make me feel better," he said, cupping a breast.

She made a sound of pure arousal even as she shook her head. "Josh—"

He tugged her bra cups down and pulled her over him so he could suck her into his mouth.

"Oh. Oh, that feels so good," she said shakily. "But you're not up for this."

Gripping her hips, he ground against her, showing her exactly how "up" he was.

"Josh, seriously. You need to be still, not—"

"I'm going to be very still." He reached out and blindly opened his nightstand drawer, producing a condom.

He knew he had her when she took it. She tugged the sheet from between them, then untied his sweats and pushed them off before rolling the condom down his length. He ran his hands along her sweet thighs, pushing her dress as high as he could. She rose up and took him inside her.

She gasped, then covered her mouth with her hands. Watching her fight to keep in her moans of pleasure drove him right to the very edge. Gripping her tight, he thrust up inside her wet heat, hard, and oh, Christ. Christ, she felt amazing.

Warm hands covered his on her hips. She pulled them from her and lifted them to the headboard above his head, tightening her fingers on his. "Still," she whispered. "You have to stay very still."

He opened his eyes to find her face only inches from his. Deep blue orbs stared down at him, and his breath lodged in his throat.

Apparently satisfied that he was going to relinquish control, she let go of his hands and skimmed hers down his shoulders and chest to his stomach and back up again. And then she began to move on him.

Slow.

Achingly slow.

Grace's hips rocked, and her head fell back as she took her pleasure from his body. Every time he so much as rocked his hips, she stopped. This was her ride, and she had places to go. And it was a hell of a ride. She nipped gently at his lips, nothing guarded or shielded in her gaze, nothing held back. He could see anything and everything in those eyes, and he didn't understand how it could be, but this between them just kept getting better.

She was going easy, clearly not wanting to hurt him, but he needed more. He rocked up, changing the angle, creating a deeper penetration. Inhaling sharply, she bowed over him, entwining her fingers with his as she kissed him, her muscles quivering as the pressure built. Lost in the sight of her, he whispered her name, and then again.

It sent her skittering over the edge, her entire body shuddering in gorgeous relief above him, and he groaned as the wave took him under right along with her.

It was the most erotic experience of his life.

"I should go," she whispered against his jaw.

"A minute." He pulled her into him and stroked a hand down her damp back. "In a minute."

Grace opened her eyes and nearly leaped right out her skin.

Toby was nose to nose with her.

And so was Tank.

Toby was on a stool leaning over the bed. Tank was actually on the bed.

On her.

At least until she sat up and dislodged him. With a reproachful look, the pug rolled aside like a boneless glob. Grace looked at Josh, who was flat on his stomach, sprawled out, and thankfully covered by the blanket.

Equally thankfully, she was fully dressed—and *not* covered by the blanket. Huh. The doctor was a bed hog.

Toby smiled at her. "Whatcha doing in my daddy's bed?"

Yeah, Grace, whatcha doing in his daddy's bed? She tried not to eyeball Josh's sweatpants on the floor behind Toby as she reached for the book on the nightstand. *The Berenstain Bears Forget Their Manners.* "Reading him a bedtime story," she improvised. Which was better than explaining the middle-of-the-night bootie call.

"It's not bedtime," Toby said.

And to think she'd been excited when he'd started using his words. "Well—"

"Hey, Squirt," Josh said, opening his eyes. "Cereal for breakfast?"

"Yeah!"

"How about you go pour it."

"By myself?" Toby asked.

"Yep."

"Oh boy!"

Toby leaped off the stool and ran for the door.

When he was gone, Grace covered her face. "Oh my God."

"He didn't see anything."

She rolled to her feet. "I was in your bed! We could have scarred him for life!"

"Grace, we weren't doing anything. Well, I wasn't. You were snoring."

"I don't—" She smoothed her dress down and searched out her sandals, shoving her feet into them. She glanced at herself in the mirror over his dresser and groaned. Hair, wild. Lips, swollen. Face, flushed.

Nipples, hard.

"Dammit!" She clapped her hands over them. "It's like they're broken!"

Josh let out a low laugh. "They just like me more than your other parts."

She didn't know about that. Her other parts liked him, too, a lot.

He got up much more slowly than she. Naked, of course. The man didn't have a single ounce of self-consciousness in his entire body. Not that he needed to. "What are you doing?" she hissed. "Put some clothes on!"

"Christ, woman." He appeared to be holding his head onto his shoulders. "Shhh."

She narrowed her eyes. "Your head didn't seem to hurt so badly a little while ago."

"The brain is motivated to avoid pain by seeking pleasure."

"The brain, huh? Because I'm pretty sure the body part that was seeking pleasure sits quite a bit lower than your brain."

He let out a low laugh, but it was weak. Softening, Grace slid her arms around him, trying to guide him back to the bed. Not a hardship, since he was warm and sleek and hard.

Everywhere.

The hardest part of him was poking her in the belly. Seemed her nipples weren't the only things broken.

Looking both amused and pained at the both of them, he extracted himself from her grip and strode butt-ass naked to the sweats on the floor, which he pulled on. "What's up for you today?" he asked.

"The usual variety of jobs. Tomorrow I have another interview."

He froze for a beat. "Seattle?"

"Yeah," she said, more than a little distracted by the way the sweats sat so low on his hips. "You have a few more nanny applicants." It was her turn to pause. "One of them is Sarah Tombs, Mindy's sister, from the florist shop. She's going to an online college and is looking for a way to work part-time. I could check her out if you'd like."

"That'd be great."

She nodded. "The other is Riley."

"Amy's Riley?"

"Yes. She's taking college classes in the mornings," she said. "She needs a job for the afternoons or evenings. She loves kids, she loves Toby, and more importantly, he loves her."

Josh said nothing to this as he pulled on a T-shirt, his

muscles bunching and unbunching in a way that made her lose her train of thought again. When he finally spoke, it was a complete subject change. "I heard you picked up a few more clients."

"Yeah, it's getting totally out of hand. Mindy brought me her paperwork. In *grocery store bags.*" She shook her head. "What is wrong with people?"

He smiled. "Lots."

The smile made her want to hug him, and maybe love him up some more. Stupid smile. She backed to the door. "I'll be back in time to get Toby."

"We'll be okay today. Do what you have to do "

"You're not going to work?" This had her heart stopping short. "You're not better."

"I'm fine. Just not fine enough to treat people."

She looked him over carefully. He had shadows beneath his eyes. His brow was furrowed. His mouth was tight. He was holding it together—the guy clearly knew no other way—but he was feeling like shit. She shook her head. "I'm going to cancel the floral deliveries—"

"No. Don't."

"You're—"

"*Fine,*" he said finally. "I'll pick up Toby from school and take him to the pier. We'll play arcade games and eat crap."

Aw. She pictured it, Toby running around in hog heaven, and Josh trying to find something to eat that wasn't a hot dog. "You're a good dad, Josh."

He didn't have any obvious reaction, but she knew him now and felt his surprise. Had no one ever told him such a thing? The thought made her heart melt. And it wasn't the fleeting kind of melt either. It was the kind that made her want to burrow into him and make him feel good some more. In lots of ways...

Which in turn reminded her that she was *this* close to a job—finally—and he was *this* close to getting a nanny, and then this time with him would be over.

And when it was, there'd be no reason to see him. At least no reason that didn't involve doing what they'd both said they didn't want to do—have a relationship.

Chapter 23

The best drug is chocolate.

The next day, Grace had her Seattle interview and got on the road heading back to Lucky Harbor. Her passenger was a big, shiny, fancy file folder with a formal offer and all the big, shiny, fancy benefits that went with it.

It was a really good offer. It didn't involve shoe boxes filled with receipts, modeling various body parts, or doggie poo. It didn't involve grumpy paraplegics or terrifyingly adorable Jedi warriors. This job would be all checks and balances, spreadsheets, and detailed analysis programs for a midsized bank with growth potential.

No messy emotions.

Now it was just a matter of deciding if she wanted it. This thought was so disconcerting that she had to pull over and stare at herself in the rearview mirror.

Of course she wanted the job. It was a good salary and had full benefits. It was what she'd been aiming for, and it would make her family proud.

But it also meant walking away from all the things and people who'd come to mean so much to her.

The break's over, she told herself firmly. Fun was fun but it was time to follow through on her life plans. *Past* time.

She headed to the pier. She'd called Sarah for a preliminary nanny interview. They were meeting in twenty minutes at the diner. She was halfway through town when she saw Anna on the sidewalk, wheeling furiously along, steam practically coming out of her ears. Grace pulled over and got out of the car. She could tell Anna had been crying, but since she didn't have a death wish, she didn't mention it. "What are you doing?"

"What does it look like?"

"Well, it looks like you're on a mission to kill someone," Grace said. "And since you won't look good in an orange jumpsuit, I thought we could discuss."

"I'd totally rock an orange jumpsuit."

"*No one* rocks orange. Talk to me."

Anna rolled her eyes. "You even sound like him now."

Grace sighed. There was no hurrying a Scott, ever. "You getting in the car or what?"

Anna took a moment to swipe the mascara from beneath her eyes. "Yeah. Sure." Once she got into the front seat, she looked at the folder Grace had set on the dash. "What's that?" she asked, opening the file without waiting for an answer.

"Hey, that's private," Grace said.

"Holy shit, they're going to pay you a *buttload*," Anna exclaimed, eyeballing the bottom line on the offer. "What is it you do again? Add up other people's money?"

Grace sighed. "Something like that."

"I want a job that pays this."

"Get a degree."

"There you go, sounding like my brother again." Anna flipped through the papers for a moment, thoughtful. Silent.

"I'm interviewing Sarah at the diner. Want to help?"

"I guess."

Inside Eat Me, Jan brought them iced tea as they met with Sarah and her nice, neat, freshly printed résumé. She was local, and everyone liked her. She had a list of references a mile long, and she could start immediately.

It was a no-brainer.

After Sarah left the table, Grace looked at Anna. "So?"

"So what?"

"What did you think?"

"She's like Mary Poppins," Anna said.

Yeah. Dammit. She was perfect. Far more perfect than Grace. Which was *not* the point, she told herself. She'd never meant for this job to become anything more than a temp position on the way to the Real World.

"You look annoyed," Anna said. "You've been looking for someone to replace you for weeks. Why aren't you doing the happy dance?"

"She's talking about getting married to her fiancé. She'll be too busy with wedding plans to play with Toby."

"She said they're planning on eloping."

"Exactly," Grace said. "Which means she'll just up and go away for two weeks. Toby doesn't need that kind of disruption; he's had enough."

"So hire Riley."

"Yes, but Riley's so…young."

Anna stared at her, then laughed. "Let me get this straight. First you can't find a viable candidate. Now you've got not one but *two*, and you don't want either?"

"I didn't say that."

Anna shook her head. "You really are as nuts as I thought."

"Pot, kettle," Grace said. "Now tell me what the hell you were doing wheeling down the highway like a Formula One driver minus a racetrack."

"You first. Tell me why you're not happy about your job offer, the one any normal person would be celebrating already by now."

They stared at each other, at an impasse.

"You first," Anna bargained with the same talent as her brother. "And then I'll tell you."

"Uh-huh," Grace said. "And I'd totally say yes, except you're a weasel and a non-truth teller—"

"Non-truth teller?"

"Nicer than saying liar," Grace said with a shrug.

"Okay, fine." Anna shifted in her chair. "Today was the day."

"The day . . ."

"With Devon," Anna said. "The day I agreed to finally . . . you know. Do the deed."

"Oh." Grace's stomach clenched. "And? Are you okay?"

"Yeah. I really thought I was ready. I'm twenty-freaking-one."

Grace held her breath. *Tell me you didn't go through with it . . .*

"I got there," Anna said. "To his place. And it was still his same stinky, old bedroom with the huge bong in a corner and the posters of Megan Fox on the walls, and no pillowcases on the pillows . . ."

Pig.

"I mean, I don't know what I expected," Anna said. "I guess I thought somehow it'd be romantic and special. You know?"

"I do know. And it should be romantic and special. What happened?"

"I changed my mind."

Grace let out the breath she'd been holding. "It's okay. It's okay to change your mind."

Anna lifted a shoulder, then shook her head. "Devon was all pissed off about it."

Tell me I have a reason to call the cops and have his ass arrested. "Did he hurt you?"

"No. Of course not. I wouldn't let a guy hurt me." Anna's voice caught. "But he was a total jerk about it. Wouldn't give me a ride home."

Asshole. "So you took your wheels to the highway?" Grace asked. "Why didn't you call someone, Josh or me?"

"Josh's at work."

"He'd have come anyway," Grace said. "And you know it. And I would have as well."

"Without killing Devon?"

Tough question. "Okay, so Josh might have struggled with that, but you can call me, Anna. *Always.* I'll pick you up no questions asked and take you wherever you need to go. Well, except the one place you actually *want* to go. I don't have enough credit on my Visa to get us to Europe, sorry. But I do have a full tank of gas, which gives us about two hundred miles in any direction."

Anna rolled her eyes, but she also *almost* smiled. "I still want to go to Europe."

"I've heard this song."

"And then after Europe, I figured out what I want to do with my life. Other than driving the people in it crazy."

"Anna." Grace covered Anna's hand with hers. Anna's was calloused and strong from spinning the wheels on her chair. As strong as the woman it belonged to. "There's no need to stop something you're so good at."

Anna snorted.

Grace smiled at her, then let the amusement fade. "You know you can do whatever you want, right? Climb mountains, cure world hunger, rule the universe?"

"I want to work with people like me. Help them, like, adjust. I know," she said quickly. "I know I'm mean and obnoxious, but that's me. That has nothing to do with my legs not working. I think I'm pretty damn well adjusted when it comes to that."

"I agree," Grace said quietly. "So you want to be a counselor? A therapist?"

"Psychologist. Specializing in obnoxious teenagers." She smiled. "Who better, right?"

"Nice," Grace said. "You'd probably have to lose the scowl, maybe turn on your self-editor, but nice. Really nice. Do it."

"It's just that I've said that I'd go to school like a million times over the past three years, and every time Josh got me all admitted and registered and everything, and I've flaked."

"So don't flake," Grace said.

"I can't tell him. He won't believe me. He's lost faith."

"Anna." Grace shook her head. "He's never lost faith in you. Have a little faith in *him*." Because Anna wasn't looking sure, Grace went on. "You're a born fighter. So fight for what you want."

Anna nodded, then smiled.

"What?"

"Your turn. You have to tell me stuff now. About your job offer."

"Well," Grace said. "It's a good one."

"Duh."

"It's everything my parents ever wanted for me. And I thought it was everything I wanted as well."

"But it's not?"

"No, it is." Grace hesitated. She didn't know how to express her feelings on this because they were so new. Her "big job" was going to satisfy her goal to be a successful career woman. But she'd discovered something during her time here in Lucky Harbor—happiness. Shouldn't that be a goal too? "I don't want to leave Lucky Harbor," she admitted. "I like it here. It feels more like home than . . . well, home."

Anna didn't laugh. She didn't roll her eyes or make a single sarcastic statement. She just nodded. "Well, then, there's really only one thing to do."

"What's that?"

"It's painful," Anna warned. "You're going to have to take your own advice and fight for what you want."

Grace stared at her as the door to the diner opened. Josh strode in like a man on a mission. He wore navy scrubs, his hospital ID hanging around his neck, and a deep scowl on his face.

Jan started toward him, order pad in her hand, before she caught sight of his expression and backed off.

He headed straight toward Anna and Grace, mouth grim as he turned to Anna. "I just got three phone calls that you were wheeling yourself down the highway and sobbing, refusing all rides."

And he'd run out of the ER in the middle of his shift to come find her. Grace's heart melted.

But not, apparently, Anna's. "That's stupid," she said. "Who said I was sobbing? I want to talk to that person!"

Josh was not amused. "What the fuck happened?"

He'd spoken quietly, but he was standing over them, and as big as he was—not to mention incredibly charismatic—people were looking.

"Look," Anna said, pointing out the window. "A puppy."

Josh's eyes narrowed, but he took a deep breath and slid into the booth. "Anna—"

"Grace got the job!"

Josh's eyes cut to Grace. They were laser sharp as always, but for an instant, just the briefest of instants, something not quite identifiable flickered. She wanted to see it again, wanted to reach for it, or better yet, have him give it to her willingly.

"Congratulations," he said quietly. Calmly. As if it mattered not one bit, when they both knew it mattered a whole hell of a lot.

"It's not a done deal," she said.

"They're going to pay her beaucoup bucks," Anna said. "She'd be crazy not to take it."

"You deserve it," Josh said quietly.

"Okay!" Anna said, turning her chair away from the table. "So who's ready to go home?"

Grace stood up and went through her purse for cash to cover their bill. Josh put a hand on hers and turned and sent a look in Jan's direction.

Jan jerked her chin in acknowledgment. She'd put it on Josh's account.

In the parking lot, Grace hesitated. She figured Anna would go with Josh, but Anna was at Grace's car, struggling with her chair. Grace looked at Josh. "I've got her."

Jaw tight, he stepped forward and helped Anna get into Grace's car before turning to his.

Twenty minutes later, Grace had dropped Anna at home and met Toby at the bus stop. They'd no sooner walked in the door than Josh showed up.

"Hey," Grace said, surprised, "you done with your shift?"

"No. I drove over there but I need to do this. Where's Anna?"

"In her room."

She could hear his phone going crazy in his pocket. Josh ignored it and headed down the hall. Not wanting to be near the impending explosion, Grace took Toby into the kitchen, setting him up with carrots and yogurt dip. But as it turned out, voices could carry.

"Just tell me what the hell you were doing alone on the highway like that," came Josh's voice.

"Coming home from Devon's."

"I told you not to see him anymore."

"That's not your decision to make," Anna said.

"What happened there, Anna?" His voice was low and controlled. Angry.

"You don't want to know," she said.

"I do want to know."

"You *don't*."

Their voices were escalating. Grace shoved more carrots at Toby, then looked around for Tank, thinking the pup could be counted on for a good diversion. Surely he'd be chewing on a piece of furniture or doing something bad. But Tank was sitting at her feet, looking wistful and sad at being left out of the carrot party.

Where was a loud "arf arf" when she needed one?

"Puppies like carrots," Toby said.

"Choking hazard," Grace said.

"Talk to me," Josh said to Anna.

"Fine!" came Anna's raised voice. "I was going to lose my virginity today! Happy now? Are you thrilled I told you?"

"Anna." Josh's voice sounded tight, like he was having trouble getting the words out. "You can tell me anything, you know that. But this…with *him*? Jesus. How stupid can you be?"

Uh-oh, Grace thought. He'd just waved a red cape in front of the bull.

From down the hall, silence thundered, so thick Grace could scarcely breathe through it.

But apparently Anna could. "I can do what I want with my life. I'm a *grown-up*."

"Then act like one." Josh wasn't yelling like Anna, but he was close. "And you're not a grown-up until you can support yourself."

"Daddy's mad," Toby whispered.

Grace again looked at a calm, quiet Tank. "Are you kidding me?" she asked the puppy. "Really, you're going to behave *now*?"

"This is stupid!" Anna yelled at her brother. "It's not like you're a saint! You don't have to follow any rules or listen to anyone! You get to do whatever—and whoever—you want."

"Anna—" He broke off, and Grace imagined him shoving his fingers into his already disheveled hair in frustration. She felt the frustration as her own because she knew that everything he did was for his family. Anna knew that too. Grace waited for him to say so, even as she knew he wouldn't.

"The way I live my life," he said, "the things I do, aren't up for discussion. Period."

"Even the babysitter?"

Grace sucked in a breath. Toby looked at her with a thoughtfulness that belied his five years, while she did her best to look innocent. "More yogurt?" she asked desperately. "Jedis need strong bones. Here, have some milk too."

"Tank's sad," Toby said. "He wants a carrot."

Tank spun in circles before sitting and offering a paw and a hopeful smile.

"See?" Toby said. "He's saying please."

Grace gave up and went to the cabinet for a doggie cookie.

"I just wanted to be normal," Anna flung at her brother, her words booming down the hall. "I wanted to feel like a woman, Josh. And Grace said—"

"Wait a minute. Grace knew?"

Oh, crap.

"She guessed," Anna said. "And it's not like I could tell *you*. You couldn't possibly have understood because you're like a machine. No feelings allowed."

This was followed by another thundering beat of silence, during which Grace hoped Josh wasn't killing his sister. But he'd taken an oath to save lives, so probably he was just grinding his teeth into powder.

"If that's how you feel," he finally said, sounding very tired, "then you should go."

"That's what I'm saying! I want to go to Europe!"

"No, I mean go. Move out. If you can't be happy here, or at college, then you need to go figure your life out and learn to support yourself."

Another silence, this one loaded with utter shock.

Grace grimaced. Perfect—an ultimatum, which, *hello*, never worked, *especially* on angry twenty-one-year-olds. Plus, Anna was so similar to Josh, down to every last stubborn hair on her stubborn head. How could he not see that?

Granted, Grace didn't have a whole hell of a lot of experience with blood ties. Actually, she had zero experience with blood ties. But even she knew that no one could tell Josh what to do. So why would he think it'd work on the sister who was so much like him?

Grace started down the hall with some half-baked idea of trying to butt in and somehow finesse the situation and ran smack into Josh coming out of Anna's room. "Sorry," she said. "I thought maybe I could help..."

"You can't," Anna said from her doorway, eyes flashing. "No one can help because he's an overbearing, uptight, rigid asshole who doesn't listen."

"I *always* listen," Josh said. "You just don't like what I say." He looked at Grace for backup, and she hesitated.

"Jesus," Josh said, and tossed up his hands as Anna wheeled past them both, heading toward the door. "Where are you going?" he asked her.

"What do you care? You told me to move out."

"Oh, for chrissakes, Anna. I didn't—"

The door slammed.

Josh inhaled sharply and turned to Grace.

She tried a weak smile. "Well that went well, huh? Talking it out..." She trailed off when he rolled his eyes.

"Okay, so it didn't. But an ultimatum, Josh? Really? You're a doctor. You're supposed to be smarter than that."

"Excuse me?"

God save her from annoying alphas. "Oh, come on," she said. "You lost that fight the minute you tried to tell her what to do instead of discussing it—"

"Discussing it *never* works with her."

"Are you sure you actually gave it a shot?" Grace asked.

Josh's eyes narrowed. "I've tried everything over the past five years. Asking, telling, begging..."

She doubted the last part. She couldn't imagine Josh begging for anything. Well, that wasn't entirely true. The night Mrs. Porter had died and he'd been drunk, he'd begged a little then. *Don't stop, Grace. Oh fuck, please don't ever stop.*

He probably didn't want to be reminded of that right now.

The truth was, his parents' deaths had thrust him into some uncomfortable, unnatural roles—being his sister's parent, the head of household, protector...everything. He'd been wearing all the hats and working an incredibly demanding job on top of it. It'd taken its toll on their relationship.

But Anna wasn't that same sixteen-year-old anymore either. "She's growing up," Grace said. "She's old enough to make her own mistakes."

"And you're an expert on family now?" he asked. "You, the queen of running away from your own family problems?"

"Okay, now that's not really fair," she said slowly, stung. "I didn't exactly run away—"

"No, you just lied rather than tell them your dreams don't match theirs."

She opened her mouth but he wasn't done. "You took Anna's side." He said this in his quiet, calm voice. His professional, detached voice, and that really got to her.

Her parents talked to her in that same voice when she'd disappointed them or had somehow—no matter how inadvertently—stepped off the expected path.

No judgment, never that, but no real emotional attachment either. No feeling.

She processed the unexpected pain of that as well.

Josh mistook her silence for something else. "You took her side," he repeated, "over me."

She found her voice, which was *not* void of emotion, thank you very much. She was getting pissed off. "I didn't realize we were taking sides."

"And then," he went on, "you pulled the passive-aggressive card by going behind my back about Anna—"

"Now wait a minute." She realized he'd been spoiling for a fight since he'd walked in the door, and ding-ding, he'd just gotten one. "You don't know what you're talking about," she said. "And I'm *not* passive aggressive. I just…"

He cocked a brow and waited with a mock patience that had her temper hitting the boiling point. She no longer had things to prove, not to anyone, and certainly not to herself. "You know what?" she said. "*Never mind.* I'm done talking to you when you're like this."

"This?" he repeated.

"You. When you're being all mule-headed and obstinate and—"

"Those are the same things, Grace."

"Smug," she added. "An overeducated, arrogant... *doctor*." After this final insult, she inhaled a deep breath and then let it out again. "Okay, never mind the doctor part. That's my own hang-up showing. I didn't mean that part."

"I thought you were done talking to me."

"Argh!" She grabbed her purse and whirled to the door. She got all the way to it before she remembered she was still on the clock. She executed an about-face. "Are you going back to the hospital?"

"Have to."

"Fine. And you should know, I interviewed Sarah. Assuming you trust my passive-aggressive judgment, she's perfect for you and could start immediately."

"Handy, since you got the job you wanted."

"Actually," she said, "you have no idea what I want."

"Then tell me."

Yeah, Grace, tell him. But he was standing there, so big and sure of himself, shoulders stretched impossibly broad, strong enough to take on the weight of his entire world.

Which he'd done.

And what had *she* done? Exactly as he'd accused her—she'd blindly followed a path set out for her, not spending time second-guessing that path or even standing up for what her own hopes and dreams might be.

That shamed her. Embarrassed her to the bone. She had no idea how to tell him that what she wanted was to throw away the only thing she'd ever been good at and start over. That what she really wanted was to keep this little make-believe world she'd created for herself. So she said nothing at all and went into the kitchen. "How about making more cupcakes?" she asked Toby.

"Oh boy!"

The front door shut, and Grace felt twinges of unidentifiable emotions.

Regret.

Anxiety.

Loss.

And something else, something that left her stomach uneasy, because it felt like heartbreak.

Are you having fun now?

Chapter 24

*Chocolate is cheaper than therapy, and you don't even
need an appointment.*

Fifteen minutes later, Josh was back in the ER, trying
to keep his mind on his patients, which wasn't easy. Why
had he picked a fight with Grace? Because she'd inte-
grated herself into his life so that he could no longer
imagine it without her? Because she'd gotten a job he
wasn't even convinced she wanted and would be leaving?
It made no sense. He'd always known she'd be leaving.
And if she took the Seattle job, she wouldn't be far.

But that wasn't the point. The point was that it
wouldn't be the same.

His fault.

All his own fucking fault. He called Riley and asked if
she was free to watch Toby so that Grace could leave if
she wanted to. Riley promised to head over to his house,
no worries.

Josh spent the next five hours working, and at the end
of his shift, all he wanted was to crash. Mallory caught

up to him in the hallway. She was in pink scrubs, hair up, looking a little frazzled. "Got a minute?" she asked.

The ER had been a mess all day. There'd been a five-car pileup on the highway, the usual heart attacks and hangovers, and a mob of strep throat infections. She'd kept up with him every step of the way. "For you, always."

She smiled. "Aw. Don't make me tell Ty I'm marrying his good friend instead of him."

"Tell him you realized you needed a real man."

She laughed, but he couldn't manage the same. She looked at him for a long beat; then her smile faded. "Oh, Josh. You didn't."

"What?"

"You screwed it up?"

He shook his head. "What makes you think that _I_ screwed it up?"

"Because you have a penis."

Josh let out a breath. "Maybe there was nothing to screw up."

"Oh my God. And how does a guy as smart as you get so dumb?"

"_Dumb?_"

"Yes, dumb! You fell for her, Josh, I know it. We _all_ know it. It's all over your face. It's all over the way you act with her."

"I don't act any different with her than I do with everyone else," he said.

"Really? So you pay all your babysitters a thousand dollars a day?"

"A _week_," he muttered.

But she wasn't listening. She was ranting on him

some more. "I mean, I can't understand how you can't see it. Have you looked at yourself in that pic on Facebook? Or noticed how much more relaxed you are these past weeks?" She smacked him on the chest. *"Relaxed*, Josh. *You!* Hell, you even sold your practice so that you could have a private life. So wake up and smell the damn cupcakes—you're crazy about her. You even let yourself depend on her. You, the King-of-Depending-on-No-One!"

"I *pay* her to be dependable."

"Yes, well, you've paid me on occasion to work in your practice when you were short an RN," she reminded him. "Does that mean we're doing it by your pool like a pair of teenagers?"

"She told you?" he asked in disbelief.

"No, actually. Anna did," she admitted. "And then both Amy and I pounced all over Grace for details—which she wouldn't give, by the way. You know why that is, Josh?"

He wasn't afraid of much, but even he knew to be afraid of Mallory when her eyes were crazy like they were now, so he said nothing.

"It's because you don't give details when you're *falling*." She drew a deep breath and studied him, hands on hips.

He held his ground in case she decided to hit him again, because for a little thing, she hit hard.

"Let me just say this. I love you, but if you hurt Grace in any way, I'm going to —" She huffed a minute. "Well, I don't know what. Depends on what you did."

Again with the assumption it was him

Because it was, you dumbass... He pinched the bridge of his nose. "Look, it's late. I'm tired. *You're* tired. Did you need a minute to tell me something important or just to yell at me?"

She sighed. "I almost forgot. I wanted to know if you could pick up a shift at HSC this week."

"Depends on when Grace leaves and if I have someone to cover Toby."

"Oh, yeah. Right." Mallory sighed and got quiet, very quiet. "I keep telling myself she's not going to really go, you know?"

He did know. He knew because he'd been doing the same thing. The thought of Grace heading off to Seattle gave him a gut ache.

And a heartache.

Which proved Mallory's point, of course. He *was* crazy about Grace, and he really had absolutely no idea how she felt. In the beginning, he'd mistakenly believed she needed him. That he was the one doing *her* the favor.

He'd been wrong. Very wrong.

Grace didn't need a man to be the center of her universe. She wasn't dependent on anyone. She would never be one more thing on any man's plate to take care of. What had he been thinking to assume that? Especially since the truth was that *she'd* been taking care of him since day one. "I'm going home now," he said. "Unless you want to hit me again."

"Do I need to?" she asked.

"No."

She studied him for a long beat, then surprised him by sighing and stepping in to hug him tight. "It's okay to be stupid in love," she assured him, patting him like he was a little boy instead of a full-grown man who was a head and a half taller than her. "*Once*," she said, this last word spoken in a definite warning tone. Then she stepped back and out the door before he could tell her that he'd already used his allotment of stupid in love.

Just over five years ago.

Except hindsight was always twenty-twenty. And he knew now that what he'd had with Ally hadn't been so much love as lust. As for what he had with Grace, he wasn't sure. It felt more like heartburn than anything else.

On the way home, he called Anna. She still didn't pick up, but two minutes later he got a text from her that said he should leave her the hell alone, that she was with friends, that she was fine, and she'd come talk to him when she was "grown up" enough not to want to kill him.

He figured that might be a while. He drove by Devon's place to make sure she wasn't with him, but it was dark and no one answered the door. Relieved, he headed home.

His house was dark, too, just one small lamp in the living room. When he walked in, Grace stood up from the couch. "Toby's asleep," she said, and handed him his mail. Actually, she slapped it to his chest. "We had spaghetti. There's leftovers, if you're able to stomach canned sauce." She headed to the door.

"You stayed," he said.

She whipped around to glare at him.

Yeah. Admittedly, it wasn't his finest opening. But he was dizzy with exhaustion and worry, and completely out of his element. Never a good combo. "I meant that I expected Riley—"

"I told her I had Toby," she said. "Because I did. Did you really think I wouldn't? That I'd just walk away?"

Whatever she saw in his face made her come close and stab him in the chest with her finger.

Ouch. Jesus, the women in his life were scary.

"You did," she said in disbelief. "You thought the going had gotten tough, so I'd get going. Well, bite me, Dr.
Scott. This job might have started out as a favor—for *you*
I might add—but it's not just a simple floral delivery or
bookkeeping job." She stabbed at him again. "This isn't
about the bottom line, or what balances and what doesn't.
It's about a dog, and a kid, and a girl, and a man, all of
whom needed me—or so I thought."

"Grace—"

"No, I believe I just told you what you can do. *Bite.
Me.*" She headed for the door again, but Josh was done
with people yelling at him and/or walking away from
him today. Done and over it, and pissed off to boot. He
snagged her by the back of her sweater and reeled her in.

She sent daggers at him but he was also done talking.
He scooped her up and took her caveman style down the
hall to his bedroom. There he set her down, shut and
locked the door, and backed her to the wall, caging her in.

She opened her mouth—no doubt to blast him—so he
covered that sexy mouth with his own. His hand slid to
the nape of her neck to hold her still while he kissed her
like he was drowning and she was his only hope.

Because she was his only hope.

Grace knew she should push free and walk out of Josh's
room, but there was a problem with that. A big one.

He had her up against the wall, held there by well
over six feet of worked-up testosterone. It should have in-
furiated her. Instead, her brain must have mixed up the
signals because she was suddenly hot as hell. She shifted
against his body and made herself hotter. "Move," she

said, the token protest, made out of a need to not set back feminism by caving to the sheer dominating force of his personality.

He held still, forearms on either side of her head, face close.

"*Move*," she repeated.

He did. He moved backward to his bed, taking her with him. He sat, pulling her into the vee of his spread legs as he did, removing her clothes with shocking speed and letting out a low, rough groan at the sight of her body bared to him.

It did something to her, the sound of his arousal, seeing it in his intense expression, like he was completely lost in her. Screw feminism, she decided weakly, trying to get his clothes off, too, but then he threaded his fingers into her hair and kissed her harder, pulling her onto his lap.

Naked, she straddled him, rocking onto his hard length, feeling him through his scrubs. She'd been mad at him, so very mad, but now that emotion morphed into something else—a desperate need for a Josh-induced orgasm.

"Grace. *Christ*." He ground his hips upward as he pressed her down onto him, sliding her along with his motions, making her moan in pleasure as the hunger began to build within her. Hell, who was she kidding, the hunger for him was always there.

"I need you." He nipped at her ear. "I've always needed you, Grace."

Her heart swelled against her rib cage. "Then take me."

In the next beat, he had a condom and she'd untied his scrubs, freeing the essentials. And oh God, the essentials were ready, willing, and able. He slid home, and they both gasped at the shocking pleasure. Then Josh claimed her mouth with his, and as he began to move inside her, he claimed her body as well. She cried out his name as he thrust up into her, drawing her tighter with every smooth stroke.

It was exactly what she needed, and exactly not enough. "More," she pleaded, digging her fingers into him.

He ran hot kisses along her jaw to her ear as he changed the pace, driving into her hard and fast, hoarsely whispering how good she felt wrapped around him, how he'd thought about doing this all day, wanting to be inside her like this, just like this, all the time.

It made her come, and as she clenched around him, he threw his head back, eyes shut tight, jaw clenched as he slowed for her to ride out the waves of pleasure. When she had, he took over, tucking her beneath him. Pressing her into the bed, he roughly grasped her ass with both hands, squeezing as he plunged deep and hard, his expression fierce. He'd held back for her, she knew, and now he couldn't appear to hold back at all. Her heart, already taxed, turned over in her chest. It undid her, *he* undid her, and the words tumbled out of her unbidden. "I love you, Josh."

His eyes flew open as he went over the edge, pulsing inside her, shuddering in her arms, breathing heavy. She was breathing heavy, too, but hers was sheer panic. *I love you?*

Josh rolled over to his back, taking her with him. "Grace."

Heart pounding, she pressed her face into his throat. *Be the bed, be the bed...*

He stroked her damp hair and pressed his mouth to her temple.

She didn't move.

She didn't breathe.

"*Grace.*"

She tightened her eyes. She was asleep. She had left the planet.

She was on a different time continuum. She—

Someone knocked on the door. Then came the little voice. "Daddy?" This was immediately followed by the knob turning, and right then and there, Grace had heart failure.

Thankfully, the door was locked.

"Hold on, Tobes," Josh called out, eyes on Grace. "We're not done," he said to her softly, then pushed up and off the bed. "I'm coming."

And she was going. Rolling off the bed, she grabbed up her clothes and dashed into Josh's bathroom.

On the other side of the door, she heard Josh greet Toby.

"I want popcorn."

"Little late for that, Little Man."

"I need water."

"That we can do," Josh assured him.

As their voices faded, Grace realized they'd moved down the hall. She shoved herself into her clothes and made her escape, not immune to the irony that she was absolutely proving Josh's "queen of running away" and "passive aggressive" statements.

And he was right, of course. Oh how she hated to admit that, but it was true. She *was* running away. She *was* being passive aggressive, both of which really chapped her ass.

But she was thoroughly unequipped to deal with this situation.

In fact, this situation required the Chocoholics. She texted both Mallory and Amy, and like the BFFs they were, they met her at the diner despite the midnight hour.

Mallory was wearing a pair of sweats that were clearly Ty's, looking like she'd just crawled out of bed. "I hope this is good," she said with a yawn. "I just left the sexiest man on the planet, and I have to be at work at six."

"I told Josh I love him," Grace said.

Mallory immediately softened into a goofy smile. "Awwww!"

"No." Grace pointed at her. "No awwww. You want to know why? Because *I* said it first! Do you know what that means? It means *I said it first!*"

"Well, hell," Amy said with a wince. "That's never a good idea."

"Ya think?" Grace asked, her voice resembling Minnie Mouse. God. It was a nightmare. And it wasn't as if he'd called or texted or come after her to try to discuss.

He'd let her go.

Okay, she knew he couldn't have come after her. He had Toby. But he might have called...

"What did he do when you said it?" Mallory asked.

"Nothing, because Toby woke up and wanted popcorn." Grace leaned over and thunked her head on the table a few times.

"Don't do that—you'll knock something loose," Amy said. "Here, have another cupcake."

"A cupcake isn't going to fix this," Grace said. "I need at least two."

Mallory handed her another. "What were you doing when you said it?"

Grace sighed. "We were... in the moment."

Amy winced again.

"Will you stop doing that?" Grace demanded. "Just tell me how to fix this."

"That's easy," Mallory said calmly. "Tell him when you're *not* in the moment so he knows it's real."

Grace's heart clutched. "You think it's real?"

Mallory took her hand and squeezed it. "Yeah, I do. But it doesn't matter what I think. It's what *you* think."

"Have you seen him frustrated and pissed off?" Amy asked.

Grace thought of how Josh had looked when Anna had fought with him over Devon. And his expression when Grace had told him to "bite me." Yeah, it was safe to say she'd seen him frustrated and pissed off. "Yes."

"Have you seen him upset?"

She remembered how he'd looked talking about the loss of his parents. How he'd been after Mrs. Porter's death. Or when he'd realized Toby wanted to be a good Jedi for his mom. Or when Anna had left. "Yes."

"Did his reactions to those emotions scare you off?" Amy asked.

"No." Grace sighed. "Actually, they made me care about him even more." Which was her answer, she supposed.

"You realize he's a package deal," Mallory said. "Right? He's got Toby and Anna. You'd be an instant family if you take him on, and that's a big deal."

"Of course I realize that. And I love them all." Grace heard the words, then clapped a hand over her mouth.

"What *is* that? Why does that word keeping slipping out?"

"It's because love is one of those really bossy bitches," Amy said. "There's no telling it what to do."

Mallory nodded and toasted a cupcake to that. Then she set the cupcake down and got serious as she turned to Grace. "Honey, just promise me something."

"What?"

"That you won't be so driven by your past that you throw away your future. You need to go back. You need to face him and deal with this or he's going to think you didn't mean it."

Go back... When she'd first blurted out her "I love you," she'd been so embarrassed that all she'd thought about was getting out of there. She hadn't thought how Josh would take her vanishing act. But she was thinking now, and she knew the truth. Mallory was right. Her leaving told him that she hadn't meant it and that her running off was her extricating herself from his life. Maybe his parents hadn't left him on purpose, but Ally had. Anna had.

Grace had. She stood up.

"Tell him you meant it," Mallory said. "Tell him—"

Amy stuffed a cupcake into Mallory's mouth. "She'll figure it out, Ace."

Grace wrapped her two cupcakes in a napkin for later. She was hoping things went well but in case they didn't, there was always chocolate. She drove home. And when exactly Josh's house had turned into *home*, she couldn't say. But Josh wasn't there, and neither was Toby. Afraid something had happened to Anna, she texted him: *You okay? Toby? Anna?*

His response came quickly: *Got called into ER. Brought Toby with me. Nothing from Anna.*

Grace turned around and drove to the ER. She found Toby in his Star Wars pj's playing with his Zhu Zhus in the nurse's station. "They have popcorn here," he said happily, clutching a full bag of it.

Grace turned to the nurse's aide watching him. "Is Josh with a patient?"

"Yes. And he's going to be busy for a while."

"Can you ask him if I can take Toby home for him?"

The aide came back with the okay, with absolutely no indication on what Josh thought about Grace showing up. She took Toby home and tucked him back into bed before making herself comfortable on the couch to wait for Josh.

But he never came home.

Chapter 25

Maybe man cannot live on chocolate alone,
but a woman can.

Grace woke up at 6:00 a.m., her face stuck to the couch, someone tugging on her sleeve.

Toby.

He'd liberated Tank from behind the baby gate. The puppy was prancing like a miniature dancing bear. A miniature dancing bear that had to go potty. Scooping him up, Grace ran for the front door, getting him outside just in time for him to race to the closest tree and lift a stumpy leg.

Toby, still in his Star War's pj's, trotted across the yard to join him in anointing the tree.

Grace didn't bother to sigh. When Tank finished, he pawed at the grass with his back feet, head high, proud of his business. Toby loped back to Grace, grinning with his own pride.

Grace gathered both the dog and child back inside and checked her phone.

Nothing.

She was playing Scrabble Junior with Toby when her cell finally buzzed with an incoming call, which she pounced on. But it wasn't Josh.

It was Anna. "Hey," Grace said, "I've been so worried."

Anna didn't say anything. Grace checked the phone to make sure she had reception. "Anna?"

Nothing, but she was there; Grace could feel her in the gaping silence. "Anna," she said softly. "You okay?"

Anna didn't say anything.

"Just tell me where you are," Grace said, heart aching. "I'll come get you. Are you at Devon's?"

Disconnect.

"Road trip," Grace said to Toby.

He immediately hopped up and grabbed Tank and his Jedi saber. Grace was too worried to argue with him. "Get the leash."

"Tank can't be a Jedi on a leash," Toby said.

"He's not big enough to be a Jedi," Grace said.

This caused Toby to beam with pride that *he* was apparently big enough, and he went for the leash.

Grace drove to Devon's building. The place looked dark and still, as if no one was there, but Grace couldn't get rid of her bad feeling. Not in a hurry to get out of the car in this neighborhood, she tried Anna's cell phone again.

It went straight to voice mail this time, so either it was off or it'd run out of juice. While she was still staring down at her phone, unsure of her next move, it buzzed.

Josh.

Oh God. She'd wanted to hear from him, *needed* to

hear from him, and now that he was calling, she wanted to fall into a big hole and live in Denial City. The phone vibrated more intently, and she imagined Josh waiting impatiently on the other end of the line. "Hey," she answered, wincing at how breathless she sounded.

"I'm off work," he said. "We have to talk."

Even knowing he was right, she couldn't go there right now. She couldn't do anything until she knew that Anna was okay. "About that…"

"What? Where are you and Toby?"

She didn't want to tell him where she was, not yet. Anna had told him she was with friends. If she turned out to be here at Devon's, Josh wouldn't be happy to know it. "Give me a few. I'll meet you back at the house."

"What's going on, Grace?"

Shit. He was too damn smart for her. "Okay, fine. I'm outside Devon's place. I got two hang-ups from Anna. I think she wants help and she's too stubborn to ask for it. I have *no* idea where she might have gotten that stubbornness, but I have a feeling it has to do with her last name."

"Stay put," he said. "I'm on my way."

"Staying put." Gladly.

"And, Grace? We still have to talk."

Oh boy. She could hardly wait. She disconnected and stared at the dark apartment.

"Is Anna in there?" Toby asked.

"Not sure." A text beeped in and she glanced at it, figuring it would be from Mallory or Amy wondering how it'd gone with Josh.

Which of course, it hadn't gone at all.

But the text wasn't from Amy or Mallory. It was from Anna.

I need you.

Grace called Josh. "I'm going in," she told him. "Anna needs me now."

"Wait for me. The neighborhood is shit, and so is that building. I'm five minutes out."

She wasn't going to wait five minutes, not after Anna's text.

"Grace," Josh said, voice tight.

"Tunnel."

"We don't have any tunnels," he said. "Don't—"

She disconnected and winced. "Whoops." She turned in her seat and eyed Toby, unsure what to do. And Josh was right; they *were* in a crap neighborhood. Leaving Toby in the car wasn't an option, but she didn't want to bring him inside with her either.

In the end, her urgency to get to Anna made her decision for her. "Okay," she said on the sidewalk, hunkering down in front of Toby and Tank. The two of them, boy and dog, stood side by side, facing her like two little warriors, both so adorable and serious that her heart swelled against her rib cage. "Don't let go of my hand," she said to Toby. "No matter what. That's your only job, to hold on to me at all costs, okay?"

Toby, holding his lightsaber, nodded solemnly. "Arf."

Oh God, she couldn't take it. He was upset; that was the only time he barked these days. Giving him a quick but warm hug, while silently sending Josh a *please hurry*, she straightened, and they went inside the building.

Devon opened the door to her knock. He took one look at the whole brigade, and a muscle tightened in his jaw. "Busy," he said, and tried to close the door.

Not thinking beyond *must get inside*, Grace reacted instinctively and stuck her foot in the door to block it open.

Devon slammed it on her, and Grace doubled over from the oh-holy-shit pain in her foot. She'd seen a foot get slammed in a door on TV a hundred times, and not once did anyone scream in pain. But then again, none of them were ever wearing wedge sandals.

Devon opened the door wide with clear intent to slam it again, but then Tank squirmed through the opening. Even through the agony radiating up from Grace's foot, she heard Toby cry out for his dog. She envisioned what the door would do to Toby's lanky little body or Tank's adorable, fat little one, and she threw herself at Devon. He fell backward, taking her down with him. She landed hard, writhing at the new fire in her foot.

"You crazy bitch!" Devon yelled. He rolled them so that he was on top, smacking her head hard on the floor. She saw stars, and then Tank was suddenly there, growling and snarling as he...

Bit Devon on the ass.

"*What the fuck...*" Devon shoved off Grace, hand on his butt, staring in shock at the little dog. "You little piece of—" Going up on his knees, he reached out and snatched Tank up by the throat.

Tank chirped in alarm, his eyes bugging out even more than usual, paws flailing like a cat on linoleum.

Toby, in his Star Wars pj's and wild bed-head hair, cried out, "Let go of my dog!"

Anna appeared in her chair from the hallway. She was out of breath, like maybe she'd just been fighting to get into the chair on her own, but she rolled directly up behind Toby and snatched him up into her lap. "*Hey!*" she yelled at Devon. "What are you doing? Put the dog down!"

Devon staggered to his feet, Tank still dangling. "It bit me on the ass!"

"That's *my* dog," Toby yelled from his perch on Anna's lap. He dropped his lightsaber and wrapped his arms around his aunt's neck.

Tank gave a sharp cry, signaling that Devon's grip had tightened, and Grace reacted without thinking. From the floor, she grabbed up the lightsaber and whacked Devon in the back of his knees. They buckled, and he collapsed to the floor.

Tank got loose and ran for Toby and Anna.

"That's assault," Devon snarled at Grace. "*Twice!* Not to mention trespassing. I didn't invite you in here. I'm calling the cops."

"Call them," Anna said. "I'll tell them it was self-defense. Grace came in to protect me."

"I didn't do anything to you!"

"You got me into your bed. You moved my chair out of my reach so that I couldn't get to it. You—"

This was the last word Anna got out because Josh had appeared in the open front door. He picked Devon up by the front of his shirt and slammed him into the wall.

Devon, feet hanging off the ground by a good six inches, gave the same sort of desperate squeak that Tank had given only a moment before.

"Grace," Josh said, not taking his eyes off Devon. "Call nine-one-one."

It was his tone that made her react. The utterly calm tone that said everything was going to be okay now that he was here. She slapped her hands on her pockets but couldn't find her phone. She sat up, moved her foot wrong, and cried out before she could bite it back.

"I wasn't doing anything to her, man," Devon said. "Nothing she didn't want done! Tell him, Anna, Jesus!"

"It's true, Josh," Anna said. "I thought I wanted to ... but I found his ex's panties in the bed and I changed my mind."

"For the *second* time!" Devon said.

Anna shook her head, like she couldn't believe she'd ever liked him. "He didn't hurt me," she said to Josh. "He's just a scum bucket."

Josh let go of Devon and pointed at him to stay put. Devon slid down the wall to the floor and wisely sat. Josh strode to Grace and crouched at her side, implacable, coolheaded, every inch of him the ER doctor now. Sharp, assessing eyes roamed over her as he gently cupped the back of her head, feeling the bump there. His jaw clenched, the only sign he gave of what he was feeling. He shifted his attention to her foot, his long, knowing fingers probing in exactly the place to make her suck in a breath.

His gaze slid up to hers. "Where else are you hurt?"

"Nowhere."

"He touch you?"

"*She* attacked me!" Devon said.

Josh slid him a look that would have had Grace peeing in her pants. Devon zipped his mouth.

"I'm so sorry I brought Toby in here," Grace rushed to tell him on a shaky breath, feeling so guilty she could hardly draw more air. "I didn't know what to do. Anna needed me and—"

"I know." Josh squeezed her hip gently. "Don't move." On his knees at Grace's side, he scooped up Toby, hugging both him and Anna close.

"Won the battle, Daddy," Toby said, and wrapped an arm around Josh's neck. Anna set her head down on Josh's shoulder, fisting both hands in his shirt, holding on, eyes closed tight. He murmured something softly to her that had her nodding but not letting go of him. Stroking a hand up her back, he palmed her head and let her cling. Grace watched, throat burning, heart warm.

The police came. An ambulance came. The fire department came, which turned out to be because someone in a neighboring apartment had seen the flash of the lightsaber and thought there was an electrical fire.

It took about two hours for everything to wind down, and when it did, Grace was taken for X-rays. She was sitting on one of Josh's ER beds when he came in, X-ray in hand.

Her heart immediately kicked into gear.

He didn't say anything at first. He simply hung the X-ray on the wall, flipped on the light to read it, and turned to her. His eyes were serious, so serious she felt the breath catch in her throat. "Grace, I—"

"Knock-knock." The curtain swung back to reveal Sheriff Sawyer Thompson. "Heard there was a party in here." He nodded to Grace's foot. "Is it broken?"

"No," Grace said.

"Actually, yes." Josh said, eyes narrowed at Sawyer. "And don't even think about it."

"Think about what?" Grace asked.

Sawyer sighed. "It's just for questioning, Josh."

"What's just for questioning?" Grace asked.

Sawyer turned to her. "I need to bring you into the station."

Chapter 26

Save Earth. It's the only planet with chocolate.

Josh was pacing the front room of the sheriff's station. Grace's broken foot had been set in a cast. Devon had been questioned and was being held. Anna had been questioned and let go. She was sitting quietly in her chair next to the bench on which Toby was perched, the two of them playing games on her phone.

Grace was still in the back with Sawyer.

Josh had no idea what was taking so long. Sawyer was definitely one of the good guys, but this was pissing him off.

Mallory came rushing through the front door. "Just heard from Lucille that Grace was arrested. *What the hell?*"

Josh didn't even bother to ask how Lucille knew that Grace had been taken in. "It's not an arrest. It's just formalities. She clocked Devon with the lightsaber, and he's claiming assault."

"Well fuck formalities."

Yeah, they were on the same page on that.

"They okay?" Mallory asked quietly, gesturing to Anna and Toby.

"Toby is. I don't know about Anna yet. She's playing it close to the vest."

"She's strong, Josh."

"Stronger than me," he said, and looked up to find Anna's eyes on him. There was something in her gaze that he hadn't seen in years.

Warmth.

Affection.

Regret.

He shook his head at the last and moved toward her and Toby, hunkering down before them. He pulled Toby in for a hug. "You did good today, Little Man."

"Better than any other Jedi?"

"Better than *every* other Jedi." He ruffled Toby's hair and turned to Anna. "Proud of you."

Her eyes filled. Swearing beneath his breath, he set Toby down and pulled her tight. Dropping her head to his shoulder, she did what she so rarely did. She completely lost it, sobbing like her heart had just broken.

Toby stepped up behind her and very gently patted her on the back.

"I'm s-sorry," she hiccupped. "I didn't mean to get Grace h-hurt or arrested—"

"She's not arrested," Josh assured her. "And you didn't get her hurt. That was Devon." He tightened his grip on her even as he pulled back enough to see her face. "You promise he didn't hurt you."

"I promise. And we didn't— God, Josh." She covered her face. "I don't want to talk to you about this."

"It's me or someone else, Anna-Banana," he said gently. "We're done with this angry shit."

She sniffed and nodded.

"Promise me."

"I don't feel quite so angry anymore," she whispered, then sniffed again and wiped her nose on the hem of his shirt, laughing soggily when he grimaced. "Watching Grace go ape-shit on Devon's ass was kind of empowering," she said. "I could do that, with some self-defense classes."

"Anna—"

"For paraplegics like me. They have classes like that, you know. Grace found them for me at Washington University."

He looked into her eyes. "Yeah?"

"And there's soccer too. I want to go there and live in the dorms, like a normal college student. And next year I want to go on their abroad program. I'm going to see the world, Josh. My way, not yours."

"Can you do it without a douche-bag boyfriend?"

"Yeah."

"Good." Josh leaned back on the bench, exhausted, and more than a little worried about Grace. But beyond that, there was something new blooming in his chest.

Or rather, the lack of something old. He'd felt like a family tonight with Toby and Anna. A real family.

That was all Grace. It was *still* Grace, and she wasn't even in the room. He'd actually believed that he didn't have anything at stake with her, that it would cost him nothing to enjoy the fun while it lasted. To enjoy her.

But he'd been wrong. He'd had his family at stake, his heart. Everything.

And she loved him. It'd been a shock to hear her say it. After she had, all he'd wanted to do was hear it again, but he quickly realized during her vanishing act that it'd been a mistake on her part. She hadn't meant to say it at all.

She loved him, but she didn't *want* to love him.

He'd found someone he'd never in a million years expected— someone who'd put it all on the line for him, someone to love *him*—not for being a doctor or a dad, but just for being Josh.

And he'd blown it.

The front door of the station opened and more people arrived. Amy. Matt. Ty. Lucille and her entire posse.

Hell, half the town.

Lucille and her gang were carrying posters that said things like FREE GRACE. One of the sheriffs confiscated the posters when an eighty-five-year-old Mrs. Burland hit one of them over the head. He said he'd arrest her for police brutality, but he was afraid of starting a riot.

Finally, Sawyer came out of the back, leading Grace, on crutches, and everyone started yelling at Sawyer at once.

"She was only protecting Anna!"

"You can't arrest her!"

"We won't let you take her!"

Sawyer held up a hand, and the din stopped on a dime. "You people are crazy, you know that?"

The yelling renewed, but again Sawyer stopped them. "She's not arrested! We just had some questions that needed answers. Seriously, you all need a life. Grace is free to go."

Grace was standing in the middle of the crowd looking a little bowled over at the support. And also a little unstable on her feet, especially when everyone began to move

in too close. Josh waded in, parted the seas, and drew her
up against him, crutches and all.

Grace hadn't seen him coming, but the minute Josh's
warm, strong arms surrounded her, she sighed. "Hey," she
said, breathless. The crutches were a bitch, and all the
people were a little disconcerting, but that wasn't what
had stolen the air from her lungs.

Nope, that was all Josh, and the way he'd somehow
pushed through the crowd to get to her. It was how he'd
pulled her in tight, as if she were the most precious thing
to him, as if he couldn't wait another second to touch her.

She liked that, a lot.

Everyone around them seemed a little crazy, but she
realized that they were here for her.

Her.

In her world, she'd always had to earn acceptance,
approval, even love. But from the very beginning, it'd
been different here. She had Amy and Mallory, who had
accepted her as is, and the rest of Lucky Harbor had eventually done the same, no questions asked. She'd never
experienced anything like it. It was humbling.

It was amazing.

And then there was Toby and Anna.

And Josh...

Behind them, Sawyer was shoving people toward the
door. "Out. Everyone out." He eyed Lucille's FREE
GRACE sign and shook his head at her.

Unrepentant, she grinned, then turned to Grace. "You
did good, hon, protecting the tot. If Dr. Scott doesn't realize what a catch he has, we'll all make sure to hit him
with our signs when he comes out of the station."

"Hell," Josh said. "I'm right here."

"He ought to make an honest woman out of you," Mr. Saunders said, ignoring Josh. "If he doesn't, *I* will."

"No, *I* will," Mr. Wykowski said, waving his cane.

"Easy, boys." Lucille looped an arm into each of theirs. "There are plenty of honest women to go around."

Sawyer pointed to the door. He wasn't the kind of guy people messed with. If he wanted the place empty, the place got empty, in a hurry. In less than two minutes, it was just Josh and Grace. Even Anna and Toby had gone outside to wait.

In the ensuing silence, Sawyer shook his head, muttered something to himself that sounded like "fucking Mayberry," and gave Josh and Grace a nod. "I'll be in the back."

Then they were alone. Nerves danced in Grace's belly.

"You okay?" Josh tilted her face up to his, searching her features as if he couldn't get his fill.

She gave herself permission to do the same. She had no idea what her future held exactly, but for the first time in her life, that was okay. She'd found herself. Here, in this town.

With this man.

And that was enough. She'd found her own way, not because of what her job title was or how much money she pushed around, but because of who she was. On the inside. Which, as it turned out, had nothing to do with numbers at all. "I'm okay. Devon's not pressing charges."

Josh let out a breath and pushed the hair from her face, tracing a finger along her temple, tucking a strand behind her ear. "I missed you last night."

Out of all the things that she'd expected him to say,

that was just about last on the list. She pulled back to meet his gaze. "But after I left, you didn't even call."

"I thought you needed some space. My mistake," he said quietly.

"No, it's mine," Grace said in a rush, the words needing to get out. "I'm sorry about what I said. It was too soon. I shouldn't have—"

Josh cut her off with a kiss that made her toes curl. "Don't be sorry," he said when they broke apart. "I love you, Grace. I think I have since day one when you jumped into my life with both feet, giving me all you had just to help me out."

She stared up at him, feeling the anxiety in her chest break free, giving way to hope and love. "You should know that it wasn't all from the goodness of my heart. It was also for the goodness of my very sad bank account."

His mouth curved. "Liar. You'd do just about anything to help anyone, even people who only a few months ago were perfect strangers." And though he kept his eyes on hers, he gestured outside with a jerk of his chin, where everyone in town was straining their eardrums trying to catch their conversation.

They're trying to see if you're making an honest woman out of me," she said.

"Working on it," he said. "It'd help if you threw yourself at me in front of them."

She laughed and did just that, flinging down her crutches and hitting him midchest. Her cast weighed her down a bit but he seemed to have no problem catching her. She wrapped herself around him like a monkey and buried her face against his throat, breathing him in. "You haven't asked me if I'm taking the job."

"It doesn't matter."

She lifted her head. "No . . . ?"

"Either way, we'll make it work."

Her breath caught as her heart filled with so much love and hope she didn't know if she could contain it all. "Yeah?"

"Yeah."

Nope. Nope, she couldn't contain it all, some of it spilled out in the form of a dopey smile. "You really wouldn't mind dating a woman who lived far away?"

His gaze roamed her features hungrily. "Hell, Grace. I'd go to Australia to visit you. I don't care about the job, or where you lay your head down at night, as long as your heart's mine."

Her heart melted. "I'm not taking the Seattle job, Josh."

He closed his eyes. "So the offer was from Portland, then. All right, so we'll get intimately familiar with frequent-flyer miles."

She slid her fingers into his hair and waited until he opened his eyes and looked at her. "I didn't take that job either."

His eyes narrowed slightly. He was catching on. "Give me a hint," he said.

"It involves shoe boxes." She drew in a deep breath and said it out loud for the first time. "I've lived in quite a few places in my life, and none of them ever felt like home. Until Lucky Harbor. For the first time, I feel like I belong somewhere. Here. I'm going to stay and open a small bookkeeping firm. I might have to supplement the income at first with other jobs, but as it turns out, I like mixing it up. What do you think?"

His smile was a thousand watts. "I think it's perfect. *You're* perfect. You know how much I love you, right? You, just the way you are."

"Really?"

He pulled her in tighter and buried his face in her hair, inhaling her in. "Forever," he said, and as he lowered his head to kiss her, a wild cheer went up from the crowd outside the window.

Epilogue

One year later

Grace woke from a Maui sun-soaked snooze when a shadow blocked her rays. She opened her eyes and took in the sight of Josh in nothing but loose board shorts, slung so low on his hips as to be indecent. His big, built body was tanned and wet from his ocean swim. *Very* wet, and he had a wicked gleam in his gaze. "Don't," she warned him. "Don't you dare—"

With a badass grin, he scooped her out of the oversized lounge chair on the private beach of their honeymoon house and up against his drenched body.

"—get me wet," she finished weakly.

"Oh, I'm going to get you wet, Mrs. Scott. *Very* wet." He nuzzled her for a moment, then dropped down onto the lounge, with her now on top of him. He made himself comfortable, his hands roaming freely over her body as he did. "Mmm. You smell like a coconut. You know I love coconuts."

She did. She knew this firsthand... It'd been a lovely few days, and they had a few more left. They'd gotten married six months ago, but this had been their first opportunity for a getaway. Anna had come home on college break to watch Toby and Tank for them.

They'd made the most of their alone time, and Grace lay there on top of Josh in sated, contented quiet. Working their way down her sexual fantasy list had proven exhausting business, and they had yet to start on Josh's, although sitting on him as she was, she could tell he was ready to get going.

Josh entwined his fingers with hers and drew them up to his mouth, kissing her palm, regarding her with a serious look on his face. "Promise me something."

"Anything."

His free hand slid to her still-flat belly. At only three months pregnant, she wasn't yet showing at all. "We skip the Star Wars DVDs with this one."

After Maddie Moore loses her boyfriend and her job, she moves to Lucky Harbor to fix up the inn her mother left as her inheritance. But the contractor she's hired is making it hard for her to remember that she's sworn off men...

Please turn this page for an excerpt from *Simply Irresistible* and see why readers first fell in love with Lucky Harbor.

Chapter 1

*"I chose the path less traveled, but only because
I was lost. Carry a map."*

PHOEBE TRAEGER

Maddie drove the narrow, curvy highway with her past
still nipping at her heels after fourteen hundred miles. Not
even her dependable Honda had been able to outrun her
demons.

Or her own failings.

Good thing, then, that she was done with failing.
Please be done with failing, she thought.

"Come on, listeners," the disc jockey said jovially on
the radio. "Call in with your Christmas hopes and dreams.
We'll be picking a random winner and making a wish
come true."

"You're kidding me." Maddie briefly took her eyes off
the mountainous road and flicked a glance at the dash. "It's
one day after Thanksgiving. It's not time for Christmas."

"Any wish," the DJ said. "Name it, and it could be
yours."

As if. But she let out a breath and tried for whimsy. Once upon a time, she'd been good at such things. *Maddie Moore, you were raised on movie sets—fake the damn whimsy.* "Fine. I'll wish for…" What? That she could've had a do-over with her mother before Phoebe Traeger had gone to the ultimate Grateful Dead concert in the sky? That Maddie had dumped her ex far sooner than she had? That her boss—may he choke on his leftover turkey—had waited until *after* year-end bonuses to fire her?

"The lines are lit up," the DJ announced. "Best of luck to all of you out there waiting."

Hey, maybe *that's* what she'd wish for—luck. She'd wish for better luck than she'd had: with family, with a job, with men—

Well, maybe not men. Men she was giving up entirely. Pausing from that thought, she squinted through the fog to read the first road sign she'd seen in a while.

WELCOME TO LUCKY HARBOR!
Home to 2,100 lucky people
And 10,100 shellfish

About time. Exercising muscles she hadn't utilized in too long, she smiled, and in celebration of arriving at her designated destination, she dug into the bag of salt and vinegar potato chips at her side. Chips cured just about everything, from the I-lost-my-job blues, to the my-boyfriend-was-a-jerk regrets, to the tentatively hopeful celebration of a new beginning.

"A new beginning done right," she said out loud, because everyone knew that saying it out loud made it true. "You hear that, karma?" She glanced upward through her slightly leaky sunroof into a dark sky, where storm clouds tumbled together like a dryer full of gray wool blankets. "This time, I'm going to be strong." Like Katharine Hepburn. Like Ingrid Bergman. "So go torture someone else and leave me alone."

A bolt of lightning blinded her, followed by a boom of thunder that nearly had her jerking out of her skin. "Okay, so I meant *pretty please* leave me alone."

The highway in front of her wound its way alongside a cliff on her right, which probably hid more wildlife than this affirmed city girl wanted to think about. Far below the road on her left, the Pacific Ocean pitched and rolled, fog lingering in long, silvery fingers on the frothy water.

Gorgeous, all of it, but what registered more than anything was the silence. No horns blaring while jockeying for position in the clogged fast lane, no tension-filled offices where producers and directors shouted at each other. No ex-boyfriends who yelled to release steam. Or worse.

No anger at all, in fact.

Just the sound of the radio and her own breathing. Delicious, *glorious* silence.

As unbelievable as it seemed, she'd never driven through the mountains before. She was here now only because, shockingly, her mother's will had listed property in Washington State. More shockingly, Maddie had been left one-third of that property, a place called Lucky Harbor Resort.

Raised by her set designer dad in Los Angeles, Maddie hadn't seen her mother more than a handful of times since he'd taken custody of her at age five, so the will had been a huge surprise. Her dad had been just as shocked as she, and so had her two half-sisters, Tara and Chloe.

Since there hadn't been a memorial service—Phoebe had specifically not wanted one—the three sisters had agreed to meet at the resort.

It would be the first time they'd seen each other in five years.

Defying probability, the road narrowed yet again. Maddie steered into the sharp left curve and then immediately whipped the wheel the other way for the unexpected right. A sign warned her to keep a lookout for river otters, osprey—what the heck were *osprey?*—and bald eagles. Autumn had come extremely late this year for the entire West Coast, and the fallen leaves were strewn across the roads like gold coins. It was beautiful, and taking it all in might have caused her to slide a little bit into the next hairpin, where she—oh, crap—

Barely missed a guy on a motorcycle.

"Oh, my God." Heart in her throat, she craned her neck, watching as the bike ran off the road and skidded to a stop. With a horrified grimace, she started to drive past, then hesitated.

But hurrying past a cringe-worthy moment, hoping to avoid a scene, was the old Maddie. The new Maddie stopped the car, though she did allow herself a beat to draw a quick, shuddery breath. What was she supposed to say—*Sorry I almost killed you, here's my license, insurance, and last twenty-seven dollars?* No, that was too pathetic. *Motorcycles are death machines, you idiot, you nearly got yourself killed!* Hmm, probably a tad too defensive. Which meant that a simple, heartfelt apology would have to do.

Bolstering her courage, she got out of the car clutching her Blackberry, ready to call 911 if it got ugly. Shivering in the unexpectedly damp ocean air, she moved toward him, her arms wrapped around herself as she faced the music.

Please don't be a raging asshole...

He was still straddling the motorcycle, one long leg stretched out, balancing on a battered work boot, and if he was pissed, she couldn't tell yet past his reflective sunglasses. He was leanly muscled and broad shouldered, and his jeans and leather jacket were made for a hard body just like his. It was a safe bet that *he* hadn't just inhaled an entire bag of salt-and-vinegar chips. "Are you okay?" she asked, annoyed that she sounded breathless and nervous.

Pulling off his helmet, he revealed wavy, dark brown hair and a day's worth of stubble on a strong jaw. "I'm good. You?" His voice was low and calm, his hair whipping around in the wind.

Irritated, most definitely. But not pissed.

Relieved, she dragged in some air. "I'm fine, but I'm not the one who nearly got run off the road by the crazy LA driver. I'm sorry, I was driving too fast."

"You probably shouldn't admit that."

True. But she was thrown by his gravelly voice, by the fact that he was big and, for all she knew, bad, to boot, and that she was alone with him on a deserted, foggy highway.

It had all the makings of a horror flick.

"Are you lost?" he asked.

Was she? Probably she was a little lost mentally, and quite possibly emotionally, as well. Not that she'd admit either. "I'm heading to Lucky Harbor Resort."

He pushed his sunglasses to the top of his head, and be

still her heart, he had eyes the *exact* color of the caramel in the candy bar she'd consumed for lunch. "Lucky Harbor Resort," he repeated.

"Yes." But before she could ask why he was baffled about that, his gaze dipped down and he took in her favorite long-sleeved tee. Reaching out, he picked something off her sleeve.

Half a chip.

He took another off her collarbone, and she broke out in goose bumps—and not the scared kind.

"Plain?"

"Salt and vinegar," she said and shook off the crumbs. She'd muster up some mortification—but she'd used up her entire quota when she'd nearly flattened him like a pancake. Not that she cared what he—or any man, for that matter—thought. Because she'd given up men.

Even tall, built, really good-looking, tousled-haired guys with gravelly voices and piercing eyes.

Especially them.

What she needed now was an exit plan. So she put her phone to her ear, pretending it was vibrating. "Hello," she said to no one. "Yes, I'll be right there." She smiled, like *look at me, so busy, I really have to go*, and, turning away, she lifted a hand in a wave, still talking into the phone to avoid an awkward good-bye, except—

Her phone rang. And not the pretend kind. Risking a peek at Hot Biker Guy over her shoulder, she found him brows up, looking amused.

"I think you have a *real* call," he said, something new in his voice. Possibly more humor, but most likely sheer disbelief that he'd nearly been killed by a socially handicapped LA chick.

Face hot, Maddie answered her phone. And then wished she hadn't, since it was the HR department of the production office from which she'd been fired, asking where she'd like her final check mailed. "I have automatic deposit," she murmured, and listened to the end-of-employment spiel and questions, agreeing out loud that yes, she realized being terminated means no references. With a sigh, she hung up.

He was watching her. "Fired, huh?"

"I don't want to talk about it."

He accepted that but didn't move. He just remained still, straddling that bike, sheer testosterone coming off him in waves. She realized he was waiting for her to leave first. Either he was being a gentleman, or he didn't want to risk his life and limbs. "Again, sorry. And I'm really glad I didn't kill you—" She walked backward, right into her own car. Good going. Keeping her face averted, she leapt into the driver's seat. "Really glad I didn't kill you?" she repeated to herself. *Seriously?* Well, whatever, it was done. *Just don't look back. Don't—*

She looked.

He was watching her go, and though she couldn't be certain, she thought maybe he was looking a little bemused.

She got that a lot.

A minute later, she drove through Lucky Harbor. It was everything Google Earth had promised, a picturesque little Washington State beach town nestled in a rocky cove with a quirky, eclectic mix of the old and new. The main drag was lined with Victorian buildings painted in bright colors, housing the requisite grocery store, post office, gas station, and hardware store. Then a turnoff to the beach itself, where a long pier jutted out into the water, lined with more shops and outdoor cafés.

And a Ferris wheel.

The sight of it brought an odd yearning. She wanted to buy a ticket and ride it, if only to pretend for four minutes that she wasn't twenty-nine, broke every which way to Sunday, and homeless.

Oh, and scared of heights.

She kept driving. Two minutes later, she came to a fork in the road and had no idea which way to turn. Pulling over, she grabbed her map, watching as Hot Biker Guy rode past her in those faded jeans that fit perfectly across his equally perfect butt.

When the very nice view was gone, she went back to studying her map. Lucky Harbor Resort was supposedly on the water, which was still hard to believe, because as far as Maddie knew, the only thing her mother had ever owned was a 1971 wood-paneled station wagon and every single Dead album ever recorded.

According to the lawyer's papers, the resort was made up of a small marina, an inn, and an owner's cottage. Filled with anticipation, Maddie hit the gas and steered right . . . only to come to the end of the asphalt.

Huh.

She eyed the last building on the left. It was an art gallery. A woman stood in the doorway wearing a bright pink velour sweat suit with white piping, white athletic shoes, and a terry-cloth sweatband that held back her equally white hair. She could have been fifty or eighty, it was hard to tell, and in direct contrast to the athletic outfit, she had a cigarette dangling out the corner of her mouth and skin that looked as if she'd been standing in the sun for decades. "Hello, darling," she said in a craggy voice when Maddie got out of her car. "You're either lost, or you want to buy a painting."

"A little lost," Maddie admitted.

"That happens a lot out here. We have all these roads that lead nowhere."

Great. She was on the road to nowhere. Story of her life. "I'm looking for Lucky Harbor Resort."

The woman's white eyebrows jerked upright, vanishing into her hair. "Oh! Oh, finally!" Eyes crinkling when she smiled, she clapped her hands in delight. "Which one are you, honey? The Wild Child, the Steel Magnolia, or the Mouse?"

Maddie blinked. "Uh..."

"Oh, your momma *loved* to talk about her girls! Always said how she'd screwed you all up but good, but that someday she'd get you all back here to run the inn together as a real family, the three of you."

"You mean the four of us."

"Nope. Somehow she always knew it'd be just you three girls." She puffed on her cigarette, then nearly hacked up a lung. "She wanted to get the inn renovated first, but that didn't happen. The pneumonia caught her fast, and then she was gone." Her smile faded some. "Probably God couldn't resist Pheeb's company. Christ, she was such a kick." She cocked her head and studied Maddie's appearance.

Self-conscious, Maddie once again brushed at herself, hoping the crumbs were long gone and that maybe her hair wasn't as bad as it felt.

The woman smiled. "The Mouse."

Well, hell. Maddie blew out a breath, telling herself it was silly to be insulted at the truth. "Yes."

"That'd make you the smart one, then. The one who ran the big, fancy production company in Los Angeles."

"Oh." Maddie vehemently shook her head. "No, I was just an assistant." To an assistant. Who sometimes had to buy her boss's underwear and fetch his girlfriend's presents, as well as actually produce movies and TV shows.

"Your momma said you'd say that, but she knew better. Knew your work ethic. She said you worked very hard."

Maddie *had* worked hard. And dammit, she had also pretty much run that company. May it rot in hell. "How do you know all this?"

"I'm Lucille." When this produced no recognition from Maddie, she cackled in laughter. "I actually work for you. You know, at the inn? Whenever there's guests, I come in and clean."

"By yourself?"

"Well, business hasn't exactly been hopping, has it? Oh! Wait here a second, I have something to show you—"

"Actually, I'm sort of in a hurry..." But Lucille was gone. "Okay, then."

Two minutes later, Lucille reappeared from the gallery carrying a small carved wooden box that said RECIPES, the kind that held 3x5 index cards. "This is for you girls."

Maddie didn't cook, but it seemed rude not to take it. "Did Phoebe cook?"

"Oh, hell, no," Lucille said with a cackle. "She could burn water like no other."

Maddie accepted the box with a baffled "Thanks."

"Now, you just continue down this road about a mile to the clearing. You can't miss it. Call me if you need anything. Cleaning, organizing...spider relocation."

This caught Maddie's attention. "Spider relocation?"

"Your momma wasn't big on spiders."

Uh-huh, something they had in common. "Are there a lot of them?"

"Well, that depends on what you consider a lot."

Oh, God. Any more than one was an infestation. Maddie managed a smile that might have been more a baring of her teeth, gave a wave of thanks, and got back into her car, following the dirt road. "*The Mouse,*" she said with a sigh.

That was going to change.

Chapter 2

"Don't take life too seriously. After all, none of us are getting out alive anyway."

<small>PHOEBE TRAEGER</small>

Turned out Lucille was right, and in exactly one mile, the road opened up to a clearing. The Pacific Ocean was a deep, choppy sea of black, dusted with whitecaps that went out as far as Maddie could see. It connected with a metallic gray sky, framed by rocky bluffs, misty and breathtaking.

She had found the "resort," and Lucille had gotten something else right, too. The place wasn't exactly hopping.

Dead was more like it.

Clearly, the inn had seen better days. A woman sat on the front porch steps, a Vespa parked nearby. At the sight of Maddie, she stood. She wore cute little hip-hugging army cargoes, a snug, bright red Henley, and matching high-tops. Her glossy dark red hair cascaded down her back in an artful disarray that would have taken an entire beauty salon staff to accomplish on Maddie's uncontrollable curls.

Chloe, the twenty-four-year-old Wild Child.

Maddie attempted to pat down her own dark blond hair that had a mind of its own, but it was a waste of time on a good day, which this most definitely wasn't. Before she could say a word, a cab pulled up next to Maddie's car and a tall, lean, beautiful woman got out. Her short brunette hair was layered and effortlessly sexy. She wore an elegant business suit that emphasized her fit body and a cool smile.

Tara, the Steel Magnolia.

As the cabbie set Tara's various bags on the porch, the three of them just stared at one another, five years of estrangement floating awkwardly between them. The last time they'd all been in one place, Tara and Maddie had met in Montana to bail Chloe out of jail for illegally bungee jumping off a bridge. Chloe had thanked them, promised to pay them back, and they'd all gone their separate ways.

It was just the way it was. They had three different fathers and three very different personalities, and the only thing they had in common was a sweet, ditzy, wanderlusting hippie of a mother.

"So," Maddie said, forcing a smile through the uncomfortable silence. "How's things?"

"Ask me again after we sort out this latest mess," Tara murmured and eyed their baby sister.

Chloe tossed up her hands. "Hey, I had nothing to do with this one."

"Which would be a first." Tara spoke with the very slight southern accent that she denied having, the one she'd gotten from growing up on her paternal grandparents' horse ranch in Texas.

Chloe rolled her eyes and pulled her always-present asthma inhaler from her pocket, looking around without much interest. "So this is it? The big reveal?"

"I guess so," Maddie said, also taking in the clearly deserted inn. "There don't appear to be any guests at the moment."

"Not good for resale value," Tara noted.

"Resale?" Maddie asked.

"Selling is the simplest way to get out of here as fast as possible."

Maddie's stomach clenched. She didn't want to get out of here. She wanted a place to stay—to breathe, to lick her wounds, to regroup. "What's the hurry?"

"Just being realistic. The place came with a huge mortgage and no liquid assets."

Chloe shook her head. "Sounds like Mom."

"There was a large trust fund from her parents," Maddie said. "The will separated it out from the estate, so I have no idea who it went to. I assumed it was one of you."

Chloe shook her head.

They both looked at Tara.

"Sugar, I don't know any more than y'all. What I *do* know is that we'd be smart to sell, pay off the loan on the property, and divide what's left three ways and get back to our lives. I'm thinking we can list the place and be out of here in a few days if we play our cards right."

This time Maddie's stomach plummeted. "So fast?"

"Do you really want to stay in Lucky Harbor a moment longer than necessary?" Tara asked. "Even Mom, bless her heart, didn't stick around."

Chloe shook her inhaler and took a second puff from it. "Selling works for me. I'm due at a friend's day spa in New Mexico next week."

"You have enough money to book yourself at a spa in New Mexico, but not enough to pay me back what you've borrowed?" Tara asked.

"I'm going there to work. I've been creating a natural skin care line, and I'm giving a class on it, hoping to sell the line to the spa." Chloe eyed the road. "Think there's a bar in town? I could use a drink."

"It's four in the afternoon," Tara said.

"But it's five o'clock somewhere."

Chloe's eyes narrowed. "What?" she said to Tara's sound of disappointment.

"I think you know."

"Why don't you tell me anyway."

And here we go, Maddie thought, anxiety tightening like a knot in her throat. "Um, maybe we could all just sit down and—"

"No, I want her to say what's on her mind," Chloe said.

The static electricity rose in the air until it crackled with violence from both impending storms—Mother Nature's *and* the sisters' fight.

"It's not important what I think," Tara said coolly.

"Oh, come on, Dixie," Chloe said. "Lay it on us. You know you want to."

Maddie stepped between them. She couldn't help it. It was the middle sister in her, the approval seeker, the office manager deep inside. "Look!" she said in desperation. "A puppy!"

Chloe swiveled her head to Maddie, amused. "Seriously?"

She shrugged. "Worth a shot."

"Next time say it with more conviction and less panic. You might get somewhere."

"Well, I don't give a hoot if there are puppies *and* rainbows," Tara said. "As unpleasant as this is, we have to settle it."

Maddie was watching Chloe shake her inhaler again, looking pale. "You okay?"

"Peachy."

She tried not to take the sarcasm personally. Chloe, a free spirit as Phoebe had been, suffered debilitating asthma and resented the hell out of the disability because it hampered her quest for adventure.

And for arguing.

Together all three sisters walked across the creaky porch and into the inn. Like most of the other buildings in Lucky Harbor, it was Victorian. The blue and white paint had long ago faded, and the window shutters were mostly gone or falling off, but Maddie could picture how it'd once looked: new and clean, radiating character and charm.

They'd each been mailed a set of keys. Tara used hers to unlock and open the front door, and she let out a long-suffering sigh.

The front room was a shrine to a country-style house circa 1980. Just about everything was blue and white, from the checkered window coverings to the duck-and-cow accent wallpaper peeling off the walls. The paint was chipped and the furniture not old enough to be antique and yet at least thirty years on the wrong side of new.

"Holy asphyxiation," Chloe said with her nose wrinkled at the dust. "I won't be able to stay here. I'll suffocate."

Tara shook her head, half horrified, half amused. "It looks like Laura Ingalls Wilder threw up in here."

"You know, your accent gets thicker and thicker," Chloe said.

"I don't have an accent."

"Okay. Except you do."

"It's not that bad," Maddie said quickly when Tara opened her mouth.

"Oh, it's bad," Chloe said. "You sounds like Susan Sarandon in *Bull Durham*."

"The *inn*," Maddie clarified. "I meant the *inn* isn't so bad."

"I've stayed in hostels in Bolivia that looked like the Ritz compared to this," Chloe said.

"Mom's mom and her third husband ran this place." Tara ran a finger along the banister, then eyed the dust on the pad of her finger. "Years and years ago."

"So Grandma ran through men, too?" Chloe asked. "Jeez, it's like we're destined to be man-eaters."

"Speak for yourself," Tara murmured, indeed sounding like Susan Sarandon.

Chloe grinned. "Admit it, our gene pool could use some chlorine."

"As I was saying," Tara said when Maddie laughed. "Grandma worked here, and when she died, Mom attempted to take over but got overwhelmed."

Maddie was mesmerized by this piece of her past. She'd never even heard of this place. As far as she knew, none of them had kept in regular contact with Phoebe. This was mostly because their mother had spent much of her life out of contact with anything other than her own whimsy.

Not that she'd been a bad person. By all accounts, she'd been a sweet, free-loving flower child. But she hadn't been the greatest at taking care of things like cars, bank accounts...her daughters. "I wasn't even aware that Mom had been close to her parents."

"They died a long time ago." Tara turned back, watching Chloe climb the stairs. "Don't go up there, sugar. It's far too dusty; you'll aggravate your asthma."

"I'm already aggravated, and not by my asthma." But Chloe pulled the neckline of her shirt over her mouth. She also kept going up the stairs, and Tara just shook her head.

"Why do I bother?" Tara moved into the kitchen and went still at the condition of it. "Formica countertops," she said as if she'd discovered asbestos.

Okay, true, the Formica countertops weren't pretty, but the country-blue-and-white tile floor was cute in a retro sort of way. And yes, the appliances were old, but there was something innately homey and warm about the setup, including the rooster wallpaper trim. Maddie could see guests in here at the big wooden block table against the large picture window, which had a lovely view of...the dilapidated marina.

So fine, they could call it a blast from the past. Certainly there were people out there looking for an escape to a quaint, homey inn and willing to pay for it.

"We need elbow grease, and lots of it," Chloe said, walking into the kitchen, her shirt still over her nose and mouth.

Maddie wasn't afraid of hard work. It was all she knew. And envisioning this place all fixed up with a roaring fire in the woodstove and a hot, delicious meal on

he stovetop, with cuteness spilling from every nook and
cranny, made her smile. Without thinking, she pulled out
he Blackberry she could no longer afford and started a
ist, her thumbs a blur of action. "New paint, new coun-
ertops, new appliances..." Hmm, what else? She hit the
ight switch for a better look, and nothing happened.

Tara sighed.

Maddie added that to the list. "Faulty wiring—"

"And leaky roof." Tara pointed upward.

"There's a bathroom above this," Chloe told them. "It's
got a plumbing issue. Roof's probably leaking, too."

Tara came closer and peered over Maddie's shoulder at
her list. "Are you a compulsive organizer?"

At the production studios, she'd had to be. There'd
been five producers—and her. They'd gotten the glory,
and she'd done the work.

All of it.

And until last week, she'd thrived on it. "Yes. Hi, my
name is Maddie, and I am addicted to my Blackberry,
office supplies, and organization." She waited for a smartass comment.

But Tara merely shrugged. "You'll come in handy."
She was halfway out of the room before Maddie found
her voice.

"Did you know Mom didn't want to sell?" she asked
Tara's back. "That she planned on us running the place as
a family?"

Tara turned around. "She knew better than that."

"No, really. She wanted to use the inn to bring us together."

"I loved Mom," Chloe said. "But she didn't do 'together.'"

"She didn't," Maddie agreed. "But we could. If we wanted."

Both sisters gaped at her.

"You've lost your ever-lovin' marbles," Tara finally said. "We're selling."

No longer a mouse, Maddie told herself. Going from mouse to tough girl, like... Rachel from *Friends*. Without the wishy-washyness. And without Ross. She didn't like Ross. "What if I don't want to sell?"

"I don't give a coon's ass whether you want to or not. It doesn't matter," Tara said. "We *have* to sell."

"A coon's ass?" Chloe repeated with a laugh. "Is that farm ghetto slang or something? And what does that even mean?"

Tara ignored her and ticked reasons off on her fingers. "There's no money. We have a payment due to the note holder in two weeks. Not to mention, I have a life to get back to in Dallas. I took a week off, that's it."

Maddie knew Tara had a sexy NASCAR husband named Logan and a high-profile managerial job. Maddie could understand wanting to get back to both.

"And maybe I have a date with an Arabian prince," Chloe said. "We *all* have lives to get back to, Tara."

Well, not all of us, Maddie thought.

In uneasy silence, they checked out the rest of the inn. There was a den and a small bed and bath off the kitchen and four bedrooms and two community bathrooms upstairs, all shabby chic minus the chic.

Next, they walked out to the marina. The small metal building was half equipment storage and half office—and one giant mess. Kayaks and tools and oars and supplies vied for space. In the good-news department, four of the eight boat slips were filled. "Rent," Maddie said, thrilled, making more notes.

"Hmm," was all Tara said.

Chloe was eyeing the sole motorboat. "Hey, we should take that out for a joyride and—"

"No!" Maddie and Tara said in unison.

Chloe rolled her eyes. "Jeez, a girl gets arrested once and no one ever lets her forget it."

"Twice," Tara said. "And you still owe me the bail money for that San Diego jet ski debacle."

Maddie had no idea what had happened in San Diego. She wasn't sure she wanted to know. They moved outside again and faced the last section of the "resort," the small owner's cottage. And actually, *small* was too kind. *Postage-stamp*-sized was too kind. It had a blink-and-you'll-miss-it kitchen-and-living-room combo and a single bedroom and bath.

And lots of dust.

"It's really not that bad," Maddie said into the stunned silence. They stood there another beat, taking in the decor, which was—surprise, surprise—done in blue and white with lots of stenciled ducks and cows and roosters, oh, my. "Mostly cosmetic. I just think—"

"No," Tara said firmly. "Bless your heart, but please, *please* don't think."

Chloe choked out a laugh. "Love how you say 'bless your heart' just before you insult someone. Classy."

Tara ignored Chloe entirely and kept her voice soft and steely calm. "Majority rules here. And majority says we should sell ASAP, assuming that in this economy we don't have to actually *pay* someone to take this place off our hands."

Maddie looked at Chloe. "You really want to sell, too?"

Chloe hesitated.

"Be honest with her," Tara said.

"I can't." Chloe covered her face. "She has Bambi eyes. You know what?" She headed for the door. "I'm not in the mood to be the swing vote."

"Where are you going?" Tara demanded.

"For a ride."

"But we need your decision—"

The door shut, hard.

Tara tossed up her hands. "Selfish as ever." She looked around in disgust. "I'm going into town for supplies to see us through the next couple of days. We need food and cleaning supplies—and possibly a fire accelerant." She glanced at Maddie and caught her horror. "Kidding! Can I borrow your car?"

Maddie handed over her keys. "Get chips, lots of chips."

When she was alone, she sat on the steps and pulled Lucille's recipe box from her bag. With nothing else to do, she lifted the lid, prepared to be bored by countless recipes she'd never use.

The joke was on her. Literally. The 3x5 cards had been written on, but instead of recipes for food, she found recipes for...

Life.

They were all handwritten by Phoebe and labeled *Advice for My Girls*. The first one read:

Always be in love.

Maddie stared at it for a moment, then had to smile. Years ago, she'd gotten the birds-and-bees speech from her father. He'd rambled off the facts quickly, not meeting her eyes, trying to do his best by her. He was so damned uncomfortable, and all because a boy had called her.

Boys are like drugs, her father had said. *Just say no.*

Her mother and father had definitely not subscribed to the same philosophies. Not quite up to seeing what other advice Phoebe had deemed critical, Maddie slipped the box back into her bag. She zipped up her sweatshirt and headed out herself, needing a walk. The wind had picked up. The clouds were even darker now, hanging low above her head.

At the end of the clearing, she stopped and looked back at the desolate inn. It hadn't been what she'd hoped for. She had no memories here with her mother. The place wasn't home in any way. And yet…and yet she didn't want to turn her back on it. She wanted to stay.

And not just because she was homeless.

Okay, a little bit because she was homeless.

With a sigh, she started walking again. About a mile from the inn, she passed the art gallery, waving at Lucille when the older woman stuck her head out and smiled. Snowflakes hovered in the air. Not many, and they didn't seem to stick once they hit the ground. But the way they floated lazily around her as the day faded into dusk kept her entertained until she found herself in town.

She suddenly realized that she was standing in front of a bar. She stepped back to read the sign on the door, tripped off the curb, and stumbled backward into something big, toppling with it to the ground.

A motorcycle. "Crap," she whispered, sprawled over

the big, heavy bike. "Crap, *crap.*" Heart in her throat, she leapt to her feet, rubbing her sore butt and ribs and mentally calculating the cost of damages against the low funds she had in her checking account.

It was too awful to contemplate, which meant that the motorcycle had to be okay. *Had* to be. Reaching out, she tried to right the huge thing, but it outweighed her. She was still struggling with it when the door to the bar suddenly burst open and two men appeared.

One was dressed in a tan business suit, tie flapping, mouth flapping, too. "Hey," he was saying. "She was asking for it..."

The second man wasn't speaking, but Maddie recognized him anyway. Hot Biker from earlier, which meant— Oh, God. It was *his* motorcycle she'd knocked over.

Karma was such a bitch.

At least he hadn't seen her yet. He was busy physically escorting Smarmy Suit Guy with his hand fisted in the back of the guy's jacket as he marched him out of the bar.

Smarmy Suit pulled free and whirled, fists raised.

Hot Biker just stood there, stance easy, looking laid-back but absolutely battle ready. "Go home, Parker."

"You can't kick me out."

"Can, and did. And you're not welcome back until you learn no is no."

"I'm telling you, she wanted me!"

Hot Biker shook his head.

Smarmy Suit put a little distance between them then yelled, "Fuck you, then!" before stalking off into the night.

Maddie just stared, her heart pounding. She wasn't sure if it was the volatile situation, ringing far too close to home, or if it was because any second now, he was going to notice her and what she'd done. With renewed panic, she struggled with his bike.

Then two big hands closed around her upper arms and pulled her back from it.

With an inward wince, she turned to face him. He was bigger than she'd realized, and she took a step backward, out of his reach.

His dark hair was finger-combed at best, a lock of it falling over his forehead. He had a strong jaw, and cheekbones to die for, and disbelief swimming in those melted caramel eyes. "Mind telling me why you have it in for my bike?"

"Okay, this looks bad," she admitted. "But I swear I have nothing against you or your motorcycle."

"Hmm. Prove it."

Her gut clenched. "I—"

"With a drink." He gestured with his head to the bar.

"With you?"

"Or by yourself, if you'd rather. But you look like you could use a little pick-me-up."

He had no idea.

He righted his bike with annoying ease and held out a hand.

She stared at it but didn't take it. "Look, nothing personal, but I've just seen how you deal with people who irritate you, so..."

He looked in the direction that Smarmy Suit had vanished. "Parker was hitting on a good friend of mine and making an ass of himself. Yeah, he irritated me. You haven't. Yet."

"Even though I've tried to kill your bike twice?"

"Even though." His mouth quirked slightly, as if she

were amusing him. Which was good, right? Amused at her klutziness was better than being pissed.

"And anyway, the bike's going to live," he said, directing her to the door, the one whose sign read THE LOVE SHACK.

"This is a bad idea."

He flashed her a smile, and holy mother of God, it was wickedly sexy. It might even have been contagious if she hadn't been so damn worried that any second now he was going to morph into an angry, uptight, aggressive LA attorney who didn't know how to control his temper.

No, wait. That'd been her ex, Alex. "Honestly," she said. "Bad idea."

"Honestly?"

"What, don't people tell the truth around here?"

"Oh, the locals tell the truth. It's just that they tell *all* the truth, even when they shouldn't. It's called gossip. Lucky Harbor natives specialize in it. You can keep a pile of money in the backseat of your unlocked car and it'd be safe, but you can't keep a secret."

"Good thing I don't have any."

He smiled. "We all have secrets. Come on, I know the bartender. It'll help you relax, trust me."

Yes, but she was in the red on trust. Way overdrawn. In fact, the Bank of Trust had folded. "I don't know."

Except he'd nudged her inside already, and her feet were going willingly. The place snagged her interest immediately. It was like entering an old western saloon. The walls were a deep sinful bordello red and lined with old mining tools. The ceiling was all exposed beams. Lanterns hung over the scarred bench-style tables, and the bar itself was a series of old wood doors attached end to end.

Someone had already decorated for Christmas and huge silvery balls hung from everything, as did endless streams of tinsel.

Hot Biker had her hand in his bigger, warmer one and was pulling her past the tables full with the dinner crowd. The air was filled with busy chattering, loud laughter, and music blaring out of the jukebox on the far wall. She didn't recognize the song because it was country, and country music wasn't on her radar, but some guy was singing about how Santa was doing his momma beneath the tree.

Shaking her head, Maddie let herself be led to the bar, where she noticed that nobody was here to drink their problems away.

Everyone seemed...happy.

Hoping it was contagious, she sat on the barstool that he patted for her, right next to a woman wearing sprayed-on jeans and a halter top that revealed she was either chilly or having a really, really good time. Her makeup was overdone, but somehow the look really worked for her. She was cheerfully flirting with a huge mountain of a guy on her other side, who was grinning from ear to ear and looking like maybe he'd just won the lottery.

Hot Biker greeted them both as if they were all close friends, then moved behind the bar, brushing that leanly muscled body alongside of Maddie's as he did.

She shivered.

"Cold?" he asked.

When she shook her head, he smiled again, and the sexiness of it went straight through her, causing another shiver.

Yeah, he really needed to stop doing that.

Immediately, several people at the bar tossed out orders to him, but he just shook his head, eyes locked on Maddie. "I'm done helping out for the night, guys. I'm just getting the lady a drink."

The other bartender, another big, good-looking guy—wow, they sure grew them damn fine up here in Lucky Harbor—asked, "What kind of wing man just takes off without proper clearance? Never mind." He slapped an opened sudoku puzzle in front of Hot Biker. "Just do this puzzle in three minutes or less."

"Why?"

"There's a woman at the end of the bar, the one with the fuck-me heels—Jesus, don't look! What, are you an amateur? She said she'd do things to me that are illegal in thirteen states if I did the puzzle in less than five minutes. So for all that is holy, hurry the fuck up. Just don't let her see you doing it."

Hot Biker looked at Maddie and smiled. "Trying to impress a woman here, Ford."

Ford turned to Maddie speculatively. "I suppose you already know that this guy here has got some charm. But did he tell you that in our freshman year we nicknamed him Hugh because his stash of porn was legendary? Yeah, he had more back issues than eBay. And maybe he mentioned that he can't pee his name in the snow anymore because the last time he did, he gave himself a hernia trying to cross the X at the end of his name?" Ford turned back to Hot Biker and slapped him on the back. "There. Now you have no hope of impressing her, so get cranking on that puzzle—you owe me."

Hot Biker grimaced, and Maddie did something she hadn't in weeks.

She laughed.

THE DISH

Where authors give you the inside scoop!

From the desk of Kendra Leigh Castle

Dear Reader,

I admit it: I love a bad boy.

From the Sheriff of Nottingham to Severus Snape, Spike to Jack Sparrow, it's always the men who seem beyond saving that throw my imagination into overdrive. So it's no wonder that this sort of character arrived in my very first Dark Dynasties book and has stuck around since, despite the fact that most of the other characters either (a) wonder why he hasn't been killed or (b) would like to kill him themselves. Or both, depending on the day. His name is Damien Tremaine. He's a vampire, thief, assassin, and as deadly as they come. In fact, he spent much of *Dark Awakening* trying to kill the hero and heroine. He positively revels in the fact that he has few redeeming qualities. And I just. Couldn't. Resist.

Writing SHADOW RISING, the third installment in the Dark Dynasties series, proved an interesting challenge. The true bad boy takes a special kind of woman to turn him around, and I knew it would take a lot to pierce the substantial (and very stylish) armor that Damien had built up over the centuries. Enter Ariane, a vampire who is formidable in her own right but really remarkable because of her innocence, despite being hundreds of years old. As a member of the reclusive and mysterious Grigori dynasty, Ariane remembers nothing of her life before being turned. All she knows is the hidden desert compound of her kind, a place she has never been allowed to leave. She's long been restless...but when her closest friend goes missing and she's forbidden to search for him, Ariane takes matters into her own untried but very capable hands. Little does she know that her dynasty's leader has hired an outside vampire who specializes in finding those who don't want to be found—and that once she crosses paths with him, he'll make very sure that their paths keep crossing, whether she likes it or not.

All of the couples I write about have their differences, but Damien and Ariane are polar opposites. She's sheltered, he's jaded. She longs to feel everything, while Damien's spent years burying every emotion. And she is, of course, exactly what he needs, which is the first thing to have actually frightened Damien in...well, ever. Damien's slow and terrifying realization that he's finally in over his head was both a lot of fun to write, and exactly what he deserved. After all, redemption is satisfying, but it's not supposed to be *easy*.

Between Damien's sharp tongue and sharper killer instincts, Ariane has her hands full from the get-go. Fortunately, she finds him just as irresistible as I do. Like so many dark and delicious bad boys, there's more to Damien than meets the eye. If you're interested in finding out whether this particular assassin has the heart of a hero, I hope you'll check out SHADOW RISING. I'll be honest: Damien never really turns into a traditional knight in shining armor. But if you're anything like me...you won't want him to anyway.

Enjoy!

Kendra Leigh Castle

Kendra Leigh Castle

♥ ♥ ♥ ♥ ♥ ♥ ♥ ♥ ♥ ♥ ♥ ♥ ♥ ♥

From the desk of Jennifer Haymore

Dear Reader,

When Meg Donovan, the heroine of PLEASURES OF A TEMPTED LADY (on sale now), entered my office for the first time, I mistook her for her twin sister, Serena.

"Serena!" I exclaimed. "How are you? Please, take a seat."

She slowly shook her head. "Not Serena," she said quietly. "Meg."

I stared at her. I couldn't do anything else, because my throat had closed up tight. For, dear reader, Meg was dead! Lost at sea and long gone, and I'd written two complete novels and a novella under that assumption.

Finally, I found my scrambled wits and gathered them tight around me.

"Um," I said hopefully, "Serena...that's not a funny joke. My income relies on my journalistic credibility. You know that, right?"

She just looked at me. Then she shrugged. "Sorry. I am Meg Donovan. And though the world might like to pretend that I am Serena, I know who I am."

"But...but...you're dead." Now I sounded like a petulant child. A rather warped and quite possibly disturbed petulant child.

She finally took the seat I'd offered Serena, and, settling in, she leaned forward. "No, Mrs. Haymore. I'm not dead. I'm very much alive, and I'd like you to write my story."

Oh, Lord.

I looked down to rub the bridge of my nose between my thumb and forefinger, fighting off a sudden headache. If this really was Meg, I was in big, big trouble.

Finally I looked up at her. "All right," I said slowly. "So you're Meg. Back from the dead."

"That's correct," she said.

I studied her closely. Her twin Serena and I have become good friends since I wrote her story for her, and now that I really looked at this woman, the subtle differences between her and her twin grew clearer. This woman was about ten pounds thinner than Serena. And though her eyes were the same shade of blue, something about them seemed harder and wary, as though she'd gone through a difficult time and come out of it barely intact.

"So who was it that rescued you, then?" I asked. "Pirates? Slavers?"

Her expression grew tight. Shuttered. "I'd like to skip that part, if you don't mind."

I raised a brow. This wasn't going to work out between us if she demanded I skip all the good stuff. But I'd play along. For now. "All right, then. Where would you like to start?"

"With my escape."

"Ah, so it *was* pirates, then."

She gave a firm shake of her head. "No. I meant my escape from England."

"That doesn't make sense," I said. "You'll be wanting to stay in England. Your family is there." I didn't say it, but I was pretty sure the man who loved her was there, too.

"I can't stay in England. You must help me."

I clasped my hands on top of my desk. "Look, Meg. I really like your family, so I'm sitting here listening to what you have to say. But I'm a writer who writes happy, satisfying stories about finding true love and living happily ever after. Is that what you're looking for?"

"No!"

I sighed. I'd thought not.

She leaned forward again, her palms flat on the desk. "I need you to write me out of England, because I need to protect my family, and..."

"And...?" I prompted when she looked away, seemingly unwilling to continue.

"And...Captain Langley. You see, as long as I stay in England, they're all in danger."

I fought the twitch that my lips wanted to make to form a smile. So she did know about Captain William Langley...and she obviously cared for him. Whatever danger she was worried about facing meant nothing in the face of the depth of love that might someday belong to William Langley and Meg Donovan.

"I see." I looked into her eyes. "I might be able to make an exception this time. I will do whatever I can to help you protect your family."

Note that I didn't tell her I'd help her to escape. Or to get out of England.

A frantic, wonderful plan was forming rapidly in my mind. Yeah, I'd write her story. I'd "help" her keep Langley and her family safe. But once I did that, once I gained her trust, I'd find a way to make them happy, to boot. Because I'm a romance writer, and that's what I do.

"Thank you," she murmured, glassy tears forming in her eyes. "Thank you so much."

I raised a warning finger. "Realize that in order for this to work, you need to tell me everything."

She hesitated, her lips pressed hard together. Then she finally nodded.

I flipped up my laptop and opened a new document. "Tell me your story, Miss Donovan. From the moment of your rescue."

And that was how I began to write the love story of Meg Donovan, the long-lost Donovan sister.

I truly hope you enjoy reading Meg's story! Please come visit me at my website, www.jenniferhaymore.com, where you can share your thoughts about my books, sign up for some fun freebies and contests, and read more about the characters from PLEASURES OF A TEMPTED LADY.

Sincerely,

Jennifer Haymore

♥   ♥   ♥   --

From the desk of Jill Shalvis

Dear Reader,

Ever feel like you're drowning? In FOREVER AND A DAY, my hero, Dr. Josh Scott, is most definitely drowning. He's overloaded, overworked, and on the edge of burnout. He's got his practice, his young son, his wheelchair-bound sister, and a crazy puppy. Not to mention the weight of the world on his shoulders from taking care of everyone in his life. He's in so deep, saving everyone around him all the time, that he doesn't even realize that *he's* the one in need of saving. It would never occur to him.

Enter Grace Brooks. She's a smart smartass and, thanks to some bad luck, pretty much starting her life over from scratch. Losing everything has landed her in Lucky Harbor working as Josh's dog walker. And then as his nanny. And then before he even realizes it, as his everything. In truth, she's saved him, in more ways than one.

Oh, how I loved watching the sure, steady rock that is Josh crumble, only to be slowly but surely helped back together again by the sexy yet sweet Grace.

And don't forget to pick up the other "Chocaholic" books, *Lucky in Love* and *At Last*, both available wherever books and ebooks are sold.

Happy Reading!

Jill Shalvis

Jill Shalvis

♥ ♥ ♥ ♥ ♥ ♥ ♥ ♥ ♥ ♥ ♥ ♥ ♥ ♥ ♥ ♥

From the desk of Kristen Callihan

Dear Reader,

I'm half Norwegian—on my mother's side. If there is on
thing you need to know about Norwegians, it's that the
are very egalitarian. This sense of equality defines ther
in a number of ways, but one of the more interestin
aspects is that Norwegian men treat women as equa
partners.

Take my grandfather. He was a man's man in the true:
sense of the term. A rugged fisherman and farmer wh
hung out with the fellas, rebuilt old cars, smoked a pip
and made furniture on the side. Yet he always picked u
his own plate after dinner. He never hesitated to go to th
market if my grandmother needed something, nor did h
complain if he had to cook his own meals when she wa
busy. My grandfather was one of the most admirable me
I've known. Thus when I began to write about heroes,
gravitated toward men who share some of the same qual
ties as my Norwegian ancestors.

Ian Ranulf, the hero of MOONGLOW, started ou
as a bit of an unsavory character in *Firelight*. All righ
he was a total ass, doing everything he could to kee
Miranda and Archer apart. So much so that, early or
my editor once asked me if I was sure Ian wasn't the re:
villain. While Ian did not act on his best behavior,
always knew that he was not a bad man. In fact, I rathe
liked him. Why? Because Ian loves and respects wome
in a way that not many of his peers do. While he fee

nclined to protect a woman from physical harm, he'd never patronize her. For that, I could forgive a lot of him.

In MOONGLOW, Ian is a man living a half-life. He has sunk into apathy because life has not been particularly kind to him. And so he's done what most people do: He's retreated into a protective shell. Yet when he meets Daisy, a woman who will not be ignored, he finds himself wanting to live for her. But what I found interesting about Ian is that when he begins to fall for Daisy, he does not think, "No, I've been burned before; I'm not going to try again." Ian does the opposite: He reaches for what he wants, even if it terrifies him, even with a high possibility of failure.

While Ian certainly faces his share of physical battles in MOONGLOW, it is his dogged pursuit of happiness and his willingness to love Daisy as an equal that made him one of my favorite characters to write.

Happy Reading,

Kristen Callihan

Find out more about Forever Romance!

Visit us at
www.hachettebookgroup.com/publishing_forever.aspx

Find us on Facebook
http://www.facebook.com/ForeverRomance

Follow us on Twitter
http://twitter.com/ForeverRomance

NEW AND UPCOMING TITLES

Each month we feature our new titles
and reader favorites.

CONTESTS AND GIVEAWAYS

We give away galleys, autographed copies,
and all kinds of exclusive items.

AUTHOR INFO

You'll find bios, articles, and links to personal websites
for all your favorite authors—and so much more.

GET SOCIAL

Connect with your favorite authors, editors, and
other Forever fans, and share what's important to you.

THE BUZZ

Sign up for our monthly romance newsletter,
and be the first to read all about it.